# Also by Grace Burrowes

# THE Duke's DISASTER

# GRACE BURROWES

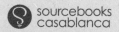

sourcebooks
casablanca

Copyright © 2015 by Grace Burrowes
Cover and internal design © 2015 by Sourcebooks, Inc.
Cover art by Jon Paul Ferrara

Sourcebooks and the colophon are registered trademarks of Sourcebooks, Inc.

Published by Sourcebooks Casablanca, an imprint of Sourcebooks, Inc.
P.O. Box 4410, Naperville, Illinois 60567-4410
(630) 961-3900
Fax: (630) 961-2168
www.sourcebooks.com

Printed and bound in Canada
MBP 10 9 8 7 6 5 4 3 2 1

*To the newly wed*

# One

"I AM NOT A NICE MAN," NOAH WINTERS, EIGHTH Duke of Anselm, pronounced.

Lady Araminthea Collins merely lifted a graceful feminine eyebrow at his self-assessment.

"Perhaps, Your Grace, a gentleman's veracity is more worthy of note than his niceness," she observed.

Noah silently applauded the lady's composure; but then, her sangfroid was one of the qualities that had drawn his notice.

"I am not *nice*," he reiterated, "but I am titled, wealthy, and in need of a wife." Direct speech was necessary if the blasted pansies bordering the garden bench weren't to provoke him into sneezing.

Noah's last disclosure didn't *even* merit a raised eyebrow.

"Hence your attentions to my employer," Lady Thea murmured.

"Marliss isn't your employer," Noah countered. "If we're to be truthful, her papa is, and now that she's announced her betrothal to young Cowper, you will no doubt be looking for another position."

That comment was a small display of his lack of niceness, but patience and posturing had never been Noah's greatest attributes, particularly when his nose was starting to tickle.

"You've heard an announcement, Your Grace?"

"Endmon was rather jovial at the club last night." Rather loquacious and rather drunk, like a papa was entitled to be when his darling girl had found another account to charge her millinery to.

Noah's solicitors had warned him that Cowper's man of business was in negotiations with Viscount Endmon, Marliss's papa. All Noah had felt was a fleeting frustration, to have wasted weeks squiring the young lady about in hopes of concluding his bride hunt.

"If you'll excuse me." Lady Thea grasped her skirts in both hands as if to rise. "I'm sure there's much to do, for Marliss will have throngs of callers—"

Noah wrapped a bare hand over Lady Thea's wrist. His forwardness earned him a two-eyebrow salute, but also had her subsiding back onto the bench.

That wrist was delicate, particularly compared to Noah's.

"A young lady's companion," he said, withdrawing his hand, "is little more than a finishing governess, Lady Thea. You are in want of a position, I am in want of a duchess, and I am offering you that post."

No eyebrows, no gasp of shock, no reaction at all as she regarded him out of puzzled green eyes. "You're serious."

To a fault, according to most women who'd ventured an opinion, including Noah's most recent mistress.

"Your papa was an earl," he said. "You're comely, quiet, past the vapid stage, and from good breeding stock. You are every bit as much duchess material as that giggling twit you supervise."

"Marliss is merely young," Lady Thea said repressively. "But because you are not nice and I am not a giggling twit, you think we would suit?"

A fair summary. "I do, at least as well as I would have suited Marliss or any of her ilk."

The morning sun caught red highlights in Lady Thea's dark hair, and confirmed that she eschewed cosmetics. Marliss had been overfond of them, in Noah's opinion.

"Marliss will be happier with Baron Cowper," Lady Thea said. "What makes you think I would be happier as your duchess than in another companion's post, Your Grace?"

Not the you-do-me-great-honor-but speech, which Noah had been prepared for—he did her a very significant honor indeed—but not a meek capitulation either. She managed to reprove without being rude—for which Noah admired her, of course.

Though he hadn't planned on having the Anselm tiara so thoroughly inspected before the lady tried it on.

"You will never know material want," Noah said, studying the privet hedge rather than her ladyship's plain gray gown. "You will never be forced onto your brother's dubious charity, and once the obligation to the succession is met, you will have as much freedom as discretion and independent wealth allow."

Though if Noah had any say in the matter, Lady

Thea would not order the gardeners to plant pansies beneath her window.

"You believe the obligation to the succession will be easily met?"

Lady Thea fired off the question crisply, but Noah wasn't sure what she was asking. His breeding organs were as happily devoid of restraint as the next man's, and the lady was comely enough he ought to be able to fulfill his duty.

"My father produced only two legitimate sons, despite taking three successive wives," he said. "Your parents managed one son in three tries, so no, I am not boasting of an ability to control all aspects of our union, but I am hopeful Providence will be accommodating. You had a number of uncles on both sides, after all."

Her ladyship fell silent, no pithy rejoinder, no troublesome questions.

Noah had sat across from her in many a carriage as he'd escorted Marliss on the usual rounds and knew that silence was one of Lady Thea's many gifts. She was also quietly pleasing to the eye. She did nothing to draw attention to herself, but any man would notice that she had lustrous sable hair, good bones, a figure politely described as suited to childbearing, and green eyes with a hint of an exotic tilt to them.

She'd *do*, though this revelation had come to Noah only two days ago, when his informants had learned Marliss was no longer on the hunt for a groom. The idea had popped into his brain out of whole cloth, with the same lack of warning that characterized some of his most profitable commercial gambits.

A proposal to Lady Araminthea was worth a try in any case, because the Season would soon be over, and that meant another year before the next crop of giggling twits was presented at court. Another year of sitting backward in his own carriage, another year of strolling through colorful, troublesome gardens.

"I will think on this," Lady Thea said. "I have no one to speak for me, so you will provide me any draft settlement documents."

Provide them to *her*? The notion offended Noah on her behalf. "What about your brother?"

"If you and I can come to terms," Lady Thea said, "you may send him a copy of the contracts as a courtesy, but I gather you seek to have matters timely resolved, and decisiveness is not in Tim's nature."

Sobriety was not in Timotheus Collins's nature, or temperance. Even a man who was not nice could keep those observations to himself.

"I can have drafts sent around to you by the end of the week," Noah said, though dealing with Lady Thea directly on marriage settlements left him uneasy. "You have no one else to negotiate on your behalf—an uncle, or even a widowed aunt?"

"The Collins family tends to live with more intensity than stamina, Your Grace." She rose, and this time Noah rose with her. "I am the eldest surviving exponent thereof. Will you walk with me?"

Yes, he would, provided they moved away from the infernal posies.

Noah offered his arm, content that Lady Thea would give him an answer within the week. Because she had no dowry, Noah could easily ensure the settlements favored her, though in the face of the lady's hesitance, he turned his thoughts to the further inducements he could offer.

She would be his duchess, after all, and duchesses, even prospective ones, were due every courtesy.

"Your sister would of course be welcome in our home," he said as they ambled away from the house—and the dratted flowers. On an early June morning, Viscount Endmon's gardens were peaceful, pretty, and softly scented—like the woman whose arm was linked with Noah's. They followed a gravel walk into a shaded bend in the trees where Lady Thea dropped his arm.

"I have a request," she said.

Noah was prepared to bargain politely over a long engagement or a fancy wedding, though neither was in his plans. "Provided it's reasonable…?"

"Kiss me."

They were out of view of the house and the stables, which was fortunate, for Noah sensed this additional, unanticipated request was the key to winning Lady Thea's hand. Kissing was a pleasant enough undertaking, usually.

"What sort of kiss would you like?" he asked, for Noah's expertise comprised the usual repertoire, plus a few extras.

Now *she* took a visual inventory of their surroundings, as if she either hadn't known or hadn't admitted to herself there were different kinds of kisses.

"A husbandly kiss."

*Women.* "Because I have never been a husband, we must refine on the point. Is this to be the kiss of a husband greeting his spouse in the morning, parting from her, offering her amatory overtures, or...claiming her?"

"Not overtures." Her ladyship checked the watch pinned to her bodice, a small, plain gold trinket apparently of more interest than Noah's kisses. "A kiss to inspire trust."

Was that the same as a kiss to seduce? But, no. She didn't mean a kiss to inspire *misplaced* trust, but rather, a kiss to inspire the genuine article. Noah hadn't taken Lady Thea for the fanciful sort, but kisses likely did not come her way often enough that she could allow an opportunity for one to pass by.

"Over here." He took her hand and led her a few steps deeper into the shade. "Close your eyes."

She had trouble with that, but eventually complied, giving Noah a moment to study her downcast, tense expression. He stepped closer and slipped a hand around her waist, bringing her against his taller frame.

The fit was pleasing, the lady's martyred expression a trial.

"This isn't kissing, Your Grace."

"Hush," he chided, "and no peeking. This is part of it, but I'm waiting for you to behave kissably." He rested his chin on her crown, more so she'd know where he was than anything else, but that presumption allowed him to inhale her sweet, meadowy fragrance, and to brush his cheek over the silky warmth of her hair.

To prevent her ladyship from fussing him for his opening maneuvers, Noah grazed his nose over her cheek, then used his lips in the same gesture.

She stiffened in his arms.

Well, damn. So their marriage was to be candles-out, under-the-covers, nightclothes-all-around when it came to conjugal duties, emphasis on the duties. Noah sighed against her temple, and what should have been a kiss to inspire trust became a kiss of longing on his part for what would not be.

⤜⤛

For six days, Thea held out, and on the seventh day she sent the Duke of Anselm a note. She'd been all set to politely reject his proposal, for she'd already contacted the employment agencies before he'd made his startling offer. She should not be his duchess. Anselm was too intelligent, too assured, too cold, too…large for her to consider his suit seriously.

The match would be appropriate though, and the temptation to accept had loomed mightily when he'd offered his home to Nonie too. Then there had been that kiss, not like any Thea had experienced, not in any way.

His Grace had given her the first kiss she'd asked for, the first one she could say in some way she'd initiated, and his kiss had been so unexpected, so *sweet*, coming from such a taciturn, dark man. More than anything, that kiss had assured Thea she was no match for the duke. Her insides still went fizzy when memories of his kiss intruded on her thoughts, which they did frequently.

So the kiss had done its job, and weighed in *against* the notion of holy matrimony with Noah Winters, Duke of Anselm. Not the way Thea had thought it would, true, but effectively nonetheless.

And now this. The settlements were generous, including a dowry for Nonie, however delicately described. Provision for Nonie was more than Thea could have hoped for, and the sum enough that one day her younger sister might have the happily ever after every girl had a right to wish for.

This generosity meant Anselm was even more shrewd than Thea had thought—or more perceptive. In any case, with Nonie's future in the balance, Thea's decision became more difficult. She was not the least bit confident she could carry off marrying the duke, and if she failed in her role, the consequences would be severe.

Still, those consequences would not devolve to Nonie, and thus Thea wavered.

"He's here." Marliss bounced through the parlor door, blue eyes shining, golden curls severely confined with myriad pins. "This will kill Mama, positively kill her, Thea. You're snabbling a *duke*, and one with pots and pots of lovely money. Shall I go down with you? I promise to giggle at all the wrong times."

"Bother you," Thea said, enduring Marliss's hug. "You had sense enough to know you'd be happier with Cowper, and you'll make Cowper happy too."

Marliss dimpled becomingly. "He's dear, and he'll grow into the barony, whereas Anselm never will be dear and doesn't care a whit for his title. Maybe you can smooth off his rough edges, Thea, but he's not my cup of tea. Regardless of his expression, one has the sense Anselm is always scowling."

"I still haven't accepted him," Thea reminded Marliss—and herself.

"You are too sensible not to. I'll give you fifteen minutes. If you want more, take him to the gardens or the mews. The staff is dodging work this morning because Mama has a bad headache."

Thea finished the thought. "And the sound of pruning shears will overset her." Marliss's mama was easily overset, hence the need for Marliss's companion to be of a sturdier constitution. "I'll keep my conversation with Anselm most civilizedly quiet."

Marliss escorted Thea to the top of the stairs, then blew her a kiss, and Thea was still smiling when Corbett Hallowell, Marliss's older brother, pushed away from the wall on the second landing.

"In a hurry, Thea dear?" he crooned.

"Yes, if you must know." Thea tried to hustle past him, but Marliss's brother-the-heir was lanky, and he snaked out a long arm to clamp a hand above Thea's elbow. He glanced around before stepping far closer than a gentleman should stand to a lady.

"She set a date yet?" he asked.

"You should discuss that with your sister," Thea said. With the servants taking an informal half day, Corbett had chosen his moment well.

Corbett's grip on Thea's arm began to hurt. "You'll be wanting another position, my lady."

"Let me go." Thea tried to extricate herself from his hold, but succeeded only in tightening Corbett's grasp.

"I have a position in mind." Corbett leaned in, pushing Thea up against the wall. "On your back, for starters. It pays well."

"Let me go, Corbett." Corbett, several years Thea's junior and only a few inches taller than she, shouldn't be posing such a threat—again. She'd kept her voice steady, but her heart was galloping, and panic beat through her veins. Jesus save her, Corbett's breath held a foul whiff of last night's spirits.

*Scream*, she ordered herself. *Pray later, scream NOW.*

"I like a little fight in a female." Corbett swooped in as if to plant his lips on Thea's mouth, but missed—thank God—and landed closer to her ear as she began to struggle in earnest.

"I like a lot of fight in a man," said a cool baritone, "except those worthy of the name are in such short supply."

Corbett's head came up, and then he was gone. One moment he was all pinching fingers, fetid breath, and slobbery lips, the next, he was flung against the opposite wall, trying to look indignant but mostly looking scared.

"If you must prey on your dependents," Anselm said, "you'd best do it where you can't be seen, overheard, or held to account. You may apologize or choose weapons. My advice would be something unconventional—whips, knives maybe—because pistols and swords no longer pose much challenge—for me, that is."

The duke spoke casually, shooting his cuffs, then winging his arm at Thea. She accepted His Grace's escort but spared Corbett a perusal as well. He was gratifyingly pale and still darting glances up and down the stairs.

"My apologies, Lady Thea." Corbett found the strength to stand up straight and nod curtly. "Your charms—"

"Tut-tut," Anselm interrupted mildly.

"Are not for me to take advantage of," Corbett finished.

"Adequate," Anselm said. "Be off with you."

Corbett left, but turned on the third stair up and shot a murderous look over his shoulder, timed so Thea caught it, and the duke, in his towering calm, did not.

"Tiresome," Anselm said, "but my apologies as well, on behalf of my gender. I gather we'll have more privacy out-of-doors, unless you need your hartshorn, or a tisane, or some such?"

"A bit of fresh air in the gardens will do," Thea said, though a stout punch directed at Corbett's nose would have been a fine restorative too.

The duke had the decency to accompany Thea outside in silence, while her emotions rocketed between gratitude that Anselm had come along, disgust that Corbett had waylaid her again, and the sinking certainty that if Anselm's offer of marriage had been only reluctantly appealing before—despite his sweet kiss—it looked un-turn-downable now.

But how on God's earth was Thea to be honest with him?

"Does he importune you often?" Anselm asked, as if he were inquiring as to where Thea had acquired her watch pin.

"Me, the tweenie, the scullery maid. Corbett's papa dotes on him, and he's at that age between university and marriage, where he has no responsibilities, and all his friends are similarly situated."

"You make excuses for him?" Anselm's tone was

thoughtful, not quite chiding as he steered Thea away from the pansies.

"Of necessity, I understand him," she said. "He's no worse than most of his kind."

"Meaning he's not the first to pester you," Anselm concluded, sounding displeased. "Shall we sit?" He'd drawn Thea into the shade at the back of the property, where they'd have privacy, at least until Marliss appeared. He chose a bench for them, then came down beside her.

"I was planning to refuse you," Thea said. "But your generosity toward my sister, and the inevitability of scenes such as the one you just interrupted have persuaded me toward acceptance, Your Grace."

"Noah," he replied, sounding no more thrilled to hear her acceptance than she was to tender it. "If we're to be married, you should know my name."

"Shall I use it?"

"You are welcome to," he said. "Why?"

"Why what?"

"Why accept my proposal?"

"I will never know material want," she quoted him, when she should have been blurting out the blunt details of her past. "I will not be cast on my brother's dubious charity. I'll have independence once certain matters are tended to." She was too much a lady to refer to the settlements directly, but they were impressive.

His Grace's expression suggested he did not like hearing his reasoning cast back at him, and Thea's resolve faltered.

"My sister will be safer under your protection

than the indifferent efforts of my brother," she said, marshalling her scruples. "As your duchess, I can see to her come-out."

"And you'll be away from Corbett's charming importuning," Anselm concluded. "You know, I would find you another situation, did you ask it of me."

Thea hadn't known that, but more glorified governessing would do nothing to assure Nonie's future.

"I will not ask it."

His Grace's features showed fleeting amusement. Thea knew what he was thinking: *She'll take my name, my coin, my protection for life provided I get breeding rights, but she'll not be beholden to me for a simple act of consideration. Women.*

"A special license, then?" he asked.

Thea nodded, as anxiety chewed at her nerves. The moment when she might be honest with the duke and suffer only his quiet disdain was passing. He would get children on her, and he had a right to know the truth of her situation.

"Shall I see to the details?" he asked in the same tone Thea used to inquire whether a guest at tea preferred one lump of sugar or two.

"Marliss will be wed fairly soon," Thea said. "I assume I'm welcome here until then."

"And leave you where Corbett can follow up on his apology?" the duke scoffed. "Not blessed likely. You will bide with my sister Patience. How soon can you be packed?"

Anselm—Noah—wasn't stupid. Maybe not nice, but singularly capable of grasping the unpleasant realities of a woman's life in service. A lady's life in service. Thea opened her mouth to speak the words that would have him retracting his proposal.

"This afternoon," she heard herself say. Anxiety rose higher, even as leaving Endmon's household also sparked relief.

"I'll send a coach at three. We'll no doubt be interrupted soon, so you'd best apprise me of any changes you'd like to make to the settlements."

Thea waved a hand as if batting away an insect. "The settlements are fine, more than fine, generous, and I thank you." *In for a penny...* "When can I collect Nonie?"

"*We* can collect your sister tomorrow. I assume you'll want her underfoot as you prepare for the wedding?"

"Of course," Thea murmured, while vividly recalling the one time she'd been on a runaway horse. The memory was unpleasant, and the sensations—stupefying panic, primarily—were reasserting themselves.

"How long will it take to locate your brother and get him into wedding attire?" Anselm asked.

His Grace was appallingly blunt, though Thea liked that about him. "A few days," she said. "The Season is reaching its apex, and he'll be about somewhere."

"I'll see to it. Anything else?"

Thea's gaze traveled to the back of the house, where all was still, not a sign of life.

"Yes." She was to become Anselm's wife, a far more daunting prospect than simply swanning about as his duchess. "It's not about the settlements."

His Grace sat back, regarding her with a banked impatience that suggested for the duke, Thea had become a piece of work in the Concluded Business category. A last-minute request was merely an irritant for her prospective husband.

*Husband*, gads. *Tell him.* "I need time, Your Grace."

"For?"

"I barely know you." Though twenty years into marriage with this man, Thea might still barely know him, and not mind that a bit.

"You've been sharing carriages and walking with me and Marliss for weeks," he shot back. "I've kissed you."

"Once. I'm not asking for a lot of time, and we can be married whenever you please, but after that…"

"You want me to woo you?" Anselm made it sound as if Thea's request were peculiar—eccentric. Interesting, in an abstract, slightly absurd way.

"Not woo, precisely." Most people would call Anselm handsome, for all his expression was usually sardonic. Dark hair, unnaturally vivid blue eyes, aristocratic features, and a nose and chin suggesting he held to his convictions. But he was too big, too robust, too *male*.

"I am marrying to beget heirs, Lady Thea," he reminded her.

"You've had years to do that," she reminded him right back. "A few weeks or months one way or another won't matter. Your proposal was unexpected. I've not been assessing you as a potential mate, though you apparently had that luxury with me all the while you were courting Marliss."

The duke's lips compressed into a line, and Thea could see him weighing the desire to argue against the constraints of a gentleman's manners.

"The vows will be consummated on our wedding night, but after that, we'll take it slowly," he allowed, his delicacy relieving a little of Thea's worry. "Not as slowly as you'd like, more slowly than I'd like. And I have a request, also not in the settlements."

More than that, Thea sensed, he would not give her, but his concession was enough, because she'd find some way to tell him the whole of the bargain before vows were spoken. She waited for his additional request—that she call on his sisters, limit her spending, let him speak with Endmon.

Men took odd notions.

"Kiss me," he said, something flashing through his eyes that might have been humor.

Odd, unexpected notions. "I've already kissed you once, Your Grace. That was quite enough."

"No, it was not." Anselm laced his fingers with Thea's. "I kissed you. Now you kiss me."

His hand was big, brown, and callused, hers grace-ful, pale, and smooth. Pretty, but ultimately useless, those hands of hers.

"What sort of kiss, Your Grace?" For kisses appar-ently had their own taxonomy.

"Any kind of kiss you like, provided it's wifely and not some cowardly little peck on the cheek."

The duke was challenging her, and Thea silently thanked him. Her worries and fears and second guesses were getting the better of her, but a challenge restored her balance.

Anselm had approached their previous kiss with a casual élan Thea could never carry off, though she could imitate his ducal imperiousness.

"Close your eyes, Your Grace."

The duke sat beside Thea, eyes obediently closed as she rose and balanced with one knee on the bench, one foot on the ground. She purposely put herself higher than him, trying to create the fiction that his size didn't intimidate. Her experience was limited though, so she had to aim her kiss by cradling his jaw in her hand before she pressed her lips to his. His skin was surprisingly smooth, indicating he'd shaved just before calling on her, and his scent was...

Lovely. As Thea settled her mouth over his, she inhaled lavender and roses, an odd fragrance for a man but fitting somehow. Anselm's mouth moved under hers, and his hand cupped her elbow. Thea let her fingers trail back through his dark hair, which was as thick and silky as it looked, and beguilingly soft, while his features were so rugged.

As his tongue seamed Thea's lips, her hand went still, her breathing seized, and she paused, listening with her mouth for him to repeat the caress.

"Now you," he whispered, before joining his mouth to hers again.

He wanted her to *taste* him?

Tentatively, Thea complied, the texture of the duke's lips against her tongue soft, plush, and...enticing. She did it again, and Anselm leaned closer, his arms looping around her waist. With her last shred of sanity, Thea grasped that kneeling over him like this put his *face* at bodice level.

She lifted her mouth from his and tried to step back, though Anselm's arms around her waist prevented her retreat.

"None of that," he chided, drawing her down beside him. "We'll bide here a moment, while you gather your wits."

"My wits?"

"It's not every day a lady accepts a marriage proposal."

"Oh, yes." Thea touched her lips with her index finger. Was the buzzing sensation from her lips or her finger or her entire body? "That."

Anselm's gaze warmed again with that fleeting suggestion of humor.

"That." He slipped his fingers through hers, and a silence stretched between them.

Unnerved on Thea's part. No doubt pleased on the duke's.

# Two

"WHY NOW?" LORD EARNEST MEECHAM WINTERS Dunholm, as Noah's only surviving adult male family member, could safely ask that question. "You've had years to find a filly, Noah, and you've not troubled yourself to do so. I had my doubts about you, you know."

"They were hardly secret," Noah said as Meech handed him a glass of very fine spirits. "And, yes, if you're interested, I sent Henrietta her parting piece before the Season even started. You're welcome to console her on my departure."

Meech's countenance brightened. "Henny Whitlow? She won't hold a little snow on the roof against a fellow. Might drop by and see what her terms are these days."

Noah took a sip of the drink for which he himself had paid.

"Her terms are expensive," Noah said. "Too expensive for you, Uncle, so don't think of taking her on exclusively."

In fact, the entire elegant apartment on an elegant

Mayfair side street was billed to Noah, as were the servants' wages and tradesmen's deliveries. Meech had tried for a time to live off the proceeds of his gambling, with notable, if elegant, lack of success.

"From one Winters to another, it pains me to say it, young man"—Meech settled into a wing chair—"but while the spirit is enthusiastically willing, the flesh is not what it once was. Though mark me, experience can compensate for a great deal of what passes for youthful vigor. Besides, with a bit of charm and guile, a man needn't be writing bank drafts."

Meech had been the dashing, blond, blue-eyed ducal spare in his youth, and he'd aged handsomely, considering how dissipated his lifestyle had been.

"Henny's easy to please, as long as your credit is good on Ludgate Hill," Noah said, which was no compliment to himself and no insult to dear Henny.

Meech took a parsimonious sip of his drink. "In my day, we were neither so mercenary about these things nor so sentimental. We understood sweetness without turning it into a business transaction, and we understood our place in life."

Which was, apparently, to lecture all and sundry at the least provocation. Noah rose, for Meech was merciless when he had a captive, well-heeled nephew for an audience.

"Now comes the speech about great-nephews being sadly absent from your golden years. Or did I leave out the part about respecting one's elders by increasing their stipends?"

"Elder," Meech corrected him with a pained smile. "Singular. But because you're putting your shoulder to the marital plow, so to speak, I'll forgo that particular homily. Do I know the lady?"

"One hopes not biblically," Noah said, almost meaning it. Meech had married once, quite young, and mercenarily enough that he was still sporting the lady's surname as a condition of the settlements. Having buried his young bride decades ago, Meech claimed he'd be doing the women of England an injustice to limit his favors again to only one wife—of his own.

The portrait over the mantel was of two men and a single woman, all three stylishly mounted, enjoying a visit under a venerable oak. Every time Noah saw the painting, he wondered where the lady's groom had got off to.

"My intended is the daughter of the Earl of Grantley," Noah said, for Meech would pester him until he delivered up the details. Meech knew everybody, being in great demand among the hostesses to even the numbers and keep morale up among the widows and wallflowers.

"A sturdy, sensible lady fallen on hard times?" Meech asked, downing the rest of the drink.

"Pretty enough," Noah conceded, though Thea was quietly lovely, "and her brother is a twit who's bankrupting the earldom at a tidy gallop."

"There's another sister, isn't there, not so long in the tooth?"

"Lady Antoinette." The bargaining chip that had likely decided the matter for Lady Araminthea. "She'll dwell with us, and yes, I know I would have had a few more breeding seasons out of the younger sister, but she and I haven't met."

Even Noah would not marry a woman sight unseen.

"So why are you marrying now, and why this Lady Thea?"

Lady Thea had something to do with the why now. "When both my father and my junior uncle did not live to see fifty," Noah replied, "I promised Grandfather on his deathbed that I'd meet a marital deadline. As for Lady Thea, she's an earl's daughter serving out her days as a companion. Given the reputation of you lot"—he waved a hand to indicate his father and uncles before him—"I want a respectable duchess. Ladies come no more respectable than the companions at the edges of the ballrooms. Then too, I like Lady Thea." Which Noah probably should not have admitted in present company. "But not too much."

"That's promising." Meech topped up his own drink, his tolerance for spirits being legendary among the college boys. "Does she like you?"

"She's willing to tolerate me," Noah said, opening a gold snuffbox on the mantel and catching a whiff of cinnamon, of all the nancy affectations. "The female who likes me has yet to be born to the human species."

"Take after your grandfather, you do. None of my charm, though I was a late bloomer too."

"Very late," Noah rejoined, for sober maturity had yet to entirely settle upon Meech. "Will you fetch Harlan from school?"

"A note will fetch him from school. He hasn't your penchant for the books, Noah. God knows who that boy takes after."

A subject even Meech should not have raised.

Noah set his drink on the mantel next to the snuff-box. "Just get him to the wedding in proper attire. Breakfast will be at Anselm House immediately after, family only, and my thanks for the brandy."

"Do you suppose Henny would like that snuff-box?" Meech asked.

Henny had better taste than that, but she was kind. "You should ask her, but please, for the love of heaven, do not bring her up at the wedding breakfast."

Meech poured the remains of Noah's drink into his own glass, something he likely would not have done had a servant been present.

"If you're intent on seeing this wedding accomplished forthwith, I will not be in evidence, Noah. Pemberton and I have accepted Deirdre Harting's invitation to a house party out in Surrey, and she would be most disappointed did we let her down. I'll give Henny your regards before I go, though."

For a man in his late forties, Meech was handsome, trim, and charming by most hostesses' standards. He and his bosom bow, Pemberton, could have passed for twins, right down to a shared distaste for weddings.

"Far be it from me to expect my nuptials would take precedence over your socializing," Noah said, though he was disappointed—or he should have been.

Meech walked with him toward the front door. "You're sure you won't take up with Henny again once the wife is settled?"

"I'm sure." Almost sure.

"Best keep your options open. Wives can be the very devil."

"You would know, Uncle. You've had so many."

"Disrespectful pup. If you're lucky, you'll grow up to be just like me."

"I could do worse," Noah graciously allowed— Meech had at least avoided diseases of vice and tiresome addictions.

Noah accepted his hat, cane, and gloves from a footman, and saw himself out, stopping by his own establishment only long enough to send the requisite note to his younger brother—half brother, in truth— then choose a ring for his bride from among those presented for his perusal.

"And for the morning gift, Your Grace?" the dapper little gentleman inquired. "Perhaps you'd like to see some bracelets, necklaces, earbobs?"

"No, thank you." Noah had forgotten this detail, but Thea Collins did not strike him as a jewelry-acquiring sort of female. She'd want independence, not ornamentation. "The lady will choose most of her own jewelry, but I will certainly recommend your shop to her."

"Our sincere thanks, Your Grace." The man bowed and took his leave with a blessed absence of further obsequies.

When Noah's town coach rolled up to the Endmon establishment, his intended was ready, her belongings stowed in one pathetically battered and small trunk. Her luggage was lashed to the boot, and amid a teary send-off from Marliss—and only Marliss—Noah collected his bride.

"Are you sorry to leave your charge?" Noah settled into the carriage while his future duchess sat across from him, cradling a small maple-wood box on her lap.

"I will miss her," her ladyship conceded, "but Marliss is destined for her own household now, so my task was complete."

"Lady Thea, does my person offend you?"

"I beg your pardon, Your Grace?"

"I'm a frequent bather, and a devoted slave to my tooth powder," Noah went on, "and I will wear only clean linen, so I must wonder why my affianced bride has left me to myself on the forward-facing seat."

She clutched her wooden box, her expression genuinely abashed. "I meant no offense, Your Grace. Habit only, I assure you."

Her ladyship didn't move until Noah held out a hand, steadying her in the moving carriage as she switched benches. He took her box from her and kept her hand in his.

"You've met my sister Lady Patience?"

"She called this morning. A very amiable woman."

"My sisters are all amiable," Noah replied. "All three of them, until they fix on some objective, and then they amiably ride roughshod over all in their path to achieve it." Including their ducal brother.

"They are each wed, are they not?"

"Thanks to a merciful God and the pudding that passes for brains in the heads of most young Englishmen, they are. Have you considered a wedding trip?"

"I have not," Lady Thea said, her gaze on their joined hands. "A journey seems inappropriate, as our union is not…"

"Not…?" Noah wouldn't rescue her from the windowless corner she'd painted herself into.

"Not sentimental in nature, Your Grace. You've

assured me we'll have time to become acquainted, and you're busy enough without having to create the appearance of doting on your broodmare."

Lady Thea would have had ample opportunity to draw that conclusion. During her weeks of chaperoning Marliss, she'd seen that a duke worth his title must needs go through life at the speed of a particularly fierce whirlwind. A duchy did not run itself.

"I do dote on my broodmares," Noah informed her. "They're more likely to catch that way, and I enjoy it."

"Doting will not be necessary." Lady Thea injected enough frost into her tone that a lesser man might dread his wedding night.

"We'll see." Noah rubbed his thumb over her wrist, which was the only inch of skin exposed below her pretty neck. "In case you're interested, I might enjoy being doted on a little myself."

"How would one go about that?"

"You'll think of something," he assured her, "but we arrive to your brother's residence. I hope you sent a note?"

"Of course. One to Tim, one to Nonie. You may leave my music box here."

Though Noah did not want to encourage his bride's tendency to issue orders, he put her box under the seat.

The coachman set them down in the porte cochere, where no footman or butler appeared at the door to greet them. Noah looked askance at her ladyship, but her chin was held high as she opened the door and admitted them herself.

"Lady Thea!" A plump older woman in apron and

cap came scampering up the hallway. "It's that glad we are to see you. Lady Nonie will be down directly now you're here, and you've brought a caller."

"Hello, Mrs. Wren." Thea bent so the lady could kiss her cheek. "Is my brother home?"

"Oh, he's *home*, my lady." Mrs. Wren's expression suggested the greatest of her earthly burdens lay one floor above. "Whether he's *at* home, I surely couldn't say. Perhaps you and the gentleman would like to greet Lady Nonie in the morning room?"

"We'll see ourselves up," Thea replied. "If you could please send along some tea, once you've let Nonie know we're here?"

"Thea!" A younger, merrier version of Thea came skipping down the stairs, dark curls bouncing with each step.

"Thea, you've come, oh, thank the saints." Lady Nonie threw herself against her sister and held tight. "Is it true? Is this your fellow?" The girl tossed a barely recognizable curtsy at Noah, and proceeded to obliterate the protocol for introductions. "You're the Duke of Anselm?"

"I have that honor," Noah replied.

"Lady Antoinette," Thea interjected, "may I make known to you my betrothed, Noah, Duke of Anselm. Your Grace, Lady Antoinette Collins, my younger sister."

"My lady." Noah bowed over the younger woman's hand, and saw a smaller replica of Thea, one not so plagued by life's injustices and realities. "It will be my pleasure to offer you a place in our home for so long as you care to join us."

Or until some pudding-headed swain came along sporting a ring.

Nonie blushed and slipped her hand into a pocket. "He even talks like a duke."

"I take tea like one too," Noah said, seeing smitten lordlings by the half dozen lounging about his parlors several years hence. "If that's the plan?"

"Of course," Lady Thea said. "The parlor is this way, and bother it, Nonie, have we not a single footman to take His Grace's hat and gloves?"

"Not a one," Nonie replied blithely. "They work until the pay runs out, then find other positions until the next quarter's funds show up. I can take His Grace's hat and gloves."

"I'll hold on to them for now," Noah said. When the party reached the morning parlor, he set his accessories on a sideboard. The curtains hung the merest inch askew, the rug needed a sound beating, and the andirons hadn't been blacked in a week.

Shabby in the details, but not yet desperate.

The sisters were desperate to spend time together, though, based on the speed with which Nonie chattered on about some cat and the boot boy, and a bird loose in the pantry.

"Are you packed, Lady Antoinette?" Noah asked when the girl had paused to take a breath.

"I am." She spared Noah a smile that was no doubt already turning heads when she walked in the park. "I'll fetch my trunk down before we go."

"You," Noah shot back, "will sit right there and sip your tea, while I see to your trunks."

He left the ladies in the morning room and found

his way to the corridor housing the family bedrooms. A passing maid—cap askew, apron stained—pointed him to Lady Nonie's room and gave him directions to Lord Grantley's quarters.

Noah found his lordship facedown on a bed and sporting one stocking only. The rest of him was sprawled across the covers, naked as a babe, snoring the day away.

"Here lies the head of the Collins household," Noah muttered. Grantley couldn't be much more than twenty, his form hardly that of a man. The abundant evidence confirmed he eschewed physical exertion, and his hands qualified as those of a gentleman—or a lady.

The young earl screamed like a female too, when Noah tossed a glass of cold drinking water on his back.

"What the blazes!" Grantley slewed up onto all fours, shaking his head, then must have realized he wasn't alone. "Who the hell are you, and why in blazes did you do that?"

"I'm your prospective brother-in-law," Noah replied, "and unless you want my boot planted on your tender and none-too-attractive backside, I suggest you get out of that bed and prepare to send your sisters into my keeping in, say, ten minutes."

"My sisters?"

Noah smiled nastily. "You have the two, Nonie and Thea. I'm marrying Thea, the taller one, and she's bringing Nonie with us for safekeeping. Your solicitors have the contracts, and the wedding is in three days."

"Three days!" Grantley bounced to the edge of

the bed, then sat very still. "Shouldn't have moved so quickly. Beg pardon."

Noah passed him the empty washbasin.

"See you in ten minutes," Noah tossed over his shoulder, heading for the door. "Nine and a half, now."

It took twenty, but Grantley managed a semblance of casual attire when he showed up in the morning parlor.

He nodded at his older sister. "How do, Thea, and who's your gentleman friend?"

"Noah, Duke of Anselm." Noah bowed politely. He held the superior rank, but they were under Grantley's roof—and the ladies were looking on. "At your service, and it is my happy honor to report that Lady Araminthea has accepted my suit. The wedding will be at eleven of the clock on the indicated date, with a wedding breakfast at Anselm House thereafter."

Grantley squinted at the hand-lettered invitation Noah passed him and ran a hand through hair lighter—and less tidy—than Thea's.

"Is this cricket, Thea?" the earl asked. "Seems hasty to me, but maybe you've anticipated the vows?"

Even Lady Nonie's expression went blank at that insult.

"Were you not so obviously suffering from the lack of couth that characterizes most with your insignificant years," Noah said, "I would call you to task for the slight you offer my bride."

"Slight?"

Both sisters were sipping tea as if their reputations depended upon it.

*Hopeless.* "Grantley, you will swill some strong

black tea and then assist me to retrieve Lady Nonie's effects from her room," Noah instructed.

"Hirschman can do it." With a shaking hand, Grantley accepted a hot cup of tea from his younger sister.

*Hopeless and arrogant.* Noah's sympathy for his bride doubled. "Where will I find that worthy?"

"He's a man of all work," Thea said. "He's been with us forever, and he'll likely be in the kitchen if he's on the property."

Noah left the three siblings to their tea and noted more evidence of poor household care as he made his way below stairs. A streak of bird droppings left a long white smudge on a window in the foyer, a carpet in the hallway bore a dubious stain, and the door to the lower reaches squeaked mightily. Fortunately, Hirschman was indeed in the kitchen, but Mrs. Wren nearly wrung her apron into rags at the sight of a duke in her domain.

"Mr. Hirschman, if you'd see to Lady Nonie's things?" Noah asked when Mrs. Wren had ceased fluttering and muttering.

"Of course." Hirschman rose, presenting a sturdy if slightly stooped frame. "But where, might I ask, is the young lady off to?"

About time somebody asked, because Grantley didn't seem inclined to delve into particulars.

"Noah Winters, Duke of Anselm." Noah bowed slightly, because this fellow was likely all that had kept Grantley's wastrel friends from bothering Lady Nonie. "Betrothed to Lady Thea, who is gathering Lady Nonie under her wing. Lady Thea is with her brother and sister now, and the wedding is to be in a few days' time."

Bushy white eyebrows rose, and the housekeeper's apron-wringing came to an abrupt halt.

"So soon?" Hirschman asked. At least he didn't inquire outright if they'd anticipated their vows.

"I cannot countenance leaving the young ladies to shift for themselves any longer than necessary," Noah said. "Or perhaps there's some hidden streak of sobriety in Lord Grantley I've failed to appreciate?"

"Not perishing likely," Hirschman scoffed. "Too much like his friends, that one. I'll fetch the trunks, but Your Grace will leave the direction with Mrs. Wren, if you please."

Noah complied, because Hirschman's request, while presuming in the extreme, was fair. If Grantley turned up missing, his sisters ought to be notified—eventually.

When Noah returned to the morning parlor, Grantley was looking a little less like a fish dead three days, and Lady Nonie's speech had slowed to a rapid approximation of conversation.

"If you ladies are ready?" Noah picked up his hat and gloves. "Lady Nonie's trunks are being loaded as we speak."

"You're leaving?" Grantley asked. He was a good-looking enough young man, but would soon lose his appeal if he remained dedicated to dissipation.

"We're off to the home of His Grace's sister, Lady Patience, until the wedding," Thea said, "and thence to Anselm House."

"Because you're getting married," Grantley recited

slowly, "to him." He blinked owlishly, likely still a
little drunk from the previous evening's revels.

"We'll send a carriage for you," Noah said, "and
some footmen. Who's your tailor?"

Grantley waved a hand in a gesture Noah had seen
Thea make. "Some fellow on Bond Street."

"That narrows it considerably," Noah said, his
sarcasm clearly escaping Grantley's notice. "Ladies,
shall we?"

"Bye, Tims." Nonie hugged her brother. "You
should go back upstairs and have a little more rest, I
think, and don't forget your tooth powder."

Thus warned, Thea merely extended her hand to
her brother. "I look forward to seeing you at the wedding, Tims, and thank you for coming down."

He bowed over her hand, his expression bewildered
as they took their leave. Some of Noah's ire toward
"Tims" abated when he saw how lost the earl was to
be parting with his sisters.

Noah knew how that felt. He'd forgotten he knew,
but he did know.

"This is the lot of it?" Noah asked as Hirschman set
down a second trunk amid a paltry pile of bags beside
the coach.

"I haven't many clothes that still fit," Nonie
explained. "This is it. My thanks, Hirschman."

"On your way, your ladyships." Hirschman tugged
his forelock. "Mrs. Wren and I will look after Master
Tims, same as we always do."

Noah shot Hirschman a speaking look. "You have
my direction. I'll send a carriage, clothing, and a squad
of dragoons to impress the pup into the wedding party.

Warn him he'd best be sober. He'll regret shaming my bride in any way."

Noah handed up Thea, then Nonie, and signaled the coachman to hold for a moment when the door was closed.

"How bad is the earl?" Noah asked Hirschman, walking a few steps toward the rear of the coach.

"For now?" Hirschman scrubbed a hand over his chin. "His lordship's not awful, he's just young and stupid as a stump. He gets took advantage of, but the solicitors curb the worst of it, and the old lord set it up so they can keep him from ruin for at least another year. Once he turns five-and-twenty, though, he gets the reins, and God help us then, Your Grace."

"If he lives that long. You and Mrs. Wren are adequately provided for?"

"We take our wages out first when the quarterly money shows up. The rest is spread around as needs must."

"Do the best you can." Noah pushed a card at him. "If the water gets too high, send word to me."

Hirschman tucked the card into a pocket. "Master Tims gambles," he said quietly. "Drinking and gaming, and running with his cronies. That's the worst of it, and many a young lord has found ruin on that road."

Ruin, disease, a tour of the sponging houses, idiotic duels, and penury. "His sisters are safe," Noah said, "and they'll stay safe as long as I draw breath."

"Good day to you, then, Your Grace," Hirschman said, stepping back, "and felicitations on your coming nuptials."

The first such felicitations Noah had received.

"My thanks, Hirschman." Noah climbed into the carriage, taking the backward-facing seat, and wondering why, though he'd known Grantley was a useless puppy, he hadn't considered that the man was also Lady Thea's useless puppy of a brother. What manner of titled brother would allow his sister into service, for pity's sake?

The young men of England, Noah silently concluded, didn't *even* have pudding for brains.

# Three

"YOU MUSTN'T LET ANSELM'S GROWLING FOOL YOU," Lady Patience said as the maid arranged Thea's hair. "He was the best of brothers, and still is, though my husband accounts him excessively willing to engage in trade. You won't mind that, will you?"

Patience was a feminine version of her brother. Dark-haired, blue-eyed, with swooping eyebrows that turned a pretty countenance toward the dramatic.

"I'm marrying His Grace," Thea said, meeting Patience's gaze in the vanity mirror. "This relieves me of any right to judge the man for decisions made prior to our union."

Thea desperately hoped reciprocal reasoning would apply, for there had been no opportunity to be private with the duke.

Had he planned it that way?

Patience smiled overbrightly. "Tolerance is a fine quality in any married woman, but once married, your husband will provoke you sooner or later. You simply learn the knack of keeping your judgments to yourself—most of the time. Not that I don't love my James, because I do, of course."

She fell silent, and Thea endured another spike of panic, for loving Noah Winters was difficult to imagine—assuming the wedding happened. She'd yet to find a moment to pull him aside and have a frank discussion with him. Since accepting his proposal, Thea hadn't been alone with the duke, and now they were to be wed.

Now, within the next couple of hours, and then their life together would begin.

Duke and duchess.

Man and wife.

The two becoming one flesh.

Gads. Thea could imagine respecting Anselm, yes, certainly, and maybe thirty or forty years from now harboring some affection for his irascible old self. But loving him? The notion was as peculiar as the idea of—what had he said?—doting on him a bit?

Once they'd had their frank discussion, what would his reaction be? How did a lady even broach such delicate matters?

"Can we not simplify this style?" Thea asked as her coiffure became an increasingly complicated arrangement of braids, curls, and hairpins.

The maid aimed a commiserating look at Patience, who had been the soul of graciousness thus far.

"It is your wedding day," Patience said. "In olden times, you would have worn your hair down. You should have it as you wish."

"Down, then." The style would surprise Thea's groom, and any lady who'd been consigned to His Grace's Concluded Business heap would find that notion appealing.

When they arrived at St. George's and Thea's gaze met that of her prospective husband, she saw the surprise go through him, followed by that little softening of the eyes she suspected meant he was amused. His amusement was tempered by something else though, something she couldn't quite fathom, but it inspired him not to offer his arm to her as she approached the altar, but rather to take her gloved hand in his.

Anselm held Thea's hand throughout those parts of the ceremony that allowed such liberties, the celebrant not daring to even raise an eyebrow. More remarkable still, when the service was concluded, Noah indulged in the modern display of kissing his bride in public. Had Thea known the duke would get up to such tricks, she might have taken evasive maneuvers, but he'd caught her unawares with another soft, almost tender kiss.

*What had she got herself into?*

"Having second thoughts, Duchess?" the duke asked as he handed her up into an enormous coach drawn by four spanking-white horses.

To whom could he possibly be—*Oh.*

"Second thoughts regarding?"

"Our holy matrimony," he said, helping her shift the yards of material of her wedding gown. "Why do females insist on donning such splendid finery when travel will immediately follow?"

Thea had worn her last truly good dress. "Was that a compliment on my gown?"

"Suppose it was." Anselm plopped down on the seat as if he'd just rowed five miles of the Thames upstream. "Will you wear your hair down all day?"

"I'll do something with it before we sit down to eat." Perhaps Thea and the duke would be given a moment's privacy before the guests arrived, and then she'd find a way—

"Turn a little." He'd taken off his gloves and moved Thea by putting his hands on her bare shoulders. "Hold still."

Carefully, he drew off her veil and coronet, then smoothed his hands through her hair.

"You are presuming, Your Grace."

"I'm tending to my bride. Who would have thought you had all this hair, so tightly do you coil it up." Gentle tugs and twists accompanied this ducal scold to Thea's tresses.

"You're braiding my hair?"

"When a mare is ridden into the hunt field, she has her mane and tail braided. Keeps the brambles and burrs from plaguing her."

His Grace had a decided fondness for female horses. "So I must permit you this liberty?"

"You'd best. Consider it a form of doting."

His hands were competent and oddly soothing as he finger-combed Thea's hair over her shoulders, then trailed it straight down her back to her hips. Despite a crushing urge to close her eyes and subside against the cushioned seat—despite equally compelling urges to bolt from the coach and to pour out her heart to her spouse—Thea kept her spine straight until the duke secured her braid with the few pins and combs she'd worn to the church.

"Thank you, Your Grace. I will have less work to do tonight when I brush it out."

"Tonight, madam, I'll brush your hair out," he said.

The butterflies that had been settling in Thea's stomach took wing again. She and her husband needed to talk, but just as she turned to address him, the Anselm town residence came into view.

The duke remained unnervingly attentive to her throughout the breakfast. To Thea's surprise, Tim appeared looking reasonably alert and sober, and quite well put together. He'd been at the church, to escort her up the aisle, but she'd hardly seen him for having been distracted by Anselm, looking so stern and proper in his formal attire.

The duke always looked stern and proper—unless he was smirking and looking stern, proper, and sardonic.

The breakfast passed in a chattery blur, for all three of His Grace's sisters and their spouses were present, and the women conversed at a great rate, managing to include Nonie and Thea in most of the topics. The men communicated apace as well, mostly with shared looks of indulgent patience, raised eyebrows, winks, and sighs. Anselm's sisters had chosen good men, and the notion comforted.

In all likelihood, *Anselm* had chosen good men for his sisters.

All too soon, Thea had changed into a carriage dress and was again seated beside the duke, his traveling coach speeding them to one of his smaller holdings in Kent.

Really, truly, the time had come to have that talk.

Anselm stretched long legs out toward the opposite bench. "You'll pardon me if I catch a nap?"

He was tired. One didn't brace a duke with bad news when the duke was exhausted.

"You can sleep in a moving vehicle?" Thea asked.

"In this one." He shrugged out of his jacket, for he too had changed into less formal attire. The coach was luxuriously appointed, the most comfortable conveyance Thea had ever been in, and marvelously well sprung.

"Come here, duchess." His Grace fitted an arm around her shoulders. "You might as well rest too. We've at least an hour before we get to our destination, and we'll have staff to meet and civilities to observe. Patience tells me you were up until all hours, fretting over fripperies."

Fretting, yes, but not over fripperies.

With that, he settled Thea against him, and to her surprise, the duke made a comfortable pillow. In the swaying coach, he held her securely, tucking his chin against her temple.

"Relax," he growled into her hair. "I would not gobble you whole on the King's Highway. There's a time and a place for that, and it isn't here and now."

He drew her hand across his waist and secured his other arm around her as well.

By degrees, Thea did relax. Her husband-cum-pillow-cum-worst-fear had indeed fallen asleep, but slumber eluded her. She'd seldom been held like this, not since early childhood. The duke had been trying to put her at ease, perhaps, but he'd left a question circling in her brain, one that robbed her utterly of a desire to sleep:

Was her wedding night the proper time and place to gobble her whole?

❧

Had Noah sprouted horns and fangs, that his bride should regard him so warily? Noah had read Thea as a practical sort, inured to the indelicacies and inconveniences of life—she'd been a companion to a spoiled twit, for pity's sake; how much more mundane could a lady's circumstances be?

And yet, his bride was dignified, or she was when awake. Now, she was curled against his chest, her hair tickling his nose as her breath fanned past his neckcloth. She'd fought the lure of sleep, and he'd feigned slumber himself for a good thirty minutes before he'd felt her gradually succumb to fatigue.

Thea wasn't as substantial a woman as he'd thought, not physically. Her dignity was substantial, her posture militarily erect, her presence as contained as the Queen's on a public occasion. But beneath his hands, her bones were delicate, and in his arms, she felt soft, feminine, and womanly.

Good qualities in a new wife, but disconcerting for being unexpected.

Noah had suggested they rest mostly because Thea had looked tired to him, and a tired female could be fractious, regardless of her species. Fractiousness did not bode well for the wedding night, which could set the tone for their intimate dealings for decades to come.

If need be. Noah had meant what he'd said about getting heirs, and then leaving his duchess in peace. He wouldn't keep a mistress until that time either, though absolute fidelity would likely be beyond him. He was a Winters, as much as he tried to ignore that legacy.

Noah untangled a strand of Thea's hair from her lips—his duchess had a lovely mouth.

She'd appreciate discretion, were he to stray. When he strayed.

Every husband owed his wife discretion, just as she owed the same to him, once the requisite progeny were safely thriving. The idea of another man braiding Thea's hair did not exactly appeal, though; probably an artifact of the morning's vows.

The new Duchess of Anselm had lovely hair, thick, silky, fragrant, and shining, another unexpected aspect of Noah's bride. His thoughts continued to racket about, until the coach passed through the estate village two miles from his main gates.

"Wife?" Noah brushed his lips near Thea's ear. "Duchess? *Araminthea?*"

That got her attention. Thea pushed up sleepily, her hand braced on Noah's thigh in a location she might not have chosen were she more alert.

"Hmm?"

"We've almost reached Wellspring. Best get put to rights. The staff will be formed up in the hall."

"Gads." She straightened, leaving a curious lack of warmth in her wake. "I slept like the dead."

"I rested as well. Our nuptials were a taxing performance. Here." He adjusted one of her hair combs. "That's better."

"Your neckcloth is off center." Thea tidied Noah up as casually as one of his sisters might have.

"Where does a lady's companion learn to put a gentleman's cravat to rights?" he asked.

If he hadn't been watching her, he might have

missed the slight flaring of her eyes, the minute pause in her hands.

"Tending to her orphaned little brother. There, you're presentable, at least in dim light."

❧

"My thanks, Duchess."

Thea's husband had the knack of making two words sound anything but grateful. Still, Thea was appreciative of Anselm's steady arm, of his ease with his dutifully assembled staff. He said something complimentary about each of the dozen or so indoor servants lined up in the entrance hall, but didn't tarry unnecessarily. The help was in good health, well attired, and cheerfully sincere in their welcome to her.

A heartening contrast to the Earl of Grantley's household.

And then the duke excused himself, promising to see Thea again "shortly." He bowed politely to her once she was ensconced in the chambers set aside for the lady of the house, and ordered a tray for her, as well as a bath.

When she'd partaken of a little food, and too much wine, Thea climbed into the largest tub she'd ever seen. She sank into the steaming water, there to try to compose the words she'd use to tell her new husband what manner of bride he'd married.

As she had finished drying herself and donned a nightgown and robe, she heard the door to her sitting room open and close, and the duke's voice, dismissing the maid. Then he was in the doorway, still attired for

the day, but regarding Thea with a particular light in
his blue eyes.

"You did not linger in your bath, Duchess?"

"I did." Was Thea to have awaited him *in the bath*?
"By my standards, in any case. I also had something to
eat, thank you." She could not have said exactly what.

"You're fortified for the coming ordeal?" His lips
quirked, as if he thought the question funny.

Thea pulled her wrapper closer and resecured the
knot in the belt. "Will it be an ordeal, Your Grace?"

"You may trust it will not be." He prowled closer,
giving Thea a whiff of lavender and roses. "Not physically, but please don't tell me I'm to briskly dispatch
with my intimate duties, Lady Thea. We are bride and
groom, and entitled to linger over our pleasures on
our wedding night."

"As to that…" Thea crossed her arms and prepared
to launch into her rehearsed speech, but when she
looked up, the duke was *there*, right there before her,
and all the air left her lungs. She hadn't heard him
move, and yet he was staring down at her, his gaze
both amused and puzzled.

"Can't you trust me a little, Thea?" He grazed a
single finger along her forearm, raising the fine hairs,
and the tempo of her heartbeat. "I would have us be
friends to this extent at least."

"Friends?"

"In bed." He drew the same finger back to her
elbow in a slow trail. "I will take care of you, you may
rely on that."

"Dote on me?"

"And allow you to dote on me, a little." He smiled

crookedly, a different smile than she'd seen on him before. Warmer, almost charming.

"We must discuss a few things first," she managed as that long, tanned finger moved slowly over her forearm, from wrist to elbow and back again. She felt that touch right down to her knees, which should not have been possible.

"We have decades to talk," he said, gently uncrossing her arms, "and if you're fretting over what's to come, talking will not ease your worries. It won't be so bad, Thea. In fact, I'll make it as good as you'll allow it to be."

"But there are matters…"

As Thea spoke, Anselm slowly, gently wrapped her in his embrace, bringing her hands up to his neck, then settling his mouth over hers.

"Later, Thea," he murmured. "Now comes pleasure."

How could a man who stomped, smirked, and ordered his way through life kiss with such languor? Thea knew the meaning of melting bones as the duke's mouth went on campaign, moving over her lips with such tenderness she could barely remain upright. Just a brush, a tease, a nuzzle, a taste, a sighing of his breath over her cheek, and Thea's knees threatened to buckle.

"Kiss me back," Anselm challenged her. "Dote on me."

His *mouth* was doting on Thea, exploring slowly and thoroughly, and then his tongue…

A man ought not to have such an appendage, and certainly not both a tongue and that other most troublesome bit of flesh. He could invite with that tongue, insinuate, flirt, encourage, and, *God help her*, arouse. Thea's fingers sifted through his hair, her body curved into his taller frame, and her lips learned the feel and taste of a man who intended to dote on her to the limit of his conjugal rights.

*What on earth had she got herself into?*

～∞～

Noah's bride was charming him, despite her inexperience, her starch, her uncertainty. Prior to marriage, he'd dealt exclusively with professionals in the bedroom, usually keeping a mistress, and occasionally sampling the charms of those other women available for a price. He was emotionally uninvested, and so were they, and he liked it that way. The bored widows and straying wives were for Meech to deal with, as were the messy endings and sad misunderstandings such encounters often led to.

Noah's partners were playing a part, and he paid them to play it well. They were to make him feel desired, inspire his lust, accommodate it, and send him on his way lighter in the pocket. Increasingly, he had not been lighter in the heart when he'd left their powdered, perfumed, diaphanously draped company. They were assessing his worth as they cooed and sighed, seeing not *him*, but a ring, a bracelet, a parure, or perhaps even rooms on Curzon Street.

Those women could smile at a man as if he were their every carnal dream personified, and yet be thinking as they panted and sighed of what to wear to tomorrow's opera. The calculation of it was almost admirable… Almost.

Araminthea Collins…*Winters* was having trouble

keeping any thoughts in her head at all. She was shyly enthusiastic about kissing Noah, and her grip on his hair was fierce. She probably didn't hear the sounds she was making, of desire and surprise, and she couldn't be aware of how her unconfined breasts pressed against Noah's chest.

Breasts whose fullness surprised him—wonderfully.

A figure suited to childbearing was also a figure suited to bed sport.

"Are you laughing at me, sir?" Thea's eyes were wary, but he didn't let her pull away.

"I'm smiling. Not that I have anything against laughter in bed. You, madam, are overdressed."

When Thea would have scampered off, Noah gathered her close.

"We'll blow out the candles, Thea," he assured her, "but you'll have to be my valet." When she relaxed in his arms, he stepped back and held out one wrist for her to undo his sleeve button.

"You didn't bring in a dressing gown," she said, staring at his hand as if it bore claws, "or a nightshirt."

"I won't need them." Noah kept his hand out and saw that Thea was inclined to argue, but she stifled her inclination with a huffy sigh and deftly unfastened his cuffs.

One garment at a time, she relieved him of his clothes, folding each item tidily over a chair. When he told her to unbutton his shirt, she stayed right where she was, his cravat in her hands.

"You are decidedly fond of imperatives, Your Grace," she snapped. "You might consider asking me to tend to your buttons."

"I just did, and you are stalling."

"You ordered me," she said, taking great care to fold the cravat before stepping closer and getting back to work. "You *told* me to remove your waistcoat, *told* me to untie your neckcloth, *told* me—"

Noah grasped Thea's hand and brought her wrist to his mouth.

"Now I'm *telling* your wrist how lovely it feels to put my mouth on your flesh," he murmured, bending over her wrist and tasting the pulse there. When he allowed her to have her hand back, she finished unbuttoning his shirt.

"My thanks." Noah offered the words as an olive branch. He hadn't intended to aggravate his new duchess when she was already understandably nervous. He was, however, trying to find the present limit of her sensibilities, so he could push her right to that limit and a bit beyond. The next time they were intimate, he'd push beyond that, and beyond that, until she was as comfortable with their carnal dealings as he could make her.

Handling a new wife was the same as acquiring a market, or the controlling shares in a business. One simply needed a plan, some resources, time, and determination.

Noah and Thea were married, after all. Thea could turn to no other for her intimate diversions, not for quite some time. Fairness required that Noah teach her pleasure, and share it with her often.

Assuming she'd allow him to.

"Why don't you get into bed?" he suggested—not ordered. "I'll see to the candles."

Thea drew off her dressing gown and climbed

into bed while Noah politely busied himself dousing the candles. He left one burning while he finished undressing. In the dim light, he took his time using the wash water, because he intended that Thea watch while he made use of it.

Considerate of him, if he did say so himself, virginal sensibilities being the tedious impediments to passion that they were.

Naked as God made him, his cock anticipating the consummation of their vows, Noah padded to the bed and climbed in. He bounced over to his wife's side and wrestled her into his embrace, all their previous kissing apparently forgotten.

His dear bride was stiff in his arms and averting her face.

"You said you'd give me time, Anselm."

Time to become even more nervous and fearful? Not likely.

"I said we'd consummate our vows and then take our dealings slowly," he reminded her. "There's no point to putting this off, Thea. None at all."

"Yes"—he heard her nervous swallow—"there is."

# Four

"WIFE, YOU WILL SETTLE YOURSELF."

Noah grazed his nose along a delicate feminine collarbone. "You are giving in to maidenly vapors. You should be trusting your lawfully wedded spouse instead, because what will pass between us in this bed is nothing remarkable. We're designed for this activity by God Almighty, and it does not require more discussion."

He seized her mouth a little inexpertly—she was wiggling—and she grabbed his hair. She'd taken off the night rail, though Noah spent a small eternity distracting her with kisses so he could ease the night-gown up over her curves. He'd just about got the dratted, endless nightgown up to her thighs when *she* distracted *him* with a foray into his mouth with the tip of her tongue.

He was so distracted, in fact, that his hand stole up over her ribs and gently shaped a soft, lush breast. Because Thea lay flush against him, Noah felt her body undulate in response, felt her spine give as she groaned softly into his mouth.

"You like that." Not a question or a ducal command, but a satisfying, whispered statement of fact. As Noah caressed that same breast a tad more firmly, Thea arched into his hand. "You like it a lot."

Surely that meant she liked her husband some too?

Thea fused her mouth to his for his honesty, silencing him. Noah sneaked a hand under the billows of her nightgown and palmed her breast with his bare hand in retaliation, feeling tremors of desire reverberate through her.

Well, thank all the gods, he'd married a passionate lady, and wasn't that just the best surprise so far?

Noah shifted over Thea, but didn't let their mouths part for more than a moment.

"Wrap your legs around me," he whispered, and when her eyes flew open and her body went still, he smiled down at her. "*Please*, rather. Would you please wrap your legs…?" He fitted her legs around his naked flanks and settled his body closer to hers.

"Your job," he said as he nuzzled at her sex with his arousal, "is to relax. There will be time later for more exuberant measures, but for tonight, you let me… Ah, there you are."

He found his true north, or her true south as the case was, and flexed forward carefully. She was damp, wonderfully, invitingly damp, and he'd not even touched her sex.

"Your Grace—"

"Noah, or Anselm if you must." He flexed again, and gained the first, blissful hint of penetration. "Or my dear or dearest Husband or—"

"Your Grace, please, you must not—"

"Hush now." He dropped to his forearms, settling in for the most pleasurable business. "Relax, just relax."

"But my...*Noah, you must stop.*" Her voice rose on a panicked note as he gave her the first solid thrust, then another, even as she pulled on his hair.

"Almost there, love." He tossed his head, liking that she didn't let go of his hair. "And I won't—oh, Jesus, that's so damned sweet." Thinking only to spare Thea a prolonged breaching, Noah thrust hard enough to hilt himself in the wicked, wet heat of her, then went still.

"That's it." He lowered his cheek to rest on hers. "That's the worst of it. You're all right, aren't you?"

"Oh, please just get *off* me."

Thea's tone held such misery that Noah stayed exactly where he was—despite the lust screaming at him—and considered coming without moving. He could do it, he was sure of it, but his passionate wife was unmoving beneath him, and that would not do.

"Did I hurt you, Thea?"

She shook her head, her movement brushing her cheek against his.

Her damp cheek.

*Lucifer in Hades.* Noah's bride was crying, her tears silently leaking into her hair as she lay passively in his arms. He withdrew, slowly, so as not to hurt her, sat on the edge of the bed, and reached for one of the handkerchiefs he'd stacked on the night table.

In the interests of marital tranquillity—and Noah's own sanity—he brought himself to a brisk and intense climax, his back to Thea as he stroked himself to completion. When he finished, he tidied himself and

gave a thought to how many other dukes were consigned to onanistic pleasures on their wedding nights.

"I did not hurt you, but you are crying." Noah
regarded Thea as she lay, still quietly producing tears.

"I'm so s-sorry, Anselm."

In a parody of his usual flashes of brilliance, Noah
realized what Thea was apologizing for. Rather than
keep his stupid, randy mouth shut, he had to know
for sure.

He'd encountered no real resistance as he'd joined
their bodies, only a bliss-inducing snugness. He'd
hardly made it a habit to lie with virgins, though. For
all he knew, Thea might have been chaste.

Except the light of the last candle was enough to
illuminate the sheer misery on her face.

*The new duchess of Anselm had not been chaste.*

"Do you love him still?" Disappointment as old
as Noah's oldest memory, as familiar as his own
hands, settled in his belly where arousal had been
moments earlier.

"I did not love him."

Thea's voice was low, throaty, and dry as ashes
with crying, and Noah felt an unwelcome pang of
pity for her.

"You might have said something." Noah climbed
back under the covers, and this at least had Thea's eyes
flying open. "For God's sake, don't look at me like
that. I've never struck a female of any species, and I'd
hardly start with my duchess."

Noah smacked a few pillows though, and settled on
his back, arms crossed behind his head.

"We will have this discussion now, Araminthea,

and then not talk of this matter again." He kept a
howling sense of betrayal at bay, only because betrayal
was eclipsed by the self-disgust of a boy who might
choose any one toy to play with, and had unwittingly
selected the broken one.

Would he never learn?

"You will pursue an annulment?" Thea asked.

Noah yanked the covers up. "Oh, you'd like that,
but one can't exactly claim inability on the groom's
part, can one? Nor adultery on yours or a lack of
adequate years or mental competence."

"But you didn't…"

Unchaste and blushing, both. Noah wanted
to howl.

"Hardly germane, madam, as the ecclesiastical
courts are not getting their prurient paws on the details
of my wedding night, thank you very much. Nor will
I have it bruited about that I was unable, or that I
chose poorly. Are you breeding?"

Noah should have asked Thea that before ruling out
an annulment. He was a duke and a Winters. He could
have any damned marriage he pleased annulled.

"I am not breeding."

"You will allow me leave to doubt that." Noah
fell silent, resenting his wife to the depths of his
stupid soul. He'd been so intent on seeing this task
accomplished, and she'd been his brilliantly insightful choice.

Bloody blazing damn.

"I expect business associates to attempt to cheat
me," he said. "I expected my mistresses to have their
dainty hands in my pockets at every turn, I expect my

family to wheedle and manipulate and beg favors, but I did not see this coming. I commend you."

Thea didn't shrink from him physically, but he might as well have slapped her, so palpably did she react to his insult.

"Nobody would leave us alone," she said. "I wasn't raised to know how to broach such a topic. I can't think when you start kissing me, much less speak coherently. My sister has no other hope of a proper match, and *I could not find the proper moment to s-say anything.*"

Nor had Noah exactly sought privacy with his bride since she'd accepted his proposal. What would have been the point?

"What would you have said?" he asked.

"That I am not pure."

"But you are chaste," Noah muttered. "You exude chastity." And virtue, and feminine grace, and dignity, and all manner of qualities appropriate to a duchess.

Thea rolled to her side, her back to him, and he suspected she was crying again.

"Stop that." He rolled too, to spoon around her. "Would you please stop crying, rather."

"I'm not crying." Her body shuddered to the contrary, and Noah felt unaccountably like a bully, for which he also resented her.

"Thea, this is not a tragedy," he said, his hand tracing the line of her spine. Even in the yardage of her nightgown, even lying in bed, she gave off an air of dignified injury, which was confounding, when she wasn't the wronged party. "Araminthea…"

"I'm listening."

Two words bearing an entire lecture on bruised feminine sensibilities, which was amazing, and ironically amusing too.

"Do you know what manner of family you've married into?" Noah went on talking, mostly to distract her as he worked his way closer. "My late uncle, from whom I inherited my title, had three wives, each of whom he esteemed greatly, to hear him tell it. Nonetheless, the love of his life was a countess he referred to as his Unattainable Muse, whom he cherished his entire life, to the extent he left at least one cuckoo in her nest, though my father suggested the tally might have been closer to three."

All of whom Noah nodded to politely in the park. "I bear a striking resemblance to both of the lady's sons. My surviving uncle continues to cut a swath through the ballrooms and house parties, often taking up with willing ladies half his age. It's either an inspiration or a complete farce, I know not which."

Thea was listening, Noah sensed, because her posture gradually eased, and she didn't flinch when he brought his legs up along hers.

"There are those who believe my half brother, Harlan, could be the result of my youngest uncle's attempt to console my father's third wife," Noah went on, "though I don't credit that rumor, myself. My uncle has consoled many a widow, though, and the resulting progeny are considered the deceased's posthumous miracles. I've forbidden him to attend any more funerals, unless the grieving widow is past childbearing age."

Thea peered at Noah over her shoulder, and he

used the moment to finish stealing a march across the bed.

"Are you serious, Anselm?"

"I was single-handedly upholding the standards of common sense among the menfolk in my family, and then you came along—I thought you an eminently sensible choice, I'll have you know—and upended my good opinion of myself entirely. I do not appreciate it."

Noah did not know exactly what to do about it, either.

"I am sorry." Thea subsided, facing away from him. "I am truly, truly sorry."

Noah believed she was sorry to be found out, but he wasn't a saint, and practicalities demanded consideration.

"We will not be intimate until you've had your courses, Thea. You will understand my reasoning, given that there's a ducal succession to consider. Unlike my father or my uncle, I believe children should be raised wherever possible by those responsible for their creation."

"As do I."

Noah had sensed that about her, sensed she'd be an involved parent, not a woman who pretended her own nursery was located in another shire.

"Please assure me you haven't any children, Duchess."

A moment of banked dread passed as Thea drew the covers up, tugging hard until they came free of Noah's hip.

"I have no children, Your Grace. For Nonie, I

would surrender all of my worldly freedom, my independence, and my dreams of a less pragmatic union. I could never leave my children, and certainly not for something as trivial as a tiara."

Noah's heart resumed beating. A child would have been… His stores of civility were unequal to considering that hypothetical.

"When I am assured you haven't played me entirely false," he said, "we will embark on relations with the intent of producing my heirs." He hoped. Even his breeding organs weren't entirely without emotional sensibilities. Anger and bewilderment did not make endearing bedmates.

Thea was back to peering at him over her shoulder, scowling, really. "You're sure?"

"You are my duchess." Also his wife. "I could rely on Harlan to secure the succession, but he's only seventeen and might turn out every bit as rackety as the generation before him. The most reasonable choice is to content myself with your charms, keep a close eye on you, and hope the good Lord sees fit to give us sons in short order."

Though getting roaring drunk seemed a fitting addition to the list too. Noah simply could not muster the sangfroid to interrogate Thea further about the details of her past now, when they were both exhausted, he was naked, and she might well be missing another man's attentions.

"And after the children have arrived?" she asked.

Noah rolled over, so they were back to back. "Enough chatter. Go to sleep, and please recall when you arise that we've passed a night exploring conjugal bliss in each other's arms. If you steal the covers, I will fetch them back."

He fell silent, and his bride took a long, long time to fall asleep, though she did not at any point in that interminable and disappointing night intentionally steal his covers.

*

As Thea lay unmoving beside her husband, she mused that her wedding night had been an exercise in humiliation, but she was mindful another man would have beat her and tossed her into the street by now. Many other men. Given Anselm's general irascibility, marrying him without disclosing her past had been risky, but he was being surprisingly decent about it.

The duke thrashed about on his half of the bed, his knee bumping Thea's hip.

She recalled him holding forth once to Marliss, explaining he'd promised his grandsire he'd marry by age thirty-two—the grandfather had been pressing for marriage in the next fortnight—and Anselm's thirty-second birthday loomed at the end of summer.

His Grace was not quite twice Marliss's age.

But he was eons older than Marliss would ever be in terms of experience and world-weariness.

And that, Thea mused as the duke's hand stole up to rest on her shoulder, was the greatest humiliation of all. Noah Winters was inured to disappointment in his familiars. His litany of role models—father, both uncles—was a pathetic recitation of all that was self-indulgent and immature about the typical privileged male.

His business associates had proven no better, nor had his sisters or his mistresses.

Plural.

That gave Thea pause, and stopped her march toward canonizing her recently acquired spouse. Anselm was far less pure than she was, far less chaste, and that perhaps was what allowed him to display such tolerance toward her.

Though for men, of course, sexual peccadilloes were just that, little indiscretions, almost humorous, and they would never be thus for women.

Anselm was absently caressing her neck, which she attributed to a somnolent habit, one he'd likely developed in the handling of his mistresses—all seventeen of them—and yet she couldn't resent his touch. She'd disappointed her husband on their wedding night, not because she was barely experienced, shy, self-conscious, and easily embarrassed, though she was all of those.

Because she'd erred, strayed, stumbled.

Fallen.

And the duke, for entirely pragmatic reasons, would catch her. His decision boggled Thea's tired mind, almost as much as the insidious languor radiating from the touch of a few warm, male fingers on a few inches of her bare flesh.

"Go to sleep, Wife," he murmured. His Grace excelled at issuing orders even when stark naked. "You can fret about it all tomorrow, I promise."

He patted her shoulder, and while Thea knew the duke graced her bed out of a desire to provide convincing appearances in the morning, she also suspected he was torturing her. If these were his casual caresses, what might it have been like to know his highest regard, his most tender intimacies?

Thea checked her unruly imagination from speculating on that theme. Bad enough she'd let matters progress as far as they had. Terrible, in fact, but also so undeniably lovely.

Who would have thought?

And because Thea would never in a hundred years have attributed such tenderness to her new spouse, it was also, despite all, the greatest kindness that he would stay with her and soothe her to sleep and smile at her as she woke in the morning.

<br>

"Arise, Wife. You are a thief as well as a liar," Noah pronounced the minute his duchess's eyes opened. When she merely wrinkled her nose and burrowed back into the pillows, he added a poor ability to take orders to her transgressions.

His duchess was not so dignified in the morning, and she'd slept on soundly as Noah had risen and shaved.

"Madam. Wake. Up."

"I do not steal." She muttered this to the pillow she clutched like a drowning sailor clutches a passing spar.

"Wake up, Duchess." Noah sat on the edge of the bed, which meant she listed toward him. "We embark on the first day of our conjugal bliss this morning, and I cannot have you wasting the hours abed."

"Tea?"

Noah passed her a steaming hot cup, with

cream and sugar—not milk, of course. Duking had its privileges.

"Drink it all." He rose and crossed to the sitting room, coming back into the bedroom pushing a tea cart. "You will partake of sustenance while we plan our day."

"Hush." Thea was at least sitting up, her cheek faintly wrinkled from passing the night in intimate congress with her pillow. Her hair was a mess, cascading down her back in a dark waterfall, and her eyes were soft. Noah saw a hint of beard burn on the side of her neck.

Well, hell, did a lying, prevaricating new wife ever look so intimately adorable?

"Butter, my lady?"

She cradled her teacup as if it held the secret to eternal life. "In quantity."

He made her a plate with a thick slice of raisin bread, halved and slathered with butter, garnished with several sections of orange and a sprig of mint.

"You steal covers," Noah said, putting together his own plate, which included bacon, eggs, buttered toast, and a single section of orange.

"I beg your pardon." Thea's voice was even as Noah settled on the bed beside her, his dressing gown gaping open when he leaned back against the headboard.

"We do breakfast so well here in England," he remarked, munching his toast. "It sets one up for great disappointment in the remaining meals."

"We have good desserts," his duchess remarked between bites, "and excellent cuts of meat. So what would you have of me today?"

"Eat." Noah put a piece of bacon on her plate. "You need some meat on your bones if you're to keep up with your spouse, Duchess. I am not a restful presence."

"Nor nice," she reminded him, then looked abruptly pained. "But I must thank you for your forbearance."

Noah shrugged and did not look at her. "I stole the covers back."

He'd already told her they would not discuss their wedding night again. He was not forbearing, he was practical, adept at making the best of a bad bargain. "More tea, madam?"

"Please."

"I will be your lady's maid this morning, and you will be my valet. My sisters will likely descend this afternoon, inspecting the ravages of our night of passion. You will smile, blush, and stammer convincingly?"

"B-b-but of course, Your Grace."

"Just so." He smiled into his teacup, despite her impertinence. "I've a morning gift for you. You needn't stammer over it, but feel free to smile."

"That is hardly necessary."

"The smiling? You must do as you see fit, of course. I am not ordering you to smile."

"Gracious of you, Anselm." She *was* smiling into her teacup as well.

They could be civil with each other, they could communicate effectively, and they could share a meal companionably.

Noah bit off another piece of warm, buttered toast, mostly in charity with the world, because despite odds to the contrary, there was hope.

෴

"This is hopeless." The duke scowled at Thea's hair, such condemnation in three words, Thea wanted to snatch the brush from his hands.

"It isn't hopeless." She held her hand up over her shoulder. "My hair is merely thick and a bit disheveled. Give me the brush, and I'll set it to rights."

Anselm passed her the brush and stomped off toward the dressing room. Despite the peevish look in his icy blue eyes, Thea had the sense her husband had been angling for that surrender. He'd actually made significant progress on the briar patch that was her unbound hair in the morning, and it had felt good, so good, to have somebody else tend to her at the start of her day.

The start of her married life.

"Given recent developments," the duke's voice rang out from their connected dressing rooms, "I'll send a note into Town and wave off the Furies."

"Beg pardon?"

"My dear sisters." Anselm emerged, clothing over his arm. "My brother was up at university doing some end-of-term studies of flora and fauna, which is likely an excuse to gape at women and swill hops. He'll join us the day after tomorrow, which can't be helped. What do you think, the white or the cream?"

"White," Thea said as in her mirror she saw him hold first one then the other shirt against a blue waistcoat embroidered with silver paisley designs.

"White it shall be." The duke laid his clothing over a chair and disappeared again, only to emerge bearing a shining pair of black tall boots. "There wasn't time to ask to whom you'd like a wedding announcement sent, but I suppose you have a list?"

Anselm was brusque, imperious, and oddly thought-ful. Thea could get used to the combination when he topped it off by asking her opinion of his wardrobe.

"I have a very short list," Thea said, a miserable comment on her circumstances. Since her parents' deaths, her circle of acquaintances had dwindled and dwindled, until her brother's unsavory cronies had kept all but the oldest associations from withering.

"Doesn't a certain gentleman need to have his face rubbed in your successful marriage?" Anselm asked, ever so casually.

Well, damn, this again. That gentleman—who hardly qualified for the name—would be the ruin of their marriage.

"There is no such gentleman, Your Grace."

He regarded Thea steadily, then whisked off his dressing gown.

"Your Grace!"

"Hmm?" Anselm disappeared behind a privacy screen, and Thea realized he'd just deliberately unnerved her with his nudity, a retaliation for disappointing him so badly the night before. He wouldn't speak of it, oh no, but he wouldn't leave her any peace over it, either.

Which was only fair, she supposed, plaiting her hair into one thick skein and pinning it to her head in a coronet. Anselm was raised to observe certain standards of behavior, and she must not allow herself to mistake civility for friendship.

Ever again.

"I had the maids brush out your habit," he said from behind his screen. "It will do for present pur-poses, but you'll need a wardrobe."

"I have a wardrobe." Thea rose and poured herself another cup of tea. The blend had to be private, because the taste was rich, smooth, spiced with jasmine, and altogether delectable. The quality of the tea had Thea wondering just how wealthy her new husband was.

And how self-indulgent. Unbidden, she recalled the smooth play of his fingers on her nape, the way his body had covered and warmed hers, the…

"That has to be the most unapproachable hair style on earth." Anselm frowned at her coiffure as he came around the privacy screen, shooting his cuffs like some actor making an entrance from stage right.

"This serves to keep my hair where it won't cause trouble."

He peered at himself in her vanity mirror, and appropriated her hairbrush. From the scent of him, he'd made use of the tooth powder and some fancy French soap as well. Not lavender and roses today, but something summery and softly floral. As he dragged the brush over his hair, his gaze followed Thea in the mirror while she took her turn behind the dressing screen.

"You aren't complaining about being up so early," he remarked a few moments later.

"It would hardly matter, would it?"

"Not in the least." Thea heard him set the brush down. She did not hear him cross the room, and so when he folded his arms over the top of the screen, she tried not to let her discomfiture show.

"You intend to watch me dress, Your Grace?"

"Such pleasures are a husband's privilege. At least that color is becoming."

And at least Thea had her chemise on, and the

riding habit's bodice secured too, though it gaped completely at the back. She hadn't wrapped the skirt into the folds designed for riding either.

"Let me do that." Anselm stepped close, and Thea stopped breathing as he hooked her habit together at the back. His breath brushed her shoulder, so near did he stand, but she didn't dare step away. To him, veteran of thirty-four mistresses, these little intimacies were likely routine, not even worth remarking. To Thea, they were...

Overwhelming, and not in a good way. A good way would have been if their marriage were not tainted with her deceit, and her past. A good way would have been if Anselm had bothered to court her for even a few socially visible weeks. A good way would be...

"Turn."

Thea obeyed, and let him—*him!*—adjust the skirts of her habit so they fell properly.

"There." Anselm stepped back and turned the ducal scowl upon her hair.

"It's just hair," she said repressively. "If you like, I can cut it into fashionable little curls, but I warn you, I will look a fright when it rains, which is most of the time."

"You will not cut your hair." Anselm winged his arm at her. "And that is not a request, Duchess. Now, chin up—you're good at that—and feel free to adorn your countenance with your secretive, cat-in-the-cream-pot smile."

"Right." Thea lifted her chin. "Conjugal bliss, smile, stammer, and all that."

"Just so."

Anselm smiled at her then, that almost-charming smile of the evening before, the one that momentarily banished the shadows in his blue eyes, made the corners crinkle with impending mirth—the smile that nearly stole Thea's breath with the sheer dearness of it.

Mercy.

She laced her arm through the duke's, and let him escort her downstairs, past the beaming maids, the smiling footmen, the giggling tweenie, and the silently nodding butler. All the while, Anselm remained quiet, inviting no comment from his staff, and Thea wondered why no one else had ever accused her of having a cat-in-the-cream-pot smile.

For that matter, what *was* a cat-in-the-cream-pot smile?

# Five

BLOODY DOUBLE INFERNALLY DIRE DAMN.

Noah made it through the house, his duchess swanning along beside him, and knew a profound relief when they reached the out-of-doors. Perhaps if he put a shire or two between his wife and himself, he might not feel so strongly the need for the pleasures he'd been denied the night before.

He was used to waking in a state conducive to procreation, and had tended to himself before Thea had even opened her eyes.

Tended to himself *again*.

Rather than ease the ache, he'd only shortened the fuse on his ever-obliging lust, such that simply brushing Thea's hair was enough to put him back into a state. Two states, actually, for he was still unhappy with his new duchess, even as he inconveniently desired her.

When had brushing a woman's hair become arousing; when had it graduated from a step in a well-planned seduction to a step in a man's own downfall?

The trouble was, Noah wasn't used to sleeping with

females. Occasionally, his house cat might steal into his bedchamber, but other than her, he knew better than to sleep with his passing fancies. They got Ideas if a fellow allowed that type of nonsense, especially a wealthy, titled fellow. Thank all the gods, wives were a more sensible breed.

"You have lovely grounds," his duchess observed, stopping to sniff a bloodred rose. "Not a subtle fragrance, but very pretty."

Thea's comment reminded Noah of Henny Whitlow, to whom he'd sent more than one bouquet of showy red roses with their cloying fragrance. This peculiar marriage of his was bringing out all the less worthy qualities of the typical Winters adult male, and he liked that not one bit.

"You're free to do with the grounds as you wish," Noah said. "We'll assemble the outside staff when we return later this morning, and I'll introduce you to our head gardener. He's a temperamental Dutchman who insists on being referred to as a botanist. I like him, because he doesn't bow and scrape, except before his flowers."

Thea made no reply, for they were approaching the stables. Although Wellspring was one of Noah's smallest holdings, it was also one of his favorites. Every detail, every building, flower bed, and window trim was finely wrought and well maintained. Wellspring was a retreat of sorts, though Noah doubted his associations with the place would be quite as restful in future.

"I haven't ridden to speak of since I was much younger," Thea said. "Papa had a weakness for horses and ended up letting out the estate houses by the time I was twelve to generate income for the sake of his hunters."

"So you'll need a gentle mount." Noah would not allow himself to be disappointed—not over such a detail, not again, not with her, so soon.

Thea smiled the very cat-in-the-cream-pot smile he'd dreamed of.

"Let's see what you have in here, Your Grace, and I'm sure we can find someone with whom I'll get along."

Someone other than *him*, Noah supposed, but had Thea been cowering and obsequious this morning, he'd have disliked that more than her serene equanimity and tidily braided hair.

Noah escorted his duchess down the barn aisle, introducing her to this hunter, that hack, these coach horses, and even a pair of enormous draft horses, visiting from the home farm because the roof to their stable was being repaired.

"They're happy to laze about." Noah stroked a bare hand over a large, velvety nose. "Planting only recently ended, and haying will start at the end of the week, then comes the clearing of ditches, and cleaning up the home wood. If we've time, we might dig a new irrigation ditch or dredge the ponds, and then the harvests start, and the wood hauling, and sometimes they must scrape snow off the drive, and life is endless work, isn't it?"

The gelding weighed easily a ton, likely nineteen hands plus at the withers, but his big lips nibbled delicately at Noah's hand, while his mate watched intently from the next stall.

"Shameless little beggar." Noah produced a lump of sugar purloined from breakfast, and let it disappear, then fed another to the second gelding.

His wife was watching him, no evidence of her smile to be found.

"Come, Duchess," Noah said, dusting grains of sugar from his palms. "Your morning gift awaits." *Please will you come, rather.* He'd have to practice that.

He took Thea's hand and towed her past a couple more stalls, stopping before a loose box housing a sleek chestnut with four matching white socks.

"This is your idea of a token offering?" Thea asked.

"Her name is Heart's Delight, though the lads call her Della."

At the sound of her name, the mare gave up her hay and came to hang her head over the half door. Big brown eyes peered at them with a combination of reserve and curiosity that put Noah in mind of his wife. The selfsame wife who just hours before had shyly let her tongue—

"She's not without spirit, but I found her quite sensible too," Noah said. The mare had also already dropped a foal, a handsome colt.

"She's lovely." Thea turned to him, her gaze so warm Noah nearly forgot to breathe, and then she stepped closer, and he could not divine her intent until she wrapped her arms around him and hugged him hard.

Not a seductive embrace, a long, tight hug.

Noah might have been about to hug her back when she stepped away and ran her fingers softly over the mare's jaw. Rather than watch that and suffer the resulting torments—what was *wrong* with him this morning?—Noah marched off, leaving the ladies to get acquainted while he bellowed for grooms and tack, and where in the hell was everybody this morning?

This was just another morning, after all.

His wife, however, was not just another lady in a faded habit perched on a horse for display. Thea rode with the natural seat of one who'd taken to the saddle early and often, and she delighted in her mare, the both of them game for any log, ditch, stream, or bank Noah led them over.

Who would have thought?

"You are a hoyden," he concluded. "The pair of you are hoydens, and what am I to do with you? Troubadour and I will never hack out in peace again."

"Troubadour has been a perfect gentleman," Thea said, her smile careless and quietly stunning as she patted her mare. "I cannot thank you enough for Della, Your Grace. She is perfect, and had I chosen a gift myself, I could not have picked out anything lovelier or more appreciated. I humbly and sincerely thank you."

*Damn.* Noah did not want Thea's thanks, he wanted *her*, and her smiles and pats and teasing.

Which would not do. "Race you to the end of the field."

He waited one gentlemanly heartbeat for Thea to tap her heel against the mare's side, then let True bound after them, holding back until the last minute so the finish was honestly in question.

"You let me win!" she accused breathlessly. "I know your scheme, Anselm. You're bent on destroying my coiffure, and it's not very subtle of you."

Her braid had indeed come free of its pins to hang in a shiny sable rope over her shoulder.

"We'll not be racing anymore with you in such disarray," Noah said. "Besides, the horses have to walk out, and our outdoor staff requires introductions forthwith." He turned his big gelding to amble along beside her mare. "What do you think of this little holding?"

"Little?" Thea blew a strand of hair off her forehead. "Wellspring must be several thousand acres, with the tenant farms, the home farms, and the woods."

Noah gave his horse, who was still puffing, a loose rein. True had endured months of Town life prior to this remove to Kent and was in want of conditioning.

"Wellspring is small," Noah said, "but I like it. My mother was fond of this place too, and I have good memories of summers spent here as a boy. By mutual consent, my parents never opened this estate for house parties or shooting parties or the like."

A shadow crossed Thea's face as she took up the reins. "A refuge, then. We all need a place of refuge."

She had needed a place of refuge, else she might not be married to Noah—lowering thought.

"We can change before you review the troops," he said, "or we can greet them in riding attire. They'll be assembled outside."

"How many?"

What did that matter? "Two dozen or so, I should think. It's summer, so more people are about than in winter."

"We'll stay here for haying?"

"That depends." True minced around a puddle, an affectation he'd never indulge in on the streets of

London. "The duration of our stay here depends on when your courses start."

Thea fussed with her skirts, adjusted her whip, petted the mare, and glanced off toward the stables in the distance.

"Well?" Noah prompted, for they'd soon have grooms hanging on their every word.

"This is the tenth," she said very softly. "Likely by the twenty-second."

The timing could be worse. Three weeks instead of two. Thea could have been one of those vexing women who pretended not to know, or not to be able to predict her cycles, one of those women who sought the title Duchess of Anselm and were never invited to Noah's bed.

"Then, yes." Noah nudged his horse around a turn in the lane. "We will be here through haying, likely through the end of the month, and possibly longer."

Though when they left, they'd be man and wife in every possible sense.

"When will Nonie join us?" Thea asked.

"Lady Nonie will remain in Town for at least the rest of the month," Noah said slowly, "possibly longer."

Gone were her soft smiles and blushes, and her expression became mulish. "The entire reason I consented to marry you was for the sake of my sister, to keep her safe, and spend—"

Noah shortened his reins, curb and snaffle both. "The entire reason, Thea?"

Her chin came up, predictably. He knew that for the battle flag it was, and they'd been married less than a day.

"Entire," she said, very pleasantly. "I was content not to marry, but Nonie's circumstances demanded attention."

"You were content to be preyed on by the likes of Corbett?" Noah's question was unkind, but Thea was being prodigiously stubborn. Every couple adjusting to married life deserved some time to themselves.

"I'd rather have been left alone," she muttered.

Thea eased her mare up into a rocking canter, and Noah let her lead him over the lanes back to the stables. They still weren't speaking as he helped her off her mare, but rather than give up the fight, he stood beside the mare, his hands on Thea's waist, holding her immobile for long moments in the stable yard, looking down at her until she took his point.

For better or for worse, she was not *alone* now.

Thea lifted her chin and without benefit of her husband's escort, swished off in the direction of the gardens.

⁂

The duke had held Thea so closely through the night.

He'd been companionable over breakfast.

He'd given her that gorgeous mare for her very own.

And Thea had foolishly, foolishly *hoped* her taciturn, sardonic husband had been showing a well-hidden tendency toward forgiveness.

She'd known a gathering sense of relief as Anselm had toured his land with her, acting like any new husband might. They'd conversed, they'd even laughed, and then like waking from a pleasant dream to a harsh reality, the pretense of civility had been abruptly dropped.

Thea was hurt, but she couldn't fault Anselm. The error had been hers, to think this gentleman who was her husband could ever be her friend. He'd told her he wasn't nice.

Why hadn't she listened?

While her heart was fracturing along a thousand old lines of pain and disappointment, Anselm was doing the pretty before his outdoor staff.

"And this little fellow"——Noah nodded at a lanky blond man wearing wire-rimmed glasses—"is my botanist, Benjamin Erikson, whom we must commend for tearing himself away from his workbench long enough to greet you."

"Your Grace." Erikson bowed over Thea's hand. "I am charmed." Brown eyes twinkled at her, and he held her hand a moment too long.

"Having met Erikson," Anselm said repressively, "we have concluded the reviewing of the troops, and a proper breakfast awaits us inside. Erikson, if you've some time, I'd like to meet with you later this morning."

"I'll be propagating," Erikson said. "Best not bother me until this afternoon."

At least somebody was propagating, for Thea wasn't sure she ever would.

"Be about your botany. I'll find you. Duchess?"

Anselm winged his elbow, and Thea obediently accompanied him to the house.

"Gardeners are to be drab little men in shabby coats whose eyes light up only when they can present a perfect red rose to a blushing young lady," Thea said. "Erikson is not a gardener."

"No, he's a botanist, but he'd better not be offering any roses to you, Thea."

She paused on the front steps and untangled her arm from the duke's. Perhaps a proper duchess would hold her fire until she was private with her husband. Thea would work on that skill—later.

"I understand you are furious with me, Your Grace, and disappointed and entitled to exact revenge in all manner of small and nasty ways. I accept this, as long as you provide a safe home for my sister, but please do not attribute to me a cavalier disregard for fidelity because of actions occurring before we even met. I am your wife, and I will not shame you, *or myself*, by flirting with your help."

"Our help," he said, frowning down at her from one step up.

They processed in silence toward their chambers, but as Anselm ushered Thea inside her sitting room, he stood for a moment by the door.

"I am furious," he said, "and disappointed, but not as much at you as I am with myself."

A ducal olive branch, the only variety of the species that came with thorns.

"Can you explain yourself, Your Grace?" Thea regarded him levelly, which was an effort when his blue, blue eyes had gone more bleak than usual.

"I should have seen you coming," Anselm said. "In this family, my job is to see disaster on the horizon and steer us clear of it."

This disclosure was supposed to help their marital

situation? "I am a disaster now, though still not quite a tragedy?"

"You are my wife."

Anselm left, closing the door silently behind him. Thea heard him moving about his adjoining chambers as she changed out of her riding attire and restored order to her hair. As she put herself to rights, she reflected on her husband, and how she had spent weeks in his company, weeks observing him, really, and still she knew him not at all.

❧

"You married yesterday." James Heckendorn, Baron Deardorff, handed Noah a drink. James, as always, was the picture of blond, blue-eyed gentlemanly decorum, while Noah's hair was probably sticking out in all directions. "And yet you present yourself in my library today, two hot hours in the saddle away from your bride?"

"An hour and a half." Noah took the drink and passed it under his nose.

James poured half a finger into his own glass, probably for the sake of appearances. "To marital bliss." He lifted his glass.

Noah lifted his glass as well, a duke being incapable of wholly discarding his manners. "You're sincere."

"I am married to *your* sister," James observed. "Patience will come directly here to seek me when she returns from her shopping, towing *your* sister-in-law with her, so, no, when I toast marital bliss, I am not being the least facetious."

"You and Patience are getting on well enough?" Noah knew they were, for Patience was the most misnamed creature on earth. If she were unhappy, her brother would have long learned of it.

"I think you're at last to be an uncle," James said, studying his drink. "She hasn't said, but the signs are there."

"Signs?"

"You know." James's smile was bashful. "A tenderness about the…" He gestured to his chest. "It's been some weeks since Patience was indisposed, she naps at odd times, and has declined bacon at breakfast."

"She is either breeding or ill." Patience adored a crisp slice of bacon. "Congratulations, I suppose. Your mother will no doubt be pleased."

"I am pleased," James said with quiet ferocity. "You marry, congratulating yourself on a good, solid match, and then you hum along for a few years, and before you know it, the good, solid match has turned into something altogether *more*. I married Patience thinking we'd suit, but I want to give her children because she's the best mother my children could have."

"Impending fatherhood is making a thespian of you." Noah set down his mostly full glass. "Matrimony has made a fool of me."

"It's only been a day since the wedding, Anselm. How could you bugger up an institution that's been around for thousands of years in only a day?"

"You assume I'm the party at fault?"

"I do," James said without a hint of hesitation. "You're the party who rode to my doorstep in the heat of summer, leaving your new bride out in Kent to fritter away the day."

Noah paced to the window, turning his back on

James and his confounded fraternal smile. "My new bride came to me in less than perfect condition."

"She's not a twit who just put up her hair, Anselm. Of course she won't be without a few quirks."

"It wasn't a quirk she chose to give to some other man, James." Though Noah didn't think Thea had given away her heart, if that mattered.

James took up the place beside Noah at the window. "Despite old wives' tales, there's no real way to tell. Patience didn't bleed, but I refuse to believe she wasn't pure."

Not what a brother wanted to hear.

"Wise of you." Outside the window, two common blue butterflies went flitting around a hedge of honeysuckle. No sooner would both light beside each other, than one would flutter to a different flower. "I wouldn't want to have to beat you senseless, and Thea would not understand why I came home sporting bruised knuckles. My duchess made sure I knew of her amatory experience when it was too late to seek an annulment."

"It's never too late to seek an annulment. Old Kimball set his second wife aside after three years."

"Because she was barren, and he the last of his line, and they did not suit," Noah said. "But the man's a laughingstock, while his barren wife is up to, what, three little darlings with her subsequent spouse?"

Noah aspired to be the first Winters male who was not, at any point, a laughingstock. A humble ambition, but dear to him.

"You are castigating yourself because you consider your wife to be used goods," James decided. "This is like you, Noah, but where's the point?"

"That's just it." The butterflies abandoned their honeysuckle and flew off toward the roses. "There is no point. Unless I want to make a complete fool of myself, I will keep my mouth shut and content myself with my used goods. I will get sons on her, I will parade her about as my duchess, and I will show her every public courtesy."

"Because," James said, "you are a damned saint who never put a foot wrong, never poached on another's preserves, never misstepped, and couldn't find a way to undo it in time to prevent harm to another—you alone of all grown men?"

Noah felt an urge to shoot at butterflies, for this very point had intruded on his ride before he'd trotted past the foot of the Wellspring driveway.

"James, you are tiresomely unsympathetic. I hardly recall why I permitted you to marry my beloved sister, and I fear for the happiness of my unborn niece or nephew."

Noah also feared a little for Thea's happiness, though he could not have said why such a wayward sympathy should plague him. His own happiness had long ago surrendered to duty, and to satisfaction in an obligation competently executed.

"Allow me to be practical as well as unsympathetic," James said, opening the window. "My wife has developed an opinion regarding the suitability of your bride."

The breeze that came in was warm and fragrant—like Thea, damn it.

"You allow this folly of freely expressed uxorial opinions?"

"Give it a few years." James patted his arm. "We'll see who is permitted to hold opinions in your household, Anselm. But as to Patience's views on your bride, she liked Lady Thea very much, and said you'd chosen far more appropriately than she expected you to."

Allowing a friend to marry one's sister had distinct disadvantages. "Of course she liked Thea—Thea has been a companion. Thea knows better than any woman how to be agreeable."

Though she could take Noah to task on the steps of his own home, which had pleased him marvelously.

"Do you know to whom your Thea was a companion before taking the post with Endmon's tender flower?"

"I do not." Noah set his drink back on the sideboard, while James was roundabouting toward some point which would be as uncomfortable as it was insightful.

"Thea's first post was with Joanna Newcomer, dowager Viscountess Bransom."

"Holy God. Old Besom herself. Papa used to threaten to sell me to her when I was lad, or leave me on her cook's doorstep."

"Lady Thea's second post was with Annabelle Handley, Lady Bransom's boon companion."

"Besom and Bosom, according to Meech. A difficult pair, but what's your point?"

"The difficult pair each left Lady Thea a small bequest and glowing references, as I'm sure you're aware."

"My solicitor is certainly aware." The butterflies came dancing in the window, as if a baron's private residence should remain open for their inspection. "What is your point, James?"

"I know of these little windfalls because Lady Thea put them in trust for Antoinette and told me I must send the bills for the shopping expeditions to her solicitor, who would pay for them out of those funds."

Those bills would, of course, be sent to Noah, now that he knew about them.

"So Thea set the money aside for her sister. Decent of her." Noah had yet to see to Lady Nonie's settlements, but he would. Soon.

James wasn't quite as tall as Noah, but he was lanky and fit, with a humming energy that matched Patience's vivacious nature.

"You feel cheated," James said, sauntering closer, "because your wife was honest enough to admit you weren't her very first. Never mind she isn't your first, or your hundred and first, likely. You will have your tantrums and pouts, as anybody who's studied the Winters male line will attest."

A low, telling blow.

"We're dramatic fellows," Noah allowed, "or the previous generation was. I am not storming about, threatening legal action, casting Thea into the street." Though part of him wanted to—the part that wasn't wondering which bounder had sampled Thea's charms and then left a gently bred lady to fend entirely for herself.

"Your pride will not allow you the typical Winters histrionics," James countered as a butterfly landed on his shoulder, opened and closed its wings twice, then flitted off toward the window. "But for one minute,

Anselm, think about *her* pride. She didn't have to say a thing, didn't have to tell you, didn't have to let on your suspicions—if your lust-clouded brain had any—were based in fact. And for God's sake, man, she was an earl's daughter *in service*, a lamb to slaughter, considered fair game by most, and completely without protection. But she took the risk of telling you, because for all that, she is decent."

The second butterfly danced a few inches from the end of Noah's nose, then joined its mate, darting out the window.

Noah thought uncomfortably of young Corbett's punishing grip on Thea's arm.

"The trouble with you, James, is that you are decent and you can't imagine a female scheming to get her hands on your title."

Noah muttered this, knowing Thea had in no wise schemed to get her hands on anybody's title. Marriage had made him daft, or the heat had addled his wits.

"Cut line," James said, taking a sip from Noah's glass. "To you, I'm a mere baron, but to some, there is no such thing as a *mere* title of any degree. You're not thinking this through—which would be gratifying to behold were there not a lady involved. You won't set Thea aside or you'd be at the solicitors, not wasting my best brandy. You know little about her, but you might like her, might find there's much to respect about her, and a lapse in her past means little."

Had it been a lapse or a torrid affair? A recent torrid affair?

*Something else entirely?*

"You want me to give her a chance," Noah said,

the very conclusion he'd been avoiding for the entire ride into Town. Their marriage deserved a chance.

*Thea* deserved a chance.

"A little forbearance could only benefit you when you're hell-bent on getting her with child," James pointed out. "Have you ever tried to swive a woman you hate?"

"Interesting question, and I see your point. Why not swive a woman I'm vaguely disappointed in? It wouldn't be the first time."

The price Noah paid for limiting himself to mercenary unions was a touch of disappointment with the arrangement, and with himself. Perhaps he simply excelled at being disappointed.

The Duke of Disappointment, as it were.

"You are afraid," James said as another soft, sweet breeze wafted through the room. "Not afraid that Thea's worse than you fear, but that she's much better than you think now, and you don't want to be proven even happily wrong."

James was noted for his cogent speeches in the Lords, the plaguey bastard.

"Isn't that my contretemps in a nutshell?" Noah asked, crossing the room to close the window. "I can't laugh off a lack of chastity in my duchess, not when it was concealed until only by risking my own reputation could I undo my mistake. Now I'm to befriend the woman who treated me thus, James? I wouldn't know where or how to start."

Just as Thea hadn't known how or where to start with a disclosure of her past.

Damn and blast.

Noah's journey home passed in the same preoccupied blur as had the earlier trip in from Kent.

James, damn his practical half-Dutch, sister-stealing hide, had a point: if Noah did not befriend his bride, he would make it that much more likely Thea eventually became his enemy.

Noah did not need enemies on any front; no man with a modicum of sense did.

James was a canny bastard too. He listened in the clubs, he read the papers, not merely the business pages, and—peculiar notion—he apparently *talked with his wife*. Noah was not about to put his children in the middle of the domestic battles he himself had grown up with, and James had likely seen this.

Becoming friends with Thea was the logical course, except friendship with a woman was something Noah hadn't experienced—not with a sister, not with a mistress, not with a friend's wife, or with a neighbor. The undertaking would be awkward, at best.

Assuming Noah's new wife was interested in having him for a friend.

# Six

ABSENCE WAS NOT MAKING THEA'S HEART GROW fonder. Her spanking new spouse of one entire day had departed after luncheon, saying he had to run into Town on business, and would finish the afternoon on the third floor with his botanist.

The presuming man had kissed her cheek, lingeringly, and promised to see her at supper.

"He's likely off to one of his lightskirts," she muttered, putting aside the menus the housekeeper had obligingly left for her review. "He likes his spices, according to Mrs. Hurley. Spices, hah."

*Araminthea, you are being ridiculous.* In her head, she endured her late father's most dire accusation, one typically followed by a cold silence so profound no self-respecting earl's daughter would remain in the same room with it.

Thea was not ridiculous; she was frightened.

She had married into a family of scoundrels, and had she a male relation worth the name, this information would have been made known to her before she took the awful leap of matrimony. The leap into Noah

Winters's bed, assuming he still wanted her there when he returned from meeting with his solicitors and his mistress.

Mistresses.

Thea had known marriage to Anselm might result in some awkwardness—a lot of awkwardness—after the wedding night, but she hadn't anticipated jealousy would complicate the emotional waters.

She tapped on a closed door, having no idea where on the vast third floor her spouse might be.

"*Willkommen!*"

Thea opened the door and peered around. "Mr. Erikson. What an interesting room."

He smiled, pushing his glasses up his nose and gesturing broadly. "Come in please, and we keep the warm with us for my little darlings."

"It is warm in here." Thea closed the door behind her, assailed by the scents of rich earth, damp, and green growing things. "This is a conservatory?"

The ceiling and two walls were glass, though some of the top panes were angled out to create the slightest breeze.

"This is my laboratory, I think you would say." Erikson untied a leather apron, his hands dirt stained. "I'm working on some crosses for His Grace, and up here, we have much light. Would you like tea, Duchess?"

What duch—Oh.

"Tea would be lovely." Thea came a little farther into the room and sniffed at a peculiar white flower growing on a shiny green vine. "That smells like biscuits."

"The vanilla orchid," Erikson said, stoking up a small potbellied stove. "More accurate to say the biscuits smell like the flower."

"I've never seen one before," Thea marveled, taking another whiff. "And what's this?"

Before the kettle was even whistling, Erikson was introducing her to each and every plant, explaining its properties and the challenges of cultivating it.

"Anselm wants to make vanilla?" she asked.

"The vanilla orchid is native to Mexico," Erikson said. "It can be grown elsewhere, but one must know how to pollinate the flowers by hand to create the fruit. I suspect there are bees native to Mexico, or small birds and butterflies equipped to do the job naturally."

The vanilla scent was delicious, both soothing and sweet. "Interesting. What else are you working on?"

Erickson showed Thea spices, medicinal plants from lands faraway, and a few that were just plain pretty or intoxicatingly fragrant. For others, Erikson could show her only sketches of the blooms.

"Not only you fine lords and ladies go to the ball," he said. "My beauties also like to put on pretty gowns, though one can't wear the finery always."

"Has my husband traveled to all these far-off places"—Thea ran a finger down a soft white petal—"searching for such beauties?"

"Anselm has traveled." Erikson passed her a plain cup of tea in a chipped white mug. "I travel more. I meet Anselm in America, when he came there for some silly lawsuit. All lawsuits are silly, though, no matter in which country."

"Anselm traveled in America?" How had Thea not known this?

Erikson downed his tea at a swallow. "As I did, looking for the plants. The natives in all lands know their plants and the magic in them. The Indians know their plants, and I studied with them. You need sugar?"

Thea held out her cup until two lumps had been deposited therein. Erikson was charming, if lacking in polish or perfect English. She suspected his English could be perfect though, because he forgot to jumble up his word order when he waxed poetic about his beauties.

"Erikson." Anselm's voice sounded pleasantly from the doorway, though the draft he brought with him was cool. "You are to cultivate my flowers, not my duchess."

"All beauties benefit from cultivation." Erikson saluted Thea with a white quill pen. "Close the door, Duke. You let out the warmness, and you'll give my babies a chill."

"He's not right in the head." Anselm ambled into the room and took up a perch on a stool. He did, however, close the door behind him first. "The poor man thinks plants are people, or something like it."

"I think they are alive and created by the same God as your arrogant self." Erikson poured a third cup of tea, added sugar, and passed it to Anselm. "You claim no little worth by association with our Maker, so my plants must surely have His constant regard as well, for they don't get up to naughty tricks like people do and He made them first."

"I come here for sermons," Anselm said to Thea.

"These plants are very pious, you see, benefiting from Erikson's sanctimony, or blasphemy, depending on your church."

"It was a *garden* from which we fell," Erikson began.

Anselm held up a hand. "Any luck with the witch hazel?"

Erikson was deftly deflected into an assessment of the conditions that might allow a North American medicinal plant to be grown locally.

Anselm set his teacup down when the botany lecture concluded. "Dear Wife, this has to be boring for you, and we're keeping Erikson from his assignations with his flowers. Let's have a proper tea in a proper location, shall we?"

"Of course." Thea rose, happy to comply with His Grace's *request*, however much it bore the scent of an order. "Thank you very much for the education and the tea, Mr. Erikson."

"You must come visit us anytime." Erikson smiled genially, reminding Thea that behind his glasses, his lectures, and his questionable accent, Erikson was a very handsome man.

"What do you think of our Benjamin Botanist?" Anselm asked as they gained the corridor.

*Our* Benjamin. They were to be civil, then. "He's possessed of a large and active brain," Thea said, "and he's happiest when among his beauties."

"You don't find him eccentric?"

Anselm was walking along beside her, but Thea had the sense he was matching his steps to her slower pace out of discipline, and they couldn't be off the third floor soon enough to suit him.

"I think he's passionate about his science," she replied, "and if you're bent on commercial horticulture, he's a brilliant find. He said you met in America?"

"I was stuck there for nigh a year and a half while I sorted out some breach of contract and trade problems with people I thought were our business partners. It about drove me to Bedlam, to be separated from home and family like that, but one can't trust a solicitor to deal effectively with a problem when one is nowhere in evidence to supervise."

One probably could, but His Grace, the Duke of Anselm, would not.

"Eighteen months to settle a lawsuit must be an achievement," Thea observed as they descended to the next floor. "Where are we going?"

"You didn't tour the house today?"

"I was shown the public rooms and the working areas on the ground floor. You have a marvelous kitchen."

"Cook has a marvelous kitchen. I have a marvelous exchequer, and a healthy appreciation for happy domestics. We're on our way to the library."

Did Anselm see himself only in terms of his healthy exchequer?

They traversed another winding staircase, made three turns, and went up a few steps to reach their destination—and Wellspring was one of Anselm's smaller holdings.

"I don't go in for formal tea very much," Anselm said as he led Thea to a brocade sofa before which a tea service sat on a low table. "We're in the country, after all. You toured the public rooms, and you discovered my eccentric botanist in the attics. What else did you do today?"

They were to be *very* civil.

"I visited Della." Thea lifted toweling off a porcelain teapot painted all over with blue flowers. Antique Sevres, from the looks of it. "I reviewed menus and discussed the kitchen gardens with Cook, and went in search of this library for a book, but got lost twice instead."

Anselm came down beside her with a sigh that might have been tired. "I'll show you a map of the place. I loved getting lost here as a small boy."

The duke had once, long ago, been a small boy. Intriguing notion. "Where did you get off to this afternoon?" Thea asked.

"Nipped into Town." Anselm's gaze was on Thea's hands as she poured their tea. "Dropped in on James and Patience, but the ladies were out doing their part on Bond Street."

"You rode two hours each way to drop in on people we saw at the wedding breakfast?" As soon as the question was out of her mouth, Thea wished it back. "I'm sorry." She set her teacup down and rose. "I have no right to ask you that."

"You don't," Anselm agreed, getting to his feet as well, "but when I'm in the saddle, I find it easier to think things through. Come have something to eat. Dinner won't be for another two hours at least."

So what was the duke thinking through, and had he also met with his solicitors?

"I've asked that after tonight we move dinner up," Thea said. "I hope you don't mind?"

"Of course not." Anselm extended a hand to Thea, but when she thought he'd merely seat her again, he slipped his arm around her waist and drew her closer. "How is it you've been racketing around here all day, and you still smell so sweet?"

A husbandly question that went well beyond civilities.

"It's the soap I use," Thea said, her arms vining around his waist. "It lingers."

"Wonderfully." He bussed her cheek. "I am keeping you from your sustenance, and me from mine."

"You're hungry?" Thea slid away, and to her relief, Anselm let her go. What was he about, kissing her that way?

"Peckish. You?"

"The same." She sat to assemble meat, cheese, and buttered bread on a plate, casting around desperately for a conversational gambit. "When did you acquire the idea of botany as a profitable venture?"

For every appearance said the Anselm finances prospered handily.

"My grandmother loved her gardens, and my grandfather kept a botanist on his staff for her. The plants became a hobby for them, though Grandfather also sold his excess inventory, and I developed it from there."

Thea passed the duke a plate and started fixing her own. "Did your father share the same interest?"

"He was more of a Town man. Move over, Thea, and we'll share a plate."

She obliged, because to refuse her husband would seem standoffish, if not…cowardly.

They ate, but the silence grew and grew and grew some more.

Anselm set the empty plate aside, his long legs ranged beside hers, and sat back to regard her.

"Is something on your mind, Your Grace?" Thea asked, for her mind had become a hash of anxieties, fears, and the odd, stray hope.

Also a few regrets.

In response, Anselm gathered Thea's hand in his and brought her fingers to his lips.

"I cannot sustain enough anger at you to make it convincing." He sounded puzzled or perhaps relieved.

"A very small display will usually convince me," Thea said. "You are entitled to your temper, in any case."

His grip was warm, almost comforting.

"But if we're both angry"—Anselm gave her back her hand—"can you imagine the eventual intimacies? I've thought about this for much of the day."

Thea did not ask: Why would *I* be angry? Because in a small, defiant corner of her soul, she *was* angry, and at him, among others, not only at herself.

Though she had materially misrepresented herself to Anselm. There was that.

"Other couples struggle through significant differences," she said.

"We're not other couples." Anselm rose and stood frowning down at her. He was an accomplished frowner, though he had cause to be. "We'll have to make a go of this, or at least give it a good try."

There he went, being *not nice* again, though he probably didn't even realize it.

"I'm not sure what to say." Thea got to her feet, but the duke moved to assist her, and so she was right next to him without planning to be there. "One expects to try to make a go of one's marriage, I hope."

He searched her eyes for heaven knew what and touched one of the pearl earrings Thea had inherited from her mama.

"We'll have to try particularly hard," he said. "I'll have to."

"I don't want that." Thea moved away, unable to tolerate the resignation in his gaze. "I don't want to be a chore for you, an obligation, a matter of self-discipline and soldiering on with your burdensome duty."

"Perhaps you should have thought of that before your ill-timed announcement, Thea."

For which she would never cease being tormented, apparently. "You would have had me *lie* to you?"

"You did lie to me, or you certainly allowed me to muddle along on the basis of a misrepresentation," he shot back. "You simply confessed the lie at the most inopportune moment."

"Right." Thea's lips compressed, and she knew, *knew*, she should keep her mouth shut. "And we will not speak of my past unless you're bringing it up to toss at me like a dead cat when you're feeling uncertain of your way in this marriage. I will take to wearing a scarlet sign around my neck: I am sorry. I am sorry, *I am sorry*, but apologizing is all I can do, Your Grace. I can't change my past. I can't unsay the things I've said. You set before me an impossible task, because your trust has been destroyed, and I don't know how to win it back, or why I should take on such a labor of Sisyphus."

The silence from before had nothing on this ringing, bitter gap in their civilities now. Tension snapped and crackled around them, rife with all sorts of bad feeling and misery.

Then Anselm was beside her.

"Don't cry." He moved in, handkerchief at the ready. "Please, Thea…"

"I'm not crying." But she was, and no matter how determinedly she thrust her chin in the air, her cheeks were wet, and Anselm was dabbing at them gently. "Tears n-never solved anything, Your Grace, and you will please desist."

"I will if you will."

The childishness of it, the slight smile he managed at the ridiculousness, had Thea smiling too.

"I don't mean to provoke you," she said, letting him finish with the handkerchief. "But you pick on me."

"Pick at you." Anselm dabbed at the end of her nose, the idiot. "You're a problem I don't know how to solve."

"A problem." Thea leaned into the hand he'd cupped along her jaw. "And a disaster, but not, thank ye gods, a tragedy."

"I would not have us be a farce, either," Anselm said, expression serious.

"What is the problem that has you so vexed?" she asked. "I need a description more specific than my very name."

The duke folded up his handkerchief, which had borne his initials and his beguiling scent.

"I'm not sure how to put the problem, but you're right that it has to do with trust."

Thea regarded her husband for a long, solemn moment as they stood two feet and a world of wishes apart.

"I've trusted you, Anselm. When I opened my mouth at that inopportune moment, I was trusting you." More fool her.

He unfolded the handkerchief and began again, this time so the monogram remained face out.

"Trusted me not to beat you?" The duke spoke as if the very words stank.

"Not to beat me, or worse."

Anselm jammed the handkerchief in a pocket, scowling ferociously. "Cast you out?"

"That too. I am grateful that my trust was not misplaced. I think you trust me a little too." Thea prayed he did. Getting him to admit it was another matter.

"Whatever prompted that fancy?" Anselm hadn't meant to sound so incredulous; Thea was sure he hadn't.

"I was behind a closed door with Mr. Erikson," she said, "and he was figuratively laying his flowers at my feet, but you did not leap to the wrong conclusions. That is an act of trust."

Viscountess Endmon would have turned Thea off without a character for such a breach of propriety.

His Grace resumed his place before the tea tray and drained the contents of Thea's cup. "You were trying to look interested as Benjamin prosed on and on, even

I could see that, and you were sitting a good eight feet from him. You forgot to sugar my tea."

Thea took the place beside the duke and passed him his own half-full cup.

"The door was closed, Your Grace, and Mr. Erikson is a comely fellow, intelligent, vigorous, and possessed of humor and a certain passion."

"For posies," Anselm said, passing her the unsweetened cup. "I don't care for the flowers so much as I do the money they can make me."

Anselm cared for the flowers because they reminded him of his grandparents. "My point, sir, is that you didn't challenge Mr. Erikson to pistols at dawn."

The duke wrinkled his nose, a splendid, aristocratic feature. "You'd have me believe a failure to issue a challenge is a step in the direction of marital trust?"

Of course it was. Thea held her peace rather than argue with her husband.

"Not a step back," he allowed, popping a strawberry into the ducal maw. "I suppose that's encouraging."

They fell into an entirely different kind of silence over their next cup of tea, until the duke took a thoughtful nibble of a slice of golden cheddar.

"I'd not challenge a man of lesser station to meet me on the field of honor," he said, passing Thea the butter knife. "The rules of honor forbid it, though I suppose a round of fisticuffs might be permitted. Perhaps I ought to remind Benjamin of this. Pour me a spot more tea, please, and don't take that last slice of bread."

Thea poured the duke's tea and cut the last slice of bread exactly in half.

# Seven

IN ADDITION TO ESCHEWING FORMAL TEA, NOAH WAS also disinclined to stand on ceremony at dinner. He and Thea dined à la française, that is, serving themselves, though this informality was clearly not what his bride had been expecting.

"You're used to a more formal meal?" he asked.

"As companion to two elderly ladies, and as Marliss's companion, yes. Those households were prone to formality."

"What about your household?" Noah asked, because they had to converse about *something*. "Was your mama a high stickler?"

"My papa was more the stickling kind. Mama was the type to tuck us in when we were too old to merit such coddling, and to read us stories on the nights when it stormed."

An image of Thea surrounded by sleepy children, reading to them as thunder boomed, came to Noah's mind's eye. The picture was sweet, and he resented it even as it drew him.

"You loved your mother," he said, pouring Thea more wine. "What of your father?"

"I've come to see that he wasn't stern so much as serious," Thea said. "He and Mama were not a love match, but they came to love each other fiercely. I saw that much before he died."

Would that Noah's parents had come to love each other *at all*. "How old were you?"

"Fourteen when he died, and sixteen when Mama died." Thea picked up her wineglass but didn't drink. "Then we were in mourning, and when I might have made a come-out, there was no money, and no one to present me. Tims was being a regular brat, and Nonie not much better."

"Siblings can be a challenge." What little Thea had told Noah grated. She'd been sheltered as an earl's daughter should be, completely unprepared to take on the raising of her siblings, and without the means or appropriate gender to do so.

And yet, she'd hesitated to accept his proposal?

"How did you become a companion?" Noah asked.

"Lady Bransom had been a friend of my maternal grandmother, and she saw the situation upon Mama's death. She shooed Tim back to school, found a governess for Nonie, and said my salary as a companion would be adequate to cover the expense of the governess. She was being charitable."

She'd apparently let Thea know that too. "How old were you?"

"Eighteen by then and out of mourning," Thea replied, tracing her finger around the rim of her wineglass. "I felt awful, leaving Tims and Nonie, though it was necessary."

Noah took a sip of his wine, lest he opine that it had

*not* been necessary, not if the trustees had been minding their duties. When he'd been left with siblings to raise, the last thing he'd permitted was for them to be separated from each other.

And from him. Noah pared off a bite of cheese and extended it to his duchess on the point of the knife.

"Speaking of siblings," Noah said, "Harlan should be down from Town tomorrow. If he doesn't comport himself like a perfect gentleman, we can send him off to Uncle Meech, and he'll endure a few months of bawdy house parties and excessive doses of summer ale."

Thea accepted the cheese and put it on her plate. "Harlan was at the wedding. A charming young fellow, and he has your eyes."

Harlan had been at the wedding, and the dratted boy still hadn't stopped growing—and Harlan had Meech's eyes.

"The hour grows late, Duchess." This time Noah held the bite of cheese up to Thea's mouth, and she dutifully accepted it. "We can review the family traits while we prepare to retire. Shall I order you a bath?"

Noah's wife would not discommode the servants at this hour by making the request herself.

"A bath would be most pleasant. I am tired, though."

"I'll light you up." Noah drew Thea to her feet. "Will you ride out with me tomorrow?"

By the dim light of the sconces she peered up at him, for his request had apparently surprised her—her too.

"I'd like that, Anselm."

"Then we'll ride before breakfast, and I'll send word to the stables to have Della saddled for you." Just as Thea began to smile, Noah felt compelled to add, "You don't need my escort, you know. Simply have a groom accompany you whenever you'd like to ride out."

Thea's smile guttered and died. "I will enjoy my husband's company at the start of my day tomorrow."

They processed along in silence until Noah pushed Thea's door open. "Your bath should be ready shortly."

When Thea might have taken the candle from him, Noah put a hand on her arm, kissed her forehead, and then stepped back.

"Good night, Husband."

"Enjoy your bath." Noah strode off, leaving Thea privacy to end her day, and he didn't return until some hours later, when he could be sure his wife was fast asleep.

❧

Thea awoke at the first gray light of dawn, aware that His Grace was abed with her. His scent was on the sheets, his arm about her middle, and his breeding organs were nestled against Thea's backside. She did not dare move.

Had her nightgown hiked itself over her hip, or had a ducal hand aided its disarrangement?

The duke rolled to his back, and the hand that had been tucked against Thea's waist came to rest on her hip.

Well, not quite her hip. Anselm had warm hands. He continued to caress her, while on his side of the bed, something else took place. A rhythmic movement—his other hand perhaps?—a slight jostle of the mattress, as if—

His breathing became deeper, harsher, and the tempo of whatever he was doing increased. The movement stopped, all was stillness, and then a soft, masculine groan wafted on the morning air.

Merciful, everlasting, gracious, benevolent—*Anselm had just pleasured himself in Thea's bed.*

The mattress shifted as the duke left that bed, and Thea feigned sleep for all she was worth, while her thoughts raced off in all directions.

Was Anselm making a point? Withholding intimacies from Thea as a punishment? Was he simply being male? Was he being *considerate?*

Somebody patted her backside.

"You're awake," Anselm accused softly as he climbed back on the bed and wrapped himself around her. "Even if you're not, you should be."

As if she could have slept through that? "Good morning. You may go away now."

"And leave my bride?"

Thea burrowed into her pillow. "Please." The sooner the better.

"You've an assignation at dawn with a handsome stranger." Anselm brushed her braid back over her shoulder. "How can you resist such a call to awareness?"

Had he bothered to dress? "This stranger of yours is too cheerful," Thea muttered. "You meet him for me." Too cheerful, too male, too bold, too close.

Too intriguing, despite his moods and bluntness.

Anselm kissed her cheek. "If you're truly too tired, we can ride later."

He wasn't leaving, but neither was he getting any more Ideas.

"Is there tea?" Thea asked, which earned her one duke, crouched above her on all fours without benefit of clothing.

"I'll fetch you two cups, and you may down them both in peaceful solitude while I dress."

"Such consideration, Your Grace."

He nuzzled her temple, then took himself off to make good on his threats. When he pushed the tea cart into Thea's bedroom, she was sitting up against the headboard, feeling not entirely rested, but at least sentient—and quite disconcerted.

Thank a merciful Deity, Anselm was in shirt and breeches.

"I had expected to sleep alone," Thea ventured. "You seem to enjoy good spirits in the morning." Good animal spirits.

Anselm passed her the first cup. "Unlike your charming self?"

"I love a nice clean, fluffy bed," she said, "and a good hot cup of tea." How Thea felt about waking up with a duke in her nice clean, fluffy bed required pondering. She was by no means ready to discuss such a topic, though in some mysterious, marital fashion, Anselm's shocking behavior had been a step in the direction of a normal union.

"What else do you love besides clean linen, Duchess?" Anselm propped a hip at Thea's side and appropriated a sip from her cup.

"Sweets. I am shamelessly appreciative of sweets."

"Isn't everybody?"

"No. Tims can walk past a plate of marzipan, or even chocolate, or chocolate-covered marzipan, and Nonie and I are incapable of his indifference."

Did Anselm enjoy sweets? He certainly took sugar in his tea.

"Ah, but can his lordship walk past a brandy decanter?" The duke stole another sip.

"I frankly worry he cannot." Thea peered at her almost empty cup. "If you filch half my tea, then you must fetch us another cup."

Anselm rose from the bed, taking the teacup with him, and poured them more. "Shall I take Grantley in hand? This isn't his first Season, is it, Thea?"

"By no means," she said. "You asked me about going into service last night, and part of my motivation was to prepare Tims to stand on his own two feet. The tactic was not entirely effective."

Had been a howling disaster, in fact, while this conversation was a cozy, even friendly way to start their day.

"Growing up takes time." Anselm passed her the second cup and resumed his place beside her. "Then you blink, and your siblings are adults, and you've nothing to say to it."

He sounded so forlorn. Thea suspected he'd married in part out of sheer loneliness for family. She risked a pat to the ducal knee.

"You are a good brother."

Anselm was off the bed in an instant, rattling lids and plates and serving spoons while Thea sipped her tea.

"Some bacon for you today, I think," he said, "and you like your oranges too, if I recall. Eggs?"

"Eggs would be good, and butter on my toast."

Anselm attacked the buttering process as if fixing Thea breakfast were an important matter of state—because she'd given him a compliment?

"Husband?"

"Your breakfast." He set a tray over her lap.

"Why did you sleep with me last night?" Thea asked as neutrally as she could when his answer mattered.

The toast was golden perfection, the eggs were steaming gently, and the scent of bacon made Thea's mouth water, but she didn't touch the food.

"Do you object to sharing your bed, Duchess?" Anselm asked in equally careful tones. He arranged food on his plate with a focus Thea suspected most men reserved for their dueling opponents.

Thea's marriage was in a difficult posture because she'd not disclosed her lack of chastity prior to the vows. She made a decision right then, among pillows and breakfast offerings, to deal with her husband honestly.

"I like sleeping with you, Your Grace." Liked his warmth, his simple male presence, his willingness to share the night with her, when distance and trouble lay between them elsewhere in their marriage.

Anselm's head came up abruptly, and then he was buttering his toast to within an inch of its life.

"You needn't say such things, Thea. I presumed when I joined you last night. We'll be expected to spend time together for the next month, but we needn't, that is to say, one hardly—"

"Noah Winters, I have enjoyed sleeping with you both times it was my privilege to do so. Now, will you march about while you demolish your breakfast, leaving crumbs all over my bedroom, or get under these covers and bear me some company?"

"I would not get crumbs on your carpet," he grumbled as he climbed into bed with her and took a sip of her tea.

"I am married to a poacher." A *shy* poacher, for all his vigorous animal spirits. "I suppose you're also partial to chocolate?"

"I'm worse with chocolate," he said between bites of Thea's toast. "If you want to hoard your morning drink, take coffee. I can't stand the stuff."

"Neither can I," Thea said, and then they were smiling at each other and sharing a third cup.

Thea's fragile truce with her husband lasted through their ride, and into luncheon, and then Harlan arrived, and the brothers made plans to tour the village together. Thea walked with them to the stables, then excused herself to pen a letter to Nonie and a surprisingly cheerful epistle it would be.

"Thea?" Anselm's hand on her arm stayed her departure. "You recall my earlier offer? The one regarding your brother?"

Made casually over eggs, toast, and purloined tea. "I do recall it."

"You never gave me an answer. I'd not make such an offer in jest."

"I know you would not," she said, "and we will discuss it. You are most generous." She searched Anselm's gaze, certain he was leaving a great deal unsaid, but he simply kissed her cheek, with Harlan standing right there, and let her go.

"Until dinner," Anselm said.

"Which will be at seven, you two." Thea shook a finger at them. "No staying for an extra pint and dragging in to table in your riding attire."

They grinned similar rascally grins and headed for their mounts, while Thea, for reasons she did not want to examine too closely, grinned too.

※

"I like her." Harlan swung up on the trusty bay he'd had since childhood, and waited politely for Noah to check True's girth. Noah had taken his second personal mount out this morning with Thea, a big glossy black whose knees turned to jelly around cats, rabbits, and anything small and fast.

Except children, upon whom Regent, idiot beast that he was, doted.

"You are a male of the Winters line," Noah said, swinging into the saddle. "You would like anything in skirts, including a Jersey Island heifer. Let's head for the hay fields."

Noah liked Thea too, which was a puzzle and a relief.

"Of course, the hay fields." Harlan sighed with adolescent long-suffering. "I curdle my brains the livelong year in Greek and Latin, not to mention French, Italian, and German, just so you can put a blighted hay rake in my lily-white hands come June."

Noah nudged True toward the driveway. "You're

familiar with French letters too, I hope, or I'll know the reason why."

Harlan aimed a scowl at Noah that was more adult than adolescent. "Is that all you ever think about, Noah? Uncle's proclivities I can understand, because he's too old to change his spots, but you're a properly married man now, and I expect better from you, despite your age."

"I'm old too?" Noah was now about the same age as Meech had been when Noah had gone to university half a lifetime ago. At the time he'd thought Meech not elderly, exactly, but...past his prime? Whatever the male equivalent of matronly was.

Jesus on the Mount.

"You think like an old man, and you always have," Harlan declared. "The sisters say it's because you were oldest when we were orphaned. I say it's because you were born crotchety."

The day was lovely, the countryside on that sweet edge between spring and summer. Noah had the smarmy, ridiculous thought that it was good to be alive.

"I wasn't crotchety until you came along," Noah rejoined. His duchess thought him capable of good cheer.

In the morning. Noah had been more asleep than awake when he'd realized exactly where and with whom he was starting his second day of married life. Thea, thank heavens, had taken his behavior in stride—once she'd stopped blushing.

"Crotchety, crotchety, crotchety," Harlan sing-songed. "Race you to the woods."

Noah won, mostly because he was the more ruth-less of the two, and Harlan's seat was rusty. Oxford did not afford a great deal of opportunity to ride, but the race settled them both into another of their awkward reunions.

"You said you liked my new wife," Noah observed as the horses came down to the walk. "What do you like about her?"

"The way she looks at you," Harlan said, patting his beast, who was breathing like a bellows. "She doesn't have a hard look in her eyes. Her gaze is soft, a little worried, but worried for you as much as anything."

"A damned poet in the family," Noah muttered. "That's all we need." Thea was probably fond of the poetical sorts.

"Better than Uncle's dirty rhymes," Harlan countered. "I wish you'd keep him from school, though the fellows all think he's a capital old thing."

"He *is* a capital old thing." An expensive capital old thing. Noah ducked forward as True sidled beneath a low-hanging branch.

"He is, until all your mates go around quoting, 'They all look the same in the dark, whether in bed, in the scullery, or the park,' and 'Never discount the charms of an older woman, my boys, as she'll be discreet, grateful, and generous with her toys.' It wears, after about the third telling. Then old Pemmie goads him to sing."

Pemberton provided the harmonies, obliging sot that he was.

"Pemberton's not so bad," Noah replied, but viewed through the eyes of an idealistic seventeen-year-old, Meech wasn't so charming, either. "He and

Pemberton claim to have come up with those rhymes when they were younger than you are now. Besides, Meech will spend the summer at his various house parties, flirting with all and sundry, swiving the maids and companions."

"Our sisters attend house parties, Noah."

"As do I," Noah said gently. "But our sisters are all safely married, Harlan, so you needn't fret, and Uncle is mostly bluster."

"Right." Harlan snorted, batting aside an oak branch. "Which is why you forbid him funerals for young widows. Why wasn't he at your wedding?"

Because God was given to the odd mercy. "Off on his rounds. What manner of grades can I expect regarding my baby brother's most recent term?"

"I took a first in Latin," Harlan said, fiddling with his reins. "My only first this year."

"Isn't there some award for the top scholar in Latin?" Noah asked casually. "If there isn't, there should be."

Harlan's gaze stayed on his reins. "Such as?"

"One never knows." A first in Latin was a fine, fine thing, particularly for a Winters male. "One might want to examine the loose box across from the saddle room when one is done moping about before one's thoroughly impressed older brother."

"Might one!?" Harlan's horse bounded forward, and Noah let him win the race to the stables.

Harlan was still bubbling over with enthusiasm for his new gelding at dinner that evening, and Thea was fool enough to encourage the boy with well-timed questions.

"How is he over fences?"

"Do you suppose you'll take him up to school in the autumn?"

"Have you seen the sire?"

As a matter of tradition, Noah challenged his brother to a billiards game after dinner, but Harlan's fondness for his sister-in-law trumped the weight of family rituals.

"I'll play you, Noah, but Thea gets to play the winner, and ties go to me."

"Ungrateful, bottomless puppy." Noah's gaze rose to the cupids sporting about on the ceiling. "This is what an Oxford education gains us, Wife. Be warned: we're having only daughters if this is what our sons will be like."

"I've never met anybody who took a first in anything," Thea said, linking arms with Harlan as they removed from the dining room to the game room. "I trust you will explain the finer points of billiards to me, Harlan?"

"She abets him," Noah said to the house at large. "My own wife, corrupting the youth of the nation, and my own heir, colluding with my duchess. The pair of you pay attention, and I will show you how the game is played."

"For form's sake," Harlan stage-whispered to Thea when the cue sticks had been chosen, "I will allow Noah to win the first game, because the elderly must be allowed their crotchets."

"Hush," Noah muttered. "I'm about to break, and this is a holy moment."

Thea giggled, causing Noah to straighten, wait her out, and then position himself again to break, only to hear her snorting with laughter as he drew his cue back.

"Stop encouraging her with your drollery," Noah warned his brother. He broke smartly, balls rolling all over the table, two finding their pockets. Though Noah hadn't planned it, he sank every ball in succession, such that Harlan got not one shot.

"This is war," Harlan said, brandishing his cue stick. "And recall, Brother dear, you taught me everything you know. I'm not elderly, like certain people, so I didn't forget half of it while eating my pudding."

Noah stepped over to his wife, and whispered with not a little pride, "He'll sink them all, just watch."

"No colluding with my sister-in-law," Harlan said as he took a shot. "She plays me next."

Because Harlan also sank every ball, they agreed Thea would break and take every other shot in the third game. Eventually they played to a draw, but it was late enough that Noah declared the game at an end.

"My duchess is tired," he announced. "She needs her rest, because adjusting to marital bliss is taxing." Adjusting to marriage was making *him* daft, in any case.

"Marital bliss?" Harlan looked puzzled. "But she's *your* duchess, last I heard."

"Go to bed, your puppy-ship," Noah said, putting up the cue sticks. "Go directly to bed, do not visit your new horse, do not stop by my room to leave a toad in my bed, do not put eggs under my pillow, and do not think for one instant to turn a rooster loose in my bedroom tomorrow morning."

"Harlan would never indulge in such childish pranks," Thea sniffed. "Really, Noah, your imagination is prodigious."

*She'd called him Noah.* This morning Thea had referred to him as Noah Winters in a scolding fashion, but this was merely talk among family.

"Yes, really, Noah," Harlan intoned gleefully, dancing away as Noah would have swatted him soundly on his backside. When they parted from Harlan at the landing, Noah slipped an arm around his wife.

"Harlan likes you." Noah liked her too, more with each passing day.

And each passing night, and each passing morning.

"I like him," Thea managed around a yawn. "Will you sleep with me tonight?"

Noah's duchess was skilled at the marital ambush. "Are you asking me to?"

"I am asking you to. I like sleeping with you."

And her aim was faultless. "You needn't harp on it." Noah opened her door. "I'll join you shortly."

"Going to cage up a rooster, Noah?"

He was off to bay at the moon, for the chicken coop was locked every night as a matter of course.

"Of course I'm seeing to the welfare of my roosters. I've missed the boy, but there's no sense leaving temptation in his path."

"There's always tomorrow night," Thea mused, tousling Noah's hair in a caress he felt straight down to his damned, idiot, demented balls. "Maybe sleeping with you will be more excitement than I bargained for."

Noah did not reply. He absolutely, positively did not allow himself to reply.

# *Eight*

THEA HAD RETIRED EARLY, ALONG WITH HER HUSBAND, as a function of exhaustion sufficient to stifle even Harlan's volubility. Haying had started, which meant both Winters men were on horseback much of the day, while Thea had supervised the preparation of food and drink for the crews. When Thea awoke, the room was still in darkness, though birds sang outside the open windows.

Her husband's hand caressed her hip, then glided over the curve of her flank. She'd had several mornings to savor that very caress, and to decide she liked it.

Wicked of her, and she shouldn't admit it, but the duke's movements were slow and soothing, but also... *not* soothing. His hand was warm on her bare skin, and she knew that hand, knew the power in it, the competence, and yet there was gentleness in his caress as well.

"Thea?"

"Hmm?"

"Let me touch you."

Not a request, more of an unacknowledged entreaty. She settled her hand over Anselm's, squeezing his fingers. He wasn't asking to couple with her, but he was asking something.

Anselm must have sensed her acquiescence, because he rolled to his side and spooned himself along her back and her legs and everywhere in between.

"You don't mind?" he asked.

A question, now that Anselm was blanketing Thea with his warmth, and his erect flesh was fitted into the juncture of her thighs. The sensation was odd, intimate, and vaguely unsatisfying too. Peculiar.

His hand paused on her hip.

"Noah, I don't know what to do."

The rest of him went still, and Thea realized she'd used his name—not Husband, not Your Grace, not Anselm. Well, he'd told her his name for a reason, though maybe not this reason.

"You relax," he said, his voice barely above a whisper. "You go back to sleep if you like. You forget I'm here."

Anselm's caress traveled over Thea's hip, up to her midriff. She was accustomed to him holding her thus, his embrace secure without being confining. This time, though, his arm was banded across her bare skin, her nightgown bunched above her waist.

"Shall I take off my nightgown?"

His teeth grazed her nape, sending a shiver down her spine and beyond.

"You must do as you like." His voice was a rasp in the darkness, and he was using his teeth again. Thea got her nightgown off by bracing on one elbow, and then Noah was *there*, the entire expanse of his chest, his thighs, his intimate parts, his arms, all naked, warm, and enveloping her from behind. The sensation was novel and overwhelming, like being possessed by a combination of primal elements.

"Are you sure?" he asked.

His lips traced the path he'd scraped with his teeth, and Thea wasn't sure of her own name.

"I'm sure," she said, her voice thready in the gloom.

"Close your eyes, Thea." Anselm's hand glossed down her face, as if to close her eyes for her. She complied, and for a long moment, the only sound was the birds' bright, silvery caroling in the cool, predawn air.

Anselm hunched closer, that warm, competent hand hiking Thea's leg up, then folding it down over him, over his most intimate flesh in an approximation of coitus. Did it hurt him, to be pressed like that?

The duke shifted and pushed against her several times, then stopped, and slipped his hand up, to cup her naked breast.

"Push back," he whispered, flexing slowly forward then retreating. Thea tried to move as he directed, but she'd never felt a man's hand on her naked breast—save perhaps for her wedding night— had never wanted to, and focusing was difficult. Noah's caresses were powerfully distracting, sending currents of wanting to places a lady didn't take notice of.

All the while, Noah kept up a slow, steady rhythm with his hips, until Thea grew damp between her thighs.

She knew so little.

"That's it." Noah's hand closed gently around her

breast, and heat uncurled in the pit of Thea's belly. "Keep moving with me, and don't…stop." He shifted up, so he was half lying over her from behind.

Thea arched into his hand, and the heat turned molten when he closed his fingers over her nipple.

"Thea, God in heaven…" Noah pushed firmly against her, and pulsed his hips hard several times before going still, his open mouth on her shoulder. "Holy everlasting sweet…" His weight eased but did not leave her. "Sweet, holy baby…Jesus."

The duke wasn't cursing, more like praying, and Thea was rendered nearly as inarticulate.

What had just happened? She was wet between her legs, which she suspected was Noah's seed. She was all jumbled inside, and she was sleepy, and yet not.

"This will be delicate," her husband muttered, drawing back. "Don't move."

*He* moved. He slid away from Thea, tenting the covers around her so she was still warm, but bereft, too, somehow. Water splashed behind the privacy screen, an odd counterpoint to the dawn song of the birds, and then the mattress dipped heavily.

"It's cool," Noah said from behind Thea, and he again carefully lifted her leg, and under the covers a damp cloth—cold, not cool—was pressed between Thea's legs. "Sorry for the mess."

"What are you doing?"

Another stillness from him, while Thea was blushing madly, and wondering how anybody found words to describe such an odd activity.

"When I spend," Noah said, swabbing at her with the cloth, "it's messy."

"That…"

He moved the cloth again, high along the crease of her sex. "Yes?"

"It provokes peculiar sensations."

"Does it?"

"Most peculiar."

A few more minutes of silence, while Thea tried to study those sensations. Noah had slowed the movements of his hand and was applying a firmer pressure.

"I could make you come like this." He sounded intrigued, and devilish, and that cloth was focused on one little spot that wreaked havoc with Thea's reason.

"I don't know what that means," she said. "Maybe you should stop."

"Maybe I should," he agreed, sounding amused now, damn him. "The first time I make you come, I intend to be inside you."

"You speak in riddles, Husband."

"Noah." He patted her bottom. "I'll give you a minute to settle."

"Gracious of you, but you sound pleased with yourself." Thea would need much more than a minute to gather her wits.

"I'm pleased with the day so far," he said, taking his pleased self back to the privacy screen.

Thea felt again the sense of loss at Noah's absence, but he was soon back on the bed, gathering her in his arms. To turn toward him, to conduct their intimate business face-to-face, was a relief.

"You are not very experienced, Wife, for a woman who came to my bed in used condition."

Noah's arms were warm and secure around Thea,

his heart beat steadily beneath her ear, and she didn't know whether to be pleased with his conclusion, insulted, or simply…sad.

"I never said I was very experienced," she replied, her voice admirably even. "You will have to explain these things to me."

"I will." Noah rested his cheek against her hair, still sounding pleased. "In due time, I most assuredly and thoroughly will. Now grab a bit more sleep. You've earned it."

Thea didn't think she could sleep, so disconcerting had the morning's developments been. But Noah was pleased, the birds were singing, and for the first time, Thea's hope progressed to the real possibility that her marriage might develop into something more than a cordial exercise in guilt and disappointment.

❧

The rains came later that morning, in sheets and torrents, and patters and showers, and in brief drippy intervals when the world seemed to wait for the next drenching. Noah hacked out with his duchess before the heavens opened up, but only just made it safely home. The first ominous crack of thunder boomed as they handed off their horses to the grooms. Noah grabbed Thea's hand, and they made a dash for the house between fat, splatting raindrops.

"Why must everything be a race with you?" Thea panted as Noah bundled her under the overhang of a balcony on the back terrace.

"Why lollygag when you can get more done if you'll apply a little speed?" Noah countered, wrapping his arms around her. Her riding habit was wool and would probably keep her warm, but a new husband was allowed some privileges.

"You don't always apply speed." Thea tucked in closer and then hid her face against his chest.

"I can take my time when the situation warrants." Too late, Noah realized the words were flirtatious. "What will you do with your day today, Wife?"

A pillowcase went kiting by on the next wet gust of wind.

"Lollygag with my husband under the eaves. Watch the rain."

Thea implied that she'd enjoy spending time with that husband. Noah held her as the wind buffeted the trees, the rain came sheeting down, and the shouts of the stableboys battening down the hatches came bouncing across the gardens.

What if Thea had been chaste on their wedding night? If Noah could risk lollygagging with her under the eaves or in their bed with no thought that his self-restraint might desert him before paternity of their first born could be safely assured?

He stepped back. "Come along. We've watched it rain, and I've neglected my correspondence while I played land steward these past few days." He led Thea under balconies and eaves to the kitchen door, and when they were in the back hallway, he drew off her gloves.

She had pretty hands, a lady's hands, and she'd used those hands just hours ago to—

"I haven't given you the official tour of the state-rooms," Noah said.

"That can wait, Your Grace, if you've correspondence to catch up on."

He leaned in close, his words only for Thea, because they were not far from all the bustle in the kitchen.

"You and your proper address. We are married, *Your Grace*. You didn't call me Your Grace this morning."

She'd called him Noah, which was apparently justification for a blush.

"You take my point." He straightened. "My day is well begun, then. Should you need me, I'll be in the library for the morning. After luncheon, if you would afford me some time, I will acquaint you with more of the house."

"Until luncheon."

Thea turned to go, but Noah's pride—or something—rebelled at how easily she parted from him. He tugged her gently back to him, kissed her on the mouth—lollygagged over kissing her on the mouth, the cheek, the chin, the forehead—and when Thea began to give as good as she got, he let her go, patted her backside, and took himself off.

If he weren't mistaken, Thea remained in the hallway, fingers on her cheek, trying not to watch a certain part of his anatomy as he retreated.

☙

"Are you our new cousin?"

Thea halted abruptly, her hand on the door of Mr. Erikson's conservatory. A little girl and a littler girl, both dark-haired and blue-eyed, stood across the corridor. They were holding hands and regarding her with the solemn intensity unique to uncertain children.

"I am Lady Thea," she said, hunkering down. In fact, she was no longer Lady Thea, but rather, the Duchess of Anselm. "Who might you be?"

"That's the name of Cousin Noah's new duchess," the younger child stage-whispered to her companion. "Lady Thee."

"Thee-a," the older child replied, keeping her gaze on Thea. "Cousin Noah said we might be crowded, with you moving in here at our house."

"It's a very large house," Thea observed. Large enough to hide two children who resembled Noah in many particulars. "So large I sometimes get lost here."

Was usually lost in some fashion or another.

"Will you play hide-and-seek with us? We know all the best places to get lost." That from the younger one, while the older looked vaguely worried.

"Before you show me how to get lost, why don't you tell me your names?" For *Cousin Noah* had already told them Thea's name.

"I'm Evelyn," said the older, "and this is Janine, but we call her Nini. We live here." This last was offered with a pugnacious emphasis.

Thea straightened and held out one hand to each child. "Can you show me where, exactly, your rooms are? I'm sure I couldn't find them without knowledge-able escort."

"She means us," Evelyn concluded, but it was Janine who took Thea's hand first.

"Come along." Evelyn took the other hand. "Maryanne and Davies are having their tea, and they never notice when we get to rambling when they're having a cup. Cousin Noah says it's our besetting sin, but we asked him to find where in the Bible it says rambling at tea is a sin, and he hasn't yet. Cousin Harlan said Cousin Noah was hoist on his own petals, which makes no sense at all, for Cousin Noah isn't a flower."

"Petard," Thea said as the girls towed her along. "Like being speared with your own pikestaff, by accident." Or by bad luck, or poor timing.

"Cousin Noah would *never* have an accident like that," Janine pronounced, clearly dismayed at the very notion. "Not Cousin Harlan either."

"Maybe when he was little, like us," Evelyn temporized. "Harlan that is, not Noah."

The girls debated the possibilities until they'd led Thea to the opposite end of the corridor, down a short cross hallway, and halfway up another corridor.

"They've done took off again," said an exasperated female voice. "The dook will turn us off for this, Davies, see if he don't."

"We'll just have to find them and hope..." The second voice fell away when the girls drew Thea into a cheerful, cozy nursery suite.

"Good morning, Your Grace." The two nursery maids bobbed nervous curtsies in unison.

"This is Lady Thea," Evelyn said, swinging Thea's hand. "We went to visit Mr. Erikson, and we found her."

"You were naughty." Maryanne closed her eyes. "You were both very, very naughty, begging Your Grace's pardon. You've been told and told not to wander, and I can only imagine what your—what His Grace will have to say about this."

*Your father?*

Thea shook her hands free and sauntered over to the windows. "His Grace has best not take very great exception. Today is a boring old rainy day, and if nursery maids can take a short break over their tea, perhaps children can be forgiven for visiting Mr. Erikson in his lonely conservatory on the same floor of the house."

The same floor from which Noah had personally escorted Thea the last time she'd ventured up here.

"I like her," Janine said, grinning hugely and looking every inch a Winters. "She's nice."

"Lady Thea gets lost, and we know where everything is," Evelyn reasoned. "She's been here for days and days, and even if Cousin said we must give her time to settle in, days and days is long enough."

"What are you young ladies working on, when you're not paying a call on Mr. Erikson's beauties?" Thea asked as she sat on a small chair and opened a book on the proportionately small table before her.

"*We're* Mr. Erikson's best beauties." Janine's tone was preening as she clambered onto Thea's lap. "He says so all the time."

"That's my old storybook." Evelyn took the opposite seat. "I can read it better than *anybody*. Cousin Noah said so."

"Rainy days are the best for telling stories," Thea said, opening the book to a drawing of a fire-breathing dragon attempting to toast an armored knight. "You must each tell me your favorites."

"My favorites," said a stern voice from the doorway, "are little girls who obey the very few orders they are given."

"Hullo, Cousin." Evelyn and Janine popped to their

feet and dipped little curtsies at the unsmiling duke. Thea didn't so much as glance up from the storybook.

"I met my new friends as we converged on Mr. Erikson's conservatory," she said, flipping a page when she wanted to fling the book at His Perishing Grace. "The girls and I were of like mind, thinking perhaps the dreary day had made him or his beauties lonely for callers."

Noah shot a glower at the maids. "Then by all means take the girls to visit Erikson for a nice long cup of tea, why don't you?"

"Aye, Your Grace." In unison. Each maid took a child by the hand, leaving Noah and Thea surrounded by pint-sized furniture, dolls, and toys.

And a huge silence.

Thea stayed where she was, perched on the sturdy little chair, looking at a book of fairy tales but not seeing the knights, dragons, or witches. She saw only a husband, one trying very hard to find a place in the room that would give him strategic advantage in the battle to come.

"They're good girls," he said, back to Thea as he stared out a rain-streaked window. "This is the only home they've known."

Thea had spent her entire childhood in pursuit of good-girlhood—fat lot of good that had done her—while Noah had been exercising the privileges of a young, wealthy, *lusty* duke.

She snapped the book closed. "His Grace deigns to pass along a tid-bit." She enunciated each syllable with biting precision. "Or perhaps, in the spirit of good sportsmanship, we can consider that two tidbits."

"Thea…" Noah turned to face her, his expression wary. "I won't have the girls unduly upset because I took a notion to marry, and I'm sure there's some compromise we can…"

He fell silent as Thea advanced on him, skirts swishing in her fury.

"You lied to me, Noah Winters," she accused in low, miserable tones. "You lied to me about your own children, and you have been living a lie with me this past week and more. You *judged me* for my past, but at least I didn't involve a pair of innocent children in my short-lived attempt at discretion."

He shoved the dragon book between other tomes on a shelf. "So you're discreet when you come to the marriage bed unchaste, but I'm a liar?"

"They are *children*," Thea spat. "Innocent, helpless children who depend on you for the stability of a roof over their heads, and you involved them in your subterfuge."

Noah had the grace to look chagrined, running a hand through his hair and again turning his back.

"I'm sorry," he muttered.

"I beg your pardon?"

"I said, I. Am. Sorry. Your Grace."

All the hope, all the possibility Thea had been harboring for their marriage evaporated in the chill spaces between his words.

"It was not well done of me," he went on, "to think the children wouldn't be curious about you, and look for every opportunity to inspect you at close range."

"You are sorry." Thea came to stand beside him,

determined he would not avoid her gaze, even if his expression could freeze boiling water in an instant.

"Yes, Araminthea, I am sorry. Shall I put it in writing for you?"

No angel of common sense appeared to slap a celestial hand over Thea's mouth, not that such a trifling impediment would have kept her silent.

"Maybe that was my mistake," she said. "I did not apologize to you in writing for my lack of chastity, and for my failure to find a way to disclose it to you any sooner than I *willingly* did."

Noah traced a finger down the glass, keeping pace with a single raindrop as it started its journey to the sea.

"You disclosed your lies when it suited you to do so, and mine have been revealed by the children," Noah mused. "The glare from your halo must be blinding me to the distinction between the two."

"And no doubt"—Thea matched him for coolness—"some night over cherry cordials, you planned to tell me about your little indiscretions, tucked away up here in the attics. You'd relegate them to the status of details, and dare me to fuss at you for your dissembling."

"Please do not refer to the children as indiscretions," Noah bit out. "They have names, and they are dear to me, and whatever your quarrels with me, you may be assured of two things."

Thea waited, for His Grace was very fond of ducal pronouncements—when they suited his purposes. His expression would wilt all of Erickson's beauties, and likely Maryanne and Davies too.

At some point in this skirmish, he'd become the

man who, without benefit of his own majority, had kept his family and estates together. The same man who coolly chose the companion when the debutante had given her hand elsewhere.

No, Thea corrected herself, not coolly. Coldly.

"First," Noah said, "you may be assured I will do what is right for those girls in all the ways that count. They aren't leaving, Thea, not to protect your sensibilities, not to spare you, of all people, embarrassment."

"You idiot man, I would not ask them to leave."

"You would ask *me* to leave?" He put universes of condescension in his question.

"Your blasted pride won't let you set me aside, Noah," she said. "I am resigned to being periodically tormented in this marriage for my mistake, or regularly tormented with your scorn and victimhood, but even you have to grow bored with bemoaning what you have unilaterally decided cannot be changed."

His drew in a breath, and Thea would not have been surprised to see him sprout scales and wings and start breathing fire.

"You are already clear on my second point, Duchess: no matter your disagreement with me for how I've handled the introductions between you and the children, no matter you feel justified in judging me for it, this changes nothing. When I am assured you aren't carrying another man's child, I will make every effort to see to it you are soon carrying mine."

He leaned in, kissed her cheek, and whirled away. His boots thumped down the corridor in an angry tattoo as the first, futile tears slid down Thea's cheeks.

# Nine

"It wasn't raining when we left Town." James Heckendorn accepted a medicinal tot from Noah as the storm raged outside the Wellspring library. "Patience insisted Lady Nonie had to see her sister. If I'd known dropping in would put you in such a foul humor, I would have come earlier."

Noah saluted with his drink. "Bugger you, James."

"The same to you," James completed the toast as he ambled around a library where he'd run tame since boyhood. Noah should ask James to give Thea the tour of the house, lest Thea become lost on purpose for the remainder of the year.

"You'll have to put off that thunderous expression," James said, giving the globe a spin. "Otherwise, Patience will insist we join you here for a protracted stay."

Noah took a hefty swallow of his brandy. "You intimate to her you'd abet such a plan, and it will be pistols at dawn, James. Rain, shine, or impenetrable fog."

Such was the hospitality of a man who'd bungled

with his duchess and knew not exactly why, much less how to fix it.

Though fix it, he would.

"You weren't in this bad a mood when last we met," James observed, giving the globe another push. "I thought maybe you'd stop by Henny's and get your newlywed spirits, shall we say, lifted."

The rest of Noah's drink burned its way to his middle. "I am newly wed, and I did ride past Henny's, though I haven't yet officially informed her of my nuptials."

"Oh, right." James peered at his brandy, as if perhaps tea leaves might be read therein. "You're the town crier now, making sure your mistress is kept apprised of your social schedule. I gather holy matrimony is now approximating holy hell?"

Noah gently set his empty glass down on the sideboard.

"For your benighted information, I cut Henny loose at the beginning of the Season, and generously so, if I do say so myself. I did not call on her last week because Meech's phaeton was in her mews, and while I do not begrudge my uncle his pleasures, neither do I want to catch him on the stroll, so to speak."

Which was nearly impossible, because Meech and Pemmie were usually trolling for custom of one sort or another. No wonder Harlan fretted over his legacy.

"One doesn't know whether to admire Meech's stamina, or shudder for his lack of adult restraint," James said. "But if you've gone for, what—three months?—without exercising your manly humors, then no wonder you're like the Regent with a bad head."

"Oh, it's worse than that." Noah poured himself a touch more libation—a generous touch. "I was trying to give Thea time to settle in before I told her about Evvie and Nini, but the girls slipped the leash and found her on their own. Thea drew the worst conclusions, and we're at daggers drawn all over again."

For Noah's duchess had gone toe to toe with him, as a duchess should when her idiot duke had bungled badly and been too proud to admit his error.

James saluted with his glass. "When you set out to muck something up, you muck it up as efficiently as you manage everything else."

"I was *trying* to be considerate," Noah shot back. "I was *trying* not to overwhelm the lady with all the changes in her life at once, to give her a chance to be my wife before she had to be anybody's mother."

With the luxury of hindsight, those rationalizations now seemed implausible to Noah—cowardly, even.

"That's the preferred sequence: wife then mother," James said. "But when you're nobody's father, why would she think she's their new mama?"

Yes, why indeed? Thea had been magnificent in her temper, and not entirely wrong. Noah had kept the girls from the notice of his duchess, which was badly done on his part. Beyond that, the disagreement had escalated on both sides before common sense could wrestle pride, hurt feelings, and mistrust into submission.

Escalated *again*.

James touched his glass to Noah's. "Anselm, you didn't."

"Didn't what?" Noah took off across the carpet,

for the drapes wanted closing lest the drafts gutter the sconces. "Thea drew erroneous conclusions, and I did not correct her. The girls call me Cousin, and Thea chose not to believe them either."

"Was she at least civil to them?"

Noah pulled two sets of curtains closed, plunging the library into funereal gloom.

"She was..." Noah flopped into a wing chair and ran a hand through hair already disheveled. "Thea was ferocious, James. She as good as told me I was free to decamp to some other residence, and she and the girls would be just fine without me, thank you very much. She berated me for involving the children in my schemes, and was generally quite impressive."

Very impressive. Had called Noah an idiot to his face.

James put a hand over his heart. "Never say you found something to respect in the hopeless jade you married? Your Grace, I am ashamed of you."

Noah threw a pillow at him, but James dodged it easily and took the other wing chair.

"What will you do, Noah?"

"One considers soaking one's head in a rain barrel and beating one's chest at such times," Noah said, staring at the fire. "Or giving the lady what she wants."

"Which would be?"

"The absence of her spouse," Noah said. "Maybe some time to settle her feathers is a good idea."

"While you leave Thea to contemplate having the marriage annulled?"

Noah got out of the chair and handed the pillow to James, who wedged it behind his back.

"No annulment," Noah said. "I've spent years living down the reputation of my elders, and the day Thea goes to the bishop, I will be a laughingstock, just as they were."

"No doubt. Bishops are the worst gossips, after all."

"You are such a bastard." Noah's favorite bastard in the world, in fact.

James adjusted the pillow against his left lower back, which an old riding accident tended to make stiff on chilly days.

"Were you really only trying to give Thea time to grow accustomed to you?"

"Of course."

James said nothing.

"Well, partly." Mostly?

"And the other part?"

"How do you tell a woman she's acquired maternal responsibility for two bastard children you neglected to mention before you so bitterly castigated her for her own silences?"

"You tell her humbly," James said. "I have been married these three years to the most adorable lady in the world, but it might surprise you to learn ours has not always been a blissful union."

Perhaps James had been making frequent use of his traveling flask and was already slightly tootled.

"I am that lady's *brother*, James."

James waved a dismissive hand. "I am her *husband*, and it is my job to make Patience's way on this earth smooth and pleasant, to protect her from all harm, including the occasional minor irritation visited upon her as a result of my own human shortcomings."

"Do your philosophical peregrinations have a point, James?"

"As a husband," James went on, "I've learned a trick you have yet to master, Anselm, and if you don't shut up, I won't share it with you."

Perhaps Noah was more than slightly tootled himself, for he was about to listen to marital advice from his brother-in-law.

"I am the embodiment of the attentive ear, Baron."

"You should be, for I am about to impart to you the same secret Wilson imparted to me, and Heath imparted to him," James said, naming Noah's remaining brothers-in-law. "Pay attention: when your wife has painted you into a corner, or your own stupidity and stubbornness have—which in present company is more likely the case—then you must use the heaviest artillery in the husband's arsenal. You must toss pride and even dignity to the wind. You must sacrifice your all for the cause. In short, you must humbly and convincingly *apologize*."

The fire in the hearth snapped cheerily for a few heartbeats before Noah gave a snort of laughter.

"Years of marriage to my three sisters, and that's all you lot can come up with? Apologize? Marriage isn't public school, James, that a virtuosic display of the civilities will impress all the fellows almost as much as a vigorous round of fisticuffs. You want me to apologize to Thea? Well, I already did, before we even quit the room."

"*We* quit the room?" James let the question hang in the air, his tone so, so innocent.

"Very well, Heckendorn, *we* did not quit the room.

I quit the room, thinking to give the lady some privacy to compose herself."

Noah was not tootled, but he was desperate enough to air grand bouncers before his oldest friend. Had Thea felt the same bewilderment as the wedding approached? The same inability to push simple, honest words past her pride?

James abandoned his chair to take the same pose by the mantel Noah's grandfather had favored.

"Anselm, you have a lot to learn and a long way to go. You *ran*. We all run. The ladies start ranting and crying and catching us out in our selfish follies, and we bluster and stomp and threaten, and then we get the hell off to high ground, go for a ride, or a pout at the club. At least be honest with yourself. You left out of consideration for your own pride, not your lady's."

Noah hadn't even left to salve his own pride. He'd simply panicked and run. "If you weren't married to my sister…"

"I'd still be one of your oldest friends," James said gently. "Apologize to Thea, sincerely, and soon. If not for your own stubborn sake, then for the children's and hers. Once you've waved the white handkerchief of husbandly humility—"

James's head came up, a hound scenting game, and whatever additional drivel he'd been about to dispense must have flown from his tootled grasp.

"I hear the carriage," he said. "If the rain keeps up, we might impose on you for the night, Anselm, so compose your delicate sensibilities, and prepare to deal with your sister and Thea's sibling as well."

"God save me," Noah muttered. "I'll warn Thea,

you warn Cook, and send a footman to let Harlan know we're entertaining."

"Of course, Your Grace." James whipped off a salute. "And you *shall* apologize to your wife."

Noah made a rude gesture and stomped off in search of the lady to whom he'd already planned to offer *another* apology.

❧

"Thea?" Noah shook her shoulder gently. "Wife? Time to wake up."

"Not yet."

"We've company, Thea."

Her Grace snored softly on.

"Araminthea, Duchess of Anselm." Noah tried for a more stern tone, but God in heaven, she was adorable in slumber. "Sweetheart, your sister's coming to call." Seeing Thea snoozing away, her cheeks streaked with tears, Noah was hard put to recall why he'd been in such a towering temper with her.

This time.

"Just let me catch a few more—Nonie?"

"No need to panic." Noah brushed a lock of hair off Thea's forehead. "The coach was just coming up the drive a minute ago. You've been crying."

She looked confused for an instant, then her eyes narrowed, and she flopped to her back.

"You made me cry, you odious man, keeping your children from me, while you strut about in righteous indignation over my own lapse. I don't like you very much right now."

James's daft sermon rang in Noah's ears as did all his

own rehearsed apologies. "You have some insight into how I felt on our wedding night. I hadn't planned for you to feel deceived, but here we are."

Thea twitched at the folds of his cravat. "And where, precisely, is that?"

Noah turned and sat on the edge of the bed long enough to pull off his boots, and then climbed up to sit beside Thea, his back to the headboard.

Where it left them was hurt, mistrustful, and married. "We are both angry, misunderstood, and weary of it."

"Very weary."

"I propose a truce. The children are innocent of any wrongdoing, and we must put their welfare ahead of our squabbles."

As apologies went, that effort was pathetic.

"This is not a squabble, Noah."

"It's not the Siege of Rome, either, Thea. We're unhappy with each other, but we can either acknowledge what can't be changed, or cling to our miseries. I honestly do not want to make you miserable."

Which was a relief and a disappointment both. Shouldn't a marriage have a higher ambition than not-miserable?

Thea began rummaging between the sheets. "What I want is to keep the vows I spoke before the vicar, Noah."

Love, honor, obey. Interestingly, nothing on that list overtly required absolute honesty—or apologies.

"Those vows seem daunting now, don't they?" Noah mused.

"Challenging." Thea tossed a white, balled up

handkerchief onto the bedside table. "I relish a challenge, usually."

"As do I." Something positive passed between them, and the tension Noah sensed in Thea relaxed.

"I have too much pride," Noah said, "but sometimes pride is all one has. I don't know how else to be."

"I understand pride, Noah, and when I wasn't either crying or sleeping off my tears, I realized you don't know me well at all. If you knew me better, you'd know I'd love to be a mother to Janine and Evelyn. You and I are *married*, we are supposed to be the foundation for an entire family, and the girls are part of that family."

Thea clearly aspired to higher ground than not-miserable, which ambition was a worthy attribute in a duchess.

"I could not predict your reaction to not one but two bastard children in the nursery," Noah said, taking Thea's hand, "and I'm more comfortable with situations I can predict. Still, I should have told you. I'm sorry I didn't."

Noah expected some cataclysm in response to his apology—the bed canopy to fall, perhaps—but Thea merely withdrew her hand and patted his knuckles.

"And I overreacted, for which I'm sorry," she said easily, as if apologies were nothing unusual between spouses. "I know why you're here, though, acting the diplomat and spouting sweet reason, Noah. If we're to have company, you're concerned I'll rant and sulk, and embarrass you before others. I won't. Never, not unless you push me to it with everything in you."

Noah had needed that reassurance, for his own parents had staged rows that had made Drury Lane look boring and Waterloo a friendly skirmish.

"I will try not to provoke you, Thea, but I am by nature a cautious man, and our marriage is off on a bad foot."

"It isn't the Siege of Rome," she said, tossing back the covers and bouncing to the bottom of the bed, "and we haven't come to blows or embarrassing the servants yet."

"Nor shall we."

As the words left his lips, Noah didn't know if he were uttering a promise or a prayer.

❧

"Marriage must agree with my brother." Patience offered the observation casually, but Thea understood it as a warning shot prior to an interrogation. Harlan was showing Nonie the third-floor conservatory, while Noah and James were closeted in the game room, leaving Thea to fend for herself.

As usual.

"I'm not sure marriage agrees with His Grace," Thea said, "but he likes to accomplish what he sets out to do, and he set out to find a bride this Season."

"Well put." Patience slipped her arm through Thea's. "And most of these fellows"—she waved her other arm at the portraits marching the length of a fifty-foot wall—"set out only to wench, swive, and occasionally take up arms for King and Country. Noah is a changeling in our family."

"Do you mean that literally?"

Patience paused before a dark-haired, blue-eyed, laughing courtier in hose and ruffed collar.

"This one was supposedly a favorite of Good Queen Bess," she said. "A particular favorite, whose exertions to please his monarch resulted in elevation of the title from viscountcy to earldom. Noah is a Winters by blood. Of that, there can be no doubt."

The fellow had a handsome smirk and looked on the verge of winking.

"Noah would never do such a thing?" Thea asked.

"He would not." Patience moved on to the next portrait, an equally rascally looking fellow. "Noah seldom comes to the portrait gallery, in fact, because these rakish fellows make no sense to him. I'm sure he tells himself they were from an earlier time. They weren't evil, they might not have enhanced the family coffers, but until recently, they didn't decimate them either."

They all certainly dressed well. "Until recently?"

"I shall be blunt," Patience said, pausing before a portrait of a smiling couple in elaborate wigs and embroidered finery. "I doubt Noah spelled it out for you when he was doing his, what, three days of wooing?"

Whatever he'd done, he hadn't spent those days wooing. "Four."

Patience moved the frame half an inch, so the portrait hung squarely. "You let him get away with this, Thea. What could you have been thinking?"

"Honestly? I was thinking the settlements were very generous, because they provided not only for me, but for Nonie and any daughters of our union as well. If I asked it of the duke, I believe he would take my brother in hand too."

Though Thea hadn't wanted to ask Noah for much of anything lately.

"Ask it of him," Patience said, strolling along. "Noah thrives on responsibility. You want to know about our family finances? When Papa was alive, the duns were circling, threatening to foreclose on the unentailed properties, for he'd mortgaged them all to pay for his lightskirts and queer starts. My late uncle was no better, though of the three, he was the least profligate. Uncle Meech is on a stipend, and while it's generous, Noah is adamant that Meech manage within it."

"I have not met this Uncle Meech," Thea said. "He was rusticating at the time of the wedding. Noah holds him in affection, though."

Noah held his brother, his sisters, the little girls, his roosters, his horses...all save his duchess in great affection, or so Thea felt.

"Meech was one of Noah's guardians when Papa died, and he's not a bad sort." Patience frowned at a portrait of a lady holding a small, walleyed dog wearing a jeweled collar. "My grandmother in her salad days."

The one who'd loved flowers? "She must have adored that dog. Noah has retrieved the finances from ruin?"

"I was only a girl when Papa died, and Harlan wasn't even born," Patience said. "I knew the servants were always exchanging portentous looks over the mail tray. I noticed the frequent callers from the City who were received only in the parlors that had no windows, that sort of thing. Noah dealt with it all, and

James says the situation was frightful, because he and Noah were barely out of public school."

"Then Noah never had those useless years," Thea said. "The ones immediately after university, when young men get into so much trouble and nobody holds them to account?"

When they had fun, made mistakes, got their hearts broken, and made silly wagers.

"Noah has never had the fribbling years, while Uncle appears trapped in them, along with his other cronies and partners in mischief."

Thea took a seat on a velvet-cushioned bench, not wanting the conversation to end prematurely, for Noah would never share this information with her.

"Is he received, your uncle?" she asked.

"Oh, everywhere," Patience said, peering at a painting of a woman with a shepherdess's crook and several fat, woolly sheep about her. "Meech and his set are a regular fixture at the house parties, in the ballrooms during the Season, and in the autumn reprise of the Season. They circulate all the best gossip, and are considered minor arbiters of fashion."

Even the mention of house parties made Thea uneasy. "While for your family, Rome might have been burning."

"Well, the footmen certainly weren't being paid as promptly as they should have been. Nor the maids, or the merchants."

Thea rose to inspect the shepherdess, because from a distance, the sheep appeared to be smiling.

"Do you suppose Noah thinks he must buy his way through life?" she asked.

Patience linked their arms again. Like Noah, she was apparently a toucher. "What a lonely notion. I would say Noah believes he must work his way through life. He's too serious by half, and doesn't know how to go on unless he's solving some problem or other."

*Or creating a problem.* "But you love him."

"Oh, yes." Patience's smile was radiant. "I love him, so do my sisters, our husbands, and so will our children. Noah's tenants love him, and household staffs love him. We owe him a great deal, and always will."

Thea wasn't sure what to say to that, because a man so thoroughly loved and appreciated should not be limited to buying his bride.

Across the gallery, the laughing courtier smirked at Thea, the walleyed dog eternally panted, and the sheep milled about at the feet of their titled shepherdess.

They all seemed to say the same thing: the duke who'd bought his bride, however much Thea might lament his approach to courting, did not deserve damaged goods for his coin.

❦

At dinner, true to his word, Noah's demeanor gave no hint of discord between him and his wife. Thea held up her end of the bargain, smiling and steering the conversational barge to topics of general and cheerful interest. Patience excused herself from the drawing room civilities when the ladies rose to take their tea, and a particularly tender look passed between James and his lady.

What would Thea have to do to earn such a glance from her husband? Noah was watching her, not tenderly, but with a regard Thea couldn't quite discern.

He tucked her hand over his arm as they approached the drawing room.

"Dear Wife, you must not wait up for me. Subduing James over the cribbage board might be a lengthy undertaking. He is to be a papa, you see, and his pride needs a sound drubbing."

Hence that tender look.

"Here we go," Harlan said from where he was escorting Nonie behind them. "The battle of the gods, but they leave the decanter undefended in their absorption with the hostilities."

"Tomorrow morning," Patience observed, "you will be expected to ride out with these old warhorses, and in your case, the decanter will have been painfully victorious."

"Heed your sister," James said, "for the rain has stopped, and I've a notion to see how Wellspring is getting on."

Noah paused outside the parlor door. "Thea, I bid you a pleasant evening, and please do not think to give up your slumber in the morning for a soggy ride. I'm sure you'll want to visit with your sister." He kissed her cheek and departed after good nights all around.

Nonie had been oddly subdued for most of the day, but when Thea closed the door to the drawing room, Nonie wrapped her in a hug.

"Oh, Thea, you truly are a duchess, aren't you?"

She was and she wasn't. "What does that mean?"

Nonie gestured to the room in general. "This whole house is what I mean. Did you know Noah has been to North and South America? Harlan said he'd been to Egypt and the Levant as well. That's four continents, Thea, and he's rich as a nabob and owns property in seventeen different shires and counties, including Ireland, Scotland, Wales, and France."

"Five continents," Thea countered. "But no, I wasn't aware he was so well traveled. Tea, dearest?"

Nonie plopped down onto a sofa. "Please, for I must settle my nerves, Thea. Harlan is absolutely delicious, and so is James. I've called upon the others too, since the wedding breakfast, and they are all lovely, and they all wanted to descend on you here at Wellspring, but James wasn't having any of that."

Thea let Nonie prattle on until two cups of tea later, when she finally sputtered to a pause.

"But are you happy, Thea?"

Thea was married. *Happy* didn't signify. "I am pleased. Anselm has dowered you generously, Nonie. Very generously, and you are welcome to live with us when I've found my bearings here."

"I haven't spent a summer in the country for ages," Nonie said, glancing about as if heaven might have sported the same wallpaper as this very drawing room. "Will Harlan be here?"

For the next twenty minutes, Nonie's conversation was peppered with references to Harlan-said and Harlan-told-me and Harlan-thinks.

Thea smiled into her tea, wondering if she'd ever, ever been that innocent, particularly where a male of the species was concerned.

"James says we aren't to think of wandering the house parties while Lady Patience is in a delicate condition," Nonie went on. "Patience said she doesn't want to be tied to the foaling shed until she's at least having to alter her gowns, but James can be very firm without even raising his voice."

Thea's tea tried to go down the wrong way. "House parties are much overrated, Nonie. I've told you this."

Nonie popped a tea cake into her mouth—a pink one. "You can speak from experience, because your employers dragged you hither and yon while they made the rounds. Isn't the gossip at least entertaining?"

No, it was not. Gossip was a weapon that could destroy a young lady overnight.

"Gossip might be entertaining to some, Nonie, but it's nasty talk about people's lives, and it serves no purpose."

Another pink tea cake met its fate. "You should never have gone into service. You didn't used to be so serious, Thea. You enjoyed a little gossip. You even flirted with Tim's friends."

"They were younger than I, and I thought it was harmless." Tim's friends had flirted with Thea, rather. She went to the door and signaled a footman to take the tea tray. "I'll show you up to your room, Nonie. You have to be exhausted after all the excitement today."

"I am," Nonie said, wrapping two more tea cakes in a serviette and tucking them into a pocket. "Today has been a lovely day, Thea. Still, I wish you were a little more *in love* with Anselm. He's a good-looking fellow, if somewhat deficient in charm and overburdened with muscle."

And Nonie had seen the duke only fully clad.

"That good-looking fellow is deserving of your humble gratitude, Antoinette Collins. He is making it possible for you to have the security of a decent match, rather than be parceled off to whichever of Tim's friends he owes the most money to."

Nonie halted in the middle of the stairs. "Is that what sent you on such a flight, Thea?"

Nonie was approaching the age at which Thea had accepted employment from Lady Bransom. She was so painfully young, and yet Nonie was no longer a child.

"Something like that, though Tims never overtly threatened me."

"Threats are more effective when they're subtle," Nonie replied. "Every governess and tutor knows this."

How had Nonie learned it?

"All's well now," Thea reminded her as they reached Nonie's bedroom. "You're enjoying your visit with James and Patience?"

Nonie wrapped her arms around Thea. "Oh, absolutely. Life has become quite lovely, Thea, and all thanks to your marriage. You'll be happy with Anselm, won't you? I couldn't bear it if you weren't."

"I will be happy," Thea said, her smile never faltering. She was a duchess, after all.

Nonie padded off to bed, and Thea took herself to her own room, there to bathe and retire without any sign of her husband. Hours later, she thought she heard the door between their dressing rooms creak open, then slowly close. She caught a whiff of Noah's lavender-and-rose scent and anticipated the familiar sounds of him undressing, then washing.

But she waited, and waited, and still heard no

Noah-going-to-bed sounds. His weight didn't dip the mattress; his arms didn't slide around her and pull her into the warmth of his body.

For the first time since their wedding, Thea tried to sleep through the night without her husband. Despite their differences and troubles, she was unable to banish a certain new and profound sense of loneliness caused by his absence.

# Ten

"You are a traitor of the most shameless sort, to me, to your calling, and to your kind." Noah lowered himself to Thea's bed and passed a steaming cup of tea through Thea's field of vision. "If you didn't catch the occasional, and I do mean occasional, mouse, you would be relegated to the stables for the rest of your indolent days."

"Tea." A plea disguised as a groan. Noah was growing wise to his duchess's habits.

"Good morning, Wife." Noah leaned down to kiss her cheek. "You've allowed a trespasser into your bed."

"We're married." Thea struggled to rise, her expression bewildered and grumpy. "It isn't trespassing if we're... Oh, aren't you a *lovely* little kitty."

"She's two stone if she's an ounce," Noah groused. "One never sees her eating, though, because she subsists entirely on huge bowls of cream, which she charms Cook into leaving in conspicuous locations."

Thea set the teacup aside after only a single sip. "What's her name? She's magnificent."

"She's a disgrace, and her name, accordingly, is Bathsheba. Evvie smuggled her in from the stables two years ago, a bedraggled, pitiful excuse for a kitten, and now *this*."

Bathsheba, a glorious specimen of quintessential feline in long black fur and brilliant green eyes, squinted contentedly at Noah, then delicately licked the finger he extended toward her.

"We'll shear you next spring, cat," he threatened. "You'd better perfect your bleating."

"She kept my feet warm," Thea said, retrieving her teacup, "when a certain husband was absent from his proper location."

Had Noah really expected Thea to let his absence go unremarked? Part of him was pleased she'd bring it up; another part of him was tired from a bad night's rest.

"You weren't supposed to mention that, Thea." Noah took her teacup from her and appropriated a sip. "I was trying to be considerate of your exhaustion, and now you complain. I expect at least a touch of gratitude for my thoughtfulness."

Though a touch of pique was acceptable too.

Thea gave the pillows a smack. "I expect the comfort of my husband's nocturnal company."

"You are entirely without civilities first thing in the day, aren't you?"

"I was without my husband all night." Thea sat back and appropriated her teacup, though it was now empty. "And you say this dear kitty is a disgrace. I like sleeping with you, Noah."

This again.

"You won't be sleeping with me tonight." He rose to pour a second cup of tea from the service on the cart. He prepared it exactly to Thea's liking—cream and a mere gesture of sugar—then propped himself at the foot of the bed, where he commenced petting his traitorous cat. "I've some business in the City, and I'm accompanying James and Patience back to Town."

"Without your untrustworthy wife," Thea muttered.

"Even were we in Town," Noah said gently, "you would not accompany me to the solicitors' offices, but if you're determined to force the point, then you're right: I do not want us socializing until certain matters have been resolved beyond doubt."

Or a certain duke had found his balance with his duchess.

"I don't blame you for your caution, Noah, but I'd like to look in on Tims. He can be difficult, and Mrs. Wren tends to dither and then the maids feud, so the footmen—"

Sibling anxiety Noah understood very well. "I'll look in on dear Tims. You might have asked."

Thea narrowed her gaze at him over her second cup, like a dragon might yawn and stretch outside her lair.

"*When* might I have asked? You're telling me your plans only now, when you're on your way to the very stables."

Noah crawled up the mattress, past the cat, and settled in beside his wife at the head of the bed.

He held up a stocking-clad foot. "I'm not quite ready to ride away. I'd look silly saddling up without my boots, wouldn't I?" He took Thea's hand, while the cat sat at their feet and groomed her long black whiskers.

Thea closed her eyes and leaned her head back on the pillow. "I have a latent talent for bickering, and marriage has brought it to the fore. I am sorry."

Another apology, a genuine, remorseful apology, and Noah resented Thea for being the first to offer one.

"You aren't generally quarrelsome, Thea, or surely Marliss would have remarked upon this shortcoming. I really do have business in the City, and I frequently will. That's part of the reason I typically summer here and not at one of my grander holdings. Harlan likes Wellspring, and I'm not far from Town."

Or from his sisters, and their fellows.

"Patience said you thrive on your commerce."

What else had Patience said? James might know, and he might not. "The family coffers thrive on commerce, but you are sworn to secrecy, of course."

"Of course."

Noah settled back on the pillows. "No one of significant standing must be seen to engage in trade, but in any given ballroom, I will be approached by no less than six gentlemen, some of whom outrank me, asking me if I've heard of any interesting opportunities lately, or if my man of business is available to meet with theirs. Perhaps I have a pound symbol painted onto my evening jackets."

"And on your riding jackets when you hack in the park?"

"Yes." Noah turned onto his side, the better to

regard his duchess, to whom he was whining. "How badly was Hallowell bothering you?"

This had bothered him as he'd tossed and turned for hours in a cold, lonely bed.

Thea tugged the covers up a good half a foot. "Now who lacks civility first thing in the day?"

"I'm your husband," Noah said quietly. "Tell me."

Thea turned to her side too, so they faced each other. "He was getting worse, but I knew Marliss would soon marry, and my days in that household were limited. I resolved to be very cautious, and Marliss understood what was afoot."

The conspiracies of women never failed to impress— and surprise—Noah. "Marliss?"

"You gentlemen often think you see *the* truth, when what you see is only *a* truth, and a version of it that you want to see."

Noah rolled off the bed rather than wade into that verbal swamp. "I cannot argue that point in present company. Harlan will bide with you here. He hates Town unless his mates are about, in which case he loudly professes to love it."

"What about you? Do you hate it?"

"I don't…" What did it matter if Noah loved or loathed the crowded, stinking, hectic social cesspit that was Polite Society in Town? "I don't hate it. One does what one must. You may reach me at the town house. I'll take care of appointments this afternoon, have dinner with Wilson and Prudence, and likely ride out with Heath in the morning. For the sake of domestic tranquillity, I will break my fast with Penelope tomorrow, tend to more appointments, and likely be back here by late afternoon. You'll manage?"

Thea gestured for Noah to pass her the wrapper hanging from the privacy screen. She flipped her braid out from the collar of the dressing gown in a gesture at once sensual and brisk.

"If you've no objection, Noah, I'd like to discuss the girls' routine with their nursery maids, and maybe ride out with Harlan when the roads are dry. I'd also like to tour the vegetable garden, meet with the housekeeper, look in on Mr. Erikson, and so forth."

"Erikson?" Noah poured wash water into the pot suspended from a swing on the hearth, and pushed it over the coals, then set Thea's slippers by the side of the bed—pink slippers embroidered with white rosebuds. "What need have you of his company?"

"He's a brilliant botanist." Thea untangled herself from the bedclothes and made her way to the edge of the mattress. "His conservatory is a few doors away from two very curious little girls. I want to make sure they don't pester him, unless he's willing to be pestered, in which case I will suggest he turn their visits into botany lessons."

"See that he isn't willing to be pestered in any regard you'd come to regret, Thea."

Noah's comment should have merited him pursed lips, Thea's chin in the air, and a mighty, wifely huff of indignation.

His duchess was apparently getting wise to his tricks.

She smiled wickedly and tossed a pillow at him. "Enjoy your appointments in Town, Husband, and don't worry about us here. We'll contrive without you somehow."

The dragon was awake and ready for a serving of toasted duke. Noah considered stomping out in high dudgeon, stocking feet notwithstanding. He picked up the pillow, put it back on the bed, and wrapped his wife in his arms.

"You will behave," he said as she bundled into his embrace. "I want no reports from the magistrate about my womenfolk when I return, no petty rebellions among the servants, no wild starts from my brother. The peace of my kingdom rests in your dainty paws, Wife."

"Safe journey." She kissed his cheek. "My regards to your sisters, Husband."

❧

"Running." James gave the word a gratingly musical inflection as the horses plodded toward Town. "Run, run, running."

"I've business in Town, the same as you," Noah replied, "and Thea asked me to check in on her brother." Well, she had, more or less.

"Grantley," James said, humor disappearing. Their horses splashed along the mucky road for a few paces. "Not an impressive specimen, from what I've gathered."

"The earl is young, but he worries my duchess, and I cannot have that."

"So you'll charge forth to vanquish her worries," James surmised, "when she'd really rather have you toddling about underfoot at the castle."

True took exception to a rabbit darting across the path, or to having an inattentive rider in the saddle.

"Being on the nest has curdled your meager store of brains, James. You've grown besotted with domesticity."

The remainder of the journey into Town was a testament to how badly James had been longing for a child, for James's conversation was sadly peppered with musings about how many names the baby might be reasonably given. He'd toss a crumb in the direction of business matters, then veer right back into whether Patience would be better served by a son or a daughter as their firstborn.

By the time Noah reached the City, he was relieved to be free of his brother-in-law's company.

Though what would it be like, to be that enamored of one's future, and one's mate?

Noah dispatched with business matters, then turned True toward the outskirts of Mayfair. At midafternoon, Henrietta Whitlow would likely be rising from her bed.

Henny, and very possibly some lucky, toothsome, well-heeled fellow with her.

The thought should have given Noah a pang, for he liked Henny tremendously, but his reaction was curiously uninterested.

Henny was not uninterested in her former protector She welcomed Noah with kisses to both cheeks, then stepped back and gave him a stern look over folded arms.

"You mustn't start presuming, Anselm. The bracelet was extravagant, but your privileges are at an end here. You know that."

The male half of Polite Society had likely known it too. Noah tucked Henny's hand over his arm.

"I would have humbly accepted the butler's admonition that you were not home, my dear. I'm sorry I did not send a note." Apologies weren't that difficult, once a man had some practice with them.

"I am glad to see you in any case," Henny allowed. "Join me for some tea."

Henrietta Whitlow was a woman fashioned by male gods, on their scale, to their specifications for what was most desirable in a woman. With masses of flaming hair and big green eyes, she was majestic. Noah had always liked that she was shamelessly indulgent in all her appetites. Honestly indulgent.

"Tea would suit," Noah said, particularly because tea with Henny meant sustenance as well.

"How is married life?" Henny asked as she slid gracefully into a padded wicker seat on her shaded back terrace.

"Trying," Noah said, reluctant to embellish in any way that might reflect poorly on his wife. "I am not accustomed to being in double harness."

"You aren't." Henny paused mid-reach for the teapot. "Do sit, Anselm. You're more likely used to being the leader of a six-in-hand."

Noah took the place opposite her, when for nearly a year, he'd taken the place right beside her. Thus did marriage reach into every corner of his life, though not as uncomfortably as he might have guessed.

"You've concluded I'm a poor candidate for marriage?" he asked.

"You have been head of your family for half your

life, Anselm." Henny poured him his tea and passed it to him. "You don't realize how much time you spend picking up after Meech, checking on Harlan up at school, harrying your brothers-in-law on the subject of your sisters' happiness. You'll adjust to being married, but I don't envy your duchess. Toast?"

Henny had forgotten Noah liked his tea with cream and sugar. A small oversight, but reassuring, because it implied her focus was no longer on him and hadn't been for some time.

Thea would not have forgotten how Noah took his tea, not after three decades, much less three months.

"Toast with jam and butter," Noah said, stirring his own sugar into his tea. "You're faring well?"

"You didn't believe Meech's reports?"

"I have not seen my uncle since before my nuptials." Noah hadn't missed him either.

Henny ran a pale finger around the rim of her teacup, stirring a memory Noah couldn't quite place.

"Meech is sniffing about, more so he can boast to Pemberton that he's visited here than because he's of a mind to take me on. I haven't permitted him past the parlor, though I don't find him egregiously offensive."

She found Meech mildly offensive, then, as Noah occasionally did.

"Meech can't afford you, Hen," Noah said gently. "Not consistently." Henny also deserved better than Meech, whose grasp of politics, international affairs, and literature paled compared to Henny's.

"I do prefer consistency." She reversed the direction of her finger circling the teacup's rim. The gesture

might once have appeared erotic, though Noah no
longer found it so. "One man at a time is trouble
enough, but I'm taking a repairing lease."

What did one of the most sought-after courtesans in
London consider a repairing lease?

"Henrietta Whitlow, do I need to send my man of
business around?"

Her finger stopped its endless circling on the gilded
lip. "You are so dear. I'm considering retiring."

London's bachelors would go into a collective
decline. "You're that well fixed?"

"I'm that lonely."

A silence stretched between them in the warm
afternoon air. They had been friends, after a fashion,
but Noah would have described it as a friendship
where each party was burdened with a loneliness the
other never intended to assuage.

"I will be known as the man who drove you from
your business," Noah said, trying for a touch of levity.
"Not well done of me."

"Or you will be known as the man who brought
me to my senses in time?"

"Henrietta?"

"My menses approach." Her bluntness might
have shocked other men; Noah was used to it.
"Welcome as always, of course, but don't mind
my mood. You did not stop by here to renew our
arrangement, and if you did, you will please pretend
you did not."

"I did not. What do you know of Grantley?"

"Timotheus Collins." Henrietta nodded, a lady
about her business. "Useless, intemperate, but not

mean. Yet. Shamefully negligent of his sisters, but did adequately at school, funds still managed by his solicitors, which will soon end. He's not quite pockets to let, unless it's the end of the quarter, but he's foolish in his choice of friends."

God bless a woman who took her work seriously. "Who might they be?"

"The typical studies in uselessness," she said, listing a half-dozen names. "Lately he's been in company with Corbett Hallowell a great deal."

"Of course." It would be Hallowell, who was likely spoiling for an excuse to call Noah out. God spare a hapless duke from silly young men whose antics made the little debutantes look like seasoned diplomats. "Does anyone hold Grantley's vowels?"

"Hallowell, to the greatest extent." Henrietta buttered herself a piece of toast. "You're married to Grantley's older sister. Pretty girl. Poor thing went into service."

"Fled into service, I'm coming to believe."

Henrietta aimed a basilisk stare at him over her toast. "Are you being decent to her, Anselm? Lady Araminthea is an earl's daughter and deserving of every consideration."

A faint echo of James's lectures sounded in Noah's memory. "*You* are giving me marital advice, Hen?"

"If more men were better prepared to become husbands, I'd have far less trade to choose from, Anselm." She tossed her flaming mane over one shoulder in a gesture that earned the attention of royal dukes across a crowded theater. "One can't expect these gently bred young ladies to know what's what in bed. You have to show them, and you're perfectly capable of explaining—Are you laughing at me?"

Noah would miss her, though not in his bed. "You accuse me of being a mother hen, *Hen*?"

"You are impertinent," she said, taking a regal sip of her tea and reminding him of Bathsheba, or even a little of Thea, when her chin came up. "You courted the woman for less than a week, then spirited her off to your peasant abode, and you've no doubt executed your marital duties with all brisk dispatch. Didn't I teach you anything?"

"Henrietta, a change of topic is in order."

"No, it is not." She rose and glared down her undainty nose at him. "You are a good man, Anselm, better even than you know, but you're mucking this up. I can tell."

Noah was coming to loathe the verb *to muck*.

"How can you tell?" He rose as well and not only because manners decreed he must. A man wanted to be on his feet when his former mistress impugned his intimate skills.

"You're here, aren't you?" Henny asked.

"Here," Noah agreed, "on your back terrace, not inside. Not inside your house, not inside you."

She regarded him for a long, thoughtful minute, and Noah knew a frisson of unease. Henny in a rant was magnificent. Henny with that look on her face made a man leery.

"I suppose that's something," she conceded, resuming her seat. "More toast?"

More toast? Noah paced off, his back to her, while

the sounds of cutlery and porcelain tinkled through the fragrant summer air.

"I sleep with my wife." Now where in the hell had that come from?

"Do you, now?"

Noah traced the petals of a blushing pink rose, his back still to his hostess. "That's about all we do between the sheets."

"She's shy?"

"She's—Hen, I was not her first."

Cutlery clattered onto a plate and a chair scraped back. Henny soon stood behind Noah. He could sense her there, could smell her fragrance. If he turned, she'd allow him to take her in his arms.

"You would be upset about something like this," she said, "because you are a goose—or a gander, I suppose. I gather you did not know before the vows were said?"

"That's just it." Noah moved away a few steps and half turned, while Henny remained by the roses. "I think my wife tried to tell me, but she just…couldn't, Hen. Then she did, a few intimate moments too late, but she knows nothing. She barely knows how to kiss, and she… What?"

"You are assuming your lady had an affair, Anselm, but women in service are considered prey by every man under the age of eighty, including their employers. I know this firsthand."

Henny had leaped to the very conclusion Noah had avoided for several days. "How come you to this knowledge, Henrietta?"

She flounced back to the table, and Henny could flounce with the best of them.

"Do you think I woke up one morning and decided to be the Whore of Mayfair, Anselm?"

Noah had never considered Henny's past, hadn't wanted to consider it, but, yes. He'd assumed Henny enjoyed being naughty and somehow always had.

"You're not a whore."

"Anselm…" Her tone was infinitely gentle. "I have two brothers and a grandmother. I am an aunt twice over, I have cousins. Do you think their regard means so little I would gaily toss aside my virtue for even this?" She held up her wrist, where a gorgeous bracelet of gold and emeralds winked in the sunlight.

"I'm…sorry, Henny. I had no idea."

"You aren't supposed to have any idea." She dropped her hand back to her side, shaking her arm so her dressing gown covered Noah's parting gift. "The fiction that I'd choose this life above all others is part of what lets you and others of your ilk bed down with me. But back to your duchess, with whom you sleep. Are you asking me for advice?"

"I suppose I am." What else was he to say? Henny Whitlow had a grandmother, and brothers. Plural. Cousins, some of them no doubt quite small, maybe all of them dependent upon her.

"Do you know what I like about you most, Anselm?"

Noah snapped off a pink blossom and passed it to her. "I am loath to speculate, when you have already called into question my amatory skills."

"Don't sulk." She gave him the queen of all unsympathetic grins and set the rose behind her ear. "You are frightfully competent in bed, Anselm. You even taught me a thing or two, but you can wipe that smirk off your face. What I liked most about you, and you may freely note the past tense, is your affectionate nature."

The entire world had gone stark raving tootled. "I am a duke. I do *not* have an affectionate nature."

"I am not accusing you of the randy foolishness that characterizes your uncle, Anselm. I am telling you, just this once admitting to you, that what I looked forward to most about time spent with you was when you would hold me, afterward, and ask me about my day and tell me about yours."

A look passed over Henny's striking features, one Noah wished he hadn't seen, an expression of longing and vulnerability.

"You went to bed with me to *talk*?"

"I did." Her gaze was appallingly serious, even wistful. "To talk, to cuddle up, to visit, to be with you, not simply with your manly exuberance or your skills."

"This has to do with that loneliness you mentioned," he ventured. "You're a *professional*, Hen." An admonition, or an expression of disappointment. The observation sounded bewildered to Noah's own ears.

"I am a human being, Anselm. A person, and so, my friend, are you."

Henrietta showed Noah out soon after, but she'd gone up on her toes to kiss his cheek, reminding him starkly of his wife.

Who was a person too.

To know he wouldn't be dropping in on Henny again should have made Noah sad—married men weren't welcome to drop in on her, Henny had her rules—but mostly as he swung onto True's back, Noah felt relief. Like finding the tea cakes weren't sitting on their usual shelf in the larder, when the temptation to ruin dinner was calling loudly.

The call had served its purpose nonetheless. Henny had told Noah what he needed to know about Grantley, and many other things he hadn't wanted to know.

About himself.

# Eleven

"So you've met my demon cousins?" Harlan asked as he patted his new gelding, upon whom he'd yet to bestow a proper name.

"You mean Evvie and Nini?" Thea was up on Della, their choice of riding paths limited by the recent rains.

"The demons," Harlan said. "They blink those great blue eyes at you, exuding such innocence, then steal a sip of your tea and hare off in a storm of giggles, but you can't be angry when they're so adorable with it."

"Stealing tea seems to be an inherited trait. Have you always known about them?" Thea asked. The girls were technically Harlan's nieces, if Noah was their father—which he had not denied.

"Of course I've known about them." Harlan's assurance sounded much like his older brother's. "They are family. Noah would no more fail to acknowledge them than he would me." Harlan speared Thea with his own innocent blue-eyed gaze. "I gather you and my brother are having a rocky start?"

Brave lad.

"I hope you gather nothing of the kind, Harlan Winters, and if you did, it wouldn't be gentlemanly to remark on it."

He held his mount back to allow Thea to steer Della down the only dry patch between two puddles.

"Perhaps not gentlemanly," Harlan said, slight color rising from under his collar. "Maybe brotherly. You should give Noah a chance."

"Marriages are complicated," Thea said. "Your loyalty to Noah speaks well of you both. Shall we turn back? We'll not get in a gallop in this wet footing."

"We could stick to the road," Harlan said, eyeing the damp track before them. "The rain stopped last night."

Thea had her own reasons for taking their time on the way home.

"We neither of us know our mounts that well," she pointed out. "The better part of sportsmanship would be to show caution. Then too, we are without grooms because you are my escort, and I don't think you brought a firearm, if one of the horses should break a leg in this mud."

Harlan made a very adolescent face, but he turned his horse at the walk beside Della.

"What a cheering thought. Noah tells me, when I'm out of patience with the demon cousins, to get used to it, because the adult version is even more wily. I see him with our sisters, and now with you, and I believe him."

Little girls were not demons. "What do you mean?"

"You didn't ask, what if a horse breaks a leg in the

mud? You noted that I'd neglected to bring a gun—
and you put the matter with all possible diffidence.
Diabolical of you."

"So I'm a demon too?"

"Noah's demon." Harlan used his crop to thwack at
the branch above his side of the lane, sending a shower
of drops down on him and his horse. "Noah's the
best brother, Thea. I had tutors until I was fourteen,
and then I went up to Rugby, and I was one of the
new fellows."

Maybe the male equivalent of being a debutante.
"That was hard?"

"I made it worse. I'm taller than most, and I've
always been fast."

"You brawled." Thea tried not to sound dismayed.
Tims and his friends were always debating pugilis-
tic science.

"The headmasters look the other way, because boys
must sort themselves out. I'd got a fine education at
home, and hadn't the sense to keep that fact to myself.
Somebody's older brother must have said something
to Noah, because I usually sported a black eye or two,
a split lip, and so on. I had a bad few weeks."

Weeks seemed like forever to the adolescent—or
the newly married. "What happened?"

"My brother dropped everything and came to visit
me," Harlan said. "Noah inspected my rooms, met with
each of my professors, took me off for a round of clothes
shopping, brought my horse up to stable locally, laid in a
supply of food, and somehow quietly let the lads know
my allowance was adequate to maintain that supply."

"You never suffered another black eye?"

"If I did, it was in a fair fight, Thea. Not a matter of four of the fellows jumping me while two others whaled on me with their riding crops. No one used my nickname after it became obvious the Duke of Anselm's visit wasn't an isolated occasion."

Thea was fiercely glad Noah had not believed boys should be left to sort themselves out through endless violence.

"What did the food have to do with the situation, Harlan?"

"At public school, we never have enough food, much less enough good food," Harlan said. "Growing boys can eat like grown men only dream of, and the headmasters say it teaches us self-discipline to be on short, bad rations. I say it made us mean, tired, and irritable, and I think Noah agreed. I made money off it, in fact."

Engaging in trade, like his ducal brother, because trade had been the family's salvation. "You sold your stores."

"At a modest profit. All the boys had allowances, and food was a better use of their money than the watered ale at the local posting inn. When I went up to university, I passed my enterprise on to a pair of the new boys, whose older brothers were leaving with me."

"Did Noah give you the idea for this tactic?" They were approaching the stables, and Thea hadn't asked the things she'd wanted to, about Noah, and the dem—the little girls, and his trips into Town.

"I can't decide if the scheme was Noah's." Harlan turned his horse up the drive beside hers. "I've decided Noah planted the idea but let me think it was mine."

"He's a good big brother, then." Noah was a good duke, too, and possibly even a decent, if aggrieved and cautious, husband.

"He's a good *man*," Harlan countered. "Noah isn't as charming or easy to spend time with as other men, not for a lady, anyway. I've told him he should have practiced his flirting before he tried to get a wife, and he laughed."

Harlan helped Thea dismount from her mare and then offered his arm as the grooms led the horses away.

"Harlan, what was your nickname?"

"Not fit for a lady's ears," Harlan muttered, posture straight as they made their way toward the house.

"I could ask Noah."

The pink was creeping up his neck again. "One forgets you have a brother, so you're not without guile."

"I'm also sister to Lady Antoinette, whose company you seemed to enjoy."

"You must never tell her," Harlan said, sparing Thea a single uneasy glance.

"I will never tell her," Thea said, thinking that boys were really too serious over something as inconsequential as a schoolyard nickname.

"Harlot," he said very quietly. "They all, all of them, at every turn, called me Harlot. Excuse me."

On his long legs, he turned and headed back to the stables, his face averted from Thea's horrified gaze.

❧

"Tell me you didn't visit your harlot less than two weeks after your wedding, Anselm."

Heath Carruthers had waited the duration of a dawn

hack through Hyde Park to spring his question, which was typical of him. He was married to Penelope, who as the baby sister, had been ever so slightly spoiled by her older siblings.

Carruthers had a Gypsy darkness about his lean height, and a mind equally given to dark twists and skewed humor. He characterized his wife as the embodiment of sweetness and generosity, for example.

"I needed information from Henrietta," Noah said, "and she provided it."

Carruthers kneed his mount—a stolid gray by the name of Horatio—to a more brisk walk, because True set a faster pace—not that Noah was in a hurry to end the conversation.

"Would this be the same variety of information I've provided your sister almost nightly for the past four years?" Carruthers inquired.

"Must you, Carruthers?"

"When my informing has born consequences, yes. Your sister and I are in anticipation of an interesting event. You may congratulate me, Anselm."

Hyde Park was beautiful in the early morning. Sunshine bounced off the Serpentine, mist rose from low-lying ground, and the occasional rabbit snatched a few last nibbles of sparkling green grass.

All of London was stirring and stretching into a new day, hundreds of thousands of souls, and yet, Noah felt alone.

"Penny is doing well?" Noah asked, because that was what a brother asked. Penny had the constitution of a plow horse to go with her demanding nature, and she had Carruthers to spoil her rotten.

"She's taking good care of herself," Carruthers said. "She, Patience, and Pru are very much in one another's pockets."

While Noah had removed to Kent, with the bride who hadn't trusted him until it was too late. The bride he did not trust, rather.

"Your papa must be pleased," Noah managed. "Congratulations, and if anything happens to my youngest sister, I will geld you."

"And Wilson and James?"

Well, of course. "Them too. I gather Prudence is also on the nest?"

"I think the ladies planned it this way," Carruthers said as Park Lane came into view. "When you announced your intention to go bride hunting, they all grew quiet, and *affectionate*. Wilson and James noticed the same thing. More affectionate even than usual."

"Women." And sisters, turning up more affectionate than usual, causing Noah to wish his marriage were different. Thea would enjoy a hack through the park first thing in the day, and she'd look very fetching on her mare too.

"You'll be next, won't you, Anselm?" Carruthers had to nudge his horse again. "That was the purpose of the marriage, as I recall. Time to set up the nursery, see to the succession, but if you're visiting Henny, perhaps there's trouble in paradise already."

If Carruthers were speculating, then Noah's situation was hopeless, because unlike James and Patience, Heath and Penelope had no discretion. They discussed *everything* with each other.

"Tell me, Carruthers, has James been bearing tales?" James, Noah's oldest and dearest friend. Impending fatherhood apparently made traitors of otherwise good men.

"Tales about you? Of course not, but Penny is worried for her oldest brother, and she's off in corners with Patience and Pru. I'd be least in sight if I were you. Maybe time to visit the holdings in Cardiff with the new duchess, if you know what I mean."

Cardiff would mean days in a coach, with Thea dozing by Noah's side. Thea's feet in his lap. Thea sharing the wild, beautiful Welsh vistas with him...

"I'm lucky all three sisters aren't camped on my doorstep right now," Noah said. "Lucky, and fortunate in my brothers-in-law."

Carruthers waggled a gloved finger. "See that you never forget it, Anselm, and heed me when I tell you now isn't the time to be crying on Henny's milk-white shoulders."

They were actually freckled shoulders, and a trifle mannish in their breadth, not like Thea, whose proportions were feminine perfection itself.

"I dropped in on Henny to gather information on Grantley," Noah said. "It's time to buy the boy's vowels and bring him to heel."

Carruthers's horse chose that moment to come to a complete stop, lift its tail, and leave a steaming pile of manure at the park's entrance.

"Even Horatio has no respect for Grantley," Carruthers said as the gelding toddled on. "One fears for a young buck without anyone to reel him in from time to time. I well recall those uncomfortable lectures from the marquess—temperance, dignity, economy, family name, and all that."

In his turn, Carruthers would deliver the same pointless lectures to his own son.

"Because you are the spare," Noah said, "I'm sure the occasional admonition to marry found its way into the quarterly sermons."

Grantley was of age. Why hadn't he contracted marriage with some sweet, young, well-dowered thing?

"Papa never harped on marriage." Carruthers's nonchalant tone belied the sensitivity of the topic. "The marquess has always expected my older brother to find a bride, regardless that Owen states clearly he will not."

Because Owen had left-handed tendencies, as was known to all save the man's own father.

"You'll not outrank me even if you inherit," Noah said. "Make sure my sister is reminded of that fact regularly."

"She outclasses you, old man, and always will."

"Besotted," Noah spat. "On the nest and besotted, the bleeding lot of you." He cantered off, Carruthers's happy laughter ringing in his ears.

❧

Thea took herself to her bedroom, the only private space she could reliably find in Wellspring's rambling interior. She needed solitude and a sense of Noah's presence to recover from Harlan's disclosure.

*Harlot.*

She curled up on Noah's side of the bed, felt the impact of the word physically, felt the biblical enormity of the scorn it embodied. If not for ladies

Bransom and Handley, that vile word would have been applied to her.

Should have been, or so she'd thought at the time.

Thea clutched a pillow to her middle, though it was little comfort compared to Noah's strong arm about her waist.

She'd had years to consider her past, years to watch how little Polite Society did to prepare its daughters for times when no chaperone was on hand. Such moments were inevitable, when even the most protected of young women might dash off to the retiring room between sets to have a hem mended.

Thea was struck anew with how audacious—how desperate—she'd been to accept Noah's offer of marriage. She'd become his duchess, and Noah's consequence would be enough to protect Nonie, in even unguarded moments.

For the first time, Thea realized that Noah's consequence would protect *her* too.

His consequence would protect her, as would Noah himself.

To the extent that she could, Thea would protect Noah as well.

She rolled off the bed, smoothed over the wrinkles on the counterpane, and made her way to the third floor.

Thea approved of Noah raising his illegitimate daughters under his own roof, where they'd be safe and watched over, where they'd learn a sense of their value in the duke's eyes.

No wonder he summered here, and had Harlan do

likewise. Harlan was his heir, for the present, and the girls' protection would rest on Harlan's shoulders in Noah's absence.

Thea made a quick stop in the conservatory, where Erikson assured her he enjoyed the visits from the girls, and was already using the time to bring botanical matters to their notice.

"They love the flowers as Anselm does," Erikson said. "So we learn about the flowers together, and thus they become little scientists. My uncle was the same with my brother and sister. We learn by enthusiasm and example, and his enthusiasm was catching."

The vanilla orchid's scent blended with the earthy, herbal aromas of the laboratory to create a fragrance both peculiar and exotic.

What had Noah learned from the example of his profligate progenitors?

"Your enthusiasm is contagious too," Thea said to the bespectacled Erikson, "though small children can be taxing, even when fascinated with their lessons. Do you speak in your native language to your flowers?"

Thea couldn't quite refer to them as beauties, though the rest of the Winters family apparently did.

Erikson's expression turned thoughtful. "I think my tone of voice matters to them, not my language. Why?"

"Might you also share some Dutch with the girls?"

"Tea words, my aunt called them. Please and thank you, good day, and how do you do? I can start them off on tea words, and when we are chattering in Dutch, maybe then some French?"

Exactly how Thea's governess had eased her into

French. "They'll like the Dutch, because they'll share it with you and your beauties."

When Thea took her leave, Erikson was beaming as if she'd told him the Regent sought a Royal Botanist of Dutch extraction.

In the nursery, she found Nini and Evvie were napping, an unusual occurrence, but not unheard of, and that gave her the chance to ask Davies and Maryanne what exactly the girls were studying.

"A bit of this and that," Maryanne said. "More to keep them out of trouble than anything else."

Which scheme was meeting with mixed results, apparently.

"His Grace trusts us," Davies added, exchanging a glance with Maryanne. "We take good care of the girls, and they're good girls."

The nursery maids also took care of a prodigiously nutritious tea tray, the remains of which would have made Harlan several nice snacks.

"I'd say Evvie and Nini are very good girls," Thea replied, helping herself to a ginger biscuit. "Though staying up here all day is confining to their minds and their bodies. Do they have ponies?"

"That's just it, Your Grace." Davies's expression grew earnest, and she and Maryanne were still finishing each other's sentences, and trading impatient glances thirty minutes later.

"We thought about writing to Lady Patience," Davies said when Maryanne let her get a word in, "but she might take it amiss, you know? She does dote on the duke something fierce. The girls have needed a guiding hand, and His Grace already provides them so much, but they're *girls*, and he's, well, he's Anselm."

Except for those moments when he was Noah, stealing Thea's tea or lending her his cat.

Thea appropriated a second ginger biscuit, the last on the tray. "One comprehends the difficulty. Did you two teach them to read?"

"They just picked it up," Maryanne said. "I don't have much reading, though Davies has her letters. His Grace reads them bedtime stories, or he used to, and they'd cuddle up, one on each side, and he'd ask them to pick out words, and that sort of thing. They're frightfully bright."

Another Winters family trait.

"And the little one, Nini," Davies said around a mouthful of tea cake, "she can mimic anything you say, while our Evvie has a wonderful eye. They need a drawing master, and it isn't too soon to start them on the pianoforte."

"Make me a list," Thea said, as "I'm awake now" rang out from the next room. "A list of supplies and subjects. You've both done yeoman duty, but we need a governess, at least, if not a governess and some tutors. Surely we have a drawing master in the area, and a music teacher. His Grace will see the need, and it will be addressed."

Noah would see the need when Thea pointed it out to him, which she would do immediately upon his return from Town.

"Yes, Your Grace," they chorused, but as Thea retraced her steps to the main staircase, she realized what neither maid had said. Evvie and Nini were little girls, but they were *illegitimate* little girls, and their welcome could not be assured, even on the rolls of a piano teacher's students.

Noah had dealt with such complications now for years as best he could.

For the next phase in his campaign, however, he needed a wife. A lady to call upon the neighbors, to take the girls shopping in the village, to sit with them at services and stare down the small-minded bigots of the shire. Noah's wealth and title could do a great deal, but some doors only a determined lady could open.

And Thea was nothing if not a very determined lady.

# Twelve

"Jesus spare me," Timotheus Collins groaned into his pillow. "Not you again."

"Be warned, Grantley: your sisters are not underfoot to intercede for you," Noah replied. "Are you trying for the dissipated scoundrel look, or living the part in truth?"

If anything, the boy looked worse—man, rather. Grantley was again sprawled on his counterpane in all his skinny, naked glory. His eyes were sunken, his hair greasy, and his chin sported at least a day's growth of dark whiskers.

"For the love of God, go away." Grantley hunched into his pillow, then his head came up, and he turned bleary eyes on Noah. "Thea's all right?"

"A glimmer of brotherly concern," Noah observed to the room at large. "Thea thrives in my care, and Lady Antoinette is similarly enjoying my sister's hospitality not three streets over in the direction of Mayfair. I take it you have no valet?"

A knock on the door interrupted Grantley's reply, and then Hirschman trouped in, rolling a large copper tub before him.

"Water's nice and hot," he said. "Morning, Master Tims."

"Thank you, Hirschman. His lordship will need strong tea in addition to his bath," Noah said. "Where's his shaving kit?"

"I'm awake." Grantley swirled the sheets over his nakedness, then lay flat on his back and closed his eyes. "I'd rather not be, but I am awake, which suggests I'm alive too."

"You're still drunk," Noah said as Hirschman emptied buckets into the tub, "and you're the worse for it. This is a particular folly of young fellows, but you've been down from university long enough to outgrow it. Out of bed, now."

"Go to hell." Grantley rolled over and buried his head under his pillow.

Noah used a riding crop to swat his lordship on his backside through the sheets. Thea had asked him to look in on Tims, after all.

"For shame, your lordship," Noah said. "You have company, and you are not displaying your company manners."

"Holy perishing saints." Grantley rubbed his posterior and he sat up. "In what jungle did Thea find you, and how soon can we ship you back there?"

Noah slashed his crop through the air, as if testing a foil at Angelo's. "A spark of wit, however feeble. Out of bed with you, now."

"Out of bed with you, *my lord*," Noah's host muttered, slogging to the edge of the bed. When Grantley gained his feet, he dropped back onto the mattress like a puppet whose strings had been cut.

"Does *your lordship* need the basin?"

"I need the damned room to hold still."

Hirschman reappeared with the tea tray, and while more buckets were added to the tub, Noah poured tea down Grantley's skinny gullet. Thank goodness Thea wasn't here to see her brother in all his disgrace, for she was a good sister, and she'd be more concerned than outraged.

Three cups later, Grantley scrubbed a hand over his face. "What's all this in aid of?"

This exercise was in aid of Noah's matrimonial good will. "We are family now. Your days of useless fribbling are over. You have responsibilities."

Grantley hoisted himself back against the pillows. "I most assuredly do not. I have sense enough not to be getting bastards all over the place, like certain other people I could name."

"We are not discussing certain other people, we are discussing you, and you might be surprised to learn you are Lady Nonie's legal guardian." For the present, in any case.

Grantley blinked, then blinked again. "I am about to be sick."

"You are not," Noah shot back. "Get your arse into that tub and close your eyes."

On unsteady feet, Grantley complied, more falling into the water than sitting in it. His eyes slammed shut, and if Noah hadn't shoved a hot cup of tea into his hand, he'd no doubt have gone right back to sleep.

Charming. And this malodorous, inebriated stripling had been Thea's source of masculine protection?

"Now, *your lordship*, you will attend me."

"I'm attending." Grantley kept his eyes closed. "Might I have more tea while I'm being tormented with your pontifications?"

"You are worse than your older sister," Noah pronounced. "With respect to Lady Nonie, you are an outright disgrace. She had not one dress that fit, much less one that was acceptable for making calls. She had no gloves that hadn't been stitched, and no mount suitable for hacking in the park. Were you thinking she'd not live to turn eighteen?"

"I won't live to see her turn eighteen. My thanks for the tea."

Somebody—Thea, no doubt—had put the manners on Grantley, which was fortunate, for he appeared without other redeeming features.

"Drink it," Noah snapped, "and then get busy with the soap, for there's a deal of you in need of a thorough scrubbing. I am prepared to provide a home for Lady Antoinette, and Thea and my sisters can see to her come-out next year."

Grantley set his teacup aside, the saucer and cup clattering in his unsteady grip. "That's all right then, if Thea's taking Nonie in hand."

"You are their *brother*. You were in no shape to review Thea's settlements, were you? Have you even read them yet?"

"Been a bit busy." Grantley sank lower into the water, then grunted when Noah fired a hard-milled bar of French soap at his chest.

"You don't know busy, Grantley. I have three sisters, and they all required launching. You will call on Lady Nonie this afternoon, you will drive her in the park tomorrow, and you will take her to visit my sisters Prudence and Penelope by week's end. You will take her shopping on the Strand by Saturday."

Grantley stared at the soap, which bore a strong scent of lavender. "In daylight?"

"Civilized society conducts most of its business in daylight," Noah replied. "Now dunk." He emphasized his command by shoving Grantley's head under the water and holding him there for an instant.

"You bloody bastard…" Grantley came sputtering up, flailing for a towel. Noah slapped a dollop of soft soap—rose was such a lovely scent—onto his palm instead.

"Your hair reeks," Noah said. "Wash it thoroughly, or I'll wash it for you."

Grantley complied, while Noah rummaged in the wardrobe for clean clothes. Mrs. Wren's sense of duty was to be commended, for at least his lordship had decent linen.

Noah laid the clothes on the bed and stalked over to the tub. "I'll rinse you off, assuming you can stand unaided." He poured the rinse water over Grantley's head, taking care not to splash on the floor. By the time Noah had finished, Grantley was shivering, naked, and a great deal more sober than he had been.

"Close the bloody window, for God's sake," Grantley muttered, belting the robe Noah tossed at him. "Do you want me to catch a lung fever?"

"This room reeks," Noah said. "Your life reeks, and lung fever would be a mercy, if it would give you time to grasp the extent of your own folly. Now, you may eat something."

"Couldn't possibly."

Noah passed him a plain piece of toast. "A show of petulance isn't the same thing as a display of spirit. Eat."

"I do hate you," Grantley said, eyeing the toast. "Some dark night, you'll hear a twig snap behind you, and that will be your only warning I've come to exact my revenge."

Noah suppressed a smile from long practice dealing with Nini and Evvie.

"You'll exact your dread revenge by sneaking up from behind? In the dark?" Noah went to pour himself a cup of tea and found the pot empty. "Hardly sporting. One shudders for your honor."

By degrees, Noah bullied, teased, reasoned, and forced Grantley into a semblance of order, then all but dragged him out into the midday air.

"Where are we going, now that I've been tortured to your satisfaction?" Grantley asked as they headed out the town house door.

Noah snapped off a rose from the trellis near the door and tucked it into the younger man's lapel.

"Anselm, are you daft?"

Anselm as a form of address was a presumption, but—may God have mercy on dukes with marital schemes—Noah and Grantley were family, so Noah tolerated it.

"You look a fright, your lordship," Noah replied, which did not directly answer Grantley's question. "A cadaver has more color than you, smells better, and exudes more charm. A boutonniere will distract the unwary from your ghoulish countenance and provide a hint of scent. We are off to Tatt's, where you will do as I say, bid as I say, and otherwise impersonate a young man with enough sense to accept a decent influence on his life when it resists the urge to drown him at his bath."

Grantley pursed his lips and sniffed at his lapel.

"Damask," he said. "Emphasis on the damn. Tatt's it is."

❧

Noah wasn't coming back to Wellspring, not that night anyway. Thea folded the note brought by one of Noah's grooms, silently congratulating herself on not crumpling the paper and tossing it on the dung heap. Married less than two weeks, and the duke was "delayed by the press of business" in Town.

*Business* likely sported an impressive set of bosoms, while Thea had merited two lines of scrawled information.

"Thank you." She managed a small smile for the groom. "No reply, but you should take yourself to the kitchen, where you'll find food and drink."

"Thank you, Your Grace." The groom tugged his forelock, showing Thea a sort of deference she found difficult to accept.

Harlan would be disappointed Noah wasn't rejoining them at Wellspring, as would the girls. Thea's guess was they noted the comings and goings on the property far more intently than the adults around them surmised.

"We shall have a picnic." Even saying the words made Thea feel better. "Harlan can take up one little girl, I'll drive the other in a cart, and we'll bring blankets, kites, and a storybook. My husband will regret that he was so sorely pressed by his *business*."

A bold claim, and sincere. Thea suspected she'd cry herself to sleep that night anyway.

◦❧◦

"At least you have your late papa's sense of horses," Noah allowed as he and Grantley mounted up to leave Tatt's.

Thea had horse sense too, and she smelled a good deal better than her brother.

"Hunters were his specialty," Grantley replied as he clambered aboard his gelding. "Some of my best memories are of being up before him for the family meets. You think Nonie will like her mare?"

That Grantley would ask was encouraging.

"She will like that you thought of her," Noah said, "and Thea will approve as well."

"Approve of you?" Grantley bent his head at an angle that allowed him to sniff at the rose in his lapel. "For rousting me out of bed and spotting me the blunt for the pony? Was my morning's rest sacrificed on the altar of marital politics?"

Which question also did not merit a response.

"You'll have the next quarter's funds within two weeks," Noah said. "As loans between family members go, that's short term enough, I don't need a note of hand. When we've had some lunch, we'll call on your solicitors. For your information, your sister has no idea how I've wasted my morning."

But she would. Noah would make a full report within an hour of returning to Wellspring.

"Meet with the solicitors? And spoil a perfectly good tot of gin?"

Noah fell silent, because Grantley was serious. Many young men consumed spirits in great quantity, but Grantley was in deplorable condition. His hands shook, he yet smelled of the previous night's imbibing, his complexion was waxen, and his eyes were bloodshot.

From a distance, the earl was the picture of the successful young man about town. Up close, he was the image of inchoate ruin. He would have made a fine addition to the Winters line.

"You have a choice, Grantley, barely."

"Now he gives me choices. Be still my joyous heart."

Noah tipped his hat to the Duchess of Moreland as she tooled along with her youngest daughter on the bench beside her. Grantley was too busy fussing his posy to notice the ladies, though with a glance, Her Grace had noticed—and disapproved—of Noah's companion.

Duchesses had that ability—most duchesses.

"You have the barest hope of a choice, Grantley. One option is to climb into the gin bottle and pickle away the few years remaining to you. In that case, you will be at the mercy of the solicitors, though they will be free to pilfer your funds, and no one will stop them. You will console yourself with the company of your drinking companions—you will have no real friends, of course—and they will find great sport in goading you to increasingly dangerous wagers, all for their entertainment."

Noah drew True up, Grantley's horse shuffling to a halt as well while they waited for a crossing sweeper gathering horse droppings.

"To soothe your troubled spirit," Noah went on, "you will seek the company of the whores willing to service you in your stuporous lusts. One of them will know to turn the lamps down, so you won't see the evidence of the pox that eats her alive. You will die alone, stinking, penniless, and brokenhearted. If God is merciful, you will also die soon, so your sisters needn't be humiliated by this debacle."

Grantley kicked his horse back into a trot. "You pronounce me dead in the gutter because I want a bit of hair of the dog? God help Thea should she spike her tea."

Somehow, Noah knew she'd never do that, and he need never worry she'd abuse spirits. Not ever.

"If that option does not appeal," Noah went on, as if Grantley hadn't spoken, "then the first step you ought to take is to shift your associations. When Corbett Hallowell comes around offering to stake you to a few wagers or buy you a few drinks, you decline."

"*Hallowell?*" Grantley looked genuinely confused. "He's a friend. He's the one who found that last position for Thea. She was at loose ends and refusing to come home when old lady Besom or Bosom—I forget which—went to her reward. You suggest I cut him?"

Noah would have insisted upon it, but his experience with Thea suggested the Collins siblings dealt poorly with ducal insistence.

"Hallowell's papa is a viscount. Your papa was an earl," Noah said. "For Thea to be a glorified governess to Hallowell's sister was a humiliation for your sister, not a coup. Thea was not respected in that household."

Grantley's gelding slowed to the walk. "Not… respected?"

There truly was hope. Grantley yet reasoned, and he wasn't indifferent to his sisters.

"I will spare you the details, Grantley, because I am the lady's husband, and her protection falls to me now."

What Noah left unsaid penetrated the fog of drink and youthful bluster that passed for Grantley's awareness.

"Are you saying Hallowell did not respect my sister?"

Noah turned True toward the Anselm mews. "More to the point, he does not respect you. He's a few years older, has had a few more years to acquire his town bronze, and you are a toy to him. He's broken other toys, but they at least had family to repair them. My guess is he would rather have broken your sister. You'll join me for lunch."

"Couldn't possibly," Grantley said. "Not feeling quite in the pink. You said I had a choice."

"Live or die," Noah said simply. "Hallowell has your vowels. I will pay them off and deduct installments from your allowance to amortize the debt over, say, a year, without interest. If you incur more debt to Hallowell, I'll collect the total you owe me in a lump sum. And Grantley, I will find out if you borrow from Hallowell. I will know before you've staggered home and fallen facedown, bare-arsed into your bed."

Though Noah would not trouble Thea with such a disappointment if he could avoid it.

"Why bother me like this, Anselm?" The put-upon bonhomie of the young man about town humoring a brother-in-law's queer starts was gone. In its place was pathetically genuine bewilderment. "I drink, I gamble, I chase skirts. My money is not yet my own, though my excesses are consistent with those of my peers. Why are you intent on scolding me like the schoolboy I no longer am?"

Noah brought True to a halt and struggled for what to say that Grantley could comprehend.

What would Thea want him to say?

In the gathering heat of the day, beneath the aromas of the stables and the garden, the reek of gin rolled off Grantley in subtle waves, and the sweat forming under his arms bore a sour stench. The earl wasn't an evil man, not yet, but he was…going bad.

"Your sister would have me believe she went into service to give you the breathing room you needed to leave the schoolroom behind, Grantley. You might swallow that pap, but I cannot. Thea is pretty, she's an earl's daughter, and she had no one—not one damned soul—to look out for her interests. Can you imagine the unkindness of the gossip she bore?"

Noah had shied away from imagining it himself, but he'd seen how Polite Society treated a lady fallen on hard times. He had counted on Thea's misfortunes to inspire her to accept his proposal, in fact.

"Thea's stubborn," Grantley protested as he half slid, half fell off his horse. "You can't tell her a blessed thing, Anselm. I know her. You don't. She gets the bit between her teeth, and she's off. Will you, nil you. Even Nonie tried to talk sense into her, and Thea was simply…"

Grantley fell silent as the grooms approached to take the horses. He fiddled with the wilting rose in his lapel, perhaps having lost his train of thought.

"Come try to eat a little," Noah said, because arguing Thea's motivations would get them nowhere. "You at least need to drink something besides blue ruin, and in quantity, given the heat."

Grantley fell in beside Noah as they crossed the shaded gardens behind Noah's town house.

"Hallowell's off to some boating party," Grantley said. "I think that's what he said. In any case, I won't be seeing him for some time."

God help the women trapped aboard the boat with Hallowell. Perhaps the Endmon heir couldn't swim.

"Hallowell's absence makes your decision easier," Noah said, "or buys you time to gain perspective. You may nap after lunch, but then we're for the City."

"I'm not a little boy—"

Noah merely treated Grantley to a slow, head-to-toe perusal. A breeze scented with honeysuckle wafted past, and Noah's longing for Wellspring, for the fresh air, for Thea's grousing first thing in the day, cindered the last of his patience with this dreadful excuse for an earl.

"Perhaps a short lie down," Grantley said. "Very short."

Two hours later, he was snoring soundly when Noah went to rouse him.

❦

"Noah is our cousin," Evvie explained, sitting cross-legged beside Thea on the picnic blanket. "But he's really like our papa."

Nini nodded emphatically on Thea's other side. "He really is. Harlan says so too, and so does everybody, but Harlan is only our cousin."

Harlan was "only" their cousin, but Noah was their cousin, and "really like" their papa. The distinction did not bother the children, so Thea refused to let it bother her.

"Cousin Noah is the head of your family, in any case," Thea said, turning the pages of the storybook that seemed to feature dragons on every third page. "The head of our family."

"That's why he's never here," Evvie said, as if repeating a frequently cited conclusion. "Cousin Noah must do things, and see people, and talk to Prinny about his roads, and ride in the park, and deal with the Furies."

A bee made a lazy inspection of Nini's discarded boots, then buzzed on its way.

"Who are the Furies, dear?" Thea asked as she came upon a story about a troll and a witch. What a delightful variation.

"Our aunts," Nini chimed in. "Cousin Noah says they're better now that they've found husbands to occupy them, but they were fear…"

"Ferocious," Evvie supplied. "I shall be ferocious too when I grow up."

"Me too."

While Thea was simply married. Noah, however, could lay claim to a deal of ferocity. His note from yesterday crackled softly in her pocket when she put the book aside.

"We'd better tend to this ferocious business inside," Thea said, rising from their blanket and gathering up the detritus of their morning's outing. "Firstly, I am growing peckish, and secondly, rain could soon be upon us."

Thirdly, Thea was lonely for her husband, and a moment resting on his side of the bed seemed like a fine idea.

"I'm growing peckish too," Evvie said.

"*J'ai* famished," Nini added, grinning.

Thea gently corrected the toddling French, and arranged their books, hairbrushes, and sketching implements in the hamper.

"When will Cousin Noah be home?" The lament, for Thea heard it often enough, came from Nini as she tugged on her boots. Evvie, older and more inured to disappointment, never asked, just as Thea at a young age had understood never to ask for new dresses.

"I haven't had a note from him since Tuesday," Thea said, shaking out the blanket and folding it over. "It's midday, so perhaps he'll be home later today, or perhaps not for some time. I simply don't know."

Not that these mornings with the children were unpleasant.

"You have to break him to bridle," Evvie said, finding a stray pencil in the grass. "I heard Aunt Patience explain this to Uncle James. She said men take longer than horses to civilize, because men have fewer brains."

"You shouldn't be eavesdropping, Evelyn Winters."

Thea tried to sound stern, but Noah would have made a much more impressive job of it.

"I wasn't eavesdropping," Evvie said, tossing the pencil into the hamper. "They knew I was there, and Uncle James winked at me." She gave an exaggerated demonstration, which had Nini giggling and doing likewise.

"What is all this mirth at such an early hour?"

"Cousin!" the girls shrieked in unison as they pelted across the grass into Noah's waiting arms. He rose with one girl on each hip, bussing first one then the other on their cheeks.

Would a mere cousin offer the little girls such an enthusiastic greeting? Thea's own father had never shown her that warm a welcome.

"What a pleasure to know I was missed, at least a little. Hullo, Wife." Noah leaned around Nini and kissed Thea's cheek too. "You look in great good health."

While Noah looked tired and road weary.

"I've been taking the air with the girls," Thea said. Had the duke's observation been a question? And if so, how personal a question?

"Why don't I let these beauties walk about on their own"—he set them down—"while I relieve you of that bundle?" Noah reached for the blanket, and Thea gave it up rather than deny him this exhibition of manners before the children.

He slipped his free arm around Thea's waist. "What have you young ladies been doing in my absence, and tell me the truth, because Lady Thea will peach on you in a heartbeat should you dissemble."

Two pairs of guileless blue eyes turned to Thea. "Will you, Lady Thea?"

"In a heartbeat," she said solemnly, but she winked too, and the girls were off again, laughing, winking, and giggling in their boundless pleasure at Noah's return.

# *Thirteen*

THE RAIN DID START AFTER LUNCHEON, DENYING THE girls the chance to picnic with Noah, but he promised them a picnic later in the week, a story at bedtime, and a visit to the stables the next morning.

"You think I'm spoiling them," Noah said as he handed Thea a finger of brandy in the library that night.

"I think you love them," she said. "You aren't having anything to drink?"

"I would not make you drink alone." Noah wrapped his hand around Thea's and took a sip of her drink. "When I've been gone, the girls need reassurances on my return. Their earliest years were not settled, and that still shows. The story tonight was because of the storm. They will be inordinately interested in my schedule for the next few days, and they will probably break a few rules to ensure I'm still on duty. I've been absent a great deal in recent months, and I've brought them an additional adult to figure into the household."

Thea's own mother had read to her on stormy nights.

"You know a great deal about raising children," Thea said. Did Noah recall the first thing about *being* a child himself?

He ambled over to the sofa before the hearth, sat down, and tugged off his boots. Next, he loosened his cravat, slipped his sleeve buttons free, and rolled up his cuffs.

How many people saw the Duke of Anselm in his stocking feet? Saw the dark hair dusting his forearms? Did his two-dozen mistresses watch this same process when he called upon them?

"What mischief have you got up to in my absence, Thea?" Noah patted the place beside him, and Thea sat.

The moment should have been pleasant, the fire crackling in the hearth, the children tucked up in their beds, the rain pattering softly against the windows.

"My menses haven't started, but they're not quite due."

Noah crossed his feet at the ankles. "That wasn't what I asked."

"That was what you wanted to know."

"It was what you wanted to tell me. Did you miss me?" He kissed her cheek again, which made Thea want to bolt from his embrace. She could not read his mood, had no idea what he'd been about, leaving her side for nearly a week, and had not the first clue what manner of discussion they were to embark upon.

"The girls and I managed," she said. "I told you we would."

Noah sighed as if the fate of the kingdom weighted

his spirit, then shifted so he half reclined right next to Thea. He gave off heat and weariness, and Thea let herself rest against him.

"I saw Grantley, at some length and on several occasions," he said.

The pair of them had probably gone out on the town of an evening or two or three. Disappointment joined the fatigue and weepiness plaguing Thea. "I suppose Tim enjoyed that."

Noah nipped another tot of Thea's brandy. "Grantley will hate me before it's all over. The man needs to stop drinking and grow up."

The very same conclusion Thea had come to several years ago, but it applied equally to most young men of title and wealth.

"Why should Tims hate you?"

Noah was positively bundled against Thea—or she against him—and the warmth and bulk of him felt... wonderful. They shared a concern for Tim, and they shared the weariness common to day's end.

Tonight, they also shared a roof.

"I've put the fear of God into his solicitors," Noah said. "I wasn't sure you'd approve, but they need to know somebody will look over their shoulders if they abuse the trust placed in them."

"They're the same firm Papa used," Thea said, giving in to the need to close her eyes. "They also have a small trust for Nonie." Smaller, after Lady Patience had taken Nonie's wardrobe in hand.

"What about for you, Thea?"

"I haven't a trust."

Noah grasped her neck from behind, between

his fingers and thumb, and exerted the slightest warm pressure.

"That feels divine, Husband."

He shifted his grip and repeated the pressure higher up her neck. "The girls adore you, Wife. I leave them in your hands for less than a week, and they've forgotten their old cousin entirely."

Their cousin who was "really like their papa." Thea batted that thought aside.

"You don't always have to change the subject when I offer you a compliment," she said, stifling a yawn. "The girls won't adore me so much when I hire them a governess, a drawing master, a piano teacher, and so on."

Thea should thank Noah for intimidating the solicitors, for that task had been beyond her.

The hand on her neck went still. "You'd involve the girls in all that folderol so soon?"

A young lady's life included nothing more than folderol, if she were fortunate.

"I told you I would see to them, Husband. You were gone for days, and—"

A finger on her lips silenced her.

"You are testy tonight, Duchess. One might think you missed me. What I meant was so soon, because they are so young yet."

Sitting beside Noah in the dim, cozy library, Thea's heart suffered a small fissure. Noah would be a loving and conscientious papa to their children. He'd be— contrary to how he was likely raised—a noticing and attentive parent.

To Nini and Evvie, he was a noticing, attentive, even doting parent.

Why hadn't Thea confided in him before she'd spoken her vows? Why hadn't he shown the least hint of approachability, of sentiment, when proposing?

Pointless questions. Nonie's future was assured, and that was what mattered. "Girls younger than Evvie start as apprentices, Anselm. Both children can already read, and they both have an ear for languages. It's time."

Noah gently brought Thea's head to his shoulder, whether for his own comfort or Thea's, she did not know.

Noah likely hadn't gone carousing with Tim, not if he was bent on setting a sober example for her brother. Taking Tim in hand was beyond decent of him.

"The girls were very glad to see you." As much as Thea could admit. Beside her, Noah seemed to relax a little.

A log settled on the andirons, the ducal budget allowing for wood fires in the library and the bedrooms.

"I'm always glad to see them, to be home," he said, stroking Thea's shoulder. "You're yawning, and the bath I ordered for you is no doubt ready. Let me light you up."

Noah drew Thea to her feet, but rather than slip her arm through his, he stood before her, his expression serious.

"What, Husband?"

"You're tired." He led her by the hand from the library, taking a carrying candle from the sideboard. "You have my thanks for your efforts with the girls, Thea."

Noah's thanks satisfied some need in Thea his

apologies hadn't touched. He cared for those girls, and Thea could look after them in ways even a duke could not.

Graciousness was in order. Thea was Noah's duchess, after all.

"You have my thanks too, Noah, for the time you spent with Tim. He's stubborn, but not without sense. Even if he doesn't manage much of a change in the near term, you've planted seeds and warned him he's being watched."

"He is," Noah said as they gained the stairs. "My sisters and their husbands have been recruited to this task. Every few days, he'll be invited to ride out with one of them, or needed to escort Lady Nonie somewhere. My spies will report if his evening activities get out of hand."

He pushed open the door to Thea's rooms, and lit a few candles in her sitting room. The bedroom candles were already lit, the tub steaming before the fire.

"I'll leave you in peace, Wife."

"Will you join me later?"

To ask that had cost Thea, cost her a great deal. She might as well have admitted she'd missed him.

"I wouldn't be very good company. Town was late nights and early mornings, and you steal covers."

Disappointment, keen and vexing, replaced the lassitude Thea had found in the library.

"Suit yourself, Anselm." He looked so forlorn, and tired himself, that Thea went up on her toes and kissed him. "I'm glad you're home." She settled back and gave him a little shove toward their connected dressing rooms. "Into bed with you. You've a date with Evvie and Nini in the stables tomorrow morning, and you'd best not oversleep."

He gave a tired, and possibly relieved, smile. "I won't face the Vandal horde alone."

"No, you will not." Thea patted his backside and started laying out the things she'd need for her bath. The door to their connected dressing rooms quietly opened and closed, and then she was alone.

❧

Like the Duke of Wellington, Noah had never seen the point in having a man's man about, a fawning toady to dress him and undress him, to brush his hair, tie his cravats, and otherwise reduce him to the level of an incompetent six-year-old.

He'd very nearly let Thea undress him, let her lure him under the covers with her warmth, her quiet, her soft, generous curves. In his present mood, he couldn't trust himself to behave, and truly, she'd had that fidgety, blighted look of a woman anticipating her courses.

Another few days, he admonished his lustier inclinations, and he could exercise marital rights free from doubt regarding the patrimony of his firstborn.

In truth, the doubts had died somewhere between Wellspring and London. Thea wasn't a virgin, but Noah's gut told him she wasn't given to duplicity or false promises generally. She might have a flaming affair in a fit of temper, but she'd do her duty to the title first, and she'd have a damned good motivation for her tantrum.

As he undressed and washed, Noah's hand lingered over his breeding organs.

"What the hell."

He brought himself to a quick, mindless release that did little to resolve the unrest inside him. He'd spent more time pleasuring himself since his marriage than any new husband in the history of new husbands.

As he finished his ablutions, Noah thought back over his parents' marriage, a long procession of tantrums, fits, pouts, sulks, scenes, and general misery. Matters hadn't gone any more smoothly with his sisters' mother, or Harlan's. Petty drama on every hand.

"I refuse that legacy."

He said it quietly, though Bathsheba, who'd been contemplating profundities at the foot of the bed, opened her eyes.

"You are my witness, cat. This will remain a civilized house, no thanks to your refusal to pursue the vermin, and I will have an orderly, civilized marriage."

Sheba squinted at him serenely, and then rose and hopped off the bed.

"You are not to ignore me," Noah muttered, shrugging into a dressing gown. "I am lord and master of all I survey, including your great worthless self. Where are you off to?"

She went exactly where she'd gone the last time she'd graced his bedroom, and pawed once—no claws—on the door to his dressing room.

"Fraternizing with my wife?" Noah opened the door to the dressing room, knowing the cat would only scratch and yowl and wake the dead did he deny her. "She can likely use some company. See that you recall your whereabouts, and respect my carpets."

Noah opened the door to Thea's dressing room, Sheba strutting regally before him, then he opened the final door, to Thea's bedroom. The cat slipped through into a chamber plunged into near darkness. Thea had finished with her bath, and banked the coals in the hearth. Her scent lingered in the air—fresh, meadowy, and clean—and Noah could see her shape under the bedcovers.

Thea must have already been asleep, for she gave no indication she sensed Noah's presence. Just as well, now that the cat—

A hiccup came from the vicinity of Thea's pillow. Not a hiccup, more of a catch in the throat, as if she'd been—

"Thea?" Noah took a step into the room. "Wife? Are you in difficulties?"

"Go away."

Her tone was miserable, reminiscent of Noah's sisters suffering one of their countless adolescent heartbreaks. He shed his dressing gown, and climbed under the covers.

"You're peevish," he said, shifting across the bed to lie beside her.

"I asked you to leave."

Her back was rigid, her tone brittle.

"I'll leave soon," he assured her, because no sane man lingered in the vicinity of a peevish woman. "Is it a megrim?"

"What manner of question is that?"

Noah stroked her nape, which had worked well enough in the library. "Take a breath, Thea. I've touched you more intimately than this."

"What are you trying to prove?"

"Perhaps that my wife's suffering matters to me?" Noah pulled Thea onto her back, and in the dying firelight, silvery tear tracks glinted on her cheeks. "Perhaps I'm suggesting—no orders, you will notice— that when my wife cries, I'm concerned?"

Resentment tried to wedge itself into Noah's heart—and failed. Thea had not conjured tears to manipulate him.

"You are better company when you're silent." She tried to roll away again, so Noah caught her by the shoulder.

"Why the tears, Wife? Have you been so miserable here, trapped on my peasant estate, having to deal with my brats and my brother?"

"I cannot tell if you offer genuine understanding, Noah, or if you're preparing me for a vicious set down. Your family is lovely, and well you know it. My tears are merely a passing sentiment, such as women are prone to."

Like a fire blazing up in a sudden gust, inspiration struck.

"My notes," Noah said. "They were not husbandly."

She brushed his hair back from his forehead. If Noah had been a cat, that caress would have provoked him to purring.

"Your notes, Anselm?"

"Informing you, most courteously I thought, that I was detained in Town. Hold still."

Noah threaded his arm under Thea's neck, to prevent her from squirming away. This put her head resting on his shoulder, and gave him time to mentally arrange words of contrition.

"You speak in the plural," Thea said. "I received one note."

She apparently hadn't been very impressed with it, either.

"I sent one to you, one to Harlan," Noah said. "I should have sent two to you, at least. I am sorry. I will be more attentive in future."

Apologies still weren't easy, but Noah was getting the knack of them.

"It isn't the notes." Thea sighed, though Noah heard relenting in her sigh.

"So tell me what troubles you." He planted an encouraging kiss on her temple. "I'm new to this marriage, in case that escaped your notice, and I would not distress you avoidably. If it wasn't the notes, then what?"

"Tell me about the girls' mothers."

A queer start, but something Noah could work with.

"I barely knew them," he said. "Both women enjoy tidy stipends, and are even passing acquaintances somewhere in Dorset. I'm legal guardian to both girls, and Winters is the name they'll be known by."

"You're their guardian?"

"Somebody had to see to it." Noah grazed his nose along Thea's hairline, because this—this physical closeness, this conversation in the dark—was part of what he'd missed while in London. "Evvie and Nini do not enjoy legitimacy, so their mamas could have cast them off anywhere, and had the legal authority to do so. Children are trying, and I could not have their mothers' whims dictate their futures."

"I don't know whether to hit you or commend you. Did you love them even a little?"

"The mothers? Of course not. I love the children. You've pointed this out yourself." Noah resisted the temptation to sniff Thea's hair, though the fragrance of meadow grass was a nice addition to the lavender-scented sheets.

She shifted, so her weight lay more heavily against his side. "Didn't you care even a little, Noah? They are the mothers of children whom you love."

Noah abruptly realized that Thea wasn't asking about the girls' mothers, so much as she was asking about their *father*. Noah ought to clarify the situation for her, explain exactly who was father to both girls, but Thea's voice had grown sleepy, and her hand rested distractingly at Noah's waist.

Best to end this entire discussion rather and save the sordid family history for a more opportune occasion.

"I will always esteem both women greatly for their maternal status, Thea. They could have ended their pregnancies, could have left the children in foundling homes, could have attempted blackmail, or worse. When I contacted the ladies, they agreed to terms, and each is kept informed regarding her daughter's welfare. Should the girls wish it, when they are older, their mothers will know them. I respect their mothers. Is that what you're asking?"

"I hardly know. I can't keep my eyes open."

Thank God. "Go to sleep, Thea."

Angels defend him, Noah had just *ordered* his duchess to sleep. A charged silence ensued, during which Noah fumbled about mentally for some other way to phrase his *suggestion*.

"My courses started. At my bath."

Then Thea turned her face against Noah's neck, and her tears seeped hotly against his skin. Had he made her cry? Did she miss her first love, though she denied having feelings for him?

Talk of the girls had called forth Noah's protective nature. Surely that was why he gathered Thea in his arms and held her close until sleep claimed them both.

∽

"Just the man I was hoping to see."

Giles Pemberton flicked a dismissive glance up from the *Times*, then returned to the society pages.

"Hallowell."

The younger man pulled up a second wing chair, a poor reflection on the boy's upbringing. These days, a youngster took his papa's title for a license to run roughshod over manners, decorum, and common sense. A fellow couldn't even read his paper in his own club in peace.

Hallowell, eyes sunken, cravat wrinkled, settled back into the chair. "Tell me, Pemmie, what sort of fellow does nothing to aid a friend in trouble?"

Pemberton lowered the paper, leveled a flat stare at Hallowell, then raised the paper back up.

"And mind," Hallowell went on, shooting dingy cuffs, "I'm not talking about a passing acquaintance whose off wheeler looks a trifle uneven. I'm not talking about a chap one knew at school who's playing a tad deep."

"You are talking at tiresome length, however," Pemberton said, "when you ought to be stumbling home after a night of raking, and leaving me to read my paper in peace."

"What if I'm talking about a friend of yours, old man?" Hallowell's smile was perfectly nasty, and Pemberton's breakfast beefsteak threatened to rebel. Nobody else graced the reading room this early except the aging Duke of Quimbey who was poring over the financial pages as if they were the Regent's tea leaves.

Pemberton gave the social pages a shake. "You're choosing a deuced rude time and place to do it, young man."

"Suit yourself." Hallowell rose, a slight stench of gin and cheap perfume wafting from him. "If one of my castoffs had just married into the family, I'd hope my friends were seeking a way to address the situation on my behalf. While there's still time."

Pemberton folded his newspaper but remained sitting, lest Quimbey take notice. The most recent marriage in Pemberton's circle was Anselm's surprise courting raid among the ranks of the lady's companions.

Unease congealed into dread. Companions could be a troublesome lot. Meech quite agreed—now.

"*If* I had a friend in that unfortunate situation, Hallowell, then the very last thing I'd do is bruit my friend's troubles about where all might overhear the gossip, overreact to it, and give my friend cause to sue for slander. Good day."

Pemberton rose and left at a dignified pace, making sure to greet Quimbey genially on his way out.

Old man, indeed. Fifty wasn't old, and it wasn't stupid either. Pemberton still had his teeth, his hair, and his brains, by God, and a few other noteworthy parts in working order.

But as he left the peaceful confines of his club for

the damp heat of a June morning, Pemberton realized if Hallowell knew of the situation with Anselm's wife, then others likely knew as well.

Something would have to be done. Pemberton owed it to Meech to see that something was done.

◈

"Your tea, Duchess."

Noah had woken up beside his wife—again, despite all plans to the contrary—creating another first for him. Thea had risen several times during the night to tend to herself.

He hadn't realized that monthly courses caused a woman's rest to be interrupted. Crashingly bad planning, for a lady's sleep to be disturbed when she most needed rest.

This aspect of the female body was one Noah had largely ignored, insofar as any man could ignore the moods of three sisters as they navigated the shoals of young womanhood. His mistresses had dealt with their calendars in discreet innuendo, and Noah had been perceptive enough to take the hints.

But this…

Thea hurt, her mood was off, her rest was poor, and still, she would expect herself to get up, meet the girls in the stables, and to *manage*.

"You're not about to steal my tea?" Thea held out the cup, her gaze shy as she sat propped against the headboard.

"Where's the fun in stealing what's freely offered?" Noah settled in beside her and filched a bite of her cinnamon toast. "Would you rather have chocolate this morning?"

"Because?"

"You're"—Noah waved a hand in the direction of her middle—"indisposed." While he disliked that Thea was uncomfortable, her indisposition confirmed that she wasn't carrying.

She'd been honest, in other words. The relief of that was enormous, the size of an entire duchy, in fact.

"I am not indisposed." Thea set her teacup down with a little clink. "The discomfort has passed, as it always does. You needn't be concerned."

"I am not concerned, Thea." Not greatly concerned, now that she'd stopped ordering him to go away and was ready for a proper spat. "I am attempting in my bumbling way to dote. You will allow it."

*Drat.* He'd given another order.

"You couldn't bumble if one gave you written instructions, Anselm. You were probably born instructing your nursery maids on the exact best means of mixing your gruel," Thea said, and to Noah, she looked a little less peaked for having run up her flags. "That was my toast you appropriated."

"Appropriation is what happens when one's wife can't appreciate a little doting. You're being stingy with the tea, just as you were stingy with the covers."

"I am the Duchess of Anselm." Her chin came up. "I am not stingy with anything."

"You swilled that tea right down," Noah went on. "Pardon me while I play footman to our personal exponent of porcine nobility." He let Sheba out, and when he turned back to bed, Thea was smiling.

*Better.* "You're feeling more the thing, Wife?"

"Yes, thank you." She passed him the teacup for a refill. "I do prefer chocolate when the weather's colder."

"How much longer does this non-indisposition last?"

"You are a very presuming husband." Thea leaned back against her pillows, her smile nowhere in evidence.

"Doting." Noah passed her the second cup, and took her free hand long enough to kiss her knuckles—lest she mistake his point. "In need of my duchess's guidance on this one marital matter. We didn't cover it at school or university, and even my sisters kept a few things to themselves."

Thanks to a merciful Deity.

"This is so personal." Thea's gaze was on their joined hands—for Noah had not turned her loose to go haring off in a fit of mortification. "I didn't think you'd be a personal sort of husband. You were supposed to appear in my dressing-room doorway a few nights a month, quietly lift the covers, silently take a few marital liberties, and then leave me in peace. We'd trade sections of the *Times* over breakfast the next morning, I'd ask how your ride was, and you'd hold my chair when I rose to see to my correspondence."

"Prosaic." Boring, and exactly what Noah himself had envisioned. "Hard to see any doting going on, though."

"You only mentioned a little doting when we were negotiating," Thea said. "A little is…"

"Yes?"

"Letting me borrow your cat."

"She goes where she pleases. Like most of the females under my roof."

"Husband?" Thea's tone was hesitant.

Noah forgot whether he'd added sugar to his own damned cup of tea, so he stirred in another two lumps.

"Thank you," Thea said, her hand glancing over his shoulder and down his arm. "For keeping me company. I would not have known how to ask."

Noah's duchess was shy, which shortcoming bore some responsibility for her lamentable reticence until their wedding night.

A duke didn't have the luxury of shyness.

"I suppose that's the definition of doting." Noah lingered at the cart to assemble a plate. "It's the little things you can't bring yourself to ask for, that an attentive spouse will enjoy providing to you. Bacon or ham?"

"A little of both, please."

"Feeling carnivorous?"

"I'm a trifle indisposed. I need the sustenance."

Noah piled both ham and bacon on Thea's plate, and stole better than half of it, because he needed the sustenance too.

# Fourteen

"You're quiet," Harlan said as the horses were brought around.

"My ears are recovering," Noah replied. "Have your cousins always been so damned noisy?"

Harlan gave him a good shove to the shoulder. "Nini and Evvie are *little girls*, and you just promised them ponies this summer. Of course they'll make heaps of noise."

The happiest noise Noah had heard from them. Ever.

"You may blame Thea for that nonsense," Noah said. "She has informed me we're to hire tutors and governesses and all manner of masters for the girls."

Noah's wife had been kind but firm, exactly as a duchess should be—when she wasn't stealing covers.

"You won't have Evvie and Nini all to yourself," Harlan said. "You're pouting because you'll have to share."

Noah swung up on True. "Where is it written that a grown man mustn't pout? Seems to me one of the few privileges of adulthood is a good, cranky pout from time to time, or a fit of private ranting, with a tot of brandy consumed to settle the temper. Did Thea seem pale to you?"

"She seemed quiet," Harlan said, mounting his new gelding. "The girls were making a racket, and nobody would compete with them when they're fresh from their slumbers. Where will we find these ponies?"

Where, indeed? For not just any pair of ponies would do.

"I'm loath to return to Town," Noah said, "despite all three of our sisters needing more supervision, and our brothers-in-law more moral support. Tatt's will have plenty of ponies as the beau monde leaves Town for the pleasures of murdering Scottish grouse, but there has to be something closer to hand."

A source of ponies that wouldn't require Noah to leave Thea yet again, even though she was *not* indisposed.

"Greymoor's estate is on the other side of Guildford." Harlan led them to the left as they quit the stable yard, in the direction of the cultivated fields. "Greymoor's no farther than Town, and he has a capital reputation for ladies' mounts."

Greymoor's name had come up at Tatt's, when Noah had dragooned Grantley into purchasing a mare for Lady Nonie.

"How do you know about Greymoor's ventures?" Noah asked.

"I've spent the past two years at university," Harlan said patiently, as if the elderly were prone to forgetfulness. "The true purpose of a university education is to teach a fellow how to hold his drink, and who among his set has the best gossip and the prettiest sisters."

An appallingly accurate summation. "Does Greymoor have sisters?" The name brought to mind a vague image of blue eyes, height, and a miscreant past. Greymoor's older brother had been brought to heel by matrimony—poor sod—but neither brother had been in Noah's form at school.

"Greymoor has no sisters that I know of," Harlan said, standing in the stirrups then settling back in his saddle. "Might I have some company down here over the summer?"

Not bad for a casual change of subject. "You might."

Harlan's expression remained quite diffident.

"Does this company boast of pretty sisters?" Noah asked.

"Possibly."

Noah sighed loudly enough to have True flicking his ears around. The day was pretty, the corn coming along nicely, the hedges ripe with honeysuckle, and Harlan had apparently fallen in love.

Drat the luck. Would Noah be the only Winters male to escape a legacy of unbridled folly where the ladies were concerned?

"You are too young to contemplate matrimony, holy or otherwise, Harlan. If you need certain itches scratched, you have only to accompany Meech on his rounds, and the matter will be addressed before you can finish unfastening your falls."

A common blue butterfly flitted around Harlan's gelding's ears, and the beast remained perfectly calm.

Noah had tried twenty different horses before settling on the bay.

"The less I am seen in Uncle's company, the better," Harlan said as the butterfly went on its way.

"You are out of charity with Meech?" Noah occupied himself with organizing True's unruly mane so it lay—more or less—on the right side of the gelding's neck. Boggy conversational ground so early in the day called for a touch of fraternal tact.

"I love my uncle," Harlan recited, "but he's a damned embarrassment, Noah. There's more to life than chasing skirts, bragging about chasing skirts, joking about chasing skirts, and trading reminiscences about chasing skirts."

Noah drew True to a halt in the shade of a spreading oak and crossed his wrists over the pommel. On the new horse, Harlan sat as tall as Noah, possibly an inch or two taller.

Why must they all grow up so quickly?

Harlan pirouetted his gelding to face Noah. "Don't scold, Noah. I'll be eighteen next month, and I hear things at school."

Eighteen was such a tender age. Thea had been eighteen when she'd accepted her first post as a companion, which thought, gave Noah an uncomfortable pang.

"You hear the best gossip and all that," Noah said. "I want to defend Meech, but at your age, I had the same reaction to him. I told myself not to be so missish and judgmental, and I let Meech lead me into several situations I regret. Instead of defending him, I will admonish you to stick to your guns. Uncle is damned lucky somebody hasn't blown his brains out on a foggy meadow dotted with cow dung, or worse."

Noah nudged his horse forward, knowing he'd surprised his brother. He'd surprised himself, which had something to do with this business of not wanting to go back into Town. Yes, his sisters needed some extra attention, but they had husbands for that.

Thea had never admitted what had put her in tears last night. Maybe passing female sentiment was to blame, maybe the discomfort of her menses.

Noah couldn't shake the nagging sense her low spirits were the result of something he'd done, or failed to do.

Perhaps he shouldn't have insisted on waiting to consummate their union, but he'd said they'd wait, and going back on his word was unthinkable.

In future when he was called from Thea's side, his notes would be of greater frequency and more…husbandly.

∾

"I married a grasshopper," Thea accused, unwilling to be swayed by Noah's stoic expression. "And, you, Lord Harlan Winters, are a bad influence on your brother."

Two grooms led the horses out, the elder man smiling at Thea's scold.

"Don't be too hard on Noah," Harlan replied. "Greymoor's stud is said to be all the crack, and you want the girls to have the best possible ponies, don't you?"

Thea wanted her husband to admit he'd miss her.

She crossed her arms rather than give in to the urge to touch him. "The best possible ponies would have to be thirty-odd miles away. Not a single pony in all of Kent, or at the auctions in Town, would do."

Based on Noah's disgruntled expression, he would have preferred to go pony shopping in darkest Peru rather than endure Thea's displeasure in public.

"I wasn't looking for ponies when I dragged your brother to buy a mount for Lady Antoinette," Noah replied, slapping his riding gloves against his thigh. "My wife had yet to inform me I'd been remiss in the matter of ponies."

"Oh, her." Thea groused. She wanted badly to smile, which was ridiculous, because Noah was haring off again, but this time he was dragging Harlan with him—or perhaps Harlan was doing the dragging. In any case, they were away to Surrey, though promising to be back the next day, or the day after, "at the latest."

"You disparage my wife at your peril, Duchess," Noah said, looking stern despite the glint in his blue eyes. "She is an estimable lady."

"And very determined," Thea reminded him. "If you do not reappear as scheduled, Husband, I will hire the crankiest governess I can find for our daughters, and you will have to pension the old besom off at considerable cost upon your return."

Noah pulled on his gloves, though Thea had seen something—humor, bashfulness, what?—in his gaze before he'd looked away.

"What did I say?" Thea straightened the lapel of his faultlessly tailored riding jacket. "I wouldn't hire them anybody terrible, Husband. You know this."

Noah stepped closer and planted a smacking kiss on her mouth, while Harlan made a production of cinching up his horse's girth. Thea might have wiggled away for form's sake—both grooms were grinning now—but Noah held her close long enough to murmur in her ear.

"See that you look after *our daughters* in my absence, Wife. My womenfolk matter to me."

Thea stepped back, her fingers going to her lips to mask her pleasure. Harlan winked at her, swung up, and began castigating Noah for how slowly old married men moved when there were horses to be bought, and perhaps his brother wasn't getting enough rest, or perhaps the *heat* was disturbing his slumbers—

Noah gently tapped Harlan's mount on the quarters with a crop, which had the animal trotting off more in indignation than surprise, and Harlan laughing out loud.

"You have my direction," Noah said as he settled into the saddle. "Mind you don't let the girls explode with anticipation. They're merely ponies."

"Be safe, Husband." Thea petted True's sturdy neck. "They'll miss you."

"Right." He leaned down and kissed Thea again, and that kiss held a promise. A very marital promise she wasn't at all reluctant to fulfill.

When Noah cantered off to catch up with Harlan, Thea was still standing in the stable yard, the taste of her husband's kiss lingering on her lips. What did it mean, that Noah's womenfolk mattered to him, and why had he been surprised Thea had referred to Nini and Evvie as their daughters?

The girls were family, and little and dear. How else was she to refer to them, except as *our daughters*?

Knowing the children were likely watching from the nursery windows, Thea marched herself back into the house. The day would be hot enough to do a little gardening, and then perhaps go wading, to maybe teach the girls the rudiments of fishing... No, not fishing. Anything involving worms on hooks was paternal territory.

The nursery maids reported that the girls were paying a call on Erikson, so Thea doubled back to the conservatory.

"We are dissecting," Erikson said, looking up from his worktable. "It is very scientific work."

"What hapless creature are you dissecting?" Thea knew to close the door behind her, lest the botanical beauties get cold. Erikson's little assistants were ranged on either side of him, sitting on stools the better to view the procedure.

"A chocolate éclair." Erikson's fair skin colored. "Or half of one."

"Very scientific, indeed." Thea pulled up a stool across the table from the specimen. "But here we have a discarded sample." She lifted the remaining half of the éclair, and took up a butter knife from the tea service. "I abhor waste."

Nini nodded, her cheek sporting a smear of chocolate. "Me too."

Thea cut the sweet into fourths, and forked the little bites onto plates for the girls. She speared the remaining bite—one rich with drizzled chocolate and a fat dollop of cream between the layers of flaky pastry—and held

the fork across the table to Erikson. Rather than take
the fork, he wrapped his larger hand around Thea's,
and ate the éclair directly from the tines.

"I will let Evvie make the first cut," he said dra-
matically. "Recall, child, to cut across, not toward
you, and to have your assistant note the order and
dimensions of your incisions."

"Who's my assistant?"

"I am," Erikson said, passing Evvie a clean butter
knife.

"What's a 'cision?" asked Nini, who now also had
chocolate on her upper lip.

"A cut," Thea said, dabbing at Nini's face with a
serviette.

"Quiet," Evvie ordered, butter knife poised. "Is this
a holy moment?"

"All science is holy," Erikson said. "Particularly
when chocolate is involved, and such good Dutch
cocoa in the chocolate too."

"You say everything good is Dutch," Nini said.
"Like the Holland bulbs and chocolate and the wind-
mills and canals and the—"

"Ni-ni." Evvie waved the knife. "Will you hush?"
She mashed the knife into the éclair, and peered at
her work as the filling oozed onto the cloth spread
beneath it. "I made an incision. The patient bled.
Write that down."

"That's not blood." Nini's finger made a pass
toward the filling, only to be trapped in Erikson's
big paw.

"You're an observer," he chided. "You sit in silent
awe of the wonders to be revealed."

Nini frowned at the specimen. "How long does this take?"

"Not long," Thea said, sending Erikson a look. "Not when we've spelling words and French vocabulary to learn, and wading to do."

"Wading?" Erikson's expression came alert. "In the lake?"

"We can go wading?" Evvie was off her stool, followed closely by her sister, but not before Nini cadged a taste of filling.

"I thought we might," Thea said. "After it warms up a little more and we've done our schoolwork."

Evvie arched a brow in a gesture reminiscent of Noah. "*Our* schoolwork?"

"You have to write the words, but I have to think them up and check them and explain if you've got them right or wrong," Thea said. "So, yes, it's our schoolwork. Now come, for you'll need play clothes if we're to study outside."

Thea shooed them toward the door, and they thundered past in a happy rush.

"Such small feet." Erikson said, licking Evvie's discarded butter knife as Thea closed the door. "And such big noise, while our little science lesson is forgotten." He popped the squashed éclair half into his mouth on a philosophical sigh.

"You're good to be so patient with them."

"Children are fine company for such as myself, but you should have company on this outing too, Your Grace."

Would Noah have joined them, or been too busy with his ducal responsibilities?

"I can't see bothering the footmen to stand about while the children splash each other," Thea said. "Davies and Maryanne need every break they can get."

"Those two." Erikson's normally genial expression shifted to a scowl. "They are too young for their responsibilities, but Anselm will not take them to task, because the girls are attached to their nursery maids."

"You resent the interruptions when the girls come calling," Thea concluded. "I'm sorry, Erikson. We'll keep a better eye on them."

"I resent not the children," he said, patting at his lips with the same serviette Thea had used on Nini. "Little girls should not wander off when they have not one but two nursery maids. I have told Anselm this, and he says he'll put a stop to it, but nothing happens, and they wander again."

Noah doubtless grumbled, blustered, and threatened, but when it came to the children, that was likely all he'd do.

"Wandering within the confines of the house isn't likely to get them in much trouble," Thea said, for the girls knew the place better than she did, "and I'm hopeful if they have more time out-of-doors, with me, with Anselm or Harlan, on their ponies and so forth, they won't be as restless."

"You are right." Erikson's smile was back, though muted. "You think like a woman. You think of ways around a problem, while we fellows try to smash it to bits. You are on the other side of it while we're still bashing away. I would like to go on this outing, if you don't mind."

How often did Erikson leave his aerie to be among the flora and fauna of Wellspring's lovely surrounds?

"I couldn't possibly mind that you want to share the company of two loud, busy, and likely grubby little girls," Thea said.

"And you," Erikson said. "Your company too, Duchess."

Thea said nothing, for Erikson was merely being Continental.

He had the great wisdom to bring butterfly nets with him to the lake, which resulted in both girls racing around madly at great length, and then napping on the blankets Thea had spread under the trees.

"You are what was needed here." Erikson made this pronouncement from his corner of the blanket. "I shall apologize to Anselm."

Offered with the same Teutonic resolution that had resulted in the fall of Rome.

"Apologize for what?" Thea asked.

Erikson plucked a long grass flower, folded the stem around the head, and used that to fire the head several yards off toward the water. Had Noah ever indulged in such casual botanical destruction as a small boy?

"I told the duke he was...I don't know the word—upset in the head?—to marry a lady he had not courted, but you English, you like to do things backward."

"Backward how?"

Another missile was sent toward the shore. "You conquer a land first, then get to know the people and the riches, if any there are. This is how you end up with places like Canada, which is full of wolves and bears and terrible winters."

"I've also heard it's very beautiful." Thea settled back to brace herself on her arms, when she wanted to pluck at the grass to see if she could fire her projectile farther than Erikson's. "Canada is, of course, not as pretty as the Low Countries."

"You make families backward too," Erikson went on, smoothing a hand over soft green grass. "First you marry, then you have the babies, and finally, sometimes, you are friends. Backward. But what do I know? I am only a Dutchman who talks to flowers."

A big, handsome Dutchman, though Thea sensed no untoward overture from Erikson.

"You also talk to little girls, sir. Anselm and I are not strangers. I knew him for several months before he proposed. We shared many a carriage ride, strolled every park in West London, and even danced on occasion."

Was that how a woman learned to know the man she'd marry, or did courtship have more to do with tears, cinnamon toast, and trying discussions?

"The duke is managing in Surrey. You're managing in Kent." Erikson affected a puzzled expression. "I do not understand the English. Shall we carry the little ones back to their beds? The footmen doubtless hover at the windows, waiting for you to crook your finger at them."

Two footmen had taken up posts on the terrace within view of the lakeshore without Thea even asking it of them.

"We'll manage here if you'd like to go back to work, Benjamin," Thea said. "We're within sight of the house, and I know you're busy. I suspect Noah put you up to nursemaiding us, but it isn't necessary."

"I will stay," Erikson said, getting to his feet. "I will take a few moments to contemplate the day, and leave you to your book." He shook out a blanket and spread it several yards off, between the two girls, then settled himself on his back, hands folded serenely on his flat stomach.

Erikson hadn't denied that Noah had charged him with chaperone duty. Hadn't even tried to.

Thea stared at her book—an uncharitable treatment by Miss Austen of impoverished sisters grappling with the challenge of finding suitable mates. Nobody should be expected to focus on such a dreary tale on such a lovely day.

Perhaps Noah didn't trust his own wife, for which Thea ought to resent him. She'd proven she hadn't carried a child into the marriage, and still Noah could not give her even the freedom of the Wellspring grounds.

Give the marriage time, she admonished herself, setting Miss Austen's sermonizing aside and fashioning herself a little missile of grass. Rome wasn't built in a day, and Noah Winters's marital trust would not be restored any time soon either.

❧

Noah stood in the doorway to his wife's sitting room, watching Thea as she worked at her correspondence. The white feather in her hand made a slow progress in one direction, returned, and again worked its way across the page in a soothing, captivating rhythm.

The new Duchess of Anselm was pretty, and not merely in the ornamental fashion of a younger woman.

Noah had missed her.

Had Thea missed him? Was she missing some other fellow, a youthful indiscretion, a passionate interlude, a mad lapse from conventional decorum?

"Husband."

She smiled, likely as much answer as Noah would have to that conundrum. Better not to know if Thea pined for another. Far better.

Thea rose and came to him, her smile growing shy. "You are safely returned, and after only three days."

Noah took her in his arms, drew in a lungful of uxorial fragrance, and felt more at *home* than he had a moment ago.

"You received my notes, Wife?"

"Two of them, a husbandly number for a three-day absence," she said, rubbing her cheek against his chest. "The ponies are secreted in the village livery, and the girls will be insensate with joy if they know you've returned with your booty."

"They're good ponies," Noah said, nuzzling Thea's ear. "I've misplaced my brother for at least the next week, though."

A delightful state of affairs, really.

"This Greymoor fellow must be genial indeed if he sought Harlan's company as a houseguest on such short acquaintance," Thea said, making no move to leave Noah's embrace. "I like Harlan, but I'll like, as well, having you to myself."

That pleased Noah inordinately, so he was the one to step back. A single step, only.

"Greymoor will put Harlan's willing backside on every piece of green, unruly equine stock he has. A good use of a young man's bravado and hard head, and Greymoor's countess said to tell you she would feed the boy at least eight meals a day, so you're not to fret."

Noah would not fret either.

Thea wore small gold earrings that caught the light and emphasized the curve of her jaw. Noah could not recall seeing her wear any gold jewelry previously. Had she worn them for him?

"Harlan is a credit to his upbringing," Thea said. "Greymoor is getting the better end of the bargain."

Her hair was done more softly too, still tidy, but her braid was in a bun rather than a ruthlessly secured coronet.

"I am loath to ask, Wife, but are you still on speaking terms with the girls?"

She regarded him quizzically. "Of course. They've been delightful. They are likely one floor above us, rocketing about their rooms in anticipation of seeing you."

Responsibility tugged Noah toward the nursery. Other sentiments kept him lounging in the doorway with his wife.

"How would they know I've arrived?"

"This house has a surfeit of windows, Your Grace." Thea slipped her arm through Noah's and tugged him into the sitting room. "You deserve to eat and perhaps wash off the dust of the road before you confront our daughters."

Noah was hungry; he simply hadn't realized it. "You'll join me?"

"Teatime approaches," Thea said, drawing Noah through their adjoining dressing rooms. "So, yes, I will join you. The tub is already set up in your sitting room, and we can send word to heat the water while you eat. Now tell me more of this Lord and Lady Greymoor, and why the grooms brought home not only two ponies, but that pair of gorgeous mares as well."

"Because Greymoor could sell piety to the Pope," Noah groused, though it was strangely comfortable to recount the details of his trip to Thea, to remark on the abundance of bridle paths in Surrey, and describe how Harlan had stood taller when Greymoor had asked the boy's opinion of this or that horse.

"Harlan rejected a pair of ponies I would have been happy with," Noah said as Thea pushed his hands away.

"I can undo this more easily than you," she scolded as she loosened his cravat. "What didn't Harlan like about the ponies?"

"He liked them well enough—Greymoor showed us only first-quality stock." Noah stood docilely, hands at his sides, letting Thea undress him as if he were too tired to see to it himself. Come to that, he was tired. He'd ridden the entire distance in a single afternoon rather than send along yet another note to his duchess.

"So were these ponies the wrong colors?" Thea asked, draping Noah's neckcloth and waistcoat over a chair, then pushing him onto the bed so she could tug off his boots and set them outside the door.

"They were dainty gray ponies, but small." Noah lifted his chin as Thea went to work unbuttoning his shirt. "Harlan pointed out that the girls will be very attached to their first mounts, and won't want to part with them. The ponies should thus be as large as can be safely managed, so they will have at least several years' use before the girls outgrow them."

Thea's ensemble was brown with red piping, not a dress Noah recalled seeing on her before they'd married.

"Harlan's a thoughtful young man," Thea said, slipping the sleeve buttons from Noah's cuffs and drawing his shirt over his head. "You've done a wonderful job with him."

Noah's wife might soon be doing a wonderful job of unbuttoning his falls, and abruptly, his fatigue vanished. He was hot, tired, hungry, and road weary, but he was also *married*.

"I've yet to ask you how you fare, Wife." Noah captured Thea's wrist and kissed the heel of her hand. "Lady Greymoor sent a letter for you."

"Thoughtful of her." Thea stepped back, perhaps because she realized Noah was naked, except for his breeches. Rather than lose the last of his camouflage, he tugged her down to sit beside him on the bed, the faint scent of horse and weary summer traveler coming to his nose through her much sweeter fragrance.

Her slippers were red, also apparently fascinating, for she stared at her toes. "I am…well, since you ask."

"Well enough to entertain your husband, should he prevail on you tonight for your company?"

# Fifteen

NOAH HEARD THEA'S SWIFT INTAKE OF BREATH AND the summery sort of quiet thereafter—birds singing in the oaks beyond the balcony, a groom calling the horses in from the pasture, insects faintly droning.

While color flooded up Thea's neck. "I am that well, Husband."

Noah looped an arm across her shoulders. "I don't mean to rush you, but I'd like to see to this."

What he could *see* was that his word choice had been inappropriate. His wife's gaze was full of consternation, and then, a heartbeat later, stoic acceptance.

"It is time, I suppose." Thea rose, and Noah let her go. "Your food is out on the balcony." She rummaged in his wardrobe, then returned with a dark blue silk dressing gown, and held it out to him.

Noah stepped out of the last of his clothes, and accepted the dressing gown, though he took his time figuring out how to belt the thing, and in that little while, his wife watched him.

Warily.

Noah wasn't aroused, but he was by no means uninterested, either.

"I'll tell the footmen to fill the tub," Thea said.

Noah was grateful for a few minutes to evaluate his options. He took his meal out on the balcony, enjoying the late-afternoon breeze, and the view of the back gardens coming into their full summer glory. The ham, cheese, and bread on the tray were more than adequate to blunt his hunger, and by the time he'd finished eating, the tub was full and gently steaming on the hearthstones.

"Wife?"

"In here." Thea emerged from his dressing room, clothing draped over her arm. "I'll leave you in peace. When you're bathed and dressed, will you come up to the nursery?"

She made a production out of arranging Noah's clothes on the bed, though in what she didn't say, in how she wouldn't meet Noah's gaze, he detected something amiss.

"Are you nervous regarding our evening, Thea?"

"No." She fussed at his blue paisley waistcoat—one of his favorites—when she laid it over his shirt. "Well, yes. Are you?"

Valid question.

"Suppose I were to admit to some trepidation." Noah shrugged out of his dressing gown, once again sensing his wife's surreptitious perusal while he rearranged soap, flannel, brush, and shaving gear by the bed. "If I were nervous of this evening, what reassurances might you offer me?"

Thea twitched at his clothing and turned to sit on his bed. "Assurances. For you."

She studied her hands while Noah lowered himself into the soothing bliss of the tub.

"Regarding the proper consummation of our vows," he added helpfully. "You've had this water scented."

"With lavender. It's blooming all around the laundry. I could tell you I'm not missish, and you need not worry overmuch about my sensibilities."

"I have your leave to simply fall upon you and start rutting?" Noah worked up a lather—more lavender— while Thea regarded him as if he sharpened an assassin's blade. "For God's sake, Wife, I am not serious. I would not fall upon you had we been parted for weeks. Will you be so kind as to scrub my back?"

The duchess remained across the room on the bed. "Your back?"

Noah had been an idiot to tease her. This looming consummation was not a detail to Thea, not merely the next thing on the list of duties. For the first time, Noah wished he might have elicited a few specifics from her regarding her earlier experiences.

Except those specifics might not have been altogether pleasant, and what was he to do then?

He held out the soap and a wet flannel to his wife.

"My back." Noah gestured over his shoulder, and Thea approached the tub as if it held a quantity of snakes.

Noah sat forward, passed her the soap and cloth, and hunched his shoulders. Tentatively at first, then more confidently, Thea set about scrubbing his back.

"I won't hurt you," he said. "You have to know that much already." He offered what he expected was the most basic of assurances while Thea bent over his back, the slide of the soap and the cloth kneading muscles beat to soreness by miles in the saddle.

"You are disappointed in me," Thea said, sitting back on the stool beside the tub. "I cannot expect intimate consideration from you beyond a certain point. I'll rinse your back if you hold still."

"No need." Noah slouched down into the water, effectively rinsing. "Might I prevail upon you to wash the rest of me? Sitting here, I've grown prodigiously comfortable, if tired."

"You want me to touch you."

Noah wanted her to *enjoy* touching him.

He leaned back against the tub, took the hand in which she held the soap, and put it against his chest.

"Why wouldn't you expect every courtesy of me under intimate conditions, Wife?"

Thea muttered something as she set to scrubbing his chest, but all Noah heard was "…typical man," in tones not suggestive of respect.

"Thea, stop."

Her hand went still, and she stared at his knees where they formed wet, bony islands of male flesh in the water.

Noah leaned forward the few necessary inches, and kissed Thea's cheek. "Hello. I'm glad to be home."

Thea dropped the soap into the water and regarded Noah's right knee. "Hello, Husband."

Now what? Noah took a wild shot, "I missed you."

"You don't need to do this." Thea sat back again, a line of dampness across her chest.

"What don't I need to do?"

She waved a hand. "Turn up sweet. Put on airs and graces, as if we're enthralled with each other. I know my duty."

"Your duty?" The situation was growing more complicated, not less, which was a road to marital disaster. "Lock the door, Thea, and start undressing. We might as well clarify this dreadful duty of yours sooner rather than later."

Noah had considered this option while he'd had solitude on the balcony, and saw now that it would be the kinder choice for them both.

Thea rose, for once doing as he bid.

Noah made short work of the rest of his bath, kneeling up so Thea could rinse his hair, then rising from the tub and accepting a towel from her. He didn't bother with the dressing gown, but stood behind her, naked and damp, and saw to the hooks of her dress. The cut was high-waisted, a summery fabric that wafted around her gracefully but did little to hint at her curves.

Thea took the dress off over her head, and passed it to him, then stood still while he unlaced her stays. She let out a great sigh when she stepped free of the corset, then rubbed at her waist.

"Why do you wear it so bloody tight?" Noah asked. Thea's belly would bear the imprint of the chemise's wrinkles.

"The intent of the corset is to preserve modesty."

A true duchess could lecture on propriety when wearing only her chemise.

"Modesty, bah. Torment, by another name." Noah studied the abundance of Thea's unbound breasts beneath her chemise, the sweet, soft taper of her unconfined waist. "If I forbid you to wear that corset, would you abide by my guidance?"

Thea nodded, once, watching him the way a mouse would watch a visiting hawk. "At least at home, I would. That corset is hot, and…constricting of the lungs."

"Get rid of it."

When Thea started untying the bows of her summer-length chemise, Noah stepped closer and stilled her hands with his own.

"I meant the corset, Wife. You can wear country stays or jumps, or three chemises instead. We will discuss this other business." Noah gestured at her chemise, the plainest piece of sacking ever to conceal a man's dearest fantasies.

Without benefit of his clothing, he led Thea by the wrist up to the bed. A breeze came in from the balcony, the house and grounds had the profound quiet of a lazy summer afternoon, and the room was redolent of the lavender scenting the tub.

Such ordinary domestic circumstances, and such an extraordinary moment in their marriage.

Noah sat with Thea on the bed. "You are willing, Wife?"

"You are kind to ask," she said, her gaze brushing over him. "I am willing."

"So am I, were you inclined to inquire. How would you like to proceed?"

"I don't know what you're asking."

Clearly, she did not. Thea's shoulders were hunched as if to ward off blows or blushes; Noah knew not which. That she should be so unknowing pleased him, that she worried, made conversation rather challenging.

"I'm asking how to pleasure you," he said, which

was masterfully delicate of him, if he did say so himself. "I'm asking what you like, and what you don't like."

"I like it when you kiss me."

Noah delighted in her kisses too. "Fortunate for me I used the tooth powder then. What else?"

"Your hands…" Thea looked away, as if her words had gone leaping over the balcony in pursuit of a dip in the lake.

"These." Noah held up the requisite appendages, one of which was wrapped in one of hers. "What about them?"

"When you touch me, you're not in a hurry."

Noah was barely in his right mind half the time he touched her. "Interesting. Where do I touch you when I'm dawdling so reprehensibly?"

Thea closed her eyes and shook her head. "It isn't reprehensible, when you take your time with me."

Her neck betrayed a tension, and the corners of her mouth and eyes did too. This interrogation would have to end soon if she wasn't to expire of mortification.

"Not reprehensible?" Noah mused. "Tell me what it is, then, when I'm lazy and indulgent, touching you wherever I please, however I please? A fellow can grow confused, dealing with women."

"It's…" Thea dashed the back of her free hand against her cheeks, suggesting to Noah she was near tears, if not crying. "Irresistible. You leave me no dignity, Husband. None. When your hands are on me, I don't want you to stop, and I can't imagine who this shameless woman is, to want a man so badly who can hardly want her."

What on God's earth was Noah to say to that?

Entire realms of mystery, confusion, and female unfathomables lay in those few sentences, and Noah was but a man who couldn't bear to see his duchess cry on this of all occasions.

He kissed her gently, in answer to the insecurities Thea had only alluded to. That she wasn't attractive, that she wasn't attractive *to him*, that she could not be of interest to her own husband. Noah's tongue went on to reassure the soft, damp bounty of her mouth, to trace her lips.

He brought his free hand up to cradle Thea's jaw, then slipped it back to bury his fingers in her hair.

"This has to come down," he muttered against her mouth. "Your hair, down."

Thea rested her forehead against his. "If you like."

Noah sat back enough to tug the pins from her braid, piling them indiscriminately on the nightstand. Her hair ribbons came off next, and then he was combing his fingers through the dark silky river of her unbound hair.

Noah brought a strand to his nose. "More lavender. It's so long." Long enough that he could wrap her hair several times around his wrist, long enough that he could pull Thea in for another kiss and anchor both hands in her hair while he did.

Slowly, she warmed to this kiss, not merely waiting for Noah to explore and taste and suggest, but making shy forays into his mouth on her own initiative.

Thea tasted sweet, like mint tea and cool morning breezes, and her hair was long enough to pool in Noah's lap, the silk and scent of it driving lazy arousal to blazing desire.

"I want you," Noah whispered as his mouth opened over the soft spot beneath Thea's ear. He moved her hand to his arousal. "This is proof of wanting."

Thea tried to jerk her hand away, but Noah had closed his fingers around hers, and held her grip snugly about him.

"Thea, I want you to touch me." He kept his voice low, kept the longing and lust threatening to swamp him from his words—mostly. "In time, you'll find that if you're patient and willing to try—"

His duchess wasn't listening to him; she was frankly eyeing his arousal, her hair pooling softly around the base. She used her free hand to brush her hair away.

"Take your time," Noah managed. "The broad light of day has many advantages for a woman bent on appeasing her curiosity."

Thea was curious; Noah saw that in her eyes, in her furrowed brow. Felt her curiosity as she ran her fingers all over him, then traced the vein running the length of his shaft. His most intimate parts were terra incognita for her.

What in the hell had her previous affair consisted of? Hasty couplings in broom closets? A literal roll in the hay?

Thea deserved better, for God's sake. Whoever took her virginity should at least have shown her pleasure and given her some confidence.

She had none. None. Her touch could not have been more tentative, or more curious.

"Araminthea." Noah brushed her long hair over her shoulder as she regarded him gravely. "I won't gobble you whole, or castigate you, or heaven knows what, not in bed."

A delicate circling with her finger sent lightning straight up Noah's spine.

"And out of bed, Noah?"

"If I thought you were taking chances with the girls' safety, or abusing the help, then perhaps we'd argue. For God's sake, we won't fight."

"What does that mean?" Thea sat back, her chemise gaping, and Noah had to concentrate mightily to decipher her question when he could see her breasts, unfettered and gently moving under the material.

He shifted to rest against the headboard, for he needed the distance if he was to speak in coherent sentences.

"When we have a difference of opinion," he said, "we'll discuss it, hopefully in private if strong feelings are to be aired. I won't beat you, for Christ's sake, and when we're in bed…"

"When we're in bed?"

They *were* in bed, and Noah was naked, aroused, *and lecturing his wife.*

"Come here." He closed his hands around Thea's arms and lifted her to straddle him. She curled down to his chest, which was obliging of her, when Noah wasn't entirely sure what they were discussing. Nonetheless, this was the most personal conversation he'd ever had, and cradling Thea against his naked length provided him an odd increment of privacy.

"When we're in bed, you must trust me," he said.

"Trust you?" Thea tried to draw back, to meet his

gaze—now, she tried to meet his gaze—but Noah held her gently in place.

"Trust *me*." He stroked his hands down the waterfall of her hair, slowly, gathering his thoughts as he gathered her hair. "The men in my family are profligate rakes. I know this, but you are my wife."

"I am."

Thea was hinting at a question Noah wasn't sure how to answer: How did being his wife make her different?

"I am a gentleman, Thea. I will not betray your bodily trust. In our bed, you are safe, from hurt, from humiliation, from violations of privacy even."

Said the naked duke to his shy duchess? Lust had made Noah daft, but this much he grasped: a certain degree of trust was necessary if they were to go on with the next part of their marriage. Nothing profound, just the practical respect of two people responsible for a ducal succession.

"My privacy is safe in this bed?" Thea asked.

If she made Noah wait until that evening to conclude their business, when the candles could be blown out, he'd find a way to accommodate her.

"I have given my word, madam. Your privacy is utterly safe here."

"Then may I keep my chemise on?"

❧

James Heckendorn, Baron Deardorff, had lost his best friend when Noah Winters had assumed the title Duke of Anselm. At the age of seventeen, Noah had gone from being a serious-minded friend with a hidden hint of devilment, to obsessed with his responsibilities. Each of the Winters siblings had coped with the death of the former duke differently, while James had struggled for the rest of his university years to tempt Noah back to the land of the fun-loving and carefree.

Patience had been the one to point out to James what he was about, and to inform him that his objective was futile. Noah had become *the duke*, and James's best prayer of remaining his friend was to become *the baron*.

He'd dismissed her insight, in his youthful arrogance, and yet she'd caught his attention in a way other young ladies had not. He got around to offering for her, thinking that fondness and familiarity were an adequate foundation for an aristocratic marriage.

Patience had sent him packing with a flea in his young, baronial ear.

Eventually, James had sorted himself out and made a better job of the wooing, but in hindsight, he could see that as a new husband, he'd had much to learn.

"You're brooding," Patience said, tugging his glasses from his nose. "Evening approaches, and Lady Antoinette cannot be subjected to your brown study at supper."

James drew his wife down into his lap, for they were in the small sitting room adjoining their bedroom and James had taken the precaution of locking the door.

"You had a good nap?" Breeding women were given to napping, something else James had had to learn.

Patience tucked her feet up over the arm of James's reading chair. He couldn't feel the baby, but he could feel a *difference*. Patience had a secret, inward glow, a quiet good cheer that drew James like a candle in the window on a long chilly night. Heath had mentioned the same thing about Penelope.

"I have the oddest dreams these days," Patience said. "I see Noah riding a pony, for example, or you in my best Sunday bonnet. The images are very vivid. This afternoon, I dreamed I saw Lady Antoinette jousting with a parasol."

Patience was very fond of bonnets, also shoes, gloves, and parasols.

"A parasol is hardly an adequate weapon for a lady's defense," James observed. "What did Lady Nonie get up to today, anyway?"

Having a young lady underfoot was interesting. Patience had mustered maternal inclinations in the blink of an eye, while James had been daunted. Nonie was lovely, but she noticed everything, asked the damnedest questions, and was frightfully well read. On a whole new level, he realized he was about to become a father, possibly of a *daughter*.

"Penny took Nonie off to Hatchard's," Patience said, "and I'm sure a stop at Gunter's was planned as well. Nonie frets less if she gets out."

James smoothed a hand over Patience's hair, for it tickled his jaw when she moved about.

"What has Lady Nonie to fret over? You look after her every need, she loves to read, and she hasn't yet made her come-out."

Noah would see that all in the girl's path was rose petals and doting swains, just as he had for his own sisters. How a taciturn and overworked duke arranged rose petals, James did not know, but if he and Patience had daughters, he'd acquire the knack himself.

*And* the ability to summon nightingales.

"Nonie frets over her sister and brother," Patience said. "Grantley's predicament is obvious, but for Lady Thea, Nonie's concerns are more subtle."

James had no secrets from his wife, but where Noah was concerned, Patience often didn't ask, and thus James wasn't called upon to dance between competing loyalties.

"No marriage that starts with less than a week of courtship will have an easy time of it," he said. "Perhaps we should hold a ball to welcome Thea to the family."

Noah might thank him or kill him for that suggestion.

"I thought we should repair to Haverland for the rest of the summer," Patience said, "and have a house party when Town empties out, but Nonie didn't like that idea at all."

James roused himself from increasing fascination with the curve of Patience's shoulder, and the shadowy treasure half-hidden beneath the lacy décolletage of her chemise. Pregnancy had made her breasts intriguingly sensitive, or maybe James's hands had become intriguingly skilled.

James kissed his wife's ear. "Nonie was chattering nineteen to the dozen at breakfast about the invitations you received to Darnley's gathering later this summer. Now you tell me she won't enjoy a house party we host at our own very pretty country house. Women are fickle."

Patience bit his earlobe, gently of course. He was the father of her child, after all.

"Nonie isn't keen on house parties, but Thea apparently loathes them. There's something there, James. We ought to ask Meech if he's heard any gossip concerning Thea and unfortunate incidents at house parties."

Meech would know, and what he didn't know, he and Pemmie could casually unearth from their wide circle of acquaintances, former paramours, and servant-familiars.

"I'll suggest Noah have a word with Meech," James said, "because it's none of our business, Patience. We should be focused on choosing names, decorating the nursery, and cosseting you."

"I like the cosseting part," she said, squirming around to straddle his lap. "I think the cosseting ought to go both ways. I should cosset you too."

James should have argued. They had a houseguest, and they'd been late for breakfast that morning as a result of cosseting each other.

"Nonie's with Penelope," Patience whispered, "and I've moved dinner back an hour."

James had been warned by other fellows. When the baby came, the cosseting bit was set aside for months, another daunting thought.

Patience worked the straps of her chemise down, and James's hands ached.

"We have months to come up with names," he whispered. "For now, let the cosseting begin."

# Sixteen

"THEN MAY I KEEP MY CHEMISE ON?"

Late-afternoon light slanted across Thea's features, revealing doubt, wariness, and genuine bewilderment. She apparently didn't know if a chemise was expected, permitted, tolerated, or bad form entirely.

Noah ran his finger along the lace of her collar.

"Of course you can keep your..." He stopped as inspiration struck. "I *want* you to keep your chemise on, if that's how you'll be more comfortable. What goes on here is not about appeasing my lust and shooing me out of your hair. Not only about that."

"It isn't?"

"For God's sake..." He touched his lips to Thea's again, whisper light, at variance with the exasperation that made him want to shout: "Kiss me."

Amid the lavender-scented sheets, Noah waited, flat on his back, stark naked, his wife straddling him and his rampant arousal. Fortunately for his sanity, Thea deliberated for only a progression of heartbeats before she leaned forward—not far enough to give Noah the sensation of her breasts brushing his chest, but far enough—and touched her lips to his.

She withdrew after the merest pressure, then her lips returned, a shade less hesitant.

"Delicious," Noah whispered. "More, please, or I will beg, and you don't want a begging duke on your conscience, Thea."

Neither did Noah. A begging duchess, however, became his sole objective.

Thea covered his mouth with hers, probably to shut him up.

Noah was happy with the result. Thea braced herself on her hands, and put herself at that height most conducive to his mouth plundering hers. By careful degrees, Noah transformed a kiss of the lips, mouths, and tongues, to a shared bodily caress.

The better to signal his intentions, he framed Thea's face with his palms, her golden earrings dangling against his knuckles.

Noah traced her neck and shoulders, and on down her sides to her waist, then back up. By increments, he coaxed Thea closer, until she lay on him, the smooth expanse of her belly meeting his, her breasts pressed to his chest.

She must have realized Noah had become her ducal fainting couch, for she sat up. He let her, and the resulting view was lovely.

"You want me to take my chemise off." Thea's voice had gone smoky, her gaze unfocused.

Noah would have given his oldest horse—yes, his second mount, dear Regent, to a good home anyway—to get that damned chemise off of her.

"The fate of the chemise is entirely in your hands, Wife." Noah leaned up and nuzzled her breast through the thin material. He contemplated chewing the thing off of her, but contented himself with getting his mouth over one of her nipples through the cloth. He dampened her flesh and suckled gently until Thea whimpered.

Noah desisted and lay back against the pillows. Thea looked so torn, so balanced between inchoate arousal and mortification, that Noah gathered her in his arms rather than continue to study her.

At least in terms of confidence, Thea was the very next thing to a virgin. The very, very next thing, and this inaugural marital romp abruptly became serious business. Noah rolled them so Thea was beneath him, and buried his face against her neck.

"This is better," Thea said, stroking Noah's hair.

"Because I can't gawk, stupefied by your feminine bounty?"

She kissed his cheek, which gesture Noah felt in low and lovely places. "I like your weight, Noah."

"You like fifteen stone of husband mashing you into the bedclothes?" Noah lifted his head to regard her, and damned if Thea wasn't blushing again. He could feel the heat rising from her chest, past her neck, and flushing her cheeks. The sensation was lovely, as if her sentiments bloomed right next to his skin.

"I like fifteen stone of husband keeping me safe and warm." She raised her knees, the movement emphasizing how her body cradled his.

"Kiss me, Araminthea."

"We did that already, Husband. Are you stalling?"

Noah was savoring, not the same thing at all. "I'm having an intense and highly philosophical internal debate," he said, using a golden earring and his teeth to tug delicately at Thea's earlobe. Maybe he *would* gobble her whole, because she tasted like sunshine, flowers, and goodness.

"A debate about?" she asked.

"My wife's well-being," he replied, switching ears. "In a moment, lest I part with my few remaining wits, we will join our bodies."

"One suspected you were depleted in the wits department." Thea's breathing had grown a tad pantish.

"This part of me"—Noah flexed his hips so a certain aspect of his anatomy slid slowly over Thea's sex—"wants to remain more or less where we are, with a few significant adjustments." He repeated the caress of his sex over hers, and God bless her, she shifted her hips, as if trying to follow his movements.

"If we resume our prior position, though"—he kept at her with his hips, for his sanity would mutiny did he stop—"you would have more control over what followed."

More control over him.

Thea's thumb brushed across Noah's nipple as she trailed her hand from his chest to his throat. Noah mentally seized on Caesar's letters from Gaul.

*Gallia est omnis divisa in partes tres...* Noah's wits were dividing into parts innumerable.

"I wouldn't know how to go on," Thea murmured. Her thumb was back, and then two thumbs were parting Noah's reason from further scholarly maunderings about the dratted French.

"Thea, I can't...that is to say..." Noah fell silent while she levered up and kissed his jaw. "Jesus save me."

She found his mouth next, and twined her tongue with his, in the rhythm he'd set up between their bodies.

"Please, Wife…" he managed, "you have to tell me."

Two more languorous, torturous, slick slides past heaven.

"Yes, Noah. Now."

Thea's hips stilled, and Noah mentally promoted himself to prospective sainthood by going immobile as well.

"You're sure?"

"I'm sure, Noah. With you, I'm very sure."

He closed his eyes in thanksgiving, and probed at her gently, until he'd threaded shallowly into her heat.

"You're all right?"

Thea nodded, her earring tickling Noah's jaw.

Noah cradled the back of her head in one hand, and tucked her face against his shoulder. "You say, if you're not, and I'll…sweet heavenly choruses."

Thea had moved her hips, taking another inch of him for herself, and Noah let her, then he took over the business, because that was the point of their position, for him to control this part, this delicate, fraught, *holy* moment.

"Noah, please…"

He stopped, and Thea moved restlessly beneath him.

"You can't stop, Husband. *Please.*" Begging, and not a moment too soon.

"Hush," Noah ordered. "I won't stop, just hush." Inch by slow, careful inch, he joined their bodies, with Thea matching his rhythm awkwardly at first, then more smoothly, then with a wondrously instinctive ease. Noah's arousal ratcheted up, and he hauled it under control by listening to his wife's breathing.

He paused when he was hilted in her wet heat.

"Are we finished?" Thea asked.

"Holy, ever-loving, benighted…we are not finished." Noah brushed Thea's hair off her forehead, then kissed her nose. "You are comfortable?"

"Not particularly."

"I'm too heavy." He made to shift away, but Thea locked her ankles at the base of his spine and prevented him from unjoining them.

"I don't mean that kind of not particularly," Thea said, sifting a hand through his hair. "Move some more."

"Your wish, and so forth." Noah moved carefully, savoringly, then levered up on his arms to see Thea's face. Her expression was distracted, as if she were listening to their bodies, trying to place a distant melody.

"I like it better when you move," she said, "but it's still…incomplete."

Incomplete. Noah was balls deep in his wife, and it was incomplete.

Well, hell, of course it was.

"I can complete it for you, Thea. I will complete it for you."

Noah moved with more purpose but kept his tempo slow until Thea met him thrust for thrust, bowing up tightly against him.

"Better?" he rasped.

"Yes, and worse." Thea was panting, her legs scissored tightly around him, her body reaching for what it instinctively knew lay ahead.

"I want to touch your breasts, Thea."

"Uhn."

By no means was that a refusal of Noah's request—for he'd been *asking*.

She arched her back when his fingers closed over her nipple, and Noah felt the first flutters of her release stir. He stroked into her hard, drew on her tongue, and gently rolled her nipple in a concerted choreography of arousal.

Thea keened softly in his ear as she found her pleasure.

"Let go," he whispered. "Take all you need."

He drove into her, until she was limp and quiet beneath him, then he eased his rhythm to slow, gentle movement.

"Complete now?"

"Gads, Noah."

"I'll take that as a yes, for the nonce." He folded his arms under Thea's neck, caging her with his body.

"Now are we finished?"

"What is this preoccupation you have with finishing, Duchess?"

Thea blew a stray lock of hair off her forehead. "This is all new to me, Husband. I feel…" She ducked her face against Noah's throat.

"Pleasured?" He nuzzled her temple, kissed her cheek.

"Confused."

That almost threw Noah off stride, but he was learning this husband business, and waiting was part of it.

"You seem to be completely composed," Thea went on, "but I feel…"

"Yes?"

"I could cuddle up and drift off, but my mind is whirling, and my body is humming like a bowstring that's been plucked *hard*, and the sensations are too much to contemplate experiencing again this century, but also so…"

"Pleasurable?"

"Overwhelming, though *you* don't seem over-whelmed, Noah. You are *inside me*, and still your savoir faire has not deserted you."

Well, actually… "You can rob me of my savoir faire," he said, and too late it occurred to him he was giving Thea weapons she might never have learned to use had he kept his mouth shut.

"I have no wish to rob you of anything," she said, patting his backside. "Somebody in this bed had better know how to go on."

"The sensations you refer to?" Noah kept his rhythm smooth but let himself penetrate more deeply. "A woman can enjoy those many times in succession, if her lover is considerate and has a bit of restraint."

A universe of restraint.

"You have restraint," Thea said, closing her eyes and hitching her ankles against his back. This had the effect of tightening her inner muscles.

"I am also considerate. Do that again."

"Yawn?"

Ye whimsical gods. "Not yawn, Thea. Inside, try to stop me from withdrawing."

She experimented, and Noah saw heaven from behind closed eyes.

"Like that?"

"Exactly, precisely like that, as hard as you like."

Thea continued to test and refine until they were rocking steadily, and Noah's control was turning to fairy dust.

"This time," he whispered, "I'll be overwhelmed too, just keep... Holy everlasting powers, just like... damn, *Araminthea*..."

When her pleasure hit, she sank the nails of one hand into Noah's backside and bucked against him, until his own pleasure flooded out into every particle of his body, and even beyond that, as if his skin were dissolving, and his satisfaction and Thea's were one unified experience of ecstasy.

And yet all the while, Noah had been aware of his wife, aware of her breathing, aware of the panting groans of pleasure escaping her natural reserve, aware of her breast pushed into his hand, aware of her supple length undulating in counterpoint to his greater strength. Then Noah felt the bodily peace radiating from Thea as pleasure ebbed, and her sighs fanned past his ear.

This joining had been *different*, and part of the difference lay in Noah's attention to Thea, his unwillingness to lapse into even a moment of complete selfishness, complete oblivion to his partner and her pleasure. Thea was his wife, and relying on him to see to her satisfaction, and oddly, doing that had enhanced his pleasure as well.

"I'm squashing you."

"Hush, Husband. Please."

Thea's hand closed again on his fundament, as if she could keep him where he was with that touch alone.

"Somebody ought to fetch us a wet flannel, Wife, and because you have a large, useless fellow draped over you, that leaves me to see to it." A large, useless, husband. "Do not move, and I mean do not."

Noah eased from Thea's body, and she remained obediently still while he crossed the room and retrieved a cloth. He used it on himself, then dunked it in the tub and wrung it out before returning to the bed.

Thea was on her back, knees up, legs slightly spread, her gaze directed at the strawberry leaves and leaping stags cavorting about the molding.

"You said not to move."

Noah sat at her hip and kissed her, so brave was she. Without breaking the kiss, he eased the cool, damp cloth over her sex, and held it there, until Thea started against his mouth.

"I can do that." She tried to push his hand away, but Noah ignored her and rested his cheek on the slope of her breast.

"Your heart is nigh galloping, Wife."

"You appropriate some very personal tasks to yourself, Husband."

"This is personal." Noah sat up, then lifted the cloth, refolded it cool sides out, and repositioned it. When Thea bore that, he swabbed gently at her sex. "With you, it is personal." A few more dabs for form's sake, because she was allowing it, and then Noah tossed the cloth onto the rim of the tub. "Now you must evaluate my maiden attempt at providing my duchess her marital pleasures."

"One can't evaluate something beyond words," Thea said.

Noah climbed onto the bed. Thea neither squeaked nor squawked when he pulled her across his lap and wrapped his arms around her.

"Try anyway." He gathered her hair in his hands, mindful that he'd issued yet another order in bed. "Your silence exacerbates my manly insecurities."

Thea snuggled onto his chest. "That is a grammatical impossibility, there being no such things where you are concerned. What would you have me say?"

"That you enjoyed it," Noah *suggested*. He'd enjoyed it. "That next time you want to be on the top, and the time after that we'll flip for it, or try it on our knees, or standing up with me behind you, or maybe against a stout wall, or—"

Thea put a hand over his mouth. "They must be very trying, those manly insecurities."

"Vexing in the extreme," Noah said against her fingers. "You're all right?"

Now she traced his lips with a single, diabolical fingertip. "Dazed with pleasure I didn't even know existed. Badly done of you, Noah."

*Noah.* Not my lord, or Anselm, or Husband. Here in their bed, she'd called him Noah.

"What is badly done of me?"

"You did not warn me about this part, when you listed your attributes as a husband," Thea mused. "Marliss said you had a knowing quality to you."

"Marliss? Who is this Marliss creature, to put such fancies in your head?"

Thea kissed his jaw and subsided with a happy little sigh, her breathing soon indicating she'd dozed off in his arms. Noah arranged them spoon-fashion in the middle of the bed, then drifted toward sleep. His last thought was that the term *marital bliss* had graduated from being one of those grammatical impossibilities to something else entirely.

❧

Thea curled up on her side, Noah's heat warming her back. He slept with her, a source of both comfort and confusion on this, their first night of true marital intimacy.

His kindness literally stole Thea's breath. He was brusque, and shy, and his humor was a tad ribald, but ye gods, she'd known so little about her intimate duties, and he'd taken such care with her.

Even through a quiet dinner on the back terrace, Noah's attention had been constant and considerate.

*Doting?*

Thea hadn't known marriage could be like this, hadn't suspected, hadn't wanted to know. She'd hoped consummating the vows wouldn't be too uncomfortable or take too long. God knew her experience suggested five minutes could be too long.

With Noah, years would not be long enough, and yet, Thea clung to a thread of caution. Noah had been honest about his tomcatting antecedents, and he didn't love her. Thea wasn't romantically enthralled with him, and she suspected Noah had chosen her in part for her unwillingness to be tempted into such follies with even her husband.

Especially with her husband.

So Thea resolved to guard her heart closely, despite these bodily pleasures she shared with Noah, despite how he'd troubled over her, and how his touch made her common sense melt. With luck, she'd conceive his heir and his spare in short order, and frequent relations wouldn't be necessary beyond the next while. She'd enjoy her marital duties, as Noah no doubt enjoyed his, but she'd never forget they were duties—for both of them.

"Go to sleep, Wife."

"How can you tell I'm awake?"

"You're not stealing the covers." Noah buried his hand in the hair at her nape and massaged gently. "You steal covers only when in the arms of Morpheus. Does something trouble you?"

Someone troubled her. "I'm sorting matters out."

Noah's hold shifted, to that firm, delicious squeeze that dissipated tension as if a purring cat had just curled against Thea's belly.

"This sounds serious, madam. Perhaps you'd better have help with your sorting."

Noah sounded serious. Even when he was teasing, even when he was poking fun at himself, he sounded serious.

"You nominate yourself to provide assistance?" Thea asked.

"Bathsheba had the good sense to abandon your bed tonight, so yes, because I am all the assistance to be had. Come here." Noah hauled Thea over him, so she straddled his lap, then his hand was back at her nape, urging her down to his chest.

"What manner of help is this, sir?"

Noah was silent, his caresses lulling Thea to sleep, though he'd settled her such that her sex would be right over his breeding organs, did she allow it.

"If it's any consolation," he said softly, "I'm sorting out a few things too."

"Such as?"

"You found pleasure," Noah said with characteristic bluntness, "and that matters to me."

His tone was gruff, his caresses tender.

"Pleasure. Such a tame label for a complete loss of wits, and sensation too intense for words."

"Ah, Wife." Noah kissed Thea's crown.

"And you take all the credit." She ran her nose up his sternum. "The credit belongs to a Creator who fashioned me so accommodatingly."

"The credit goes to you," Noah said. Thea wished she could see his face, see the exact shade of blue in his eyes, but she wasn't about to suggest they light a candle. "You trusted me, and yourself."

She'd trusted him, yes, for in his way, Noah had in the weeks of their marriage proven himself consistent, rational, and, well, trustworthy.

Thea swiped her tongue across his nipple. "That trusting part wasn't even in the vows, was it?"

"Don't suppose it can be compelled. Are you truly troubled, Thea?"

She had vowed that her marriage would go forth more honestly than it had begun. "Yes, a little."

"Because?"

"That trust..." She weighed her misgivings against the sensation of Noah's hand burrowed so gently into her hair, the tenderness of his touch, the patience in his questions, and decided to trust him in the dark one little bit more. "It's difficult, and different, for me to trust."

But not impossible for her to trust, not in some regards. A revelation, that.

"For me as well."

Noah had apparently reached the limit of his husbandly tether, because he framed Thea's face in his hands and settled a kiss on her mouth that turned into kisses and caresses and sighs and a slow, slow joining of his body to hers. He guided her in this position, and let her find her way too, and Thea took to it immediately. Noah's hands were free, but so were hers. Thea could wrest some of the control from him, and she could kiss him or not as she pleased.

When pleasure bore down on her, Noah anchored her snugly with an arm low across her back, and let her flail and pitch and carry on until the storm broke, and she was keening against his neck, and surrendering herself completely to his mouth and hands and loving.

And again, he took care of her afterward, scolding and taking the Lord's name in vain about wives who would need soaking baths before breakfast, and trials to his manly self-discipline.

Thea drifted into slumber on Noah's chest, the scent of him soothing her to sleep. Her last thought was a question: What would it take to obliterate His Grace's much vaunted manly restraint?

❧

"They've escaped."

Noah hated to wake his sleeping wife—he'd worn her out last night, bless her heart—but the thunder of little feet in the corridor above demanded immediate action.

"Tea." Thea's voice was a cranky mutter from the depths of the pillows.

"Dressing gown." Noah said it very distinctly, right into her ear.

Thea mooched over to his side of the bed to appropriate the warm spot left in his absence, sighed mightily, and snuggled into the pillows, all without opening her eyes.

"Araminthea," Noah began, "you will be found naked in bed by two innocent children if you do not open your eyes *now*."

"No need to shout." She opened her eyes and struggled to sit up. "And no need to take that Mean Papa tone with me before you've even fetched my first cup of soon-to-be-pilfered tea."

Noah tossed Thea's dressing gown at her head, the better to keep her from seeing his smile. She sorted herself into it as he secreted a plate of cinnamon toast in the wardrobe, and only then did he set about making her tea.

"Husband, did you hide food from our children?"

"You'll thank me," he said as the door to the sitting room opened, followed by a patter of feet, then a thumping on Thea's bedroom door.

"Lady Thea! We're out here, because Cousin is not in his bed, and we get to meet our ponies This Very Morning. Cousin Noah promised."

Noah opened the door and stood back as Evvie and Nini bounded across the room and scrambled up onto the bed to flank Thea, one on each side.

"She hasn't had her tea yet, my dears, so shout quietly," Noah said.

"We can't shout quietly," Nini bellowed. "We're to meet our ponies today, aren't we?"

"We will when my duchess has had her breakfast." Noah joined them on the bed, and even with two little girls and two adults in it, the bed wasn't quite crowded.

"May *we* have breakfast?" Evvie was eyeing the tea cart as Wellington probably surveyed battlefields. "Maryanne and Davies weren't about yet, so we couldn't pinch their sweet rolls, and Nurse says we must eat only tea and porridge for breakfast."

"I hate porridge!" Nini announced. "Unless it has honey in it. I'm hungry!"

For once, Noah let Thea finish her first cup without him filching half of it, though not until her third cup did he take pity on her and shoo the girls off to dress for their trip to the stables. When the door was safely closed behind the children, Noah retrieved the toast from the wardrobe and passed Thea a thick, buttery slice.

"They are a force of nature," Noah said, taking the last sip of Thea's tea. "Shall I fix you another cup?"

"Please."

"You needn't accompany us to the stables, Wife. The girls are only meeting their ponies today. The little beasts no doubt need to rest before taking on the challenge of training their new owners."

"I wouldn't miss this, Noah. When a girl meets her first horse, it's a holy moment."

"So it is." Thea had pleased him with that observation, just as she'd pleased him by good-naturedly sharing breakfast with a little girl on either side of her in bed. Noah had stopped allowing the girls to storm his bed a year ago, as it didn't seem…it wasn't appropriate. With a wife, he could again have the pleasure of warm, happy, little people wiggling right beside him like puppies at the start of the day.

A pleasure he'd missed, but missed without realizing it.

He put extra butter on his own slice of toast.

"We might need to move to my bed," he observed. "It's larger, and marital intimacies can eventually lead to entire hordes of children charging across the bedroom drawbridge first thing in the day."

That thought pleased Noah too, until he realized Thea had taken his toast right off his plate.

"I've married a thief. Shame on you, madam." He drained the last cup of tea in retaliation.

# Seventeen

In the following days—and nights—Thea's view of the world pivoted on new and fascinating axes. Her one experience with sexual intimacy prior to marriage had been furtive, uncomfortable, and humiliating, but mercifully brief.

With Noah, she could not imagine a furtive coupling. He strolled about as God made him, and by stealthy degrees, accustomed her to being glimpsed in her own natural state by the light of an entire branch of candles—provided they were across the room from the bed.

Noah's lovemaking was the furthest thing from uncomfortable, at least physically. He was careful, deliberate even, sometimes to the point that Thea wanted to pull his hair, or smack him, or otherwise make clear to him the desirability of a certain urgency in conjugal relations. But he'd smile that sweet, crooked smile, admonish her to wifely restraint, and steal her very wits, slowly and thoroughly.

And as for humiliation…

Shame had become a second skin for Thea when

she'd lost her virginity. In the intervening years, she'd tormented herself with a thousand lectures—she should have seen the whole matter approaching and prevented it. She should have screamed. She should have married the man who'd intruded into her body and her life, because as an earl's daughter, she could have forced him to the altar. She should have shrugged off the whole sorry little business. She should have extorted money from the miserable scoundrel and put it aside for herself or her siblings.

She should have run away to the North and begun her life anew with some semblance of privacy and dignity. She should have, should have, should have… All the things she didn't, wouldn't, and couldn't.

Moment by moment, marriage to Noah was repairing damage all Thea's fortitude and determination hadn't made a dent in previously. His lovemaking was part of it, a precious, curious part, but not all, or even the greatest part.

Thea puzzled on that conundrum, and puzzled on it. Her improved outlook on herself had to do with Noah and his rare, sweet smiles and his gruff scolds and his relentless devotion to his family. She resolved to study on the matter and get to the bottom of it, because it was important.

Thea was worrying at this very riddle while pretending to work at her correspondence when she felt Noah's index finger slip down the center of her forehead.

"My duchess is vexed."

"My duke has returned from riding with the Cossacks across the wild steppes of Kent."

He settled beside her on the day couch in her sitting room, his sigh put-upon and weary.

"They want to gallop, the pair of them. They've had their ponies but two weeks, and already we're to gallop, jump, and race about. True has been corrupted by the influence of a pair of miniature equine delinquents. Only Regent retains a hint of dignity, though one senses his resolve weakening."

"Noah, you didn't allow this wild behavior?" Males were different from females. Thea's one younger brother was enough to drive home that point, if experiences with Corbett Hallowell and his ilk hadn't. Men thought they were indestructible, and every time they survived hurt or injury merely proved to them their durability.

Women knew better.

"The girls can carry on however they please," Noah said, "provided their ponies are on one end of the lunge line, and I am no more than eight feet away on the other."

"Eight whole feet?"

Noah had had more sand spread in the riding arena the week before too.

"And tomorrow," he went on, "if they are good, I will consider ten, and so forth. Negotiation is everything when you're dealing with a Winters. What has Lady Antoinette to say for herself?"

Noah leaned forward and took a sip of Thea's lemonade, giving her a whiff of horse, manly exertion, and the underlying fragrances of roses and lavender. An odd combination, but pleasing. Husbandly.

"Nonie is agitating to attend a house party, as is

Lady Patience," Thea said, folding up the letter and tucking it aside. "I'm not sure how to respond."

"Patience agitates for form's sake," Noah said, tippling another sip. "Her spouse claims it's a bid for attention, and one must not argue with a man on the subject of his wife."

"You'd disagree?"

"Patience likes to agitate," Noah replied, setting the empty glass down. "It's in her nature, like Uncle Meech must flirt, and Harlan will gravitate to the beasts and the land."

"I haven't thought of Nonie having propensities like that. She's drawn to books." Or had Nonie retreated to books because Tims hadn't provided her a proper governess?

"You didn't raise her, not entirely," Noah said, sitting up to wrestle off first one riding boot then the other. "I was as much papa as brother to my younger siblings, particularly with Harlan."

"Which is why you're so good with the girls." Maybe even why Noah was such a conscientious duke?

"Right." Noah snorted. "So good, the girls have me dancing around in a dusty arena on the end of an eight-foot rope in this infernal heat. You are not keen on Antoinette trying her social wings at some informal gatherings?"

Noah did this, hopped around from topic to topic, while stealing Thea's drink, while removing his clothes. Just to be in the same room with him was sometimes dizzying, while to be in the same bed with him—

"What makes you think I disapprove of house parties?" For Thea did, utterly.

She pushed Noah's hands aside and unknotted his cravat, which had acquired both dust and creases in his morning's labors. His riding jacket came off next in a series of maneuvers they'd perfected a week ago.

Noah drew his finger down Thea's forehead again. "You were frowning in thought, or maybe frustration."

In vexation. "I've been to enough informal gatherings as a companion to know exactly what functions they serve for guests and hosts alike," Thea said. "They can be perfectly wholesome, lovely occasions, or the next thing to a rural bacchanal, and one doesn't know until one arrives which way they'll lean."

Though eventually, most of them turned unlovely.

"Part of their charm, to hear Meech tell it." Noah sat back. "Why not compromise?"

"How?"

"We'll have a house party here, a welcome to the family for you, and we'll invite mostly family, but include Lady Nonie and a few callow swains to dance attendance on her."

Thea's first reaction was frustration, because Noah's suggestion was too reasonable to be rejected. Negotiation was everything when dealing with a Winters, provided the concessions came to their side of the table.

"Where will we find these callow swains?" she asked, for they invariably caused the most trouble.

"Harlan can round up some of his more presentable friends," Noah said, "show off his new horse, practice getting drunk and losing his allowance over cards. We'll have some dancing to truly torment the young fellows."

Which sounded harmless enough...except: "Won't we have to invite a few young ladies to balance up the numbers?" Callow swains got up to their worst mischief when in proximity to drink, each other, and young ladies.

"God above, Wife, how should I know about such details? I have a duchess on hand to tend to such earthshaking matters now. I suggest you consult with her, and she will no doubt alert my sisters, and then we poor old hapless fellows will trot about on our lead lines, as usual." Noah kissed Thea's nose, then rose. "What does a man have to do to get some cold libation in his own home on a hot summer day?"

Thea watched Noah stomp off, poor, thirsty, put-upon, little fifteen-stone duke, and knew he was smiling—as was she. By the time the girls thundered in to regale her with tales of the day's mounted adventures, Thea had the *family gathering* guest list drafted in her head.

For they were *not* having a house party. Noah's duchess had made up her mind about that.

∽⌇∼

"I'll fetch you some punch, shall I, kitten?"

Henrietta Whitlow's escort for the evening was an earl going thick about the middle and thin on top. Poor Melmouth had been drinking steadily enough to need every chamber pot in the men's retiring room. He was still handsome in a blond, blue-eyed way, but losing his wife two years ago had nudged him into the grip of a firm and—Henny suspected—lonely middle age.

"Punch would be delightful," she said, beaming at him. "Take your time, and don't worry about me.

You must allow the puppies and rakes a chance to pay me their addresses."

Melmouth blew her a kiss—something he would never have done sober—and departed.

Henny's head had begun to pound halfway through the overture, and when some obese Italian fellow had commenced caterwauling, she'd nearly gone home. That early in the evening, Melmouth would have been sober enough to be a problem, though, and thus Henny had endured the tenor, the mezzo, and the contralto, who appeared suspiciously masculine.

"Consoling yourself with fellows of lesser rank now that Anselm has wiggled free of your clutches?"

Ignoring Corbett Hallowell would have been like ignoring a fly circling a tray of desserts. He'd pester Henny until she swatted him away.

She mustered her public smile. "Mr. Hallowell, do come in. Melmouth has decamped, perhaps never to return. Are you enjoying the performance?"

Hallowell was exactly the kind of man who'd drive any sensible courtesan to retire. He was not particular about his hygiene, the company he kept, or his manners. Before he joined Henny in her box, he glanced out into the passage, probably to make sure his mama wasn't spying on him.

"Your performances are always enjoyable," Hallowell said. "I'd heard rumors you were moving to Paris."

Exactly what Henny intended for people to believe, though in truth, Yorkshire was calling her home more loudly with each passing month.

"Paris is lovely," she said, "particularly for people of taste and refinement. Surely you'd agree?"

Hallowell remained leaning against the wall near the door, in shadow, where he wouldn't be seen, but plenty close enough to conduct an insolent visual inspection of Henny's person.

"Some say you're carrying Anselm's bastard, Miss Whitlow, and that's why he threw you over. Maybe you got rid of it."

Had Henny been lucky enough to conceive Anselm's bastard, she'd have been set up for life.

"Have a care, sir. His Grace takes a dim view of slander."

Henny missed Anselm, but had been relieved he'd gone wife hunting. No self-respecting courtesan permitted herself to become attached to her protector. Loyal to him for the duration, of course, and discreet forever after. Fond of him, protective, attracted to him, friends with him, even.

But a wise courtesan kept her heart to herself. Anselm had threatened Henny's professional reserve, and his marriage to a sensible earl's daughter was good news all around.

Especially for the earl's daughter.

"His Grace can go bugger himself," Hallowell said. "He tossed you over for mutton dressed up as lamb, and I'll bet you had your sights set on a tiara. Devonshire married his mistress. Berwick married his before she was even of age."

Henny rose, because in her heeled evening slippers, she was taller than Hallowell, and the scent of his rotten gin-breath was threatening to turn her headache into a megrim.

"Why does every titled man think every woman,

regardless of her means or her station, longs to marry him?" Henny tipped her chin up, the better to peer down her nose at this reeking embarrassment to manhood. "Do you know how hard Anselm's duchess will work? How much entertaining she'll have to do? How many households and charities she'll have to oversee? In what world could I ever be accepted in those roles, Hallowell?"

Hallowell puffed up like a bantam rooster preparing to take on a mongrel in the barnyard.

"Thea Collins is no better suited to be a duchess than you are," he spat. "Anselm will rue the day he married her, and I'll be the one to see to it."

Hallowell would have maundered on as long as the tenor and the soprano both, making vague threats that probably had to do with Anselm snatching the morsel Hallowell had coveted.

*Well done, Anselm*, if he'd preserved a decent woman from Hallowell's advances.

"I say, don't believe we've been introduced." Melmouth, bearing two cups of dreadful punch, stood in the doorway to the box.

"Melmouth, may I make known to you Corbett Hallowell, Endmon's heir. Hallowell, the Earl of Melmouth has the pleasure of my company tonight."

Melmouth, who was no fool even drunk, passed Henny her punch. "Miss Whitlow is too expensive for you, my boy. Don't tell anybody, but she's too expensive for me as well."

The earl had struck the right note, between confiding and condescending—though being referred to as expensive would ever grate on Henny's nerves. Had

Hallowell half a brain, he might have left on some quip, or even a graceful bow.

"Anselm might take you back," Hallowell said. "Just you wait and see. He's married the wrong duchess, and soon everybody will know it."

Hallowell marched off, a boy in men's tailoring.

"Was he bothering you, kitten?"

Being called kitten bothered Henny. The scent of the chandeliers bothered her. The weight of her earrings bothered her.

Henny put her lips to the rim of the cup but did not sip. "Yes, Dickie, he was. Nothing is so vile as a gin-soaked little bully in anticipation of a title. Anselm will probably be forced to call him out."

Melmouth emptied the contents of his flask into his punch. "Anselm's an excellent shot, and I hear he's besotted with his new bride. Bought her a prime little filly at Tatt's, has barely been seen in Town since the vows were spoken."

*Good for you, Anselm. Good for your duchess.*

"If Anselm's ruralizing with his new duchess, then Hallowell's lack of couth will likely go unpunished," Henny said. "Would you mind very much if we left, Dickie?"

Henny's feet hurt, her head hurt, her eyes hurt, her earlobes hurt; most of all, her heart hurt. Anselm was deserving of every happiness, but that didn't mean Henny had to sit about, like a streetwalker on her preferred corner, and troll for custom.

Melmouth drained half his cup. "Are you inviting me to join you at home, kitten?"

The question was stone sober, and pathetically

hopeful. On stage, the portly tenor and the equally substantial soprano were warbling away at volume in Italian, despite the lady's supposedly mortal wound.

Henny was abruptly homesick for the green, windy dales of the West Riding and the bleating of her uncle's fat, woolly sheep.

"Dickie, I don't think I'll ever invite another man to join me at home."

The earl set his punch down unfinished and slicked a hand over his thinning hair. "I'll have the carriage brought round. Opera has always struck me as so much noise anyway."

He took himself off, an aging knight who still had a few turns in the lists left, but Henny wouldn't allow him to squander them on her.

She'd done Melmouth a favor, but she'd also made up her mind. When Polite Society went grouse hunting, Henny would leave Town as well. Until then, she'd keep an eye on Hallowell, for a duke besotted with his new bride might not notice a threat skulking about his own garden.

༝

One floor below Thea's darkened bedroom, the long-case clock in the library let go a single, resonant *bong!* that reverberated through the house and through her wide-awake body.

Noah hadn't come to bed.

He'd given Thea a particularly enticing kiss in the library before she'd gone up to read the girls their bedtime story. His usual routine took him out to the stables after dinner, there to confer with his grooms, pet his beasts, and walk off some of his supper.

Thea grabbed a candle, and opened the door between her dressing room and Noah's, then crossed from his dressing room into his bedroom.

She didn't often go into Noah's bedroom, feeling as if his presence, or at least his permission, was needed to justify such an intrusion. His canopied bed sat in dark, ducal splendor along one wall, raised up three steps for both winter warmth and sheer impressiveness.

Had a woman at any point shared that bed with Noah? A guest at a previous Wellspring house party perhaps?

Thea closed the door. She wasn't allowed to have such thoughts, lest Noah have them about her. He hadn't asked, hadn't made any more allusions to her past, but sometimes she caught him looking at her, a question in his eyes.

Her thoughts careened in another equally foolish direction: maybe Noah had been kicked in the head while visiting the horses, and was even now lying unconscious in True's stall, overlooked by the grooms.

Maybe he'd decided to take a late evening ride in the moonlight, and come to grief hours ago.

Maybe…

"You are being ridiculous." Papa's admonition didn't quell Thea's worries now any more than it had when she'd been a girl. She grabbed a dressing gown, scuffed into a pair of old slippers, and made her way to the kitchen. There, she lit a closed lantern and let herself out into the summer night.

Crickets chirped, an owl hooted far off in the

direction of the home wood, and down at the stables, a faint light came from the horse barn.

The night air didn't carry any human voices though, so Thea hurried across the gardens, sternly lecturing herself about borrowing trouble.

No grooms were stirring, but outside Regent's stall, a lantern hung on a peg. Thea made her way down the aisle, a low murmuring coming to her ears.

"...not well done at all, to die when we're still in our prime. Seventeen isn't that old, not for a fellow who's enjoyed the best of care all his lazy, shiftless days. My duchess just met you, you filthy beggar. She will think you took her into dislike, when we both know you dote shamelessly on females of any species. Let the mares push you around, you do, which is probably why you're in such a taking. No biting, unless you're my duchess, which you decidedly are not."

Noah was talking to his reserve mount, a huge black coal barge of a beast named Regent, who could barely turn in a twelve-foot loose box without brushing both walls. Advancing age had seen the gelding demoted to status of second mount, though Noah still rode him regularly.

"Noah?"

He left off lecturing his horse, and came to the stall's half door.

"Great God Almighty." He ran a hand through hair that sported a wisp of straw. "My duchess has taken to wandering half-clothed in the dead of night without benefit of escort."

"My duke has taken to staying up past his bedtime,

leaving me to pine for his company, strange as that notion might be. Is your horse sick?"

Noah turned to survey the gelding, who stood with his head drooping, the look in the animal's eye dull and pained.

"Goddamned colic," Noah said. "He was listless this morning, which isn't unusual when it's hot, but he declined his oats at dinner, and as is predictably the case, in hindsight the grooms recall him kicking at his belly, though at the time, they thought he was grouching at the flies."

"You're worried about him," Thea said. Noah was a prodigiously competent worrier too.

"I shouldn't be. He has gut sounds on both sides, his gums are a perfect, horsey pink, and he isn't dehydrated."

Noah lapsed into silence, studying his horse, while Thea studied her husband.

"You're worried sick," she said, "and the night grows coolish. Let me bring you a jacket." Let her do anything to help, because Noah—her duke—was alone in the dead of night with a suffering animal.

Noah looked torn, as if the decision to stay with his horse or escort his wife was too difficult, so Thea kissed his cheek and took her leave. She returned less than ten minutes later, Noah's oldest riding jacket over her arm, and a tray in her hands laden with a fat ham and cheese sandwich, some hulled strawberries, and a tall glass of lemonade.

"You can't neglect yourself to care for him," she said, balancing the tray to open the half door. Noah sat on a low, three-legged milking stool in one corner, the horse standing with its head down, close enough that Noah could pet and scratch and comfort his ailing beast.

"You brought food." This seemed to puzzle Thea's husband.

She nudged a pile of clean straw together with her foot, and sank down beside him. "Food is for eating, Noah."

"You will get straw in odd places, Wife," Noah said, shifting off his stool. "Take the throne, there, and let me relieve you of your burden." He hefted the tray into his lap, sitting cross-legged in the straw. The horse looked vaguely interested in the goings on, but didn't stir so much as a hoof.

Thus did a duke recall how to impersonate a boy who was worried for an old equine friend.

"He's still listening to my voice," Noah said. "Even though his symptoms aren't severe, when they aren't listening anymore, it's time to clean your gun."

"I noticed the pistol on the trunk outside the door. Is he in such bad shape?"

"Hard to tell with horses," Noah said between bites of sandwich. "They're an odd combination of delicacy and power, much like duchesses." He settled his jacket around Thea's shoulders. "What possessed you to come haring down here in the dead of night?"

The stable was dark and quiet, save for the sounds of horses shifting sleepily in stalls thickly bedded with straw. Thea was alone with her husband. She could be honest.

"I came looking for you because I missed you."

"Hmm. Strawberry?" Noah held a ripe berry to Thea's lips, and she took a bite.

"You could have had the lads look in on him, Noah."

"When a pony has served his boy loyally for all his equine days"—Noah popped the other half of the strawberry into his mouth—"he deserves loyalty in return. These are good."

"You've had Regent that long?"

"He was the last gift from my father," Noah said, stroking the horse's nose, which had a sprinkling of pale hair. "I was leaving for university at the end of summer, and Papa gave him to me as a yearling, so I might spend the summer getting to know my horse. I spent the next two summers with him, every break and holiday, and we came of age together. When I went up to Town three years later, Regent was the envy of all my fellows. He's won me some money, and more than once, he saw me home when I was too drunk or tired or befuddled to know where I was going."

This recitation had the horse's interest, as if he understood the content, not simply the affectionate tone of voice.

"He likes your panegyric," Thea said. "I've always thought horses' noses were magic, like four-leaf clovers and fairy rings."

Noah traced a clover on the gelding's forehead. "What a fanciful notion."

"Their noses are so soft." Thea stroked her fingers over Regent's graying muzzle. "Velvet isn't this soft."

"None of that." Noah tone was stern, but directed at the horse. "He's making eyes at you, the worthless flirt. He's the same way with the girls, has no dignity whatsoever around females."

"Lucky for him he has you to protect him from his misguided nature. Do you think he'd like some hay?"

"We tried at supper," Noah said. "He looked at it and made pathetic eyes at us. The lads left in disgust."

Doubtless, the lads had been ordered to leave by a certain shy, tenderhearted, imperious duke.

"You've been sermonizing at the poor beast half the night. Shall we try again?" Thea asked.

"You try." Noah rose and took the tray from the stall, coming back with a bundle of fragrant hay.

"That smells good," Thea said from her perch on the stool. "Like mown grass."

Noah froze and scowled at the hay in his hands as if it were noxious.

"Bloody hell." The horse lifted his head at his master's tone. "It isn't cured," Noah spat. "The lads will answer for this." He tossed the hay into the aisle, and stood in the dim light, fuming, his hands on his hips.

Vulcan probably looked thus when at his forge: more shadow than light, and ready to hurl lightning bolts.

"What's the problem, Noah?"

"It's my fault," Noah said. "We went through this with him years ago. Most horses will eat hay cut last week if you give it to them, but the better practice is to cure fodder for at least a month. Regent must have his cured, or he becomes dyspeptic. I *know* this about him, and every year I remind the lads. I didn't do that this year, and now…this."

As if to emphasize Noah's diagnosis, Regent stomped a foot in the direction of his belly.

"Perishing, blasted, infernal damn." Noah took a

lead rope and halter down from a peg. "He'll try to drop and roll if we don't walk him, miserable beast."

What followed was hours of walking the gelding, letting him stand around in his stall, offering him water, talking to him, and, Thea was sure, praying for the beast's recovery. She prayed as well, for the horse, but also for her husband to be spared the misery of having to put his old friend—the last gift from his father—down.

# Eighteen

Morning came, and the stable hands went about their tasks, mucking, turning in, turning out, raking the aisle, topping up water buckets, and offering oats to the horses in work.

While Thea remained at her husband's side, and Regent grew no better.

The gelding lipped at some hay, took the occasional sip of water, but mostly stood, head down, looking pathetic and worn. Based on the muttered rumblings from the stableboys, the horse hadn't passed manure for nearly a day, and Thea gathered that was symptomatic of a looming tragedy.

"Duchess," Noah said, "you should not be about in dishabille with the fellows on hand. You will distract them, and you need your rest. Up to the house with you."

Noah was asking as gently as he could, but Thea did not want to go.

She'd seen him conferring with his head lad and cleaning his gun in the last hour, and her heart broke for him, and for the very young man who'd first fallen in love with Regent years earlier.

Thea went to her husband as he stood beside his horse, and put her arms around him. At first he did nothing, but then his lips moved against her temple, and his arms encircled her. For the space of one long, deep breath, he held her, drawing strength, she hoped, from her nearness.

"I'll bring you some breakfast," she said.

"I'll manage without," he replied. "Keep the girls away for a bit, would you? They can see their ponies later this morning."

Thea nodded and made for the house, unwilling to let Noah see her cry. Three of the stable hands passed her in the yard, not meeting her gaze—and they were carrying dirty shovels. She stopped in the back hall-way, tears streaming down her cheeks, for the horse, for the man, for the boy.

The girls would be devastated too, even True would likely grieve for his fellow, and poor Harlan—

Thea changed clothes as quickly as she could, determined that Noah not have to deal with this alone. She was his wife, his duchess, and he'd allowed her to stay beside him the entire night. They'd taken turns, walking the horse, talking to him, and spent hours sitting side by side in that stall, silently fretting when they should have been catnapping.

She hurried back to Regent's stall, leaving her hair in a single ratty braid.

"The girls aren't awake yet," she said before Noah could ask, though a gunshot would rouse them, of course.

He rose off a trunk, a long-barreled pistol in his hand. "I didn't expect you back."

In the stall, a groom was slipping the halter onto Regent's head. Panic welled in Thea's heart at the sight of the horse's weary docility. She moved to the beast's side, and Noah followed her into the stall.

"Wife, perhaps you should return to the house." Noah's tone was infinitely beseeching, his gaze sad.

"You'll put him down?"

"The lads are done digging, so, yes, it's time. He isn't recovering, and he's in pain."

*No*, Thea wanted to shout. The horse was no worse, his symptoms weren't severe, and he was Noah's friend. They couldn't just shoot him and push him into a cold, dark hole.

"I'll take that lead." She reached toward the groom, who looked first to Noah's expressionless face, then passed her the rope. "Where do we do this, Anselm?"

"The back paddock," Noah said. "Wife…Thea…I won't ask this of you."

He hardly asked anything of anybody, ever.

"Husband, you are wasting time while this dear beast suffers unnecessarily."

Noah blinked, as if Thea had spoken in some foreign tongue, then he spun on his heel and opened the stall door for her.

The stableboys watched them pass, two doffing their caps as if a funeral procession were going by.

Tears formed a hard ball in Thea's throat. The horse came along meekly, almost as if he knew Noah would relieve his suffering one way or another.

Noah led them across fields still glistening with dew, to the side of a yawning, ugly hole freshly gouged in the earth.

"Do you want to say good-bye?" Thea asked.

"I have nothing more to say," Noah bit out, then more softly, "He knows I'll miss him."

"Well, I want to say good-bye."

Noah looked pained, but nodded, and let Thea lead the horse a few steps away from the grave.

"You were a good boy, Regent," she said, stroking his neck. "The best boy. You took good care of your master when his mama and papa were gone, and he'll always love you, and so will I. You're going somewhere wonderful now, where your tummy won't hurt ever, and you can play with all the mares, and they won't order you about. Don't be afraid. Be proud of yourself. You were a good boy."

Thea was repeating herself, and Noah was looking at her so sadly, she didn't even try to stop her tears. She leaned over and kissed the horse on his big, soft nose. A long, lingering, smoochy kiss that seemed to provoke a sigh of contentment from the depths of the horse's body.

Or something.

Noah cocked his head and regarded the horse. He did not cock his gun.

"The ruddy bastard's farting," Noah said, wonder in his voice. Thea straightened, even as she perceived the distinctive sound of a horse breaking wind, and breaking wind, and breaking wind.

Over along the fence, two stables boys stopped walking, one pointed at Regent, and they both smiled sheepishly.

And still the animal farted.

And farted.

Then stopped, and dropped his tail on a sigh.

"Is he better?" Thea asked as Regent picked up his tail again and let go with a procession of staccato little reprises. The morning air took on a noxious, sulfurous quality.

"He's not worse," Noah said, the corners of his mouth kicking up. "Maybe you'd better kiss him again."

"Husband, that is not funny."

The flatulence ceased as the horse hunkered and grunted like a cow, tail up. This time, he emitted a sibilant, odoriferous breeze, and then began dropping manure.

"Praise Jesus," Noah said, shoving the gun into the back of his waistband and taking the lead rope from Thea. "Praise Almighty Jesus." He gave the horse a solid pat on the neck as Regent walked a couple of steps forward and continued to heed the call of nature.

"He did this last time he colicked too," Noah said, inhaling gustily through his nose. "I'd forgotten. Damn, but that stinks wonderfully. It was the new hay, had to be." He kept the lead rope in one hand, slung an arm around Thea's shoulders, and pulled her in close, kissing her cheek as the horse decisively ended a bout of horsey constipation.

"We'll be asphyxiated if we stay here," he said. "God bless you, Wife. You'll become the talk of every stable in the shire."

"Kissing him good-bye had nothing to do with"— Thea gestured behind them—"that."

"Tell it to the lads." Noah kissed her again. "Please

understand if, when I take my leave of you in future, your kisses will not be needed."

"Shame on you, Anselm!" Thea smacked his arm, and was still grinning like a fool when he stopped and kissed her *again*, this time on the mouth, with Regent, the stableboys, and all of creation looking on. Noah didn't stop until the stableboys started hooting and cheering, and Regent gently butted the duke with his head.

The girls' morning ride was turned over to Erikson, who professed to need a break from his science, and Thea and Noah took successive baths, ate a huge breakfast characterized by thievery at every turn, and then collapsed into bed together for a much-needed nap.

❧

Noah's wife had kissed him good-bye, their partings already having some of the comforting predictably of a domestic ritual. The little girls had tossed him their farewells from the depths of the ponies' stalls, which defection gave him a pang, one he suspected his duchess sensed.

When Thea might have trundled back to the house, she instead walked Noah to the mounting block, where True waited, one hip cocked.

"I married a nomad," Thea groused, her arm linked with Noah's. "You need a herd of camels, or perhaps you're like the American natives wandering the plains in nothing but a loincloth."

"A loincloth. A peer of the realm attired in a loincloth. Your imagination, Wife, will give me nightmares while I tend to my business in the City." Noah sat back onto the mounting block and pulled his duchess down beside him. "You are familiar with my schedule?"

"Appointments this afternoon with your solicitors, dinner and breakfast with your sisters, more appointments tomorrow, and you should be back tomorrow evening. Don't expect me to stay up late, sewing your loincloths while I await Your Grace's return."

"My daughters forget I exist," Noah informed Troubadour. "My wife would rather sleep than await my homecoming. I will be a nomad *sans* loincloths do I tarry too long on the business of the duchy. I am a man to be pitied."

Thea slipped her hand into Noah's, her predictable mercy explaining why Noah hadn't yet donned his riding gloves.

"I'll dream of you," Thea said. "Does that help?"

"I'm sallying forth on your errands, you know."

Now the dratted woman rested her head on Noah's shoulder. "How do you conclude my errands compel you to visit the City?"

"I'm off to Town at your behest. We need some ladies at this house party who can distract Erikson from his science. Patience must be canvassed for ideas, because you are sadly lacking in familiarity with your peers, madam."

Thea picked a piece of hay off his sleeve and flicked it to the ground.

"What is it, Wife? Do not send me into battle against the weasels with that sighing glance on my conscience." More of a glower, really.

"Are we procuring for our botanist, then? Turning our family gathering into something else?"

Thea was a veritable Puritan when it came to who would be allowed under the same roof as the girls. Noah liked that about his duchess, among other things.

"You truly have no use for these sorts of gatherings, do you?" Noah cast his mind back over their several discussions of who should attend, and what the activities should be. In hindsight, he could see the tracks of Thea's delicate heels, dragging in the conversational sand.

"I have no use for Polite Society in general," Thea said.

The Duchess of Anselm was dodging. Noah sought for a compromise, for something to say that wouldn't have them parting on a bad note.

"I will find some errands for Erikson to do in Town when I get back," he suggested. "He can attend to his manly urges when he's on the duchy's business, how's that?"

"I will leave his biology to you," Thea said, though Noah's suggestion appeared to have her approval. "And thank you. I really would like this to be more of a family gathering than anything else."

She'd all but insisted, and Thea was a mostly agreeable sort of female.

"Then that's how it shall be, but, Thea?"

"Husband?"

"I vote my seat, more than occasionally. If we need to do some entertaining later this year, in Town, I'll expect your assistance."

"You'll have it." She kissed his cheek. "Give me

plenty of warning, so I can interrogate you on the pressing political questions of the day."

Much more of her farewell affections, and she'd have Noah in such a muddle, he wouldn't know the Lords from the Commons.

"Take Erikson with you if you're to wander the property with the girls." Noah phrased the order—request, really—as casually as he could, checked True's girth and bridle, then looped the reins over his wrist and took his wife in his arms.

"You'll dream of me as I slay the dragons of commerce?"

"Weasels, you called them. I might dream of you."

Noah kissed the daylights out of Thea—not as if the lads hadn't seen them kissing before—and then Thea kissed the daylights out of him, which really wasn't very helpful when a hapless duke was spending the next little while in the saddle.

"Safe journey, Your Grace," she said, stepping back.

Somebody had patted the ducal bottom. Noah hadn't a clue who that might have been, but *he* patted the duchess's fundament, for the lads knew better than to gawk.

He mounted up, saluted with his crop, and let True lope down the driveway, but not before he caught the head lad smirking at him from the yard.

In truth, Noah didn't want to head for Town again, but his last will and testament needed revision, and such tedious tasks never saw to themselves. Then too, he had to invite his family out to Wellspring, and that meant taking personal notice of the state of Thea's brother.

When Noah had dispensed with the legal business,

he dropped in on Meech for tea and found his uncle not only in, but without other callers, which suited Noah perfectly.

Meech ordered the tea tray, shooed the butler off, and smiled a knowing and not entirely attractive smile.

"Is married life going well?"

Noah took a wing chair uninvited, for he technically owned the damned chair.

"Married life goes splendidly. You haven't acquired your customary dusting of summer sunshine. Didn't the Harting house party get you out into the fresh air?"

"Sometimes, the routine grows tedious," Meech said, pouring out for them both.

"You could hie out to Wellspring. You're always welcome." Meech was always family, anyway. Welcome in theory, at least.

"Wouldn't want to intrude." Meech passed Noah his tea, though when Noah took a sip, he found Meech had forgotten to sugar it. The oversight was unlike him. Meech was as comfortable being a host as he was being a guest, and Meech wasn't Henny Whitlow, to whom tea preferences were a detail.

"You're invited to intrude," Noah said, stirring in his sugar. "The duchess and I are having a family gathering, and I know a pair of little girls who will drag you bodily to the stables to show you their new ponies."

"Ponies for the girls?" Meech dumped a quantity of sugar into his own drink. "Aren't they a bit young for that?"

"Nini is two years older than I was when you and Papa first put me aboard Charger."

"That fat little miscreant? Haven't thought of him in

ages. Do they groom their beasts eight times a day, stuff them with apples, tell them all manner of nonsense?"

"Those girls are your family, Meech." Now Noah's tea was too sweet. "You should put in the occasional appearance for form's sake, and we'll have Harlan underfoot again soon too. You missed the wedding, and he has a new pony to show you as well."

Meech chose a biscuit from a Sevres bowl, biscuits being the only sustenance on the tray. "Harlan's been larking around in Surrey, hasn't he?"

"News travels, apparently."

"If a fellow his age is invited to be a guest at Greymoor's place, he tends to send around notes to his chums, because a little gloating is in order. One of Pemmie's nephews passed along the word."

Meech bit into his biscuit, crumbs sprinkling his cravat as he munched.

Pemmie had nephews on both sides of the family and both sides of the blanket, some as rackety as their uncle.

"The gloating tendency, Harlan gets from you," Noah said, though Harlan at least knew better than to scatter crumbs in the parlor. "Aren't you offering cakes and sandwiches and whatnot with your tea these days?"

Meech needed a wife, was the trouble, somebody to look after the hospitality and after Meech himself, who looked a bit peaky.

"You expect me to set out all that?" Meech scoffed. "When it's hotter than blazes? Even tea's a stretch in this weather."

Meech had a collection of porcelain teapots,

probably the only items he valued more highly than toothsome, willing chambermaids.

"Meecham, am I keeping you from an assignation, perhaps? You're twitchy, your cravat is wrinkled, and you haven't insulted me even once yet. A newly married man likes to know he can depend on some aspects of his life to remain reliably fixed—some uncles, that is."

Noah had only the one living.

Meech took a sip of his tea and set it aside. "How fares your duchess?"

Noah wanted desperately to brush the crumbs from his uncle's linen. The elderly could be untidy at table, and the very young, though Meech qualified as neither.

"So you're preoccupied with a woman," Noah muttered. "Well, best of luck with that. My duchess is settling in nicely. The girls adore her, and she is taking them in hand."

Meech had no reaction to that pronouncement, other than to fuss the crease of his trousers.

"They're to have governesses and dancing masters and piano lessons and heaven only knows what," Noah went on. "Seems to me they already know everything they need to know to go on in life."

Meech started on another biscuit. "Which would be?"

"How to read, write, and negotiate. How to sit a horse, and how to get along with each other. The rest will come from sheer curiosity."

Meech rose and rearranged the half-dozen gold snuffboxes displayed on his mantel. Noah was plagued by the notion that these had been parting gifts to Meech from fond inamoratas.

"Stuffing the female head with figures, ancient cultures, and foreign languages never struck me as useful," Meech said, opening a pearl-encrusted snuff-box and sniffing at it. "A bluestocking is a sad sight. Pemmie agrees with me."

"Come stay with us for a few days," Noah said, rising, because clearly Meech had no time to spare for ducal nephews. "We haven't all been together in an age, and your visit will make Thea feel welcome."

Noah tossed a written invitation onto the tea tray—Thea had made him write out half of them.

Meech went on to the next snuffbox—silver and lapis—rather than open the sealed epistle.

"I'll consult the schedule, Noah. Summer is a busy time when you're as much in demand as I am, and then too, one likes to head north well in advance of the hordes, or the best grouse moors will be taken."

"You can shoot birds at Wellspring, for God's sake," Noah said. "You must suit yourself, and we will muddle along with or without you."

"That you will."

Noah took his leave, unsatisfied with the exchange. Meech liked his victuals, and Meech liked a good gossip. Maybe he was pining for Henny Whitlow; maybe he was expecting a lady to discreetly call upon him. Maybe a lady awaited Meech in his very bedroom.

Noah had nearly reached the mews when a voice stopped him.

"Anselm."

"Pemberton." Noah extended a hand to the man who could have been his uncle's twin. "I left Meech brooding over his teapot and inventorying his snuffboxes. If you're expecting to linger, I don't think he'll be in the mood."

"He'll perk up when the sun drops," Pemberton said, handing his horse off to a groom. "I understand good wishes are in order. Felicitations on the nuptials and all that."

"My thanks," Noah said as True was led out. "Will you head north with Meech here directly?"

"Head north?" Pemberton paused, one riding glove on, one peeled off. "Gracious, no. Never did fancy alcohol and firearms mixed in any quantity. A bumper of nonsense, if you ask me, sitting about in the damp and fog just to scratch and reminisce with a bunch of fellows you can see in any ballroom. Then you have to eat the hapless fowl and pretend you're not picking buckshot from your teeth between courses."

"Excellent point," Noah said, snugging up True's girth. "See if you can't talk Meech into visiting out at Wellspring, then. You're welcome to tag along, but be warned my sisters will attend our gathering, and they're all in a delicate condition."

"The three of 'em?" Pemberton shuddered. "Thank you, but I will pass. Not that your sisters aren't lovely, but to see their husbands brought to billing and cooing in public… My bachelor constitution can't take it."

"One becomes inured," Noah said, though he rather looked forward to the day when he and his duchess added billing and cooing to their doting moments.

❧

The nightmare began as the reality had, with man-scents of bay rum, stale pipe smoke, and starched linen blended with the sweat resulting from a summer night's dancing.

And pressure, as a weight bore down on Thea's body. Male weight, followed by sounds, whispering, then grunting, and the sensation of Thea's nightgown being hiked up over her thighs.

"You just relax, my dear, this won't take but a lovely little moment."

Bed ropes creaking, while in Thea's mind, panic tried to beat away a touch of the poppy and an over-indulgence of punch.

*Wake up, for God's sake, wake up now!*

An intrusion, and discomfort, low in Thea's body, where a chaste woman wouldn't hurt. More weight, enough to bring her struggling to awareness.

*Scream, Thea, scream now!*

"Almost there, almost...stop that, my dear, unless you'd like a bit of the rougher..."

Thea had managed to thrash, and tried to wiggle aside, but he was big, and just as she'd perceived the true nature of his intent, she'd also recalled two ducal heirs were at that house party, and neither one would be brought to account should she scream.

Her hands were pinned on either side of her head as he began thrusting in earnest.

"Damn but you're wonderfully snug, my dear... God in heaven!" He went still, but Thea was too dazed to seize the moment, and then a dreadful sensation—his hand brushing gently over her fore-head. "My dear, you should have told me. I might have gone about things differently. Suppose you'd like me to finish now, eh?"

He began to move again, more slowly, almost carefully, and Thea didn't hurt so much now, not physically.

She cried in silence while he finished, and then he lay on her, panting, while her tears seeped into the pillow.

"I don't know why you chose me, my dear, and I'm honored and all that, but you know how the game is played from here, don't you? We bow and curtsy like perfect strangers over breakfast, and wish each other well?"

In the dark, his voice was barely above a whisper, but he sounded anxious.

Not panicked, not ashamed and horrified and all muddled.

"Get off me," Thea managed, though all she knew was that she'd just been ruined, and by a man she couldn't even properly see. Her breath was growing short, as if a pent-up scream were blocking her airway. She wanted to breathe, to shove him away, whoever he was, to get up and wash and wash and wash.

Though she had a very good notion who'd ruined her.

"I'll just be going then." He kissed her forehead, climbed off her, and then Thea was alone.

The only mercy in the entire five minutes had been the darkness. He hadn't been able to see her, and she hadn't been able to see him, though the scent and feel and sound and *shame* of what he'd done would plague her for years to come.

*Wake up, for God's sake, wake up now!*

As always, Thea couldn't wake up, not fast enough, not soon enough.

*Thea, Wife. Wake up, now, for the love of God.*

Nobody called Thea wife, or used her name in those gruff irascible tones except—

"Noah." Thea pitched into him hard, clinging to him like the welcome reality he was. In a shaft of moonshine, she caught the concern tightening the corners of his eyes, and wanted to weep with relief. "Husband."

"One hopes I'm not unexpected. I said I'd be back tonight." He'd already disrobed, for moonshine gilded bare, muscular shoulders, and Noah smelled of flowers and herbs, as if he'd recently completed his evening ablutions.

"I didn't sew you any loincloths." All Thea could think to say, an inanity. She was rewarded with the sensation of Noah chuckling as she stayed plastered against him.

"You were engaged in nocturnal larceny again." He shifted to his back, pulling her over him. "I gather you steal covers when you're thrashing with a nightmare." His hands started a slow pattern on her shoulders, and Thea's galloping heart began to calm.

"I'm prone to them. I'm sorry."

"You should be sorry. I suffer enough worries without you pounding on me in my sleep."

"Did I strike you?"

"A glancing blow."

Then a little silence, while Thea let the pleasure of Noah's hands on her back soothe her nerves.

She grew more comfortable, sprawled on him more loosely.

Noah was home. Her duke, her husband, her Noah was home. "How was Town?"

"What do you dream of?"

"You first."

"Town was hot," Noah said, for once obliging Thea without a show of stubbornness first. "My sisters send their regards, and James is forever in your debt, because the womenfolk were threatening to drag him to Brighton in lieu of the rural rounds, and one avoids Brighton when His Prinnyness is in residence."

"I've seen his Pavilion, or the unfinished version of it."

"His folly," Noah said, applying a slight, scrumptious pressure to Thea's neck. "I don't begrudge the man some beauty, or the nation, but too many soldiers have gone begging who didn't begrudge their country an arm or an eye."

"Hence you vote your seat."

"Hence, I do." He tugged the covers up over Thea's shoulders. "Now you, Thea. What troubles your sleep? Before you prevaricate, recall that I am your husband, to whom you must transfer title to all your woes and worries."

More and more, Noah's orders sounded like endearments. "I don't recall that as part of the vows, sir."

He snuggled her closer and spoke very near her ear. "Tell me, Wife. If it breathes fire and has scales, so much the better. The little girls will be so impressed when I vanquish this beast, they'll recall who I am and forget those blasted ponies."

Thea faced a decision, one that might cost her the hands so gently stroking her hair, the embrace keeping her snug and safe, the voice teasing and reassuring her in the darkness. Those were precious, and at that moment she needed them.

Needed *him*.

"It's hard to recall a dream when one wakes." Hard to forget a nightmare, though. "In the dream, I can't breathe, and I can't scream, and I can't make sense of what's afflicting me."

"Are you anxious over something? Does this family gathering truly oppress you?"

"It does not." The upcoming gathering hardly oppressed Thea, not like a house party among strangers would.

"You shudder, Wife, and give the lie to your words. Our gathering will be for a short span of days, and the young people will provide the entertainment for the curmudgeons."

"You aren't a curmudgeon."

"A certain part of my anatomy has come to its figurative feet to make that same point." Noah kissed Thea, and she was never so grateful to put his mouth to such use.

When Noah rolled them and rose above Thea to join their bodies, she was grateful for that too. Noah wasn't a faceless buffoon casually appropriating her virginity in the dark. He would never hurt her, never truly steal anything from her.

Much less rob Thea of the last gift a young woman in her circumstances had left to give.

"You've been deuced poor company all week,"
Pemberton said as he sank into a wing chair after a
long night at the opera. "Fetch a fellow a nightcap,
would you?"

Pemmie was still spry, while Meech's left hip had
begun to ache at the end of any day that involved
travel by horseback.

"I've been meaning to ask you," Pemmie went on,
"what was Anselm going on about?"

Meech poured them both bumpers of brandy,
and brought one to Pemberton before taking the
other chair.

"Anselm was going on about something?"

Noah wasn't given to rants and tantrums, something Meech rather liked about his nephew. The duke
was more of a pistols-at-dawn sort—which was not
likable at all.

"When I last came 'round"—Pemberton paused to
take a hefty swallow of his drink—"you told Anselm
we'd be heading north. I thought we'd agreed to avoid
grouse moors and the near occasion thereof."

"All those weapons, all that drink, and a paucity of
pretty women," Meech mused. "My brothers took
to it."

"Here's to your late brothers." Pemberton lifted
his glass a few inches. "Go if you want to. I'll bide
here in the south until you come home sneezing and
sporting chilblains."

Sometimes, Pemmie was not much of a friend.
"Giles?"

"Yes?"

"Sooner or later, somebody will put it about that

Anselm married used goods." Some idiot, of which Polite Society had an abundance, and they all tended to congregate at house parties. Meech was feeling idiotish himself.

Pemberton set down his drink. "Anselm did marry used goods. You might have warned him."

Oh, right. Excellent notion, if a tad on the mortally stupid side.

"I had virtually no notice of his plans, and Lady Thea—*Her Grace*—should have turned him down flat," Meech said. "The boy is too serious by half, and on the large side. Any earl's daughter should have been insulted at his offer. Anselm didn't court the lady, and he did court her charge."

"Maybe he was courting them both."

Pemmie could also be tiresome in the extreme.

"Noah wouldn't know how to court anybody, in truth," Meech said. "Brains he has, charm he does not."

Noah also had wealth and an overly refined sense of protectiveness toward those he esteemed.

Pemberton shifted in his chair, as if perhaps he too had a sore hip—or something. "Now Anselm has a wife to go with his brains and lack of charm. What would you have us do?"

*Pray.* "Head for the grouse moors and pack a hogshead of decent brandy."

"We can run," Pemberton said, getting up to poke at the fire. He knelt a trifle stiffly, which gratified Meech, even as it suggested running literally was a doomed plan. "Anselm is deucedly noticing at all the wrong times, Meech. You've been close to him and

Harlan for years, and now you'll hare off with no explanation? Simply take a notion to spend years on the Continent?"

"Anselm's new wife will keep him distracted," Meech said, not even tasting his drink. "Maybe she won't connect the puzzle pieces."

Pemberton rose, setting the poker back among the fireplace set. The whole lot threatened to upend in a noisy clatter, but Meech moved swiftly enough to catch them.

"The new duchess will connect all the puzzle pieces, Meech. She's a female, and she was in company with Besom and Bosom for her impressionable years. There was talk at the time, and that means people have at least speculated. Suppose the grouse moors will have to do."

Meech flopped back into his chair, his hip plaguing him like a guilty conscience. Thank God Pemmie was feeling reasonable.

"Grouse moors it is—for now. Whom do we know with a decent estate in Yorkshire, and a well-stocked cellar?"

# Nineteen

Enduring a house party as a companion run off her feet by two demanding older women had been hard on Thea. She'd hated dodging the winks and leers of the gentlemen—married, single, or in between—rising above the squabbles of the other servants and companions, and yet appearing as cheerful and relaxed as any invited guest. By the second day of her first house party, she'd known they were so much rural, social trouble.

Planning such an ordeal at Wellspring, and battling all the bad associations Thea had for them, was harder still. *This is family*, she kept telling herself, a chance to spend time with Nonie and Tims—hopefully with Tims too—and to get to know Noah's relations as well.

Meanwhile, the little girls were becoming increasingly distracted and querulous, Davies and Maryanne were similarly afflicted with bouts of flightiness and feuding, and Cook had decided her megrims were acting up with the summer heat.

"You need to take a break," His Grace decided one hot afternoon. "Come wading with me."

"Wading?" Thea slapped down her pen in the middle of revising the menus so the undercook could manage them if need be. "I have one hundred and twenty things to do, and you want me to come for a romp?"

The duke lounged in the doorway of her sitting room—how long had he been lurking there, and why?

"Not a romp, Thea, and I do not merely want it, I insist on it." He drew her to her feet by her wrist, and stopped only to pluck her oldest shawl from a hook in the back hallway.

In the kitchen, Anselm snagged a hamper with his free hand, provoking Thea to plant her feet and haul back against him.

"I am not a dray to be towed along at your whim, Your Grace."

The duke was the only person in the household who outranked Thea, which also made him the only permissible target for her temper.

"*Your Grace.*" He resumed his towing. "You forget whom you married, madam, so hard have you been working, and no, I did not marry a dray, but neither did I marry a drudge. Come along, for the sooner you humor me, the sooner you can get back to your fretting over the merits of peas compared to beans."

"Not peas or beans." Thea wanted to stomp her foot as her husband marched with her across the back terrace. "The *sauces*, you overbearing, inconsiderate, hopeless… Where are you taking me?"

"One usually wades in the stream," His Grace observed, not breaking stride but slowing. "As hot as it is, a particularly deep stream would do nicely."

Thea let Noah lead her along, because he was intent on his way, and she wasn't a complete simpleton. She *was* hot, tired, cranky, and resentful, and she'd cataloged at least twenty other bothered adjectives when her husband brought her around a clump of towering rhododendrons to a grassy embankment along the stream.

"Shoes off," he ordered, folding her cloak at one corner of the blankets already waiting for them.

"You planned this," Thea accused, dropping to her knees. "This was premeditated."

Why did that make her angrier? That Noah had planned to wreck her schedule, to frolic when the work piled up faster, no matter how early Thea rose or how late she retired?

"Do you suppose you're the only person in this marriage capable of forethought, Duchess? I did court you for at least three days."

A silence stretched, steamy, still, and fraught, the unpleasant droning of the insects marking the escalation of Thea's temper.

"You did not court me." She yanked off her half boots. "You waited three days between proposal and vows. That is not courting."

Noah fell silent, getting his own boots off, and in his lack of response, Thea's headlong tantrum paused for a deep breath.

For Noah, for her husband, *this* was courting. He'd had the hamper packed, he'd had the blankets spread, and he'd probably left orders not to disturb them for anything less than riots in the village.

"I don't recall this particular spot," Thea said. "We take the girls to the shallows closer to the stables."

"You do," Noah said, putting his boots and stockings off to the side, and starting on his neckcloth. "You might consider unbuttoning a bit, Wife. It's hot, in case you hadn't noticed."

"Unbuttoning."

"Because it's hotter than Vulcan's forge. There's lemonade in the hamper, which should be cold—it was kept in the springhouse this morning."

Noah had been plotting this outing for hours. Why hadn't he simply issued an invitation?

"What else have you stashed away in here?" Thea asked.

"Eye of newt and fairy wings," Noah said, stuffing his sleeve buttons in his pocket. "Have a look, why don't you? You missed luncheon and have to be peckish."

"Peckish." Thea tasted the word and found it such a bland description of her hunger, she nearly had to argue over even that. "I've been an utter virago."

Noah arranged his cravat neatly atop his boots. Thea would have bet her pin money he was trying not to smile.

"You may laugh," she said. "Sometimes laughter helps, and I might as well be entertaining. Oh, look, you had Cook put in some cold chicken and pickles and a salad of cold potatoes and buttered bread, and what have we here…" She went plundering through the hamper, her stomach growling, her mood improving.

Noah let her eat mostly in peace, interrupting only to feed her a pickle or two, or to snitch a bite of chicken from her.

Not thievery, Thea decided, but rather, Noah's version of *sharing*.

Interesting.

"Is this where we wade?" she asked.

"Always in a hurry," Noah chided, leaning back on his hands. "I'll put the food in the stream to stay cold. You will see about those buttons." He tidied up, and Thea had to admit he was right: the day was hotter than blazes, and their location quite, quite secluded. She'd reached around to undo some buttons at the back of her dress, when Noah dropped down behind her and brushed her fingers away.

"*Droit du* husband," he muttered, kissing her nape.

"I'm not exactly fresh," Thea said, pulling away, but Noah's busy fingers kept undoing buttons.

"Neither am I," Noah said. "But God in His wisdom has provided water, and you will find soap and towels in the bottom of the hamper. Come bathe with me." He pushed Thea's dress off her shoulders, and she realized he'd undone every blessed button. He next untied the shoulder bows of her chemise and pushed that down too.

"What a wise, kind husband you have, madam"— Noah pressed his lips to her shoulder—"to allow you to eschew your corset in such weather."

"Allow?" Whatever mood Noah was trying to create, it was passing Thea by. Doing up all those bows and hooks and buttons would take forever. "My husband orders, if at all possible, and all creation snaps to obey. Did you say there was soap in here?"

Thea retied her chemise, for she wasn't about to go in the water in a state of complete undress. When she sat back, soap in hand, Noah got to his feet behind her.

"Soap and towels," he said. "If you look hard enough you might also find your broomstick."

He brushed past her and sauntered to the water, not a stitch on him.

Thea gaped, soap, towels, mood, everything forgotten but the pagan glory of her naked spouse on a hot summer day. Noah had been working in the sun without his shirt, for his back, shoulders, and arms were tanned, and his legs and other southerly parts were not as dark. He must have known the spot he'd chosen for his swim, for he climbed onto a protruding boulder and dove into the water.

And stayed under for an inordinate amount of time. Thea was growing anxious when Noah's head broke the surface, dark hair sleeked back as he stroked toward the bank.

"It's cold," he said, "particularly a few feet below the surface. Might you toss me the soap?"

Thea brought it to him, crouching near the water on a wide, flat rock, and trailing her fingers across the surface.

"Come in, Wife," Noah said, treading water in the middle of the pool. "We'll save the servants having to haul our baths tonight, and you can resume fussing over the menus when you return in an hour."

Fussing. Thea was planning to graciously and economically feed, house, and entertain a small army for days, and the duke called it fussing.

"I concede the sense of your point, Anselm, except we'll be overheated and miserable again by tonight."

And the family gathering would still loom over Thea, as oppressive as the heat and darkness of a summer night.

Noah said nothing, but got to work on his ablutions, while Thea envied him his ease in the water. When he dunked to rinse, she slipped from her chemise.

Dressing over a wet chemise would be a trial, and she was sick to death of being hot and bothered. She dove off the same rock Noah had used, and bliss enveloped her as the cool water closed over her.

A short swim was a good idea. Not a well-timed idea, but wonderfully refreshing. When Thea broke the surface, Noah was lathering his hair in the shallows.

"One assumed you could swim," he observed. "You came off that rock like a sea otter in spring. Soap?"

"I'll paddle around for a bit," Thea said.

"Where did you learn to swim?"

"My mother taught me," Thea said, flipping to her back for a leisurely float. The sensation of the hot sun on the front of her, the cool water around her, and the hint of a breeze in between was delicious. "She had a cousin who drowned, and decided her children would know better. I don't fancy sea bathing, though."

"Damned lot of nonsense," Noah agreed. "At least in Brighton." He waded out to Thea and put the soap on her belly. "I'll leave you to your frolic, and even save you a tea cake or two if you'll join me on the blankets before you turn blue."

"Shoo," Thea said, relieved Noah wasn't turning up amorous just because they were alone, naked, and finally cool on a hot summer day.

And wet.

And alone.

With blankets nearby.

Thea watched Noah hoist himself up onto a rock, watched the undulation of his naked flanks, the power and grace in his horseman's thighs, saw his sex nested in dark, wet curls…

And promptly dunked herself down deep enough to reach the colder water. When she joined Noah on the blanket later, he was lying back, stark naked, one arm over his forehead. He tossed Thea a towel without getting up, and she made gestures in the direction of drying off.

"You truly do not want to get back into your clothes," Noah said, not opening his eyes. "You will remain in a state of undress because you are sane, not because you are a wicked, shameless, sinful hoyden."

"You are apparently a sane man," Thea retorted, stretching out beside him. "You were right about the deeper water being colder."

"A fellow learns these things."

Thea hiked up on one elbow, caught by something in his voice. A duke was one variety of *fellow*.

"Does that observation have significance?"

Noah opened one blue eye and lifted his forearm about two inches to peer at her, then closed his eye and replaced his arm.

"The cold helps," he said.

"With?"

"Christ in heaven, Wife." Noah sat up in one smooth, feline move, and instinct prompted Thea to do likewise. They were naked, and his tone was not…cordial. "You refuse every overture I can think to make, and for the life of me, I cannot name my transgression. Answer me something."

"Ask." Thea drew the towel to her and let it cover her breasts and sex while she dabbed at her damp skin.

"Did you not know how to dissemble on our wedding night, or were you determined to be honest with me?"

"Not know?" Thea wasn't sure what he was asking, but sensed that in her preoccupation with her own troubles, she'd lost track of her husband. She'd been too busy battling her own demons to recall that Noah was beset by devils of doubt Thea had helped unleash.

"Did you not know how to provide a replication of chastity?" he asked tightly. "A false replication."

"You have wondered about this?"

Did Noah suppose, when Thea was deciding between hydrangeas and roses for the dratted center-pieces, that she was instead pining for some old love? That she wrestled with happy memories rather than with a budget Noah had only glanced at?

"Any man would wonder at your motivations. You could easily have lied, and you didn't." Noah held Thea's gaze, his blue eyes guarded.

She abruptly wanted to toss him into his damned trysting pool. This blighted gathering was his idea, Thea was wearing herself to Bedlam over it, and now he wanted to revisit her past?

"When was I supposed to learn this courtesan's trick?" Thea asked, glaring at him. "Perhaps when I was fourteen, and Papa gave me such a nice compliment on my hair at dinner, then was dead by break-fast? Maybe I should have learned when I was sixteen, except Mama was such a wreck by then, I was too busy looking after my younger siblings as their de facto governess."

Thea had Noah's attention, which saved him a dunking at least.

"Maybe I should have acquired this sophistication when I was seventeen," Thea went on, "and out of mourning for what felt like the first time in ages, but alas for me, I went into service lest the trustees sell me off to some well-heeled lecher. Perhaps I should have acquired such lewd and useful information from my elderly employers? But no, you think I should have acquired it when I became some flaming strumpet taking her pleasure of one man after another. Surely, *then*, I might have learned such a basic trick."

"I didn't say any of that," Noah replied. His gaze had gone measuring, and Thea flinched back when he brushed his thumb along her cheekbone. "You've been upset lately, even in your dreams, Thea. I can't think why, and fear you have regrets about accepting my proposal."

Thea knocked Noah's hand away, because she hated, *hated* that she was crying in front of him again, and over nothing.

"There was one man, Noah, on one occasion, and it was…pathetic and fumbling and disgusting, do you hear me? That is the extent of my benighted experience, and of my regrets. I would not have lied to you about my chastity even if I'd known how, no more than you would have attempted the pretense of courting a woman you could not possibly be enamored of."

Noah regarded Thea steadily as the tears slipped

down her cheeks, then he took the towel from her, slowly winding it into his hands. When Thea sat naked, mortified, and hanging on to her anger for the sake of pride more than anything else, Noah draped the towel around her shoulders and assumed the place beside her.

Thea resisted the urge to fall upon him weeping, and that took effort, because Noah settled one long arm around her shoulders and tucked her closer. A day that had been oppressively hot now seemed chilly, and Noah's warmth had become necessary to Thea's continued ability to breathe.

"I apologize for having annoyed you," he said. "Now, tell me about these sauces that are vexing my duchess. I've a preference for anything made with butter, and have long believed garlic and leeks lack subtlety."

❧

"I have died, and all my tutors' predictions have come to pass," Grantley informed his pillow. "I am in hell."

"You look like hell," Noah observed as he opened the heavy drapes. "You smell like hell, and you probably feel like hell."

"My own personal demon genius." Grantley rolled into a ball. "Capable of speaking only profound truth."

"Up you go." Noah whacked him smartly on the backside with a riding crop. He'd come prepared, for Grantley responded to the crop—typical English schoolboy. "You've reparations to make."

"Haven't you a wife to keep you out of mischief?" Grantley rubbed his fundament and managed to sit up, hair sticking out in all directions, eyes bloodshot and ringed with shadows.

"My dear duchess needs her rest," Noah said, which was the truth, particularly lately. Thea might also need a respite from the company of her ham-handed duke. "You need to get back on the horse, so to speak."

"Was on him last night." Grantley studied his own bare feet. "He's probably in the mews, still under saddle. Unless somebody stole him. I shouldn't like that."

"He's enjoying his morning oats, or his noon oats," Noah said, tossing Grantley a dressing gown. "Your help is more honorable than you are."

"My help?"

"It now being July, and thus the third quarter, your help has resumed their posts in hopes of earning the occasional wage. Now, what have you to say for yourself, Grantley?"

Thea would be heartbroken to see her brother in such a condition, though she wouldn't like him sporting black eyes and a split lip any better.

*Ah, the frustrations of married life.*

"Myself?" Grantley scrubbed a hand over a thin, sallow face sporting an uneven crop of bristles. "Myself could use a little hair of the dog, or a lot of hair of the dog, but as myself's brother-in-law is once again impersonating God's Governess, I suppose I'd best wash and shave."

"You stood up your sister," Noah said quietly, the better to torment the damned, "and Thea can take that up with you, but you stood up *my* sister as well."

"Confusing," Grantley said, rising carefully, then

hanging on to the bedpost. "All these sisters. It's like this, Anselm, I either kept drinking, or I would have called the blighter out."

"Sit."

Grantley dropped like a brick back to the mattress, then looked green.

"Eyes open," Noah ordered, passing over the empty washbasin. Thanks to a merciful Deity, Grantley did not cast up his accounts.

"Now what is this talk about calling somebody out?" Noah used his older-brother-knows-all voice, with satisfying results.

"Eggerdon," Grantley said, setting the basin aside. "He kept insinuating my sister was not fit for a title, and if she must marry, then who better than a Winters, because whores will congregate on any corner, and so forth."

Old rage washed through Noah, and old regret, along with a bracing dose of new rage, for Thea had no part in the unfortunate Winters legacy.

"*So forth?*" Noah growled.

"So forth." Grantley started to nod, then apparently thought better of it. "Eggerdon's a crony of Hallowell's, and Hallowell was there too, I think."

"You didn't call anybody out?" Somebody needed calling out, badly.

"Drunk." Grantley waved a hand. "Even I know you don't call a man out when you're both in your cups. Not sporting, things said in the dregs, and so forth."

"No more so-forthing," Noah said as calmly as he could. His guts were churning, and not with anything as easily cured as an excess of gin. Thea's good name had been called into question, likely by Hallowell, who would have cheerfully taken advantage of her himself.

If Hallowell was behind this disrespect toward Thea, his accusations made little sense. Noah had watched Thea for most of the Season, and at every turn, her behavior had been exemplary. Propriety could be faked, but not decency.

Not goodness, and yet, on their wedding night, Noah had been disappointed in Thea. Shame tried to intrude on Noah's temper, but he hadn't time for it.

"You're removing to Wellspring come the week after next," Noah said.

"The country?" Grantley grimaced. "Don't think you have the authority to banish me, Anselm, though I likely deserve it."

"I'm not banishing you, I'm inviting you," Noah said, going to the corridor and bellowing for the bath just as two footmen wheeled it around the corner.

"Inviting me to what?" Grantley rose and ran a hand through his hair, which did nothing to tame it.

"A gathering to welcome your sister to the ducal family. Thea wasn't about to put up with a ball here in Town." Smart woman, the duchess. A ball in July would be stifling at best.

"Thea's stubborn."

"As am I," Noah said, appropriating the tea service from the maid who'd followed the footmen into the room. "We're having a family gathering, with a few acquaintances thrown in to even up the numbers. Your bath awaits."

With the ponderous dignity of the inebriated and

hurting, Grantley passed Noah the robe and lowered himself into the steaming water.

"Reprieve from my sentence," Grantley murmured. "How are the girls?"

A glimmer of gentlemanly instinct, at last. "You'll see Lady Antoinette later this afternoon when you take her driving in the park. You will travel out to Wellspring with her, James, and Patience. You weren't gambling these past few evenings, were you?"

"Don't believe I was." Grantley began to scrub. "Mostly drinking."

"And not calling out this Eggerdon person."

"He's a smarmy little blighter who usually has his nose—or some other part—up somebody's arse, knows all the gossip, but never has any coin. Smells of pomade and resentment."

"Younger son?"

"Of course." Grantley sank down to rinse, then rose back up. "I ran into your uncle too, I think."

"You're not sure?"

Grantley squinted at the soap. "I think he's the one who put me on my horse when Eggerdon started casting aspersions. I'm almost sure of it."

"Then you're in his debt," Noah said. "Time to shave. You've lollygagged long enough."

"The hell you say, Anselm. The water's still hot." Grantley's indignation was laughable, when he was wet, pale, the worse for drink, and sitting on his bare arse in a tub of bubbles. "My beard hasn't softened, and my valet isn't on hand."

"Your beard has barely sprouted," Noah said, pulling over a stool and rolling out Grantley's shaving kit.

"See to yourself, Grantley, and I might allow you a cup of tea."

"Serve you right if I cut my throat," Grantley muttered, but Noah held the mirror, and Grantley's hands shook only a little, so the job was passably done. When Grantley was dressed, dosed with strong tea, and more effectively impersonating a sentient human being, Noah dragged him to the library.

"You've staff on hand now and for the next few weeks," Noah said. "Summon Mrs. Wren."

Grantley looked nonplussed but intrigued as Noah laid out with Mrs. Wren a course of tasks for the maids and footmen, including a deal of cleaning, dusting, airing, and polishing.

"Now we get out the ledgers," Noah informed the earl.

"Ledgers?" Grantley ran a finger around his collar. "Hirschman sees to the ledgers."

"Hirschman is your man of all work," Noah chided. "He isn't your house steward. You don't pay him a house steward's wages, and a house steward doesn't get up in the dark of night to see to the horse you neglected. You look over Hirschman's work for two reasons: First, you might find an error, because every man can make a mistake. Second, you want him to know what he does for you matters, and your supervision is a way to do that."

"You don't mention he could be cheating." Grantley offered this, slouched in his chair across the desk from Noah, gaze roaming the room.

"He's a fool not to be," Noah countered. "You are a pigeon waiting to be plucked, Grantley, and then you'll have to marry for money, if anyone will have you. If you think Hirschman would cheat you, you should let him go."

"Without proof?"

"Would he cheat you?"

"Of course not." Grantley looked increasingly uncomfortable. "Mrs. Wren would bash him with her rolling pin."

"Grantley…" Noah flipped the ledger around and settled into the other chair. "I came into my title when I was still a minor. I mucked up the works, royally and often. Nobody expects you to be perfect, but neither will you be forgiven if you give up without a fight."

"Give up what?"

God help the boy, for Noah wasn't sure he could.

"Your honor." Noah pulled his chair closer to Grantley's, and pointed at the most recent ledger entry. "Who is this Harold person, and why did you spend your coin on him?"

An hour and a half later, Noah admitted to a grudging respect for Grantley's grasp of numbers. The earl's appreciation for household practicalities was sadly lacking, though his aptitude for accounting was excellent.

"You see the way of it now?" Noah asked. "At any point, you should be able to open this journal and know how much cash you have about."

"Like a bank does," Grantley said. "Not complicated, but who showed it to you?"

"The bookkeeping part of it, my tutor explained. He was a younger son, and they tend to take money seriously," Noah said, rising. "The legalities, my land stewards and solicitors imparted, and some of the rest of it, James's stepfather shared with us when we came down from university."

"The rest of it? There's more?"

"The don't-call-a-fellow-out-when-he's-drunk parts," Noah said. "Which mostly amounts to decency and common sense."

"Thea has common sense," Grantley observed, peering up at Noah owlishly. "She married you."

"And I married her," Noah said, withdrawing a vellum envelope. "That's your invitation, Grantley. See that you join us, and try to cut back on the drinking."

The gin would kill him, or lead him into deadly stupid situations. Thea would mourn, and she didn't deserve that.

Grantley got to his feet and walked with Noah toward the door, pausing before they left the privacy of the library.

"Why'd you come by, really, Anselm?"

Because Thea had asked this of Noah, once, weeks ago, when in all the weeks of their marriage she'd asked nothing for herself.

"You are family," Noah said. "That means I have an obligation to you, Grantley, but it also obligates you to others. Besides, you're free entertainment, and there's little enough of that in life."

Grantley opened his mouth, then shut it abruptly and smiled a smile that reminded Noah of something he hadn't seen in a while: Thea in a good mood.

# Twenty

THEA'S HUSBAND HAD RUN OFF AGAIN, OR SHE'D RUN him off. This time, he'd disappeared like a thief in the night—or the morning—stealing away before Thea had even risen. She had a vague memory of him kissing her cheek in the first gray light of day, but couldn't be sure it was from that morning or any of several other mornings.

Noah was put off by her moods; that much was obvious. They hadn't made love since he'd gone swimming with her days ago. Thea told herself she should be grateful he'd not pestered her.

Except it wasn't pestering from Noah, and she wasn't grateful.

He'd left her a note this time, claiming he'd be back before nightfall, but full dark had fallen, and despite preferring to feel neglected, what Thea felt was worried. Men with as much wealth and influence as the Duke of Anselm had enemies. They stepped on toes, inadvertently or otherwise, and ill will found them.

Thea set down her brush, and opened the music box she kept on her vanity. The little minuet had soothed her through the loss of her mother, her home, her virginity, and her innocence. It could soothe her into marriage as well.

"You should be in bed, madam."

Relief washed through Thea. "You've taken to lurking in doorways, Your Grace." She finished winding the key and set the music box down.

"What must I do to break you of the habit of Your Gracing your own wedded husband in the very privacy of our chambers?" Noah grumbled.

He ambled into the room, freshly shaven, his hair still damp, and Thea realized she'd been so lost in her brown study she hadn't heard him in his rooms. He was in a dressing gown and bare feet, and fatigue lurked around his eyes and his mouth.

"This is a pretty little tune," he said. "An old-fashioned waltz."

"More likely a minuet. The music box was my grandmother's and then my mother's."

The melody left Thea unaccountably weepy, for which she blamed her husband. She'd been worried about him, and he'd been not three doors away.

"You want to give this to our daughter?" he asked.

Yes. No. Thea still needed the music herself. "We have two daughters. I could not choose between them."

Noah came up behind Thea, put both hands on her shoulders, then wrapped his arms around her. "This upcoming gathering has you discommoded. Shall we cancel it?"

Thea rested her cheek on Noah's muscular forearm and let herself feel his warmth and strength. How had he known, and what should she say?

The truth, of course. She was getting better at trusting him with the truth. "I'll feel like a coward if we cancel it."

"Which would leave you worse than discommoded. I've checked with the staff. Your troops are in place, their orders in hand. The house is spotless, the invitations delivered, and all is in readiness. What is it that yet bothers you, Thea?"

The music wound down, and Noah twisted the key again while Thea fashioned an honest answer to his question.

"*I* am not in readiness."

"What can I do to help?"

Oh, damn him. Noah claimed to know nothing of wooing, and that was a lie. "You shouldn't have to help. Dukes don't help with house parties."

His embrace was gentle and absolutely safe. "Husbands do."

Good husbands. He was determined to make Thea cry. "You know this how, Anselm?"

"Sweetheart, shall we debate something of parliamentary importance so I can put a little fire into my defense, or shall we bat domestic shuttlecocks between us for the next week?"

Thea heard the weariness in Noah's voice, not only of the body, but also of the state she was in. She was weary of it too. Sick to her soul of it.

"I am…anxious."

"Scared, you mean," Noah said easily. "I was scared I'd have to shoot my horse."

Thea had been frightened he would too. "This is different."

Noah studied her in the mirror for a long time, wound up the music again, and drew her to her feet.

"May I have the honor?" In his dressing gown, he swept her a courtly bow, holding her hand high, as if they were at a grand ball.

"Noah, this is…" Silly. Ridiculous. Also precious.

He assumed the waltz position and slowly twirled Thea around the room. She was stiff at first, his folly was ill timed, and her mind was still stuck on nothing more than a few guests for a few days. Then Noah held her closer, the music slowed more, and thinking became less compelling.

"I haven't known quite how to go on with you lately," Noah said when they were merely swaying to the last few notes. "I had the great, profound, and brilliant insight on the way home from Town that perhaps I ought simply to ask."

Thea had come to associate lavender and roses with Noah, with a sense of homecoming, and he'd called Wellspring home.

"I wouldn't know how to answer."

Except Thea would, if she had the courage, know how to tell Noah she'd missed him in bed at night. Not only the marital relations—that was a whole different kind of complication. She'd missed *him*.

"Then let me make this simple for you, Thea: I'd like to sleep with my wife tonight. What would you like?"

What was Noah asking? What was he saying?

He shifted, as if to step back, and involuntarily, Thea's arms tightened around him.

His chin came down on her crown, and his hand splayed across the middle of her back.

"Can you find the words for me, Wife? My manly insecurities are at spring tide of late."

"Would you please stay with me tonight, Husband? I have…"

"Yes?"

"You want more?"

"I am a lot of duke to be wrestling insecurities on such a late and lonely night."

"I've missed you."

Noah didn't make her repeat it, for which Thea silently thanked him. Instead, he kissed her sweetly, at length, though he remained only moderately aroused. She kissed him back, trying to tell him she really had missed him, really, truly, even if she couldn't be gracious with the words.

When they went to bed, Noah loved Thea slowly, almost reverently, and then held her in the darkness, while Thea found the first decent rest she'd had in a week.

❧

"I am surrounded by shameless laggards," Noah announced as he stirred sugar into Thea's tea, took a sip, and passed her the remaining half cup. "And you." He glared at the cat. "Don't be eyeing the cream pitcher, shameless wench. Your figure is showing alarming signs of your weak morals, and you do not deserve cream."

"For God's sake, hush." This from Thea, who was clutching her teacup with bleary-eyed desperation.

"A sign of life, God be praised for His endless miracles."

"Now you think to offer prayers, Anselm. Pray silently until I've finished my tea."

Noah gave the cat a scratch under the chin and busied himself pouring a dish of cream and placing it on the hearth. Bathsheba washed her paws, her ears, and her whiskers before deigning to break her fast. By then, Noah had the second cup of tea ready, and cinnamon toast liberally buttered as well.

"You really ought to rest more, Wife." Noah had assayed a few exploratory caresses and provoked not even a sigh from his duchess.

"You *woke me up* to tell me I should rest more?"

Her Grace was speaking in complete sentences before the second cup of tea. Noah took encouragement from that.

"How else was the message to be conveyed," he asked, "when you sleep like the dead? We have business to conduct today."

"You have business." Thea accepted the second cup of tea, which was also not quite full. "I have a nattering magpie for a husband."

"Who has brought you a present from Town."

"Another horse?"

"Must you sound so hopeful?" Noah tore off a corner of toast, then passed Thea the rest. "My womenfolk are equipped with mounts. This is a present, just for you."

Thea was grouchy and slow about it, but Noah could tell he'd piqued her interest when she made short work of the toast and her third half cup of tea.

"I might sew you a loincloth if I like this present,"

she allowed as Noah did up the hooks at the back of her dress ten minutes later. "Or if I don't."

"Have some faith, Wife." Noah escorted his duchess through the house at a decorous pace, though their objective made him a trifle nervous.

For her part, Thea was getting better about coming along peaceably, or perhaps she was keeping her powder dry.

"Where are we going?" she asked.

"You'll see."

Noah led her down the stairs and out the back hallway, pausing only long enough to fling her old cloak over her shoulders, for the morning was blessedly cool. Out on the back terrace, a box sat on a chair, the box wrapped in decorative blue paper.

"Have you done something I won't like, Noah?"

"Many things," he said. "You make your displeasure evident when I transgress. This is a gift, Thea. A present, a token, from your husband to you."

"You are doting?"

Noah gave her credit for courage, and himself too. "I am doting shamelessly, and you will endure this hardship like the duchess I know you to be. Now open your gift, and I'll show you how to use it."

Thea eyed him dubiously, eyed the package just as carefully, and picked it up.

"Before noon, if you please," Noah said. "The day will grow too hot to gallop."

Thea shook the box, and sniffed it, and as Noah watched her, he gained a new appreciation for how reticent his wife had become regarding the joys of life.

"How long has it been since you had a present, Wife?"

"My husband gave me a lovely mare only a few weeks ago," she said, untying the ribbon around the package.

"Before that?"

"My music box, I suppose. We weren't much for presents, growing up, except at Yule, and those were either silly or practical."

Thea unwrapped a wooden box, and shot Noah a puzzled glance.

"Sweetheart, the box is not the present. The box holds the present, and I can assure you what's in there is neither noisome nor wiggly. If you don't like it, you can simply thank me for the thought and hit me over the head with the box."

For Thea's sake, Noah had kept his tone light, but his heart had begun to beat harder against his ribs, almost as if he were afraid, or very nervous.

"A knife?" Thea held up the elegant little dagger, and Noah was pleased to see it fit her hand beautifully. "A knife, and what's this? I don't think I've seen anything like this before."

Thea was...smiling, at Noah's gift, then at him. Not a smile he could parse. Perhaps she thought him daft.

"The blade is Italian," Noah said, because Thea apparently hadn't any more words for the occasion. "They take their weapons seriously, and their women too. You buckle the leather sheath about your leg under your skirts, if you don't want to tuck it into your bodice. Shall I show you?"

Thea nodded, saying nothing, and Noah wasn't sure

if she was humoring him, horrified beyond words, or maybe—God help her—pleased. She took the chair and daintily held her skirts up past the ankle. Noah reached the rest of the way and affixed her weapon snugly below her right knee.

"Nobody will know it's there, but you might want to get used to wearing it," Noah said, sitting back on his haunches. "I've tied it on the right leg, but you might prefer it on the left. It all depends on how easily you can unsheathe it."

Thea stared at him, an utterly unreadable stare that ought to be forbidden to any female bearing the status of wife.

"What made you do this, Husband?"

Noah studied Thea's hem, because he couldn't meet that stare. Whatever else was true about Thea's expression, her gaze held a desperation he'd never seen before, and a vulnerability he'd sensed even before they'd married.

Noah had *done this* because he could not abide that his duchess be either vulnerable or desperate.

"That regret you mentioned befell you at a house party, didn't it, Thea?"

She nodded once and turned her face away, and Noah was still at sea, wondering if he'd offended her, if he'd offended some rule of husbandly behavior no one had thought to tell him. He was already devising James's punishment for that sorry oversight when Thea's arms vised around his neck, and she pitched into him.

"Thank you. Thank you, Noah, thank you, thank you."

By sundown, Thea could throw the damned thing with deadly accuracy. At bedtime, she asked if Noah would mind if she slept with it under her pillow every night.

He assured her he would not.

❧

Noah looked his brother up and down, trying to pinpoint what exactly was wrong. "You're home a bit early."

"By one day," Harlan replied, leading his gelding into the stable yard.

"You can let the lads see to him," Noah said. "I'll not tattle to the great and wonderful Greymoor."

"Greymoor *is* wonderful," Harlan said, "or his riding is, and his countess knows how to keep her guests in victuals. She also introduced me to Heathgate, and to Moreland's heir."

"She's a conscientious hostess, or perhaps she enjoyed showing off her handsome young guest," Noah said, taking the reins from Harlan's hand and passing them to the waiting groom. "In truth, I am glad to see you, and not only out of fraternal sentiment."

Had Harlan filled out in the mere days he'd been gone? Grown taller too?

"What did you mean, Lady Greymoor was showing me off?"

The gelding was led away, swishing its tail against Harlan's side, an equine comment on the owner's mood, perhaps.

"I meant nothing," Noah said, walking off in the

direction of the house. The heat had driven his entire family daft. "You up for a quick swim?"

"No, thank you." Harlan's tone would have frozen the entire lake, complete with swans. "A bath will do. A tray in my room will suffice thereafter."

Harlan was a ducal heir, and for the first time, he sounded the part.

"You'll have to tell Thea your preferences," Noah said as they crossed into the garden. "Mind you tread lightly with my duchess. She's planning a house party, but you must not call it that."

"Where will I find her?"

Noah glared at the vast facade of his smallest country house. "Hell if I know. Raising Cain somewhere in there. You might ask the girls when you make your bow to them. They tend to keep watch over us all. But, Harlan?"

His brother stopped mid-charge for the back terrace. "Noah?"

"Whatever burr is under your saddle, I'd as soon you have it out with me now. Thea is struggling, and I'd spare her the family dramatics if I could."

Or perhaps Thea was practicing with her knife, which seemed to soothe her nerves.

"Dramatics." Harlan's dark brows, so like their father's, went crashing down. He looked like he wanted to say—or possibly bellow—a few unrefined sentiments, but he instead extracted a folded piece of foolscap from his waistcoat pocket.

"Perhaps this is dramatic enough for you." Harlan passed the paper to Noah and half turned, gaze on the distant paddocks.

*You are a harlot*, Noah read. *Your uncle is a harlot, and your brother married a harlot—or was that your father who married the harlot?*

Noah turned the note over and saw no identifying marks. He wanted to tear the paper into a thousand tiny pieces before setting fire to it and stuffing the ashes up somebody's...

"You received this while at Greymoor's?"

"One of the grooms said a fellow at the local posting inn asked him to pass it along to Greymoor's guest," Harlan said. His voice bore the studied casualness of the violently furious. "The note was folded and sealed, but had no franking, no address, and the groom didn't recognize the man who gave it to him."

Harlan's gaze remained on the far paddocks, a muscle twitching along his jaw.

"Could he describe that man?" Noah asked.

They were in a knot garden, a tidy arrangement of symmetrical green hedges and raked white stones, all of which Noah wanted to rip into permanent disarray.

"A town swell on a big bay horse," Harlan said. "This happened late in the evening, and I gather my postboy was in his cups."

"Probably chosen for being in his cups. How long ago did you receive this?"

"Three days. And, no, I did not mention it to Greymoor. He was my host, but this is...personal."

"Viciously so."

"You aren't asking why I'm referred to as a whore."

"You aren't a whore," Noah said, shoving the note into Harlan's outstretched hand.

"At school—"

Noah took a turn studying the peaceful acres beyond the garden. "Do you think I care what you did in the dormitories when the candles were doused and the door locked? There's a reason you had tutors until you were big enough to hold your own in a fight."

"It was my nickname, Noah," Harlan said, shoving him hard in the chest. "I was called Harlot."

Harlan's voice, which had changed more than a year ago, held a hint of youthful tremolo. Anger could do that to a young man, or heartbreak.

Despair dealt Noah a hard blow, for this was the Winters legacy. Foul names, anger, innuendo, and drama. He shook the despair away and applied his mind to the situation.

"Is that why you resembled the losing half of a prize fight for most of your first Michaelmas term?"

Harlan nodded, folding the note with shaking fingers.

Between Noah and the house lay the rose garden, most of which was past its prime and blown to thorny stems. Thea would see it all trimmed to tidiness before the first guest arrived.

"Christ in a boat, Harlan, I'm sorry."

"You dealt with it," Harlan said. "You came up to school, nosed about, and it stopped."

"Nobody told me," Noah said, though something had prompted him to look in on his brother. "My nickname was Flood, and I couldn't be seen around livestock without somebody making a lewd comment regarding long sea voyages and procreation."

Harlan gestured with the note. "What about the rest of it?"

The fighting? The juvenile politics, the teachers who turned a blind eye because a ducal heir could always benefit from a gratuitous beating?

"What *rest of it*?"

"Are you…" Harlan paced off, shoulders hunched, the gesture reminiscent of a child's defensiveness.

"Am I what? I am most assuredly not married to a harlot, and neither was our papa. Not at any point." Though as for Papa himself…

"That note implies something else."

Noah mentally revisited the words, a right proper rampage boiling up under his self-discipline.

"The note implies somebody wants to breathe their last facedown in grass and sheep shit one morning here directly," Noah said. "You feel this as an attack on you, Harlan, but it's an attack on the family—you, Meech, Thea, me, on all of us—and thus it's mine to resolve."

Preferably with violence, because this was a sneak attack on a woman who'd been defenseless prior to her marriage, and a boy not yet come into his majority.

"You can't blame somebody for commenting on the truth." Harlan's fists were clenched at his side, and his expression was…tormented. Purely, simply, tormented.

"What do you think this says?" Noah asked, snatching the note back. "It's malicious tripe, Harlan. A little fact mixed with a liberal portion of rumor and a greater portion of spite."

A very great portion of spite.

"Are you my father?"

"Your—*what*?"

"It says, 'or was it your father who married the harlot?' As if you might be my brother, or you might be my father. Which is it, Noah, and so help me, if you say you don't know…"

Harlan's expression said he'd cry or beat Noah half to death.

"I am your brother," Noah said calmly. "I am not your father. I could not be your father. Think, Harlan. You were born the twenty-third day of August. I would have been off at university the previous autumn, and not on hand for your conception."

"Mother might have visited you."

Harlan had apparently been tormenting himself with this possibility for days. Working out the details, lashing at his dignity, his sanity, his concept of himself. His mood now resembled the spent rose garden, all thorns and rotting blooms.

"Your mother was the last woman to bestir herself to travel," Noah replied. "Once Papa died, she'd barely leave the house, and received only family, the minister, her physician, or the solicitors. She did not hare up to Oxford to call on her stepson, for she was already several months gone with child."

Thus did a woman grieve the loss of her opportunity to become a duchess.

"So is Meech my father? Is that why it says Papa married a whore? Uncle is a whore?"

Harlan wasn't stupid, and he had more courage than Noah had given him credit for. "Why do you think that?"

"How many other fellows were visited at school by their uncle, almost every term?"

"I was," Noah said. "The same questions were asked, Meech gave the same wiggle of his eyebrows, and I felt the same urge to kill him slowly and painfully."

Noah had tried to forget those memories, but like briars, they'd dug into his mind all the deeper for his efforts to reject them. Was Thea haunted by similar memories, of events she'd been powerless to influence?

"He bothered you too?" Harlan asked.

"He and Pemmie sang the same idiot songs and flirted with the barmaids, and all I wanted to do was get back to my studies." Horticulture had appealed to Noah most strongly, and now he was doomed to revisit familiar history amid the peaceful back gardens on his favorite estate.

"Why is our family like this, Noah?" Harlan's question conveyed a wealth of pained bewilderment.

"I don't know." Noah moved along at Harlan's side when the boy began to walk toward the terrace, though Noah was torn between the desire to enfold his brother in a protective embrace and the temptation to get him drunk. "*My* family is not like this. Our father was, and Meech is, but you and I, Thea and the girls, we're not."

"What is the insult to Thea, then, that's she's a harlot too?"

"For God's perishing sake…" Noah kicked a loose pebble down the path, watching it skitter and bounce before coming to a stop against a pot of geraniums. "I can't quite promise you Meech isn't your father, but I will cheerfully kill him if he's allowed you to wonder about it all these years for no good reason."

"But Thea?"

Tenacity was a Winters trait Noah had prided himself on, more fool he. Gravel crunched beneath their boots, while out of some window or other, the little girls were likely watching this tormented progress toward the house.

"Thea has not confided details to me"—Noah hadn't *earned* her confidences, more like—"and I have not pried them from her. A single unfortunate incident colors her past. It apparently occurred where the meaner element of Polite Society was on hand to draw the inevitable conclusions. I tell you this in strictest familial confidence, and you are not to ask Meech about it, or James, or anybody."

How was it the house seemed miles, not yards, away?

"You didn't know this before you married her, Noah?"

Noah hadn't wanted to know it. "This happened years ago, Harlan, and I gather Thea's ignorance and innocence meant some charming bounder could take advantage of her."

Harlan looked puzzled, but Noah couldn't say more, because he didn't know any more himself. He'd hoped Thea might confide in him, for he'd been loath to raise the topic when it upset her so.

"Thea would be devastated by the contents of that note," Noah said, "for your sake and mine, but also on her own behalf. No hint of scandal has found her to this point, but somebody apparently resents her rise in the world bitterly."

"She won't learn of this note from me," Harlan said. "You'd call this fellow out, whoever he is?"

"In a bloody heartbeat. When this silly house party is over, we're going into Town and buying my duchess a handsome little pistol to carry in her reticule, and we're showing her how to use it. Then we'll explain bullwhips to her, and get her an archery set as well."

Harlan took the terrace steps two at a time. "Noah, what are you going on about?"

"Marital bliss, Harlan, wooing my duchess, and the kind of family we are now."

# Twenty-one

"COME, THEA." PATIENCE PATTED THE CUSHION BESIDE her. "Trust your people to do their jobs for twenty consecutive minutes, and let us interrogate you."

Patience traded a smile with her sisters that boded miserably for Thea's composure. This was exactly what Thea had wanted to avoid: the polite wielding of feminine daggers behind closed parlor doors, the condescending innuendo, the verbal elbow to the ribs over the tea service.

The thought of a dagger fortified Thea, reminding her of the blade strapped at her knee.

"Noah has kindly distracted the menfolk before dinner," Prudence pointed out, "so they might shriek and whoop and dunk each other and start on their libation, and we have civilized privacy for a cozy chat. Patience, shall you pour, or shall I?"

"Let me." Patience picked up the teapot when Thea would have reached for it. "Thea has talking to do. So tell us, Duchess, how is Noah coming along?"

"Noah?"

"You know him," Penelope said as she started

arranging tea cakes on plates. "Tall, dark, grouchy, unless you're his horse or a small child? You seem to have made some progress with that part of it."

"James said Noah reached for your hand when you greeted your first guest." Patience calmly poured the tea as she fired that Congreve rocket into a curious silence.

"I didn't notice," Thea said. "Noah's affectionate by nature, and one grows used to it." Except one didn't. *One* treasured each and every gesture, each manly insecurity and minor incident of doting.

"Heath is the same way," Penelope said. "Lately he's worse."

"Pats your tummy?" Prudence asked, her smile feline and knowing.

"Pats everywhere," Penelope said, putting a chocolate cake on each of four plates, "but perhaps we embarrass our hostess? Some husbands limit their affections to several nights a month, behind closed doors, with the candles out."

Patience passed Thea a cup of tea. "If Noah's being a dunderhead, we'll thrash him for you—gently, of course."

"Of course," Pen and Pru chorused and looked a little too happy, anticipating this *gentle* thrashing.

"Noah is…" Thea glanced from one face to another, seeing only sororal concern—for *her*. "Noah is patient, kind, and good-humored, and he steals my breakfast, and accuses me of felonies, and lends me his cat, and prays a lot, and I just d-don't know what to d-do…"

Patience shook her head, Prudence offered her

handkerchief, and Penelope wrapped an arm around Thea's shoulders.

"He's being a dunderhead," Penelope surmised. "Heath was no better, but he eventually found his way. Noah will too."

"What if *I'm* the one who can't find my way?" Thea wailed into her borrowed handkerchief. "What if I can't become the duchess Noah needs?"

The duchess he could trust and respect, the one he could ask anything and not cringe to hear the answer?

The sisters exchanged another look, this one more thoughtful. Penelope put three more chocolate cakes on Thea's plate, and the ladies settled in for a long listen. When Thea's eyes were finally dry, and nothing had been resolved except that Noah wasn't a dunderhead and he had lovely sisters, she suggested they look in on the little girls.

They found their quarry with Erikson, because the windows in his laboratory overlooked the driveway and stable yard. He'd scheduled a dissection of fragrant orchid to compete with the great excitement of company coming up the drive, and was succeeding modestly now that most of the guests were accounted for.

When the ladies joined him, he put down his knife.

"My laboratory is overrun with beauties." He greeted each sister with a kiss on the cheek, then had to kiss the little girls and Thea for good measure.

"We have to bury the flower," Nini announced. "Mr. Erikson says science should always be respectful."

"Then come." Thea held out a hand. "We were going for a walk among the flowers anyway. We can bury the orchid with its cousins in the back gardens."

"Evvie, c'mon!"

"We have to tell Maryanne and Davies where we're going," Evvie said, scrambling off her stool.

"I will tell the nursery maids," Erikson volunteered. "Here." He wrapped the flower's remains in a handkerchief, and passed it to Thea. "My thanks."

Prudence linked arms with Penelope when the ladies reached the back terrace, the little girls having already run ahead.

"Do you ever regret that you let him get away?" Prudence asked her younger sister.

"Erikson? Not now I don't." Penelope's look became wistful. "When it comes to kissing, he's a virtuoso, but as a husband? You'd always be competing with his beauties, and he'd talk longingly about protracted trips to faraway jungles and not even realize he was breaking your heart."

Thea was fascinated with these confidences, and kept her mouth shut accordingly.

"I suspect he knew," Penelope went on. "I think he gallantly indulged me in my first *tendresse*, kissed the hell out of me for a few weeks, and then said the very things necessary to let me get over him. He's a true gentleman."

Erikson had kissed the hell out of Penelope? *For weeks?*

"Or he truly respects the business end of Noah's bullwhip," Patience suggested. "Don't look so horrified, Thea. Noah likely knew of the entire business."

"Noah said Erikson gets lonely," Thea ventured. Did Noah grow lonely?

"I was stuck at home while Patience and Pru went larking about Bath with a cousin of our mother,"

Penelope said. "I was growing lonely, which is probably why Noah started inviting his friends' business associates out here for weekends, and so forth. Girls! You have to pick a spot with a bench nearby for when we pay our respects."

Penelope strode ahead, reminding Thea of Noah in both the authority of her voice and the way she moved.

"She'll make a wonderful mother," Thea said. "You all will make wonderful mothers."

"So will you," Patience replied. "You're bringing Noah along nicely, and these things tend to follow shortly in the ordinary course."

"With Noah, there's absolutely nothing short or ordinary about it."

The admission was out of Thea's mouth before she could stop the words, and a beat of silence followed, during which she wanted to disappear beneath the earth with the departed flower.

Patience started snickering, Prudence snorted, and before long, all three ladies were shrieking and whooping.

❧

"Our guests are in great good spirits," Noah said, passing Thea a cut-glass tumbler. "Your first dinner al fresco on the terrace was a rousing success, and Grantley was nearly delirious to provide Marliss an escort back to Town."

"Marliss is engaged," Thea said, taking a tiny sip of hazelnut liqueur, then getting to work on the pins in her hair.

"Thankfully not to me," Noah said, hanging up his jacket on the privacy screen. "I thought she'd be married by now."

The relief in his voice sounded genuine, as did the fatigue.

"The mothers-in-law are having too much fun planning the wedding, or so Marliss says. I think she's having second thoughts. She'll return for the ball next week. Perhaps she and Cowper will have set a date by then."

Earlier that day, Marliss had been very clear that she and the overly serious duke would never have suited. Noah *was* overly serious, when he wasn't teasing his cat, tickling the little girls, or thinking up insults for their ponies.

"Do you think Marliss regrets her rejection of me?" Noah's cravat followed his coat. "Too damned bad, my duchess has me in hand now."

Noah sounded pleased to be in his duchess's hands. Thea watched in the mirror as he moved around her room, grateful for his response, and for his presence.

"You don't wish even for a moment for a sweet young thing who waits patiently for your attentions?" Thea asked because the Duke of Anselm could have had any woman he wanted, and he'd chosen a lady fallen on hard times, without a fortune, without cachet, one far less virginal than he'd thought.

Noah paused with his cuffs undone and hanging over his wrists.

"I am content with my choice, madam," he said, stalking over to the vanity. "Are you content with yours?"

Noah had not left Thea's side for more than the requisite intervals with the fellows, and every member of the family was on their best behavior. He'd personally inspected every bouquet for Thea when she'd been too busy. He'd ordered her to take a nap and then carried her up to bed when she'd realized she was exhausted.

"I'm exceedingly *pleased* with my choice, Anselm."

His frown evaporated, replaced by a piratical smile. "Exceedingly, Wife? You will give me airs."

Thea's braid came slipping down over her shoulder. "To replace your manly vapors."

"Insecurities." Noah pulled his shirt off over his head. "Not vapors, for God's sake. Have you seen my cat? I fear the shameless baggage is getting ready to present us with more mouths to feed."

Thea loved how Noah could express abiding fondness for even a cat.

"She likely is, tomcats having insecurities too. I think Marliss does regret the loss of you in a way."

"Why?" Noah stepped behind the privacy screen, and Thea would have bet one of Sheba's kittens he'd emerge naked simply to afford his duchess the pleasure of beholding him unclothed.

Thea worked at the ribbon tied at the bottom of her braid. "Marliss knew you would be too much for her, but her young baron is likely by contrast not enough."

"Boredom is a terrible thing in a marriage." Noah was naked, his dressing gown in his hands. "Boredom fueled a lot of the nonsense in my parents' marriages. Meech said he was ready to howl at the end of the first month of his."

Meech, the lone family member to cry off the gathering.

The dratted knot in Thea's hair ribbon would not give. "We do not take your uncle Meech's standard as our guide."

"We've been married more than a month." Noah slid into his robe. "I howl occasionally, but not with boredom."

Such a naughty, lovely man. "Why haven't you exercised your conjugal rights lately, Husband?"

Noah looked up sharply. Thea caught the movement in the mirror as she slid the knotted ribbon off the end of her braid.

"Being around my sisters has made you forthright," Noah said, coming over to take the brush from Thea's hand.

"You don't sound surprised."

"My brothers-in-law are surpassingly, disgustingly happy in their marriages. I am beginning to sense why this might be."

Thea let Noah brush her hair—she'd missed having him do this for her, but hadn't thought to ask him. He was busy, and lately he came to bed later and later.

"They had the good sense to marry your sisters," Thea suggested, closing her eyes.

"Who are very forthright women. Do you want me in your bed, Thea? I come to you each night, and we cuddle up and talk a bit, but you never say what you want."

Thea opened her eyes, wondering what Noah was really asking.

"You never ask me to your bed," she said, because

she could tell her husband *almost* anything. "We've been married nearly two months, and I've never slept with my husband in his bed."

The brush stopped midstroke, and Thea was certain she'd offended him. That great expanse in the other room was the duke's bed, not their bed, and it wasn't as if Noah neglected—

He scooped Thea against his chest before her thought could complete itself.

"Get the doors," Noah said, pausing before Thea's dressing-room door. She lifted the latch, and the next, and the next, until she was flung—yes, flung—onto Noah's enormous raised four-poster.

He unbelted his robe and covered Thea with his naked body. "Wife, would you be so kind as to join me in my bed tonight?"

Thea didn't get to answer with words, only with her kisses, her body, her hands, her eager responses, and the way she fell directly asleep on Noah's chest after the lovemaking. She heard him get up in the middle of the night, thinking he was off to heed nature's call, but when he came back to bed, he pushed his hand under Thea's pillow, then wrapped her in his embrace.

Thea went exploring under the pillow, felt her little dagger there, and knew she'd fallen absolutely and irrevocably in love with her husband.

❧

"Corbett, you do not look at all well," Marliss observed, whisking her serviette onto her lap.

Corbett Hallowell crossed the breakfast parlor to

the sideboard and gestured at the serving maid to pour him a cup of a coffee. His bad luck, to have a sister who rose early, though at least his parents remained abed.

"Use that tone on your husband and see how well he tolerates it," Corbett said, though Marliss wasn't married yet, and perhaps never would be. The notion pleased him, for the expense of Marliss's damned Season was partly to blame for his troubles.

"Use that tone on your wife," Marliss shot back, "if a wife you can catch, and see what luck you have securing the succession. At least eat something, Corbett."

For that comment alone, Corbett would see that his sister did not speak her vows with Cowper. The baron was a fastidious sort, and none too bright, after all.

Corbett took a swallow of hot, strong coffee and nearly retched when it hit his empty belly.

"Corbett, do sit down. You're pale as a corpse, you look as if you haven't eaten for days, and I'll lose my own appetite if you loom over me much longer."

Corbett would lose any breakfast he attempted to ingest, though Marliss was right—he ought to eat something to help with the shakes.

He took a seat at the head of the table. "How was your visit with your friend, the new Duchess of Anselm?" Another swallow of coffee burned its way down his gullet, though it at least helped clear his head.

"Thea is quite happy with her duke," Marliss said, sipping her tea with the smug contentment of a woman whose schemes have come to fruition. "I believe Anselm is very happy with her as well."

Anselm wouldn't be very happy for long; nor would Thea Collins know much more contentment.

"Ever heard of a woman named Violette Cartier?" Corbett asked.

Marliss set her teacup down precisely in the center of its saucer. "Corbett, what sort of question is that? A proper lady doesn't admit knowledge of such creatures."

A proper sister just had, for dear Violette—Violet Carter, not too long ago—had once flown the flag of a paid companion, and had thus been an invaluable source of information about Anselm's new duchess.

A memory tried to swim up through the gin sloshing about in Corbett's brain, something about the damned duke.

"Toast, Corbett?" Marliss held the rack out to him, as if she really gave a hearty goddamn whether Corbett lived or died.

"No bloody thank you," Corbett said, foul language being one of a brother's most trusted means of aggravating an overly cheerful sister in the morning.

"No need to be mean," Marliss said, popping a strawberry in her mouth. "You'd best vacate Papa's chair too. He's been in quite a taking lately over your bills with the trades."

The encounter with Violette Cartier had been cheering in the extreme, and not that expensive. Weeks of lurking in clubs and gaming hells, listening for a shred of ill will toward Thea Collins had yielded nothing.

Corbett had been looking in the wrong places. His chance encounter with Henrietta Whitlow had reminded him of a pertinent fact. *Women* had the

worst tattle and were the most willing to share it. No
notions of honor troubled the fairer sex, bless their
avaricious little hearts.

Another swallow of coffee finished the cup. Corbett
rose, a bit unsteady from the night's activities. He
fumbled at his waist for his watch, then recalled he'd
lost it on a bet with Eggerdon.

A tattoo sounded in the hallway above the breakfast parlor, the ring of heels on hard wood hitting
Corbett's headache like so many gunshots. His satisfaction with the evening's work dimmed, because the
watch had belonged to some old dead viscount up the
family line, and Papa would be vexed that Corbett
had lost it.

Papa was always vexed, while Corbett's situation
was about to come right. A duchess with secrets was a
woman at risk for blackmail, after all.

"That's the maid with Mama's morning tray,"
Marliss said as the footsteps above faded. "Best hare
off, Corbett. If Mama's awake, Papa will be down
soon, and you do not want to provoke him with your
debts to Bond Street."

Debts. The word obliterated Corbett's good mood
like an ill-behaved dog scatters geese in the park.

"Anselm has my vowels." Eggerdon had passed that
news along sometime between the theater and the first
gaming hell. "Shite."

"Corbett, leave if you can't be civil. I'll have a tray
sent up."

He rose from his father's chair and headed for the
door, nearly catching the toe of his boot on the edge
of the carpet. He did not need the drama his parents

would ring down on his head in the next hour if they caught him below stairs.

Corbett did, however, need to think, to expand his plans for the Duke of sodding Anselm, and his blasted, damned duchess.

# Twenty-two

"THE NEW GOVERNESS IS DUTCH," ERIKSON SAID, A blush heating his ears. "Of course I prefer her influence on my little scientists to the nursery maids who are always making calf's eyes at strange men."

"Maryanne is the only one with a follower," Thea said. "She seems content to walk out with him."

"Frequently, and when she should be at her tasks," Erikson said. "Ask Davies about this, and you will be unhappy with the answer."

Very little could make Thea unhappy at the moment. She'd slept wonderfully in the ducal bed.

And in the ducal embrace.

"I won't ask them to peach on each other." Thea rose from her stool and set her teacup down. "We'll ask Miss Miller to begin her post as governess with the girls in September. I'll give her your direction so she can correspond with you regarding curriculum."

"Curriculum? Oh, certainly." Erikson was smiling a charming, bashful smile, one that reminded Thea he was a handsome man, and—thank you, Penelope—a virtuosic kisser.

Thea also smiled as she took her leave, and she had her own virtuosic kisser to thank for her good spirits. Noah had lectured and stomped and fumed and carried on as he'd stolen half her breakfast that morning, and the subject of his rant had been how much more sense it made for them to sleep in his bed.

Exclusively.

"Then I won't have to fetch that knife of yours from bed to bed, either," he'd finished. "You take my point, as it were?"

"Husband." Thea patted the spot beside her on the bed. "Come share my toast and my tea."

"That isn't an answer," Noah groused, but he'd come to bed, as she'd known he would.

Thea had put down her tea and looked him right in his gorgeous blue eyes. "I feel safer sleeping with you than I have at any time since I was a young girl too innocent to know better. There is nowhere else I'd like to sleep, ever again."

"You say that because I don't begrudge you your knife."

Thea moved the tea tray off her lap and took Noah's hand. "I say that because you had sense enough to get me the knife in the first place, and generosity enough to show me how to use it."

"Simple courtesy. Why are you keeping my tea from me?"

Oh, right. His *tea*. "You'll have my things moved in here. We'll share a dressing room?"

"Today, if you insist. My tea, if you please?"

"I insist," Thea said, passing the half cup remaining but keeping Noah's hand wrapped in hers too.

They held hands frequently after that, though Thea would not have said it was a conscious choice—it just seemed to happen, when they strolled the gardens with their guests before dinner; when they walked out to the stables early in the morning; when they visited the little girls in the afternoons.

None of the guests remarked it—they were too busy holding hands with their own spouses.

❧

The family gathering was going well, and as far as Noah was concerned, the nights were going *splendidly*.

Nonetheless, when the time came to gather with the menfolk after dinner, Noah nearly tossed the decanter to James, told him to get them all drunk, and bounced up the stairs to see if the duchess was properly ensconced in their bedroom.

*Theirs.* Where Thea had all but devoured Noah last night, and that was after he'd made a proper showing himself, and let her drift off to sleep. He'd fetched her knife on a whim, and Thea had swived him silly in response.

Noah had never—not once in years and years of enjoying the privileges of his age and station—been shown that degree of tenderness, caring, and fire in a sexual interlude. That one encounter with his duchess explained the mysterious looks passing between Noah's sisters and their husbands, and probably a few mysteries more profound than that.

Like civilization, happiness on earth, and faith in a hereafter.

James, Noah concluded, knew nothing. Wives were

complicated as hell, but the business of keeping them safe meant a lot to Thea, and Noah comprehended at least that much.

Which was why Noah had asked Harlan to bring the confounded note to the library after dinner.

"Gentlemen," Noah began, "now that you have your libation, lend me thine ears, assuming they still function after all the chattering at dinner."

They were seven, Erikson having been included, and with the exception of Grantley, Noah would have trusted any man there to guard his back. This was more serious, though.

"There's a snake in my paradise, gentlemen. Harlan, you have the floor."

Harlan had argued for this meeting, so Noah let him get down to business.

"*You are a harlot,*" Harlan read. "*Your uncle is a harlot, and your brother has married a harlot—or was that your father who married the harlot?*"

Silence, not a drink was lifted, for Harlan had captured everybody's attention.

"This note was delivered anonymously to me when I visited to the west," Harlan said. "Noah regards it as a slap of the glove to the family honor. I agree."

"You said Thea's a harlot?" Grantley's voice was thoughtful, not angry. "Same thing Eggerdon said, best I can recall."

"Meech should hear this," James suggested. Heath and Wilson nodded in agreement. "You're conferring with us for a reason, aren't you, Anselm?"

"Somebody is trying to let me know he's angry," Noah said, "but he's not honorable enough to simply take out a notice in the *Times*. Angry men do stupid things, and if he's angry at me, he might strike at Thea, or the children, or any of you."

"Or our wives," Heath concluded. "Any idea who is in need of killing, and are we convinced it's a man?"

"A lesson in manners, in any case," Wilson seconded. "Preferably involving lots of privacy."

"I can't point any fingers," Noah said, "but Pemberton comes to mind. He knows our family history intimately, though what his motive would be, I cannot say. One of Grantley's familiars insulted Thea recently when in his cups, and Thea was not treated kindly by her former employer's son. None of them have a clear motive for slandering a duchess, however."

"Giles Pemberton has no motive beyond the next soiree, weekend party, or ride in the park," Wilson said.

Wilson was the quiet one, the one who watched and sipped his drink and casually amassed an indecent fortune based on what crossing sweepers, flower girls, and drovers told him and his minions, season by season.

"I'm inclined to agree," Heath said. "Pemberton seems like nothing more than a harmless, aging lay-about waiting for his uncle to cock up his toes."

"Who would resent the addition of the duchess to your family?" Erikson asked. "Both insults included her."

"Our resident scientist asks a good question," James said. "I think any lady who had her hopeful eye on the Duke of Anselm's suit might wish Thea ill. You had a list of prospective duchesses, didn't you, Anselm?"

"You know I did." Noah had the grace to feel chagrined. A list, for God's sake. Thea would despair of him. "My sisters each picked out four young ladies. I culled the list to six total and had them investigated. That left three, whom I stood up with a few times before settling on Marliss."

A faultlessly rational and utterly stupid process.

"Who knew of the list?" Grantley asked. "I'm out and about quite a bit among the men who are standing up with the current crop of young ladies, and I heard nothing of it."

"Maybe only the ladies knew," Harlan suggested. "They can keep some things to themselves."

"You're suggesting our enemy is female?" Noah found the notion profoundly disconcerting. "That won't do. One can't call a female out, or deliver her a proper thrashing."

"Harlan has a point," James said. "The indirection, the use of a faceless intermediary, the reference to all the gossip Meech has provoked. That speaks to me of a lady who won't show her hand, a female mind."

"Not female, devious," Wilson temporized. "A powerless mind, and scheming but lazy."

"I don't expect answers tonight," Noah said. James and Wilson could argue prodigiously once they got started. "I simply wanted to alert you all to keep your ears open and your womenfolk in plain sight."

"Hear, hear." Heath held up a glass, and Erikson finished his entire drink.

"I don't like this," Erikson said, setting his glass on the sideboard. "You should tell your footmen, gardeners, and grooms, warn the housemaids of strangers who seek to flatter them in the market while asking about you or your duchess."

"Those are good suggestions, Erikson," James said. "I second them."

"I am surrounded by nannies." Noah tipped his chin toward James. "Heckendorn's on the nest. You, Erikson, have no excuse."

"I am rational," Erikson said. "A man of science, and I suggest only prudent precautions. You have treasures here, Anselm. Treasures you can't replace with coin."

He bowed with Continental flourish and left.

"Listen to him," James said when the room began to buzz with several conversations at once. "You've said your wife has a past, and maybe it's her past dredging up this ill will."

"You're saying I ought to interrogate her on the subject of enemies, my wife of less than three months?"

"Not enemies," James said, softly. "Safety. Speak to her of safety."

❧

Three long days later, Noah found his wife out behind the stables, where she usually was when the other ladies were taking an afternoon nap. The little dagger hit the post so hard the handle vibrated, but Thea wasn't smiling.

"I could get you a set of them," Noah said, standing at her shoulder, "so you could toss a half dozen before you had to retrieve them from your target."

"I'd walk funny, with three knives strapped to each knee," Thea said, and from her tone, she was serious.

"Besides, each knife would feel different. I'd rather practice six times as often with only the one."

Noah slipped an arm around Thea's waist. "With a knife, you have to make the first throw count, rather like marriage."

Barn swallows were flitting in and out of the stables' cupola with an industry that suggested nestlings awaited them.

"Interesting analogy," Thea said.

"You might like a bullwhip." Noah kept his arm around her lest she go stomping off to inspect bouquets or something of equally earthshaking importance. "You can lay about with it and not lose it to your target."

"I might like that." And still, Thea wasn't joking.

"Have you practiced enough?" Noah slid his hand down Thea's arm to lace his fingers with hers. A soft breeze whispered through the nearby oaks, while horses in the adjoining pasture swished at flies and dozed. "I've hardly seen you these past days, so busy do our guests keep us."

"It's going well, though, isn't it?" Thea brushed a strand of hair back with her free wrist, but Noah saw the worry in her eyes, the uncertainty. "We're half done with this gathering, and so far, no great mishaps."

The breeze stirred the lock of hair Thea had just put to rights.

"You don't consider Harlan's friends making calf eyes at Patience's lady's maid a mishap?"

"She's making them right back, but, yes, that worried me."

"Because?"

Again, Thea swiped at the errant lock of hair. "Because the maids and companions and governesses and younger sons at these infernal gatherings can create a host of mischief."

She sheathed her knife, giving Noah a mouthwatering glimpse of knee and calf.

"You were a companion for years," he said. "You would know."

A shadow clouded Thea's eyes, and Noah knew the urge to howl—or ruck up her skirts and rut. Thea had fallen into bed exhausted for the past few nights, and he hadn't had the heart to wake her.

And now, the day was lovely, peaceful, and perfect for a leisurely marital nap.

"Shouldn't the men be doing something with you while the ladies are resting?" Thea asked.

Thea's innocence was exceeded only by her testiness of late. "The men *are* doing something, at least my brothers-in-law are, while the ladies are resting."

Thea dropped Noah's hand. "Your sisters suggest otherwise."

Being married to Thea became more interesting by the day.

"What do my sisters suggest?" If a brother-in-law strayed, Noah would have to thrash him, at least. Marriages were private, of course, he understood that now as he hadn't previously, but the man who cheated on a sister of Noah's wasn't deserving of privacy.

A duke was a logical creature.

"Patience and Pen both complained that they were feeling neglected because their spouses were so considerate of their conditions," Thea said.

"While Wilson, the quiet one, provokes no complaints," Noah said. "Regardless what that lot is doing with their privacy, Thea, haven't you felt a need to go to our rooms and shut out the world for a bit?"

"You mean, reading or doing embroidery?"

"No, I do not."

She twitched her skirts, though the outline of the sheath for her knife was apparent upon close inspection.

"I am not much of one for contemplative prayer, Husband."

"Come with me, and I'll show you what I contemplate." Noah didn't leer, and he didn't wiggle his eyebrows, because he wasn't teasing.

"Of course." Then Thea's chin came up, as if she were being called upon to recite. "I have neglected you, and your manly whatevers are probably in evidence."

"My manly something."

But try as Noah might, kiss and fondle and caress as he might, when he got Thea to their bed, her preoccupation with menus and maids and the ball at the end of the week came with them. Noah lay beside her, his breeding organs singing a dirge to marital consideration.

"What's wrong?" Thea was up on her elbow, regarding Noah worriedly

Naked in the light of day, but worried.

"Come here, Wife." Noah curled an arm around her and dragged her over his chest. "Nothing is wrong, except my duchess is beset with worries. I've told you those belong to me now, haven't I?"

"Then to whom do your worries belong?"

"You'd like an even trade?" Already Thea bargained like a Winters. Noah searched out the pins in her hair, withdrawing them carefully one by one. "I'll trade you a worry for a worry. You go first."

"This is…not how I thought you'd want to spend this hour."

Perhaps Thea had expected Noah to make another round watering the bouquets.

"We have until tea," he said, "and I have few worries. Quit stalling."

"I am worried about this follower of Maryanne's."

That surprised Noah, because maids would have followers, the smart ones, anyway.

"Shall I forbid her to see him?" he asked. "I should think her spirits would be raised by the occasional flirtation."

Thea rested her forehead against Noah's chest, which let him continue his quest for the roughly four hundred pins in her hair.

"Erikson is right," Thea murmured. "He says Maryanne is not attending to her charges as she should, and Davies says the man is wellborn. A wellborn man won't marry a mere nursery maid, Noah."

"We don't know that," Noah said. Wellborn could mean some squire's son had taken an interest in her. "You aren't primarily worried for Maryanne, are you? She's a grown woman and knows what's what."

"Nobody knows what's what when they become enamored of another." Thea said this with some acerbity, and Noah wanted to ask who had taught her about infatuation and losing track of one's common sense.

"You're worried about the girls," Noah said instead. "You're worried this swain will spirit Maryanne off to holy matrimony, and while you'd be happy for the maid, you'd worry for the girls, who are attached to her."

Noah had demolished Thea's coiffure, so he started unraveling her braids.

"What you say is true, Noah. Maybe more true than I realized."

The duchess had admitted her duke was right. Dukes didn't gloat—out loud.

"Maryanne is a local girl," Noah said. "She'll want the banns cried and a fuss made and so forth. We'll encourage her to remain at her post until the new governess is settled in, by which time one maid will suffice in any case."

"How will we encourage her not to leave before then?"

Noah would simply order—

He was a *married* duke. He knew better now. "We'll ensure her compliance with our preferred schedule through a wedding present, Wife, for Maryanne has no one to dower her. My turn to share a worry with you."

Perhaps Noah's imagination was overly optimistic, but against his chest, Thea felt more relaxed.

"Will this worry involve your manly whatevers?" she murmured.

"Alas for me, my manliness is fatigued by a host's duties these days. This worry has to do with my duchess."

"Her."

And without planning to, Noah launched into a description of Harlan's note. He left out mention of Eggerdon's attempt to provoke Grantley, because that might be unrelated and truly the product of inebriated young manhood at its most stupid.

Or not.

"Who might wish to sully your reputation, Wife? Were other women pining for me of whom I took no notice?"

"Of course." Thea was clearly worried all over again, which had not been Noah's intent.

"I can hear you thinking." Noah could, almost, hear Thea's heart beating right next to his own.

"Three or four ladies cast Marliss envious looks," Thea said, "and went off in corners to whisper and start spiteful rumors. I made sure Marliss's mama knew about them, and the viscountess took countermeasures."

Thea's hair was the softest thing Noah had ever rubbed against his cheek. Softer than Sheba and more fragrant.

"The warfare of women never ceases to amaze me," he said.

"Don't discount it, Noah. I stumbled into the crosshairs of another lady's companion, for what trespass I know not, and it led to my ruin."

"Tell me." More a request than an order, Noah assured himself. Besides, Thea was not ruined; she was the Duchess of Anselm.

The topic of her misfortune was a digression, but Noah needed to understand Thea's past, and this way, this casual-aside way, was likely the only means he'd find of prying the truth from her.

"A woman, another companion, took me into dislike," Thea said, drawing a pattern on Noah's chest with her fingertip. "She convinced a gentleman to go to my room after everybody, including myself, had gone to sleep."

"To commit rape on a whim?" Putting the question civilly when Noah wanted to commit multiple acts of violence took every scintilla of his self-restraint.

"The man wouldn't have known I was unwilling," Thea said. "This is conjecture on my part, and the other woman probably thought I'd merely create a mortifying scene, turning a man away from my door."

Noah waited. There was more to the story, but would Thea entrust the whole of it to him?

"I wasn't awake to create any sort of scene, and apparently no one saw him come to my room," she said softly. "And for that I was thankful. I'd gone to bed with a headache, probably from too many glasses of wine punch, and when I couldn't fall asleep, I took a few drops of laudanum. When I awoke, it was dark, and I did not grasp the situation quickly enough to prevent what happened. The man who came to my room treated me to glances of abject pity the next day when he acknowledged me at all."

Noah held his wife in his arms, wanting to destroy those who had hurt her and wanting to protect her from all harm.

Also wanting to thank her for trusting him with this piece of a sordid and sad puzzle.

For long moments, he stroked his hands over Thea's hair, her back, and shoulders. The breeze lifted the curtain, and a fat bumblebee landed on the windowsill.

"Now I have another worry." Thea's voice was calm, and that reassured Noah, but when he recalled the conclusions he'd jumped to on their wedding night, he knew the urge to do violence to himself.

"Tell me this worry, dear Wife, for I have title to it as well. This is nothing less than the law of the land."

"I'm worried now, that my husband will think me stupid," Thea said, "for not locking my door, not foreseeing my own ruin in another woman's spite, for taking even a drop of laudanum in such circumstances or a single glass of wine. For not understanding what was happening until it was too late."

Thea was weeping, but she'd been so stealthy about her tears, Noah knew she cried only because of the wetness on his chest.

"Your husband—" He had to start again, because something had caught in his throat. "Your husband thinks you were brave beyond telling to suffer this assault without doing violence to those who deserved your wrath. He thinks you might have lost your reason, were you a weaker person, and gone into a protracted decline. He holds your resilience, your wits, and your fortitude in highest esteem, Araminthea, and he vows to never allow another to harm you thus. *Never.*"

The tears came more freely then, until Thea was boneless and spent on Noah's chest. He'd passed her a handkerchief at some point, and she'd fallen asleep with it still tucked in her fist. Carefully, he extracted the white linen from her grip and dabbed at his own cheeks.

When Thea rose some time later, she offered Noah a tentative smile, and he kissed her nose. After they'd helped each other dress, they went down to tea, hand in hand.

❧

"Now you're *not* going north?" Giles Pemberton's handsome features showed confusion and irritation by the light of the rising moon.

"Now I can't go north," Meech said. "Things are becoming too complicated."

"You're making them too complicated."

"Walk with me, Giles."

They moved off, through the flowers and moon shadows of Meech's back garden, and away from the ears and eyes of servants.

"All those years ago," Meech said, "when there was that awful little contretemps at Amberson's house party, people took note."

"There was nothing to take note of," Pemberton said, sinking down onto a bench. "Just the usual nonsense and the usual gossip."

How easily Pemmie ignored looming tragedy. How did he think Meech afforded this lovely house, and the servants who tended the garden?

"People saw Joanna Newcomer damn near plant me a facer in the conservatory," Meech said, taking the place next to Pemberton. "Annabelle Handley wasn't much more subtle."

The help would have gossiped too, all the maids, companions, footmen, and valets. The help always gossiped and was occasionally paid to gossip in the right ears. Then, too, the Carter woman had created far more mischief than even she could have foreseen, and she was still very much in the pockets—or beds—of several notorious club gossips.

Pemberton snapped off a late rose and tucked it into his lapel. "So we can admit to staring down somebody's bodice a little too long, or flirting too obviously with somebody's wife. Typical harmless nonsense. No one should think anything of it."

Meech was not a violent man—though he'd been a violent young man. Right now, he wanted to plant Pemmie the facer Joanna Newcomer had denied herself.

"Nothing of any moment—until Noah is issuing challenges at twenty paces," Meech said. "Then nobody will forget we left the party a week early, nor will they forget who was companion to Besom and Bosom all those summers ago."

The barest zephyr of gossip had come to Meech. On the winds of malice, that breeze, particularly when it wafted near the duchess's own brother, could blow a spark of bad fortune into a conflagration of scandal.

"If the duchess has any sense, she'll let sleeping dogs lie," Pemberton said. "They've been married for weeks, and we've yet to recruit seconds."

"Giles…" Meech scrubbed a hand over his face and thought of Janine and Evelyn, whose ponies Meech would likely never admire. "You know how much your company means to me."

Pemberton was off the bench, hands jammed in his pockets. "You'll turn up sentimental after all these years, Meecham?"

"Some things need to be said." Meech rose as well. "There needs to be a journey north, and perhaps even to the Continent, but first I should explain the situation to my nephew."

"Meech, you insist on making issues where there are none," Pemberton said. But his gaze slid away, like the small creatures who kept to the moon shadows.

"What do you know, Giles?" Meech crossed the walkway to stop Pemmie from sidling off to the mews. "You know something, and you're being reticent, and I would allow you your privacy, but my situation is in enough jeopardy as it is. I depend on my nephew for every last groat, which means you benefit from his generosity too."

"It's nothing," Pemberton said, turning away. "Nothing of any import whatsoever."

Meech resumed his seat on the bench, for he had the sense that his knees might turn up unreliable in the immediate future.

"No more posturing, Pemmie. Out with it, and we'll deal with it, the same as we've dealt with everything."

But as Pemberton gradually admitted what he'd overheard, Meech knew this situation was one they wouldn't deal with easily.

# Twenty-three

"WE'LL PRACTICE THEN," NOAH SAID, NUZZLING HIS wife's neck. "I recall leading you out at Moreland's ball when I was squiring Marliss about. You're a fine dancer."

"That was an allemande," Thea wailed, pulling from his embrace. "A slow, stately old dance my grandmother would have managed, particularly with you as her partner."

"I know you can waltz, Thea." Noah regarded her in puzzlement, because the more she told him of her past, the more successfully her little family gathering proceeded, the more nervous she became.

And the less interested in him, even when, as now, they shared the privacy of Thea's former bedroom.

"So waltz with me now," Noah said, holding out his hand. "We have only to start the dancing, and participate in the supper waltz. We'll be forgiven for sitting out the rest of the evening, because we're host and hostess."

"We haven't music."

"We'll have James play for us."

The look Thea gave Noah was for a very foolish duke, or a husband whose cajolery was falling utterly flat.

"James is with his wife, Noah. You can't interrupt their rest."

"You are being very contrary, my dear."

Her shoulders slumped, and Noah knew profound relief. They hadn't had a real row yet, and he didn't want one now, not with family lurking in every corner, and Thea feeling exhausted and uncertain.

She seemed to want a fight, though.

Noah stored that insight away in some new, husbandly part of his brain, and went to Thea's music box, the sole remaining evidence that she'd ever inhabited the room.

"Just a few turns around the room," he said. "Then we can find our bed and settle our nerves. How would that be?" He wound the mechanism rather than see her fret over even this, but something about the action of the little screw wasn't right.

"What ails this thing?" He opened the lid to see… nothing. The entire guts of the music box were missing, simply not there.

"What is it?" Thea came over to peer at her music box. "It's…empty?"

"So it is."

"Who would do this?" Thea backed away, as if Noah held a rocket with a lit fuse. "Who would destroy my only keepsake?"

"It might be a prank," Noah said, but he felt as if his own vitals were missing as he stared at the pretty, empty box. "One of the maids might have broken it and hoped you didn't notice for some time."

"Somebody had to be in here," Thea said, looking around her sitting room. "Somebody came in here and broke it. The mechanism was screwed to the box, Noah. This was deliberate."

Noah examined the maple wood box, particularly the underside, and saw tiny scorings, where somebody had inexpertly loosened the screws that held the mechanism in place.

"From now on," Noah said, "I want you to avoid this room unless I'm with you, or someone from the family."

"Because you don't think I'm safe here," Thea concluded. She crossed back to him, took the empty music box from him, and slipped an arm around his waist. "We'll say nothing about this."

"I do think you're safe," Noah replied, "because a clumsy housemaid is hardly a threat, but your approach is probably wisest. We'll watch for whoever seems intent on catching our reaction."

"Just so," Thea said, resting against him. When Noah had anticipated she'd fly to pieces over a waltz, she'd marshaled her nerves to deal with what was possibly a real threat.

She'd also come to Noah and sought his embrace of her own volition, which almost made the vandalism of the music box worthwhile.

Thea pulled back, her expression considering. "I don't suppose you're interested in having a lie down now?"

"Well, in truth…" Noah was interested in having a lie down with his wife, any damned minute of the day or night.

"Perhaps we might take your mind off this disconcerting development by getting out your bullwhip?" Thea asked.

"My bullwhip?" Peculiar images began to percolate through Noah's male imagination.

"You'll feel fewer of those husbandly insecurities if I have some rudimentary grasp of how one wields such a thing," Thea said, patting his lapel. "It's a pleasant enough afternoon, and we have no other duties at the moment. What better use could there be of our time?"

A duke went graciously to his fate. "None at all, my dear."

For the next hour, Noah used his whip-wielding stout right arm to demolish bushes, shrubs, and small tree limbs, and to show his wife how to do likewise, all in aid of marital bliss.

∼✎∽

Between Noah's moods, sheer fatigue, ghosts rising from house parties past, and the strain of being constantly around family, Thea was losing her mind.

And possibly her husband. Noah hadn't initiated intimacies in days, and when Thea had thought he'd been about to, he'd lain beside her and started prying all manner of secrets from her instead.

Trading worries. *Hah.*

Tomorrow's ball was a worry. Every neighbor and acquaintance from the entire shire would be in attendance to inspect the new Duchess of Anselm. A country ball was a huge undertaking, particularly so far from Town, where everything from ice to flowers was in shorter supply and had to be brought out from Town by wagon.

And now this—rain, which Noah said the corn would appreciate, but if it didn't stop soon, the roads wouldn't dry, even by tomorrow evening. That frustration was enough to make a woman pitch her dagger into the portraits surrounding her.

And why not?

Oh, not at the portraits, but the gallery was enormous, the light adequate, and just perhaps…

"Here you are." Patience stood in the high doorway to the long gallery, looking like she'd found the prize at a royal scavenger hunt. "Noah said you usually practice with your knife before tea. How enterprising of you. May I see this knife?"

"I usually practice behind the stables," Thea said, turning to hike her skirt and untie the dagger and its sheath. "Be careful—it's very sharp."

Noah kept the blade sharp for her, the sight of it in his hands as he slowly drew it along a whetstone having a curious impact on Thea's wits.

Patience took the dagger from its leather casing. "Where did you find such a thing, and how did you learn to use it?"

"Noah found it for me and showed me how to use it. I think he might have had it made for me." On one of his trips to Town, while Thea had mentally accused him of disporting with mistresses.

Patience traced the dragon inlay on the handle. "I am impressed. You practice with it daily?"

"I try to." Thea accepted her weapon back and retied the sheath at her knee.

Patience made a face, for an instant resembling Nini. "As little attention as my husband spares me these days, I might spend some time practicing with a weapon."

"James doesn't seem the negligent sort," Thea said, letting herself be guided into strolling arm in arm past the ancestors. "James seems like a wonderful husband, in fact."

"Oh, he is." Patience's smile became a smirk. "But James has his ways. For example, he distracts me in the morning, so it gets 'too late to ride in the heat.' He asks me to try this or that tidbit from his plate, for 'he can't possibly finish all this.' He's a very managing man, but it works out, because I am a very managing lady. Just as she was."

They stopped before a portrait of a panniered and bejeweled Elizabethan woman, one of the previous ladies Anselm, and Patience began to offer a family history. The entire line had been lusty, naughty, and canny as hell, apparently, for despite occasionally backing the wrong royal faction, the Anselm earldom and then dukedom—they'd backed the right faction that time around—had more or less prospered for centuries.

"But many of the more modern exponents are in here." Patience opened a door all but hidden in the oak paneling, and ushered Thea into a small side gallery.

"I never knew this was here," Thea said, though clearly, the servants kept the tall windows clean and the room free of dust. The sconces had been lit, as if the staff knew family might want to pay a call on this less public collection.

"These are the most recent additions to the family tree," Patience said, stopping before a portrait of three young men, all handsome, two dark, one blond, and all sporting dashing smiles and the exquisite, colorful tailoring of the previous century.

"They look like Harlan and Noah," Thea observed, focusing on the darker men. "Though Noah's and Harlan's looks are more refined."

"You think Noah's appearance refined?"

"Compared to these three," Thea said, but then she inspected the third man in the portrait, the blond, and her insides went abruptly queasy.

"These three are the previous generation," Patience said. "The former Duke of Anselm on the right, Noah's father, who was duke only briefly before his death, and Lord Earnest Meecham Winters Dunholm, known to one and all as Meech. This was probably done right before Meech married the lady who appended her name to his."

"Meech?" Thea's ears were roaring, her own voice sounding far, far away.

*Meech? This was Uncle Meech?*

She stared hard at the portrait, hoping she'd find some detail of eye color, a birthmark, a quirk of the lips, anything to suggest she was wrong. But no, this was the same man, the one who'd offered her pitying expressions over breakfast, and fine manners—when anybody was looking on. He'd flirted with her shamefully—she'd thought nothing of it at the time—and then he'd disported with her more shamefully still.

"Thea, are you well?"

"A little light-headed for skimping at luncheon,"

Thea said, easing her grip on Patience's arm. "Shall we move on?"

"Let's. We can order an early tea. I always seem to be hungry these days."

They ambled to the door, spending a particularly long time before a portrait done as Noah had approached his majority. His sisters were still girls, and Harlan a babe in his brother's arms. Noah might have been a particularly youthful papa with his brood around him, except for the absence of a wife.

"He did very well, I think," Patience said, studying the portrait. "I never felt deprived of both mother and father, not in any real sense. Noah was there, and he found us the best tutors and governesses, and kept a close eye on all of us."

"You're saying he'll make a conscientious papa?"

"I'm saying he's a good man. Let's find that tea."

Thea went along, but in her head, she was standing before the portrait of Lord Earnest Dunholm, a man she'd never wanted to see again, never wanted to hear of again, and God help her, he was now dear old Uncle Meech.

Noah was not the sort of duke to believe in chance, fate, and vile coincidences. His world was an orderly, rational place, unlike Thea's.

Noah would have every reason to think Thea had known that the charming, blond Earnest Dunholm was in fact a male of the Winters line. Most daughters of earls knew *Debrett's* page by page, but then most daughters of earls were focused on making a fine match, while Thea hadn't had that luxury.

Noah could easily believe she'd kept her connection

with his uncle secret, and Thea wouldn't blame her husband for his mistrust. Still, had Thea's dagger been plunged into her own heart, it could not have brought any more pain than she already felt.

❦

"You women have all day to visit and plot and sneak off to the parlors together, and then after dinner, it's more of the same," Noah grumbled to his wife. "I thought the ladies would never turn you loose."

Thea looked positively peaked, and all the lascivious, husbandly thoughts Noah had been harboring went scampering off to some mental parlor of their own, there to plague him all the worse for being banished yet again.

"Your sisters haven't had a family ball before," Thea said. "They each had their come-outs and engagements and so forth, but not a ball for family. They're very excited."

"While you just want it over with?" Noah came up behind Thea as she stood at their bedroom window and began taking pins from her hair. He'd be a properly credentialed lady's maid soon, at the rate his marriage was going. "What can you possibly see on such a dreary, damp night?"

"The moon's up," Thea said. "The sky is clearing off, and the roads will have a day to dry out."

Noah put his stash of pins on the vanity and came back to stand behind Thea, slipping his arms around her waist.

"I appreciate that you've orchestrated our first family gathering in years, Thea." He squeezed her shoulders gently, for a great weight rested upon them. "You're unhappy, Wife, and I know not how to repair it."

"I'm preoccupied," she said, turning and sliding her arms around him. "Hold me."

"With pleasure."

Except, hell and damnation, Thea must have really meant she wanted mere holding, because she tucked in close and held Noah for so long he was almost sure she was crying again.

"Wife? Shall you plead an indisposition tomorrow? The Furies would take over, I'm sure."

Thea shook her head and gripped Noah more tightly.

"You're tired," he said, hoping that was a safe bet. "Let's get you into bed and off your feet."

Even more alarming than Thea's fatigue was her docility. She let Noah take down her hair without even once treating him to that brisk visual inspection that had him on mental alert. She stood still while he divested her of every stitch, stood even more still while he used the wash water on her, a liberty he hadn't taken previously. When he deposited her on the bed, she rolled to her side and merely watched as he went through his own nighttime routine.

"You must be exhausted," Noah said, climbing into bed. He pulled Thea into the curve of his body. "Wife, some fool forgot to put you into a nightgown."

"Not a fool." Thea angled a leg up over Noah's hip and an arm over his shoulders. "My dearest husband."

*Dearest?*

Noah began to count days and weeks, because such

excesses of sentiment from his duchess might suggest she was breeding already. That ought to please him—it did please him, vain, shallow, insecure ducal beast that he was—but it didn't seem to be pleasing Thea, and that...

Noah made love to her, slowly, tenderly, without regard for her exhaustion or her odd bout of quiet, and to his endless relief, Thea made love to him too. She met him caress for caress, sigh for sigh, pleasure for pleasure.

In the few weeks of their marriage, Thea had already learned what to listen for, where to touch, how much pressure or speed or subtlety sent Noah 'round the bend in the shortest, most glorious time.

As he plied Thea with long, languid strokes, Noah realized that as much as he wanted to bring Thea pleasure, he wanted more to bring her *joy*, to ease whatever was clouding her heart.

When had his ducal priorities shifted from endless duty to marital joy?

This was not husbandly insecurity or a manly whatever.

This was a husband falling in love with his brand-new wife.

This was a man, for the first and only time in his busy, self-important, and oddly beleaguered and lonely life, falling in love with a woman.

And hoping like hell she could someday love him back.

∽

"We're to gather for a family buffet in the library when we're dressed," Noah said. "My duchess has commanded it."

"The little girls have seconded the notion?" James asked, holding out a wrist for Noah to insert a sleeve button in his cuff.

"The girls are bouncing about the third floor as if Father Christmas were coming to stay." Noah smiled at the recollection. "I have ordered that they are to be sneaked to the musicians' gallery for the opening waltz and gorge themselves on snitches from the main buffet, but only one dessert apiece."

"Sporting of you."

"If we keep the girls up half the night, there's a chance I might have a cup of tea with my duchess in peace tomorrow morning. There." Noah stepped back. "You'll do, Heckendorn, but why isn't your wife valeting you?"

James surveyed himself in the mirror. "For the same reason yours has cast you into the darkness of my company. The ladies are driving the maids to Bedlam, dressing each other's hair, putting the last touches on hems and gloves and corsages and all that female whatnot."

"Tending to the feminine mysteries, Meech used to call it." Noah considered pouring them each a drink, but decided against it when they'd be swilling punch and champagne for hours.

"Will Meech join us tonight?" James asked, fluffing the lace of his cravat.

"He will not." Noah almost changed his mind about that drink. "Meecham is up to something, James, and I know not what."

Outside the window of the guest bedroom, the gardeners were setting the last of the potted flowers around the drive, making Wellspring not only stately, but cheerful.

Noah's mother would have approved, but did his duchess approve?

James raised his chin and repositioned the emerald-and-gold cravat pin Noah had expertly placed not five minutes earlier.

"Perhaps Meech has been playing a little too deep and trying to keep it from you?"

Noah hoped Meech's problem was that easy to address. "He's learned his lesson in that regard. I am pleased to report Grantley seems to have as well. Not so, Hallowell."

James patted the lace cascading from his neckcloth, then turned to admire his reflection in profile.

"Hallowell who?" he asked.

"You recall Marliss's older brother," Noah said. "He was bullying Thea when I'd decided to offer for her. Once I married her, it became apparent that somebody had bullied her rather awfully, so I bought up Hallowell's gambling markers, and a few other debts as well."

"How much?"

Noah named a figure that had James's blond eyebrows rising.

"Does Hallowell's papa know?"

"His papa is so overwhelmed by the challenges of dealing with the viscountess as Marliss is launched that, no, Hallowell has not had the benefit of mature guidance of late."

"He's not an infant, Noah." James slipped a signet ring onto his left hand, more gold and emeralds. "If he bullies his sister's companion, Hallowell's enough to make a man dread the prospect of sons."

"Now, now." Noah offered a crooked smile. "You will be having sons with Patience Winters Heckendorn. No need to fret. All will be in hand."

James brightened on some note of marital mischief. "There is that."

A knock on the door heralded the arrival of Heath and Wilson, but not Grantley, Harlan, or Erikson.

"You'll give them their orders," Noah said to James. "In the library for inspection by the little girls, twenty minutes, no more."

"*Oui, mon capitaine duc.*" Heath saluted, Wilson passed James a small purple boutonniere, and James bowed with ridiculous ceremony while Noah went to find his daughters.

Evvie and Nini were in their bedroom, bouncing on the beds, literally, while Davies tried to tie sashes and fix hair ribbons.

"Ladies." Noah knew better than to raise his voice. "How will I offer you my tokens if you insist on comporting yourselves like dropped gum rubbers?"

"We're excited!" Nini bellowed.

"Very," her sister added solemnly, then dissolved into unprovoked giggles.

"I'm excited too," Noah said. "I get to dance with my duchess tonight. As we swirl through the opening waltz, my form will be subject to stern criticism, won't it?"

"He means we'll get to watch," Evvie translated. "We'll be spying. Davies said we had permission, but we must be very, very"—she dropped her voice as her eyes grew round—"quiet!"

The last was shrieked amid peals of laughter. Noah endured a pang of sweetness to see Evvie, his most serious little lady, so overcome with glee and excitement.

Thea had done this. Having Thea here to provide consistency and warmth in the children's days, to monitor what they studied and with whom, and to get them up on their new ponies regularly as Noah came and went on the King's business.

Thea had allowed Evvie to be more of a little girl, and the results were stunning. Lovely, dear, and precious. Noah grabbed Evvie out of the air, midbounce, and hugged her carefully.

"You'll crush my dress!"

"Heaven forfend!" He set her on her feet. "Will you allow me to offer you a small complement to your beauty?"

"He's got flowers," Nini put in helpfully. "They're pretty, and they smell good."

"Like us." Evvie grinned, holding still so Noah could affix a miniature corsage to her wrist. "Does Nini get one?"

"Of course." Noah sat on the bed, did the honors for Nini, and then drew them together on his lap. They were getting too big to share his lap, too big to even *be* on his lap—damn it.

"Listen, you two." He cadged a whiff of little-girl fragrance from each silky head of hair. "Take pity on Davies and Maryanne tonight. We're all supposed to have fun, not spend our evening watching the two of you cast up your accounts, or deal with bruises you earned pelting down the steps. If Erikson asks you to dance, you must gently decline, because you're not quite out yet. If I ask you to dance, you must oblige me, because I am your cousin and will be completely heartbroken if you refuse me."

"You're silly," Nini said, sniffing at her wrist corsage.

"A cousin's prerogative." While a duke, poor sod, would know little of silliness. "You'll listen to your nursemaids and spy for only one waltz, right?"

"Yes, Cousin," they chorused.

"And you'll come inspect the uncles in a few minutes. They're very nervous, hoping they measure up."

"That's what the Furies said when they came to visit us after tea with Lady Thea." Nini exchanged a look of devilment with her sister. "We'll be good."

Noah set them down and rose. "You will. Ladies who do not comport themselves as such will be twelve years old before they're invited to spy on another ball."

Noah had made his point, all teasing aside, so he winked at Davies and took his leave, thinking to find Erikson either in his chambers or possibly among the beauties in the laboratory.

He did not find Erikson in either location, and concluded his resident botanist was likely in the library, researching the possibilities on the buffet table. Noah had just turned to leave the upstairs conservatory and go below stairs himself when his gaze landed on a small mechanism sitting on the sill of a closed window.

All thoughts of the evening's festivities were shoved aside by a single, unhappy question: Why were the guts of Thea's music box here in Erikson's laboratory and left on display, where anyone might happen by?

# Twenty-four

THEA SHOOED HER SISTERS-IN-LAW ON THEIR WAY AND went into the dressing room to make sure a spare shirt had been ironed for Noah. There would be sufficient champagne, punch, and spirits on hand tonight that somebody was likely to grow clumsy enough to spill a drink.

Thea wished they'd spill it on her, that she might hide rather than serve as hostess.

The thought that somebody might whisper into Noah's ear what Thea herself dreaded disclosing to him had cindered her composure. She'd tell him, tell him exactly with whom she'd transgressed—who had transgressed against her—but not until this ball was behind them.

And then...

Then she'd cope, as she always coped, and be grateful she'd had at least a few weeks to dream of a happy future with a man who deserved a loving wife...a wife he might someday love in return.

Thea hadn't spent much time in her own chamber since Noah had decreed they'd share his bed, but thinking she'd soon be moving back there—assuming he didn't banish her altogether—she opened the door to her bedroom.

The room might be a guest chamber, so thoroughly had Noah divested it of her effects. Empty, like her.

"You are being ridiculous." She repeated her father's admonition aloud, wrinkled her nose at the very sound of it. She wasn't ridiculous to mourn the loss of a budding romance with her spouse, and she wasn't ridiculous to dread what lay ahead of her.

Thea knew that now, at least.

Intent on giving herself one last perusal before joining the family in the library, Thea glared at herself in the vanity mirror. Noah had talked her into this gown, a shimmery bronze silk that swayed beautifully with each step and looked beautiful by candlelight. The French modiste had even insisted on matching silk drawers, which completed Thea's first experience of elegance from the skin out.

Thea hated the dress now; hated the memory of Noah coaxing her to wear it, claiming the unusual color meant he'd be able to spot her among their guests without having to hunt endlessly for his own wife.

She blinked back tears and inspected herself in the mirror.

Something caught her eye, a piece of paper folded and left half-exposed, caught in the lid of her music box. Her empty music box. She extracted the note, knowing it hadn't been there while the Furies were in the room.

*If you want to see your husband's bastards again in*

*this life, come to the gamekeeper's cottage immediately,
and bring something of yours Anselm will recognize.
Warn no one.*

The first thought to register was that Evvie and
Nini were in peril and defenseless.

Thea knew that helplessness, knew the crushing
weight of hopelessness and fear. The second thought
was that half the village had been employed at
Wellspring for tonight's ball, and any one of dozens
of temporary footmen, maids, or pages might have
delivered the note without anybody the wiser.

Taking the time to interrogate staff and consider
options was out of the question.

What possession of Thea's would Noah recognize?
Her combs were nondescript, and she wasn't about to
part with her knife. Not tonight of all nights.

She should tell Noah…

Noah might get hurt… He *would* get hurt,
being protective and fierce and determined. These
thoughts and a flock of others flitted through
Thea's mind on wings of worry, anger, and sheer
terror for the girls. She scooped up her music box
and fled the room, even as panic had her insides in
an uproar.

At the back hallway, Thea paused only to trade
dancing slippers for half boots before slipping out into
the long evening twilight. No guests would arrive for
two hours, not even the nearest neighbors.

So Thea hurried across the back gardens toward the
home wood, intent only on keeping the children safe.

❧

"James." Noah kept his voice quiet, but the baron casually sidled closer to his host at a bay window. "My duchess is decamping across the back gardens at a forced march, when this buffet was to be a moment shared with all of our family."

"Nerves?"

"Has to be." Noah set his drink down, for Thea had been nothing but nerves for the past two weeks. "If I'm not in view again within twenty minutes, make a discreet effort to locate us. I have no one to thank for this but myself. The Furies might have to coax Thea into the receiving line."

Thea was heading for the trees of the home wood at a brisk walk, not a panicked run, but Noah felt a crashing urgency to retrieve his duchess.

"Noah, what are you going on about?" James asked, picking up Noah's brandy.

"My wife dreads this evening," Noah said, "has dreaded the whole ordeal of this gathering, and I would not listen to her. Now the poor woman is likely weeping into her handkerchiefs and cursing the day she married me."

For Thea had been ill-used at a house party, and somebody wanted to threaten her with that memory.

"Any woman of sense…" James began, but then he stopped. "Apologize, pet her a bit without messing her hair, and grovel, but be back here before Patience, Pru, and Pen sniff out trouble."

Noah nodded his thanks and nearly jogged through the house and out the back door. Thea had been headed onto the bridle paths in the home wood, but she hadn't much of a head start. Once Noah cleared the back door, he shamelessly sprinted in her wake. When he caught a glimpse of bronze silk turning up the path to the gamekeeper's cottage, he resisted the urge to shout.

If his wife was going to pieces, bellowing at her would hardly help the situation, and the cottage was uninhabited—a perfect place for groveling and apologizing.

As Noah reached the cottage, though, he heard Thea's voice raised in an unmistakably furious shout, and his blood turned to ice in his veins. He watched in silent horror as Maryanne ushered the little girls out of the cottage, and turned them not back toward the manor house, but deeper into the woods, away from Noah, safety, and what should have been one of the happiest nights of their short lives.

∽

"Quiet, bitch! I liked you much better when you were my sister's cowering companion. You shut your mouth now, or so help me, I'll have Maryanne tell her mother to make soup of those two little brats."

"You wouldn't dare," Thea snapped. She had no patience with Corbett Hallowell and his schemes to ruin the Winters family gathering. "You harm a hair on their heads, and Anselm will hunt you down and make you regret every moment of your misbegotten life. And God help you when Maryanne realizes you won't marry her and she's shared her favors with you for nothing."

"As if I'd marry an illiterate nursery maid," Hallowell spat. "I'm to marry a fortune, because my blighted sister is allowed to marry for love. My benighted father has a notion I'm to repair the damage done to the family coffers since I came down from university."

Hallowell wouldn't know a love match if it waltzed him down the room at Almack's.

Thea felt a glorious urge to turn the idiot over her knee. Noah would come, of that she was confident. Davies would be looking for the girls, or Noah would be expecting his wife in the library. Somebody would sound an alarm, and Noah would come.

"What did you bring me to lure your worthless duke out here?" Hallowell asked.

No duke had ever been of greater worthiness.

"A music box," Thea replied, setting her keepsake on the plank table near the door. A broken, useless music box, which was more than Hallowell deserved. "What are you about, Hallowell? Your sister will still marry happily, your debts will still require payment, and you will have made a powerful enemy of my husband with this stunt."

"Cowper won't marry Marliss," Hallowell sneered. "I told him she'd allowed Anselm liberties, and the idiot believed me because everybody knows the Winters men aren't to be trusted. Marliss will have to cry off as soon as everyone has left Town for the summer."

Thea trusted Noah, trusted him with her life, and her heart.

"Oh, well done," she retorted. Hallowell was a nasty, mad imbecile, while Thea was a furious *duchess*. "Now your parents will have the expense of a second Season, when they must entertain even more lavishly, lest somebody decide your sister didn't take. Brilliant, Mr. Hallowell."

He took a step closer. "Shut your mouth, now, or you really won't see those whelps of Anselm's again."

"They are my daughters." This close, Thea could smell drink on Hallowell's breath and see the desperation in his eyes. "You will excuse me, but guests have been invited to my home tonight, and I have responsibilities."

Noah would kill Hallowell if he knew what nonsense the fool was spouting. Marliss and her parents didn't deserve that misery, or the expense of a proper funeral.

Thea got her hand on the door latch, even though she heard Hallowell moving behind her. She wrenched it open, prepared to dash into the increasing gloom of the woods, but was stopped by two things:

First, her husband stood right in her path, scowling thunderously.

Second, she heard the distinctive sound of a pistol hammer being cocked.

"Turn around, Lady Thea," Hallowell said, "and step away from Anselm, so I might have a clear shot."

Lady Thea would have cowered; a duchess needed to think.

A beat of silence went by, just long enough that Thea could see cold, cold fury in Noah's eyes, and something else, something that looked like infernally intense determination. Noah brushed by her and murmured something like "girls...safe."

Then he stood between Thea and Hallowell, and Thea wanted to clobber her husband for his chivalry.

"You're here early, Anselm," Hallowell said, "but I can work with an audience. Move away from your wife."

"An audience to your stupidity," Thea muttered, but Noah shot her a look that silenced her more effectively than even Hallowell's gun. As Noah moved, Hallowell advanced, putting himself before the only door.

"An audience to your ruin," Hallowell countered, looking directly at Thea. "I'll have my pleasure of you, Duchess, and your husband can either give up my markers or keep them. If he keeps them, then all the world will know I've cuckolded Anselm himself, and no one will blame me for it, when the Winters men-folk have poached on many a preserve. If he surrenders my markers, I might keep my mouth shut, for a time anyway, until my pockets are empty again. By then, a man as enterprising as Anselm will think of some way to encourage me to silence."

Had there been no gun, Thea would have scoffed at Hallowell's scheme, but there was a gun, pointed at Noah.

"You think yourself capable of sexual congress with my wife while I watch?" Noah didn't so much as glance at Hallowell's gun, and his voice suggested incredulity, if not outright humor. "Have you considered how you'll hold a gun on me, pleasure yourself, and deal with the lady's reluctance all at once?"

Hallowell snorted. "She isn't a lady. She whored before she tricked you into marriage. It was only a matter of time before she flaunted her wares at some other hapless fool. You…" He waved the gun at Thea. "Tie him up with that rope, and bind him tightly, or you'll wish you had."

Noah obligingly backed up against the center post holding up the little dwelling. He held his hands behind his back, above the level of the table that stood next to the post as well. Thea did a creditable job of tying his hands, for all hers shook badly.

Then she saw Noah mouth the words, "Be ready."

Thea could deal with Hallowell's taunting, deal with his strutting and pawing and carrying on. If he'd wanted to beat her, she wouldn't have minded that so much either, but this... Her worst nightmare— intimate violation, again—made more vile by the prospect of Noah watching. Noah, whose respect Thea craved like she craved air.

*Be ready*, he'd said.

Thea managed to finish with the rope and stepped back.

Hallowell checked the tightness of the binding, while Noah stood quietly, exuding a vast indifference.

"If you're wearing drawers, Duchess, get rid of them," Hallowell said, his gaze riveted on Noah's face.

"Do as the boy says, Your Grace." Noah spoke easily, nigh yawning with boredom. "Excuse me, the *man*. Or so he'd have us believe. What do you think? Boy or man, or perhaps not even a boy."

"Shut your mouth, Anselm," Hallowell bit out. "And you, Duchess, do as I say, now!"

The only thing allowing Thea to draw breath was the steadiness in Noah's blue eyes. She bent to comply with Hallowell's command, when her hand brushed over the knife tied above her knee.

"Hurry up, Duchess," Hallowell taunted. "Your husband might enjoy your whore's tricks, but I don't need them."

Thea worked as quickly as she could, the yards of

her skirts and petticoats camouflaging her efforts. When she straightened, she had her silk drawers wadded up in her hands. Stepping beside Noah, she turned her back to Hallowell and folded her drawers tidily, laying them on the table directly behind Noah's hands.

A duchess needed to think. To be worthy of her duke.

"Over here, now." Hallowell gestured with the gun. "Prepare to be thoroughly ruined, Duchess, and behold, your husband does nothing to safeguard what few pretenses to virtue you still have. Undo my falls."

"How precious," Noah mused. "You get to undress him like a little boy. Is your heart beating in anticipation of what you'll find in his underlinen, Your Grace? Perhaps he'll be wearing nappies, and it will be my silence we're bargaining over. Then again, I seem to recall my great-grandpapa wearing nappies as his life neared its end too."

"Quiet, Anselm," Hallowell bellowed. "Shut your mouth, or she'll pay."

"As if enduring your attentions wouldn't be trial enough for any woman?" Noah scoffed. "Get his breeches around his ankles, Duchess, so I might be impressed with his mighty sword and cower in shame at the size of his weapon. Honestly, Hallowell, did you think this situation through? The duchess is *my wife*, and in a position to make detailed comparisons."

Noah was reminding Thea of something important, buying her time to think, to plan, to *be ready*—

"She'll be your ruined wife in a very few minutes," Hallowell said, his voice cracking as Thea undid a button on the falls of his breeches.

"Dearest Duchess," Noah said. "I have reading spectacles in my pocket if magnification would help."

"For God's sake, hush!" Hallowell screeched at Noah, then turned back to Thea, realizing a moment too late that his bound prisoner had won free, and his unbound prisoner, his intended rape victim, had melted out of his reach in the same instant.

For Thea, time took an odd, slow turn. Noah hooked an arm around Hallowell's neck and jerked back, using his superior height for leverage. When Hallowell ceased struggling, the knife Thea had tucked into her folded drawers wasn't held to his throat, but low, near a place Thea couldn't convince her gaze to stray.

Thea let go with a scream, a wonderfully loud, angry sound that went on and on, even as she told herself Noah was safe and screaming wasn't necessary.

While Hallowell bleated about the family succession and the Lords taking a dim view of mutilating a peer's heir, Thea grabbed for the first thing that came to hand.

She brought a solid weight down on Hallowell's head, as hard as she could, and the damned idiot jackanapes fell blessedly silent.

❦

Thanks to one brave, clever duchess, Hallowell ceased his babbling and slumped heavily against Noah. In the next instant, the cottage door swung open so hard the hinges shook, and James, Heath, Erikson, and Wilson burst in, armed to the teeth.

*About damned time.*

"My duchess has subdued this miscreant. You may

take him now." Noah shoved Hallowell at James and Heath, and then opened his arms to Thea. She flew to Noah's embrace with gratifying speed and wrapped her arms around his waist.

"I'll fetch the magistrate," Erikson said.

"You won't have to," Noah replied, arms around his wife. "Squire Sterling will be here in another hour or so, and tomorrow is soon enough to take statements. For now, put Hallowell in the groom's workroom, and set two footmen to watch him at all times. He's not to be let out even if the stables catch fire."

The knife in Noah's hand had been temptation itself, but the blade belonged to Thea, who shouldn't have her weaponry tainted by Hallowell's blood.

"Noah," Thea said. "Where are the children?"

Of course, she'd ask about the little ones first.

"Maryanne had no idea what Hallowell had planned," Noah said, "but she understood clearly enough that he was using her when he lured you here then dismissed her to take the children to the village, not the manor. She was more than happy to return them to the house."

Noah was impersonating a duke now, though his husbandly heart was going like a rabbit's, and Thea could probably feel that, so closely did they embrace.

"If we don't get back to the house immediately," Wilson pointed out, "the Furies will be on armed patrol. We'll make excuses for you as long as we can."

Into next week would do nicely.

"Come along, you." Erikson wrapped a large hand on Hallowell's biceps.

"Ouch, damn it!"

"You thought to trouble Anselm's beauties," Erikson said. "This was naughty of you, and naughty boys sometimes meet with accidents."

"No accidents," Thea said, untucking her nose from Noah's throat. "His sister is our guest tonight."

"You heard my duchess, gentlemen," Noah said. "My thanks for your assistance. Now be off with you, lest we hold our opening waltz in the home wood."

The men left, and the silence in their wake yawned widely. Noah was angry at Hallowell, angry at himself—Thea had been threatened on Winters land— and grateful to his bones that no harm had befallen her.

Noah held the dagger out to its rightful owner. "This belongs to you."

Thea clasped the knife in a shaking hand, set it aside, and pitched herself back into his arms.

Brilliant woman, for she'd spared Noah having to ask her to linger in his embrace.

"Go ahead and cry." Noah stroked Thea's back, loving her lissome strength. "You were magnificent, Wife. I doubt Hallowell will ever function normally again, not that he deserves to. You entrusted your knife to me, when it's you who deserved to slit Hallowell from his appetite to his aspirations."

Noah went on in that soothing, praising—albeit slightly violent—vein until Thea regained a measure of composure, though still she clung to her husband.

Thea had apparently heard every word of Hallowell's bile, and possibly sensed that her past was catching up with her future. Now was not the time to face that dragon, not when she'd already been through a trial.

"Wife, my sisters will fetch us and read me the Riot Act if you're in the least disrepaired. Look at me." Noah cupped Thea's jaw, so she had no choice but to meet his gaze. The tears in her eyes made him hope a very bad accident befell Hallowell.

"We have a ball to get through," he went on, "unless you'd rather plead indisposition. I won't leave your side, I won't travel more than six feet from you the entire night, and we'll end the dancing promptly at two of the clock. The moon will set at four, and people won't linger long if they want to get home safely. What say you?"

Noah offered her vows of companionship and protection, small comfort but sincere, for he needed to remain near his wife if he was to avoid doing permanent violence to Hallowell.

Thea tucked her nose against Noah's evening jacket. He wanted no gossip to touch her—no more gossip—particularly regarding the sordid doings in this little cottage, but more than that, he wanted Thea to once again feel safe and content.

Always to feel safe and content.

"I'll be fine," she said, more a resolution than an assurance. "Stay with me, though, or keep the family near me."

As if Noah could bear to let her out of his sight. "You are my duchess. Of course I'll remain by your side, and you will dance with no one save your own dear, devoted duke."

# Twenty-five

NOAH GUIDED THEA THROUGH THE COTTAGE DOOR, and kept an arm over her shoulders the whole way back to the house. They didn't speak, and that silent proximity set the pattern for the entire evening.

*What was Noah thinking? What was he feeling?*

He remained immediately at Thea's side until the receiving line was finished, then he swept her into the opening waltz.

Thea looked up at him in surprise as he drew her close in a turn. "This is the tune from my music box."

Her ruined music box, though the sacrifice had been for a good cause. In the corner of her mind not absorbed with remaining composed and coherent, she fretted about what Noah had heard in that cottage, and whether he believed Hallowell's taunts.

"Erikson recognized this tune when I played it for him," Noah said. "Some old German fellow wrote it as a minuet. I thought you'd like it."

Thea bundled herself close to her duke, despite neighbors, family, and servants looking on, and despite the disclosures yet to be made. If she hadn't loved

Noah earlier, she'd be enthralled with him now and for the rest of her days.

*He had spectacles in his pocket, indeed.*

"Have I pleased you with this tune, Wife? You never say, and a fellow is left to wonder without mercy."

"I love y—it," she said. "I simply love it."

"I love it too." Noah rested his cheek against her hair. "I'll love it more when it's the good-night waltz."

An hour after the opening waltz, late arrivals were still coming down the stairs, and the evening showed every sign of being an unmitigated success. The neighbors were gracious, the gentlemen making their bows to the new duchess, and the ladies admiring the splendor of the ballroom and terraces. Through it all, Thea felt Noah's hand in hers, his arm supporting her, or his fingers toying with her sash, her glove, or a lock of her hair.

Almost as if she and Noah were a loving couple, no scandals lurking in Thea's past, no near occasions of violence having marred the evening. Noah hovered like a shadow of foreboding at Thea's side, though if he went a mere five yards away to the punch bowl, her breath grew short, and her heart sped up.

The same miseries befell her when Lord Earnest Meecham Winters Dunholm stood before them, offering a terse greeting.

*Why him, why now, and when would this awful night end?*

Thea's nemesis had aged twenty years in less than ten, and he looked more nervous than any family member ought, given the occasion. Those realizations

slid away as Noah's hand dropped from Thea's side,
the emotional equivalent of a door banging open,
allowing a bitter cold emotional wind to obliterate
the meager calm Thea had gathered as the evening
wore on.

"If you've a minute, Anselm," Lord Earnest—
Uncle Meech—said, "I'd like to discuss a certain
matter with you, er, privately."

He'd bowed over Thea's gloved hand upon his
arrival, and Thea's throat filled with bile.

"I will not leave my duchess's side tonight, Uncle,"
Noah said, the soul of proper manners. "The ball is
in her honor, and you'd assured me of your regrets—
though of course we're pleased to include you as
our guest."

*No, they were not.*

"Yes, well, sorry for the confusion," Lord
Earnest replied, "but I'd truly like a minute of your
time, Anselm."

Thea saw the man's nervousness and knew exactly
what poison he'd spew if he got Noah alone. Her head
hurt, her belly was queasy, her heart ached, and she'd
had enough.

The Duchess of Anselm had finally, finally had
enough.

"We'll both join you in the library," Thea said,
slipping her arm through Noah's.

Noah patted her knuckles. "You're sure, my love?"

Gracious saints. She *was* Noah's love, though he'd
never called her that before. Thea raised her chin.

"I am sure, Anselm."

"So be it," Meech muttered. He held his peace

until the library door was closed, then turned to face his host and hostess. "I bring you a message from our mutual acquaintance, er, Whitlow, Noah. Whitlow has picked up talk from a certain Mr. Hallowell, claiming he'll attempt to right a wrong you did him, and your duchess will be the means by which he effects his revenge. Talk of a young man in his cups, possibly, but Whitlow says Hallowell's a snake, and not to turn your back on him or leave your duchess without protection."

"Whitlow?" Thea murmured. The name was familiar.

"A mutual acquaintance," Meech said again. "Nothing more."

A look passed between Noah and his uncle, while Thea tried to place the name.

Noah brought Thea's hand to his lips. "May I share the developments of the evening with Meech, my dearest?"

*My dearest?*

"Developments?" Meech crossed to the sideboard. "I'm not sure I want to know of any developments."

"Hallowell paid us a call," Noah said, leaving Thea's side to appropriate the decanter from his uncle's grasp. "Duchess, libation for you?"

Meech's presumption was thus subtly chastised. What was Noah up to?

"None for me," Thea said.

"I won't be so shy," Meech said, accepting a drink from Noah.

Noah explained in a few pithy sentences what Hallowell had been about, threatening to ruin Thea with vicious gossip unless Noah forgave all the man's debts. Noah managed this recitation without alluding to Thea's past, and she'd never loved him more.

Meech tugged on his cravat, the result being that it remained askew. "I'm sorry, Duchess. I hope you'll turn Hallowell over to the authorities."

"You do?" Why would Meech expect Thea to pursue severe penalties for Hallowell's bungled threats, but no consequences at all for the man who'd taken her virginity?

"Yes, well…" Meech stared at his drink.

Noah took the glass from his uncle's hand and set it on the sideboard. "Something troubling you, my lord?"

"Nothing," Meecham said. "How are the girls?"

"Your daughters are fine," Noah said. "Being young ladies of discernment, they've started to call Thea Mama."

An unexpected and bittersweet bit of news. "They have?" Thea asked, then the first part of Noah's reply registered in her tired, anxious brain. "What do you mean, *his* daughters? They're our daughters."

"I checked on them," Noah said, tugging off his white evening gloves and laying them beside Meecham's half-empty glass. "While the Furies redid your hair, my ears rang with Mama-this and Mama-that, and when did Mama cosh him, and why didn't Mama stab him dead?" Noah smiled at Thea sweetly. "Quite taken with you, they are."

Was Noah quite taken with her? Would he remain taken with her when Meecham had said his piece?

"I was no kind of parent," Meech said, perusing a

bookshelf as if literary scholarship was his new passion. "You know that, Anselm. They were girls, little girls. I hadn't a clue how to go on with them."

Thea felt as if she'd had too much wine, or was coming down with an ailment that affected her balance.

"Noah?"

"We'll discuss it later," Noah said. "For now, you have my apologies, Duchess."

"You haven't any children?" Thea pressed.

Noah's smile went from sweet to wicked. "Not yet. Perhaps soon."

"I'll just be going, then," Meech said, striding off toward the door.

*Yes, please. Leave with all haste and never return.* Lord Earnest had acted silently mortified the morning after taking advantage of Thea; perhaps his shame was great enough to guarantee his silence.

"You shall not leave just yet, Meecham," Noah said. "You'll apologize to my duchess first, then take leave of your children. Thea has an excellent point. I'm guardian to those little girls, and they are legally ours, not yours. Then you'll do as you said, and leave for an indefinite journey in the north, and perhaps points beyond."

"He'll what?" Thea glanced from uncle to nephew. From beyond the library came the sound of a hundred feet pounding on the ballroom floor in unison, and a twelve-piece orchestra lilting along to the strains of a happy reel.

Meech was being sent away—that was good—but not quite yet.

That was very bad. Fatigue and strained nerves had Thea sinking into Noah's reading chair, a capacious seat angled near the fire.

"He knows, Duchess," Meech said, hand on the door latch. "Somehow, your duke has parsed out the details, but it's not what you think, Noah. Maybe not even what your duchess has told you."

Thea had told Noah next to nothing. Now she wished that she'd told him she loved him—for she did.

"Then you tell me," Noah said, coming to stand beside Thea's chair. "My duchess should not be burdened with this retelling, for none of it was her fault."

Thea comprehended Noah's words on an intellectual level, but all her body knew was that he wasn't touching her.

"May I sit?" Meech asked, turning loose of the door latch. "This isn't a simple tale."

"Thea?"

She was nominally the hostess, though did that matter?

"Please, do sit, both of you."

Noah perched on the arm of Thea's chair, and she wanted to weep.

"So unburden yourself, Meecham," Noah said, "but if Her Grace tells you to hush, you shut your mouth mid-syllable, are we clear?"

Thea resisted the urge to lay her cheek against Noah's thigh, for what was to come offered only cold comfort.

She'd have a chance to hear from the perpetrator the circumstances of the crime against her person. At the time, she'd medicated a foul headache and wine-soured stomach with a touch of the poppy. Her room had been in nearly complete darkness, and her memories were fogged by the drug, and by her own revulsion.

Now Thea would revisit the plain facts of her ruin, and the prospect was a backhanded relief.

A duchess did not cower before the truth, no matter how her heart might be breaking.

Meech took the couch, flipped out his evening tails, then linked his hands before him and kept his gaze on his hands.

"It was just another infernally tedious summer house party," Meech began. "Stodgier than most, with the likes of Joanna Newcomer and Annabelle Handley on the guest list. An evening or two of whist with that pair, and my store of civilities was exhausted. Pemberton felt the same way, and so he went prowling, as he usually does."

"And you do too," Noah added. His hand settled on Thea's shoulder, the warmth of his touch an endless comfort.

"Pemberton doesn't misbehave as often as you'd think." Meech ran another finger under his collar though the library had no fire, and the room was far from warm. "Not in recent years."

Pemberton had been a guest at that dreadful house party. Thea recalled meeting him, for he and Lord Earnest Dunholm had been peas in a pod, twin specimens of blond, mature male charm, neither of whom Thea had seen as any threat.

She'd been so innocent, and so ignorant.

Meech went back to studying his hands. "Where

there are dowagers and older ladies, though, there are companions, and those ladies range the gamut from bona fide spinsters to strumpets who haven't been caught. I struck up a flirtation with such a one, a Violet Carter, though she's going by Violette Cartier now, and it was likely from her Hallowell learned of things he shouldn't."

Thea's hand went to her throat, for she hadn't heard that name since leaving the house party, and still it had the power to unnerve her. Noah's fingers glossed over Thea's, and her upset receded.

"Miss Carter was a dreadful little baggage," Meech said. "I didn't know that then."

"Go on," Noah said, taking Thea's hand in his, bowing to kiss her knuckles, and keeping hold of her fingers.

"I was bored witless," Meech said, "and after the usual round of flirtations, I agreed to an assignation with this creature. She seemed exactly my sort—lively, knowledgeable, and without sentiment of any bothersome degree. We set a time, she gave me directions to her room, and that was supposed to be that."

"She lied," Thea said, closing her eyes as Noah's thumb brushed over her knuckles. Violet Carter had lied to Meecham, and one woman's mendacity had caused Thea years of nightmares.

Meecham yanked on his cravat again, as if it were too tight. "She gave me directions to her room, except her room was across the hall from the duchess's. Miss Carter told me to use the door on the left, though her room lay to the right. Had I gone to the room she directed me to, I would have ended up not in her room, but in Her Grace's."

Thea did not want to be cast back into the role of the bewildered and ignorant young woman, and so she asked the next question.

"What do you mean, had you gone to the room she directed you to? Somebody came to my room, and you appeared guilty as mortal sin at breakfast."

Meech looked that guilty now, also fearful. Thea had felt fearful in some blighted corner of her soul since that night.

"Go on," she said, "and be quick about it. His Grace and I have a house full of guests."

Among whom, Meech did not number.

"Pemberton overheard me arranging this assignation," Meech said, "and as he and I occasionally did as younger men, he decided to step in. He fancied the girl, and didn't think she was the type to take offense."

"Dear God." Thea unwrapped her fingers from Noah's grip. "*Pemberton* was…in my room?" In her nightmares, in her very body. She leaned into Noah, wanting to weep, to throw things, to kill Pemberton slowly and painfully, and Violet Carter along with him.

"I'm afraid so," Meech said. "Pemberton found me afterward, shaking so badly he about cast up his accounts. He'd been played for a fool by that Carter woman and by his own idiot idea of a joke on me. Both Joanna Newcomber and Annabelle Handley had complained in open company of Violet Carter's flirtatiousness, and Pemmie never dreamed their companion would be the object of Miss Carter's retaliation. He was sure somebody would call him out for his behavior. I nearly did."

"*Nearly?*" Noah spat. "Your stupid old boy's

prank saw my wife violated, and you think it doesn't merit redress?"

*Violated.* Noah said the ugly, honest word Thea had avoided even in her mind. To hear him speak that truth ought to have sent her into strong hysterics, but to her surprise, his accusation calmed some of her upset.

"Anselm…" Thea linked their hands again. "Please don't raise your voice. I cannot—I think I'm relieved, if you must know. Sick, angry, and disgusted, but now at least I know. Nobody intended anything more than malicious mischief—very malicious mischief—such as would have resulted if I'd been seen turning a man away from my bedroom door."

Thea knew who, she knew why, she knew in a way she hadn't that *none of it was her fault.*

"For the love of God." Noah pushed away from the chair. "My uncle confesses to being an accessory to your ill usage, and you're relieved?"

"A duchess must deal with difficult truths sometimes," Thea said as the damned reel finally came to a close, and a measure of quiet descended in the library.

Noah glared at his uncle and seemed to grow larger before Thea's eyes. "You, my lord, engineered a situation others could use to wreak criminal havoc on a young lady's virtue. What reparation are you prepared to make?"

"My daughters call her Mama," Meech said, "and I will happily become this family's remittance man if that's what Lady Thea demands of me."

A duchess also asserted her authority from time to time. The guests would be on hand for hours yet, the truth had been aired, and Thea needed to put distance between herself and Meech.

She got to her feet and brought Noah his gloves.

"I will not have two grown men bickering before me at this hour. May we get back to our guests? I cannot recall this Pemberton person's appearance in any detail. I can assure you Violet Carter was an unpleasant, malcontented woman who took me into immediate and bitter dislike for the consideration shown me by my employers."

"You want to get back to our guests?" Noah posed the question as if the words made no sense, neither did he don his evening gloves.

"I don't want to," Thea said, "but we're enduring this entire ball to ensure there'll be no gossip. If we're closeted much longer with your uncle, there will be talk, and for no purpose. I cannot think, given what has been revealed here. I don't know what to feel, toward whom I should be angry, or if it even changes anything to know these truths, as opposed to other truths. Supper will soon be over, and it's late."

Thea needed her husband, though. Of that, she was certain.

"My duchess has spoken," Noah said, winging his arm at her.

She allowed herself one long moment to lean against him, to let a weight of anxiety and fear slide away, to take solace from the man she'd promised the rest of her life to.

Someday, someday in the future, matters between Thea and her husband would be all right. Maybe after five years of stumbling and groping their way forward, maybe after adding more children to the nursery. Maybe more awkward discussions were needed, but someday, their marriage would come right.

Just as Thea knew, in that moment, they were *not* right at all.

❧

"I didn't know Lord Earnest Dunholm was your uncle Meech."

Noah turned his tired, brave, amazing duchess under his arm, while their guests bowed and twirled along to the music beside them. "My dear, I can hardly recall the figures of the dance, much less attend to more revelations at the moment. Might we simply waltz?"

"If that's what you want."

Thea dipped gracefully, when Noah wanted to bellow until their infernally smiling neighbors, and confoundedly attentive family, and everlastingly helpful servants all waltzed themselves to perdition so he could be alone with his wife. She was holding up magnificently, while he, duke of all he surveyed, wanted to take his bullwhip to the idiot confined in his stables, the uncle swilling brandy in his library, and the greater idiot—safely traveling north—who'd invaded Thea's room and her peace and her body all those years ago.

Idiots, all of them, and yet Noah had been an idiot too.

He'd never told Thea he cared for her, never assured her he'd stand by her, never given her any reason to trust he'd meant his vows, never given her reason to confide in him.

Idiot, idiot, idiot.

Knowing now exactly what she'd suffered, he wanted to take his bullwhip to himself. How long would it be before she could tolerate him in her bed again? How long before they had more than two nominal daughters to parent together? How long before Pemberton's or Meech's name could come up in conversation without the both of them wanting to retch?

The music ended, and Noah threw ducal pretensions to the wind. He led Thea to the top of the steps and signaled the butler serving as herald. Etiquette, duty, and decorum could go to perdition, for Noah's wife needed to get off her feet and into his bed.

"Ladies and gentleman, friends, and neighbors, my duchess and I thank you for your company this evening and hope you've enjoyed the time spent with us. I fear, however, your host and hostess are fatigued by all the gaiety and need to take their leave of you. Stay on as long as you like. The buffet, cards, and drink remain for your pleasure, and I'm sure my family will see to your every comfort until you depart. Again, thank you, and good night."

Noah stole a kiss from his wife, who was covering her surprise with a convincingly warm smile. He smiled back when the room erupted in a friendly applause at his audacity, then he scooped his bride off her feet and made a grand exit from the ballroom.

If only reality resembled the fairy-tale ending to the evening in the least particular.

"You can put me down," Thea said when they'd reached the first floor.

"So you can fall asleep on your feet?"

"It's barely two in the morning," Thea retorted—around a yawn.

"I rest my case, Your Highness," Noah replied, treasuring the feel of her in his arms. "The day has been long and fraught, and that was without near kidnappings, attempted rape, assaults, and all manner of discommoding revelations over the brandy."

"I take it this display of muscles is a function of your husbandly whatevers?" Thea yawned again, and the informality of it, the simple humanness, reassured Noah.

"In all their feeble glory," Noah said, dipping so Thea could open the latch to his sitting-room door. "I will be your lady's maid tonight, and you will valet me."

"If you insist, which you seem to do when a simple request would suffice."

A show of spirit was a fine thing in a wife.

Thea was the soul of composure when Noah set her on her feet, undoing his cravat, cuffs, and shirt studs; letting him take down her hair, unhook her dress, and undo her tapes, laces, ribbons, and bows. He made quick work of the wash water, but insisted on treating Thea to a turn with the soap and water as well.

"The ballroom ventilates well when we open the highest windows," Thea said as Noah wrung out the cloth.

"I don't give a hearty goddamn for the ballroom ventilation," Noah growled, flinging the washcloth over the hearth screen. "I am exhausted, and I want to hold my wife in my arms and have all my fears relieved."

He couldn't believe he'd said that, and in perfect, utter seriousness. Thea, perceptive lady, knew he hadn't been joking.

He hadn't ever been joking.

"What are these fears, Noah?"

"Husband," he said, holding up the sheets so Thea could scoot to her side of the vast bed. "I like it when you call me husband."

"I like it when you call me wife," she said, giving her pillow a smack. "Sometimes, you even call me sweetheart or my dear, though. I like that better."

"God in heaven, Thea." Noah bounced down beside her and lay flat, eyes closed, forearm over his brow. "How can you stand to look at me? My uncle all but orchestrated your ruin, and his best friend's response is to lark off to the north. I want to shout down the rafters with the injustice of it, and you want me to call you sweetheart."

"Only when you're so inclined," she said, rising up on one elbow. "Does it make a difference, Noah, to know the how and who of it?"

"Yes, it makes a bloody difference!" He sat up, cross-legged, the sheet draping over his lap. "I hate the bastard, I hate all he stole from you, I hate that my own uncle did nothing to atone for his part, and I hate that there's no reparation to be made."

Noah loved his duchess though. Loved her endlessly and forever.

"I don't want to be concerned with hating, Noah," she said. "Though I agree, some sort of atonement is in order."

"Atonement." A stodgy biblical word. "If that's

a civilized way to discuss putting a man's balls in a vise—"

Thea put a finger over his lips. "Atonement, as in, I am sorry, Husband," she said. "My dear husband, dearest husband in the world, I am sorry I did not trust you with the story as I knew it the day you proposed. I thought Lord Earnest Dunholm had stolen into my room. He was charming and wry, and handsome in a distinguished way, and he made a grueling week so much more bearable. Then over breakfast, he'd barely been able to meet my gaze or pass me the toast."

"You thought it was *Meech*?" Horror elbowed its way past the rage roiling in Noah's gut.

"No." Thea brushed Noah's hair back. "I thought it was Lord Earnest. I wasn't one for poring over *Debrett's* when I had Nonie and Tims to see to. I did not research your antecedents or your social habits, though Marliss was of a more methodical bent. She approved of your choice of Henrietta Whitlow for a mistress, for example. Marliss claims Miss Whitlow has no patience with married men who stray. I admit to being cheered by that."

"Miss Whitlow loathes married men who stray," Noah said, mentally sending Henny a bank draft that should allow her to buy half of Yorkshire. "I do abhor unfaithful husbands too. You're attempting to change the subject, though, my dear. You did not connect the infernal Lord Earnest of your past with my uncle."

Thea brushed her fingers over Noah's brow again, as if she'd settle his thoughts by touch. Her tactic wasn't working, not when her caresses were so sweet and Noah's heart one great, endless ache.

"You never referred to your uncle by his proper names," Thea said. "Then just yesterday, your sister showed me the smaller portrait chamber, where I saw a youthful painting of Uncle Meech. I nearly lost my luncheon right there when I understood who Lord Earnest Dunholm was."

"Merciful God." Noah flopped to his back. "Please stop tormenting me with these revelations. You are in our bed, which I take for a sign of your clemency. I want to hold you, sweetheart, dearest Wife, simply hold you, if you wouldn't object."

Thea swung a leg over Noah's lap and settled onto his chest.

Noah's gratitude defied words. He needed to hold her, needed to feel her heartbeat resonating with his own—and he dared not order her into his embrace.

"I was so angry at Hallowell," Thea said, her sigh breezing across Noah's chest. "I didn't want you to suffer the sight of him making good on his threats."

"He could not have made good on them," Noah assured her. "Anger can sometimes serve to inspire a man's basest urges when desire won't, but shame will keep him unable to perform, and I knew James, Heath, and Wilson were less than twenty minutes behind me."

"You might have been killed," Thea said, threading her arms under his neck. "Noah, your taunting him might have got you killed."

In which case, Noah would have haunted Hallowell for the rest of his miserable days and nights.

"You would have missed me?" Noah asked. How had he endured his life before Thea had come along to make a husband of him?

"God's bones, Noah, I love you—of course I would have missed you! Who would steal my tea? Who would call me wife? Who would teach me to use the bullwhip and the dagger and a gun of my own?"

Noah was so *proud* of her. "Harlan and I will take you shopping for a proper little pistol when I've recovered from our infernal family gathering."

"Perhaps I'll be handier with a firearm, Husband. I didn't trust myself to throw my knife at Hallowell and hit my target." Thea kissed Noah's shoulder and let go a sigh. "I'm new to this duchessing business. You must be patient with me."

Noah was so *in love* with her. "You trusted me, Thea. You trust me a lot."

"I trust you with my life," she said, punching his bare shoulder. "I trust you with my heart, my body, my children, my future. Oh, you are awful when you are in the grip of these insecurities."

Noah was so *in bed* with her too. "I am awful, but I am not deaf. You love me."

"Hopelessly, though if you were in the least nice, you'd say it back."

For her, Noah could be the soul of nice.

"I love you," he said, slowly, distinctly. "I love you until my eyes are crossed with it, and I want nothing except to raise our children with you, tend our acres with you, and keep you safe from all harm. I want darling girls who pester me for little bullwhips, and darling boys who pester me for wooden swords. They can all have ponies when their mother says they're ready. I want a house full of them, and no more confounded balls, for they distract you awfully."

Thea kissed the shoulder she'd smacked, while Noah's body stirred with desire, gratitude, and sheer affection for his wife.

"If we have daughters, there will be balls, Noah."

"We already have daughters."

"Meech's daughters. Not well done of you."

Not honestly done of him. "I told you they were my cousins. You jumped to unflattering conclusions about me because I'm a Winters, and then I simply couldn't find the right time to correct the impression I'd created."

What did being a Winters, or a duke, or anything matter, compared to being Thea's husband? Noah experimented with an undulation of his hips, a husband's greeting to his wife.

"You are the girls' legal guardian," Thea said, returning his overture, "and you allowed me to draw the wrong conclusions." She drew away and lay flat on her back. "Mendacity is not endearing in a spouse, but I understand about timing and incorrect impressions."

"I'm veracious," Noah said, blanketing Thea with his body. "My wife will have it so."

"Say the words again, Noah. Please."

He nuzzled her temple, filled his lungs with her scent and his heart with courage.

"Thea. Duchess of Anselm, dearest, bravest Wife, *I love you*. I love your courage, your humor, your patience, your body." He kissed her soundly. "If you don't let me make love to you right bloody now, I shall cry."

Or issue an order, at which Thea would probably laugh.

"As if I could have that on my conscience."

# *Epilogue*

THE HOUSE WAS FINALLY EMPTYING OUT TWO DAYS after the ball, and Thea had begun to regain a sense of rhythm to her days and nights. The local magistrate had asked that they continue to confine Hallowell, while the authorities conferred regarding the charges to be laid.

"This is a gift," Noah announced, setting a wrapped box on the ducal bed as he stole a sip of Thea's tea. "Sort of."

"You touch my toast, and I will thrash you," Thea said. Threats were more fun than direct orders where Noah was concerned.

He took a bite of her toast. "I thought you said it was sharing."

Thea set her plate back on the tray and picked up the package. "You might consider asking. What is the occasion for this gift?"

"I'm currying your favor."

"You may curry my favor frequently." Thea shook the box, which was heavy and solid, though smaller than a bread loaf. "Not very subtle, though, simply plying me with gifts."

Noah had plied her with pleasure too, and that had been marvelous.

"Gifts are as subtle as I know how to be." Another sip of tea disappeared into Noah's maw. "You will be hard put not to scream when I tell you Grantley released Hallowell."

"Noah, you cannot be serious." Thea set the box down, while Noah blithely pilfered a crispy strip of bacon from her plate. "You are serious. This had better be a splendid gift."

"I knew you'd blame me, but Grantley was stealthy about it, and only told me after the fact," Noah said. "Shall I pour you another cup of tea?"

"Please." Thea ate a piece of her bacon lest it all disappear. "What was my brother thinking?"

"He called Hallowell out, but not for his behavior toward you, which was none of Grantley's business, because I am your husband."

"No dispute there," Thea said, eyeing her rapidly emptying plate. "So was Tims being foolish?"

"He was being gallant. He called Hallowell out for muddying the waters between Marliss and her former intended."

"Former?"

"The solicitors sent word the betrothal negotiations are at an end," Noah said around another mouthful of toast, "though Marliss seems to be bearing up wonderfully."

Bearing up wonderfully was what ladies of substance *did*. "Tims will offer for her, won't he?"

"If he survives the duel," Noah said, passing Thea a fresh cup of tea. "This outcome is likely, you see, because Harlan made sure Hallowell had the use of a fast horse and sufficient funds to get to France."

"At least your brother has sense. I warned you the callow swains were all a great lot of trouble." Thea took a sip of tea which was, to be honest, prepared exactly as she liked it.

"While you have a present," Noah reminded her, taking the teacup from her hand.

"Leave me at least two more sips. I adore how you fix it."

Noah looked surprised but pleased as Thea began unwrapping her gift.

"My music box?" Glued and sanded back together, a little the worse for wear, but when Thea opened the lid, the mechanism was restored to its proper location.

"The girls tried to dissect it, then took it to Erikson to repair, hoping you wouldn't notice. They are working on the precise wording of their apologies. Erikson would have forced them to admit their meddling before he'd finished restoring it, but he wanted to give them time to confess."

"This was so..." Thea wrapped Noah in a hug. "You are the best husband, Noah Winters, and I do love you."

"Have you started thinking up names yet?" He passed Thea back her teacup when she subsided, his blue eyes holding that special warmth Thea watched for.

"I beg your pardon?"

"You might consider this an early lying-in gift, though I suppose you'll want that bullwhip by then."

Noah was one of those damnably cheerful people of

a morning. Thea would learn to appreciate him for it, though it might help if he made sense.

"Want a bullwhip? By when?" she asked.

"Wife?" Noah took her teacup, set it on the tea cart, and framed her face with his hands. "Correct my math if I'm in error, but we've been married almost ten weeks, and you've been indisposed only once."

*What?* "Noah?"

"I am fairly competent with a calendar," he said, "and I keep rather close track of my duchess, especially recently. You're late, Wife. My guess is you're a little sensitive here." He gently closed his hand over her breast. "And prone to sentiment, perhaps? Maybe a tad queasy, or heeding nature's call more often?"

Thea settled her hand over his and closed her fingers, testing the truth of his words.

"Ye gods, Husband," she said, lying back. "The first time, likely the very first time, and I'm already carrying."

Perhaps Noah's body had ordered hers to conceive?

Noah came down over her, resting his cheek against the slope of her breast. "You're pleased?"

Thea didn't need to look into his eyes to confirm the worry in his voice, the tiny doubt.

"That is a ridiculous question," she said, though her hands were tender as they traced the lines of his face and jaw. She'd like sons with such features, tall, strong, laughing young men who teased and sneaked treats and made the ladies blush with their foolishness. She'd like daughters too—tall, strong, laughing young ladies who teased and sneaked treats and made the gentlemen smile with their foolishness.

"So you are pleased," Noah said.

"I am very, very pleased, Husband." Thea's tone was quite stern. "Though I warn you, a duchess dotes on her duke, a wife dotes shamelessly on her husband, and a mother dotes without ceasing on the father of her children. I hope you are prepared for this ordeal."

"All that doting," Noah said, kissing her cheek, her forehead, and her nose. "Sounds quite lovely. Sounds *nice*, in fact."

"Nice." Thea's tummy bounced, for Noah had made her laugh.

Mirth became a frequent morning delicacy for the Duchess of Anselm and her duke. His Grace's prognostication proved true too, for while the Duke of Anselm never quite got the knack of being nice, he did learn to dote shamelessly on his duchess, to treasure his darling children, to heed his duchess's every order—while stealing from her breakfast tray, of course—and for Thea, life became very, very nice indeed.

Read on for an excerpt from
*Tremaine's True Love*, the first book in
Grace Burrowes's brand-new Regency series
featuring the Haddonfield ladies

"THE GREATEST PLAGUE EVER TO BEDEVIL MORTAL MAN, the greatest threat to his peace, the most fiendish source of undeserved humility is *his sister*, and spinster sisters are the worst of a bad lot." In the corridor outside the formal parlor, Nicholas, Earl of Bellefonte, sounded very certain of his point.

"Of course, my lord," somebody replied softly, "but, my lord—"

"I tell you, Hanford," the earl went on, "if it wouldn't imperil certain personal masculine attributes which my countess holds dear, I'd turn Lady Nita right over my—"

"*My lord, you have a visitor.*"

Hanford's pronouncement came off a little desperately, but silenced his lordship's lament. Beyond the door, Tremaine St. Michael stepped away from the parlor's cozy fireplace, where he'd been shamelessly warming a personal attribute of his own formerly frozen to the saddle.

Bellefonte's greeting as he strode into the parlor a moment later was as enthusiastic as his ranting had been.

"Our very own Mr. St. Michael! You are early. This is not fashionable. In fact, were I not the soul of congeniality, I'd call it unsporting in the extreme."

"Bellefonte." Tremaine St. Michael bowed.

"Don't suppose you have any sisters?" Bellefonte asked with a rueful smile. "I have four. They're what my grandmother calls *lively*."

So lively, Bellefonte had bellowed at one of these sisters for the entire ten minutes Tremaine had waited in Belle Maison's formal parlor. The sister's responses had been inaudible, until an upstairs door had slammed.

"Liveliness is a fine quality in a young lady," Tremaine said, because he was a guest in this house and sociability was called for if he was to relieve Bellefonte of substantial assets.

"Fat lot you know," Bellefonte retorted, taking a position with his back to the fire. "If every man in the House of Lords had rounded up his *lively* sisters and sent them to France, the Corsican would have been on bended knee, seeking asylum of old George in a week flat. How was your journey?"

Bellefonte had the blond hair and blue eyes of many an English aristocrat. The corners of those eyes crinkled agreeably, and he'd followed up Tremaine's bow with a hearty handshake.

Bellefonte would never be a friend, but he was friendly.

"My journey was uneventful, if cold," Tremaine said. "I apologize for making good time down from Town."

"I apologize for complaining. I am blessed in my family, truly, but Lady Nita, my oldest sister, is particularly strong willed."

Bellefonte's hearty bonhomie faded to a soft smile as feminine laughter rang out in the corridor.

"You were saying?" Tremaine prompted. When would his lordship offer a guest a damned drink?

"Nothing of any moment, St. Michael. My countess and my sister Della have taken note of your arrival. Shall we to the library, where the best libation and coziest hearth await? Beckman gave me to understand you're not the tea and crumpets sort."

When and why had his lordship's brother conveyed that sentiment? Another thought intruded on Tremaine's irritation: Bellefonte knew his womenfolk by their laughter. How odd was that?

"I'm the whiskey sort," Tremaine said. "Winter ale wouldn't go amiss either."

"Whiskey, then. Hanford!"

A little old fellow in formal livery stepped into the library. "My lord?"

Bellefonte directed the butler to send 'round some decent sandwiches to the library and to fetch the countess to her husband's side when the fiend in the nursery had turned loose of her.

His lordship set a smart pace down carpeted hallways, past bouquets of white hothouse roses, and across gleaming parquet floors, to a high-ceilinged, oak-paneled treasury of books.

The library was blessed with tall windows at regular intervals, and the red velvet draperies were caught back, despite the cold. Winter sunshine bounced cheerily off mirrors, brass, and silver, and here too, the hearth was blazing extravagantly.

The entire impression—genial Lord Bellefonte;

his dear, plaguey sisters; roaring fires even in empty rooms; the casual wealth lined up on the library's endless sunny shelves—left Tremaine feeling out of place.

Tremaine had been in countless aristocratic family seats and more than a few castles and palaces. The out-of-place feeling he experienced at Belle Maison was the fault of the sisters, whom Bellefonte clearly loved and worried over.

Commerce, Tremaine comprehended and even gloried in.

Sisters had no part of commerce, but the lively variety could apparently transform an imposing family seat into a home.

"I know you only intended to stay for the weekend," Bellefonte said, gesturing to a pair of chairs beneath a tall window, "but my countess declares that will not do. You are to visit for at least two weeks, so the neighbors may come by and inspect you."

"A weekend might be all the time I can spare, my lord," Tremaine said, seating himself in cushioned luxury. "The press of business waits for no man, and wasted time is often wasted money."

"Protest is futile, no matter how sensible your arguments," Bellefonte countered, folding his length into the second chair. "You are an eligible bachelor and therefore, a doomed man."

The earl crossed long legs at the ankle, a fellow to whom doom was a merry concept.

"Her ladyship will ply you with delicacies at every meal," he went on. "Kirsten will interrogate you about your business ventures, Susannah will discuss that Scottish poet fellow with you, and Della will catch you up on all the Town gossip. The Haddonfield womenfolk are like faeries. A man falls into their clutches and time ceases to have meaning."

*Avoid faeries as if your life depends on it.* Tremaine's Scottish grandfather had smacked that lesson into his hard little head before he'd been breeched.

"What about your sister Lady Nita?" Tremaine asked. The sister putting the worry and exasperation in her brother's eyes and inspiring the earl to raise his voice.

Tremaine would never approach an objective without reconnoitering first. Knowing who got on with whom often made the difference between closing a deal or watching the profits waltz into some other fellow's pocket.

"Oh, her." Bellefonte's gaze went to the window, which looked out over terraced gardens in all their winter solemnity.

A tall blond woman marched off toward the stables along a walk of crushed white shells. She wore a riding habit of dark blue—no clever hat or pheasant feather cocked over her ear—and her briskly swishing hems were muddy.

Bellefonte's gaze followed the woman, his expression forlorn. "Lady Nita is very dear to me. She will be the death of us all."

꒰ꔷ꒱

The baby was small and vigorously alive, two points in her favor—possibly the only two.

"Your mother is resting," Nita said to the infant's oldest sibling, "and this is your new sister. Does she have a name?"

Eleven-year-old Mary took the bundle from Nita's arms. "Ma said a girl would be Annie Elizabeth. She wanted a boy though. Boys can do more work."

"Boys also eat more, make more noise, and run off to become soldiers or worse," Nita said. Boys became young wastrels who disported with the local soiled dove, heedless of the innocent life resulting from their pleasures, heedless that the soiled dove was a baronet's granddaughter and a squire's daughter. "Have you had anything to eat today, Mary?"

"Bread."

Thin and freckled and wearing a dress that likely hadn't been washed in weeks, Mary looked younger than her eleven years—also much, much older.

"Your mother will need more than bread to recover from this birth," Nita said. "I've brought butter, sausage, jam, sugar, boiled eggs, and tea in the sack on the table."

Nita would have milk sent over too. She'd been distracted by her altercation with Nicholas, and in her haste to reach Addy Chalmers's side, she'd neglected the most obvious need.

Mary pressed a kiss to Annie's brow. "She's ever so dear."

Would that the child's mother viewed the baby similarly.

Nita went down to her haunches, the better to impress on young Mary what must be said.

"When Annie fusses, you bring her to your mother to nurse. When Annie's had her fill, you burp her and take her back to her blankets. She'll sleep a lot at first, but she needs to sleep where it's quiet, warm, and safe."

Though the little cottage wouldn't be warm again until summer.

Mary cradled the newborn closer. "I'll watch out for her, Lady Nita. Ma won't have any custom for weeks, and that means no gin. Wee Annie will grow up strong."

Mary was an astute child, of necessity.

Nita rose, feeling the cold and the lateness of the hour in every joint and muscle.

"I'll send the vicar's wife around next week, and she'll have more food for you and your brothers, and maybe even some coal." The vicar's maid of all work would, in any case. "You store the food where nobody can steal it, and here." Nita withdrew five shillings from a pocket. "Don't tell anybody you have this. Not your mother, not your brothers, not even wee Annie. This is for bread and butter, not for gin."

"Thank you, Lady Nita."

"I'll come back next week to check on your mother," Nita said, shrugging into one of George's cast-off coats. "If she runs a fever or if the baby is doing poorly, come for me or send one of your brothers."

Mary bobbed an awkward curtsy, the baby in her arms. "Yes, Lady Nita."

Then Nita had nothing more to do, except climb onto Atlas's broad back and let the horse find his way home through the frigid darkness.

# About the Author

New York Times and USA Today bestselling author Grace Burrowes's bestsellers include *The Heir*, *The Soldier*, *Lady Maggie's Secret Scandal*, *Lady Sophie's Christmas Wish*, *Lady Eve's Indiscretion*, *The Captive*, and *The Laird*. Her Regency romances and Scotland-set Victorian romances have received extensive praise, including starred reviews from *Publishers Weekly* and *Booklist*. *The Heir* and *The Bridegroom Wore Plaid* were *Publishers Weekly* Best Books, *Lady Sophie's Christmas Wish* and *Once Upon a Tartan* have both won *RT Reviewers'* Choice Awards, *Lady Louisa's Christmas Knight* and *What a Lady Needs for Christmas* were both *Library Journal* Best Books, and *Darius: Lord of Pleasure* was an iBooks Store Best Book. Grace is a practicing family law attorney and lives in rural Maryland. She loves to hear from readers and can be reached through her website at graceburrowes.com.